Boies Penrose, Edward Pease Allinson

Philadelphia from 1681 to1887

A History of Municipal Development

Boies Penrose, Edward Pease Allinson

Philadelphia from 1681 to1887
A History of Municipal Development

ISBN/EAN: 9783337338596

Printed in Europe, USA, Canada, Australia, Japan

Cover: Foto ©Andreas Hilbeck / pixelio.de

More available books at **www.hansebooks.com**

PHILADELPHIA

1681–1887

A History of Municipal Development

BY

EDWARD P. ALLINSON, A. M. AND BOIES PENROSE, A. B.
OF THE PHILADELPHIA BAR

BALTIMORE
Publication Agency of the Johns Hopkins University

PHILADELPHIA
Allen, Lane & Scott, Publishers
1887

TO

JOHN C. BULLITT, Esq.,

WHOSE NAME, IN RECOGNITION OF HIS INTELLIGENT, PERSISTENT EFFORTS FOR BETTER GOVERNMENT IN PHILADELPHIA, THE PUBLIC HAVE CONFERRED ON THE NEW CHARTER,

THIS VOLUME

IS RESPECTFULLY DEDICATED.

PREFACE.

THE purpose of this work is to record the history of the development of the municipal institutions of Philadelphia; to trace, with considerable detail, the many changes in the powers, duties, and position of the mayor; in the election, appointment, and powers of the other executive officers; in the position and relation of the various departments; in the legislative and executive powers of councils; in the frequently shifting distribution of executive power between the mayor and councils; in the procedure of councils, and in the financial system of the city. Such a history is of peculiar interest to students of municipal questions, because the development of the government of Philadelphia begins with the most characteristic form of a mediæval English borough corporation, and, after passing through almost every system and phase of municipal institutions, ends with a charter embracing the latest ideas of municipal government.

The work is based upon the acts of assembly, the city ordinances, the state reports, and many other authorities cited elsewhere. Every act of assembly relating to Philadelphia since the foundation of the city has been carefully examined. Many of the early acts are in manuscript, and are to be found in the Historical Society of Pennsylvania. The collection of manuscript Penn papers, together with many books and documents belonging to the society, have likewise been freely consulted; and the librarian of the society, Mr. Frederick D. Stone, has furnished many valuable suggestions.

Mr. Charles R. Hildeburne, librarian of the Philadelphia Athenæum, very kindly placed the result of his large researches in the ancient documentary lore of Philadelphia at our disposal. The libraries of the Johns Hopkins University and Peabody Institute, at Baltimore, the Philadelphia Library, the Law Library of Philadelphia, the State Records and State Library, at Harrisburg, have been diligently consulted. As to the archives and library of the city of Philadelphia, it may almost be said that there are none, since the city does not even own a complete set of its own ordinances or journals. Among others, we are largely indebted to Dr. Herbert B. Adams and the scheme of institutional history introduced by him at the Johns Hopkins University, which has suggested both the idea and plan of this volume; to Mr. Thomas Cochran, president of the sinking fund commissioners; to Mr. S. Davis Page, late controller of the city; to Mr. S. C. Perkins, president of the public buildings commission; to Colonel Bosbyshell, present chief clerk of the controller's office; to Mr. Thompson Westcott and his valuable history; and to Mr. John C. Bullitt, for valuable suggestions, and the revision of special sections. Especially, however, would we take this opportunity of recording our indebtedness to the Hon. Richard Vaux, late mayor, and long time recorder of the old city, under whose administration that ancient office lost none of its old time dignity, when "the city spoke by the mouth of Mr. Recorder, the most virtuous apprentice of law in the whole kingdom—a man endowed with wisdom, and eminent for eloquence."

Until the inauguration, by the Johns Hopkins University, of the studies in local institutions of the United States, within the last four years, it is safe to say that no work similar to this had ever been attempted. The history of municipal and other local institutions had received almost no investigation whatever; and the principles which should control their modern development have, consequently, been entirely unknown or lost in confusion. The inevitable result has been the notorious evils and abuses in city governments which have caused them to be universally considered the only defective element in the American system.

The difficulties surrounding such a work have been very great. There are no text-books, or similar works, on the history of the city government, or any portion of it, to lighten and guide the labor. The whole work is based almost entirely on original authorities. Many of the early authorities are in manuscript, many difficult of access, and few indexed. Such studies, moreover, being still new and undeveloped, it has required extraordinary care in examining the acts of assembly and other authorities to ascertain the principles and significance of the successive changes and enactments. Added to these difficulties is the fact that the authors have had little over a year, in the midst of the exacting duties of their profession, in which to accomplish the work by the time fixed by the Editor of the Johns Hopkins University Studies for the appearance of the book in the series, and, what was considered especially desirable, before the new charter went into operation.

In a work of this character, embracing so many topics, it was, of course, a difficult matter to give a proper proportionate treatment to each, when all had to be treated as concisely as possible, and when many of the branches of the city government would require a separate volume for adequate treatment.

A brief introduction explaining the character of local government in Pennsylvania will give those who are not familiar with the historical investigations recently conducted under the auspices of the Johns Hopkins University some knowledge of local institutions in America, and more particularly in Pennsylvania; and consequently, a more scientific comprehension of the principles which have controlled the development of the local institutions of the city and county of Philadelphia.

E. P. A.,
B. P.

PHILADELPHIA, March 1, 1887.

CONTENTS.

INTRODUCTION.

Local Government in Pennsylvania.

While the city of Philadelphia was founded at the command of William Penn, its early government, the extent of its local powers, and its position in relation to the county and the State were determined by those leading principles of local organization inherited from the mother country, and modified by the circumstances of the new colony. By those principles the State was organized, for purposes of local government, into the town and county. Transplanted to the new world, this form of organization underwent three kinds of modifications—either the powers of local government resided principally in the town, as in New England, or in the county as in Virginia, or were divided between both, as in Pennsylvania.

The town, in New England, was the principal and, at first, the only unit of local organization. The Puritans belonged to the middle class of England, and were equal in condition. The character of their religion necessitated a settlement near the meeting-house. The physical conformation of the country compelled them to settle on the coast and rivers; and neither the soil nor the climate tempted them wholly to agricultural pursuits, but rather to trading, fishing, and manufacturing. These causes, combined with the method of division of land, led them to adopt the town system.

In that system it is very remarkable that—coming, as the Puritans did, from the England of the seventeenth century—they reproduced English institutions of a much older shape than they bore in England at that time—the institutions of the settlers of England in the fifth and sixth centuries. Those institutions were simply the earliest forms of political organization among the Teutonic race, consisting in the union of families, natural or artificial, in the clan which, when it has outgrown the predatory stage and has settled in fixed dwellings, becomes the *mark* or *gemeinde* from which is descended the town or parish. The ancient liberties and customs of that primitive organization were revived in a great measure in New England; so that the historian Freeman has said, "If you wish to see Old England, you must go to New England."

The leading feature of the New England system, and the one which affords the most striking illustration of its venerable descent, is the town meeting, the assembly of the freemen in person, and not through representatives, to legislate for their local affairs. At these annual meetings the selectmen are elected for the ensuing year, in whom is vested the principal administrative power. Among the other officers elected are, the constable, town clerk, treasurer, overseer of the poor, assessors, collectors, committeemen, road surveyors, parish commissioners, various inspectors, tithing men, listers, haywards, chimney viewers, fence viewers, timber measurers, and sealers of weights and measures. Among the many matters of local concern which fall within the jurisdiction of the township are the preservation of peace within its limits, the maintenance of highways, the care of the poor, and the voting of money for these and other local needs.

These township communities are not, as in the popular meaning of the word, a collection of houses, either forming a political community or not. They rather comprise a certain space of the earth's surface which may or may not contain a town, in the sense of a close settlement, but in which the inhabitants form a political community for purposes of local government. The incorporated municipalities in New England, as has been justly observed, are interlopers. When a city has been incorporated the ancient constitution of the township has indeed lost much of its importance, but it has not been abolished. In many cases the two constitutions of the city and township, the modern representative assembly and the Teutonic primary assembly, exist side by side, each with its peculiar powers and jurisdiction.

"The whole history of our land and our race will be read backwards," says Freeman,[1] "if we fail always to bear in mind that the lower unit is not a division of the greater, but that the greater is an aggregate of the smaller." As the union of families produced the clan, known in its territorial aspect as the village *mark*, so the union of clans, disregarding intermediate divisons, produced the tribe, known in its territorial aspect as the *pagus*, or county, while the union of independent *pagi* has produced the kingdom; and such is the remarkable analogy between the New England local institutions and their primitive originals, that De Tocqueville was warranted in saying, "It may almost be said that each of them (the townships) originally formed an independent nation. * * * Although they are now subject to the state, they were at first scarcely dependent upon it. They have not been invested with privileges, but seem, on the contrary, to have surrendered a portion of their independence to the state." And, in fact, after the separation from England, when the State government had become firmly established, the towns were still permitted to make and administer most of those laws which were of immediate concern to themselves; while the legislature of the State was composed of representatives from the towns and made laws affecting only the common concerns of the towns—which laws were executed by the town officers within their respective jurisdictions.

The county in New England was formed by an aggregation of townships to constitute a judicial district midway between the justices' courts and the superior courts of the State, and to take charge of the few matters of common interest to the neighboring communities. But the county had never had a very distinct political character, and played but an insignificant part in the administration of government. The State and the township possessed all the power requisite to conduct public affairs. The few county officers were appointed by the governor, and had only a limited and occasional authority. The budget of the county was drawn up by its officers and

[1] Comparative Politics, page 119.

voted by the legislature. The county court of sessions presided over the small number of affairs which concerned the townships in common, such as the erection of prisons and courts of justice, the county budget, the assessment of taxes, maintenance of certain highways, and acted in a judicial capacity in questions concerning the administration of the townships.

Such are the local institutions of New England, the simplest and best system of local government in existence. They are descended from the primitive institutions of the Aryan race, and especially that illustrious branch of it—the Teutonic, and have justly excited the admiration of all men. Jefferson was greatly impressed with their merits, and wrote, "As Cato, then, concluded every speech with the words '*Carthago delenda est*,' so I, every opinion, with the injunction, 'divide the counties into wards.' Begin them only for a single purpose; they will soon show for what others they are the best instruments."

In Virginia, on the other hand, the county is the unit of organization for local government. The colonists of Virginia, it is true, were, like those of New England, of pure English stock; but there was not the same equality of condition which characterized the early New England democracies. There was, in the beginning, a large body of "servants" sprung from the lowest class of London; while the early introduction of negro slavery, and the consequent debased condition of the poor whites, contributed to increase the inequality. The result was, that the upper classes took the reins of government into their own hands from the start, and rendered impossible a democratic institution like the general assembly of the freemen in the town meeting. The land, moreover, unlike the small divisions of New England, was held in immense quantities in a few hands; and the system of entails and primogeniture which, it has been claimed, reached a greater height in Virginia than in England, contributed to the same result—the complete removal of the government from the hands of the people, and the organization of the county for those small powers of local government that were granted. The climate, too, was mild, and the country was penetrated in every direction by navigable streams, forming harbors, far in the interior, where the English ship could exchange her cargo of manufactured goods for tobacco grown in the vicinity. The soil, of unrivaled richness, was peculiarly favorable to the cultivation of tobacco, which speedily became the main staple and source of wealth. Indeed, the cultivation of tobacco was so profitable in the early years of the colony, that it was grown in the streets of the only village that then existed; and it was only by means of the most stringent laws that the farmers could be compelled to grow enough food for themselves and their laborers. The character of the original government, also, had a great influence on the development of the local institutions, and is in marked contrast to the free charter governments of New England. Vast powers were secured to the crown; the whole legislative and executive power was vested in a council nominated by the crown, and guided by its instructions; and for many years laws were made and taxes imposed without a legislature, until in the course of time such concessions were wrung from the crown as to lay the foundation of future liberties.

Under such conditions the development of local government in Virginia was in remarkable contrast to that in New England. While the settlers of New England, as we have seen, revived the local institutions of the fifth and sixth centuries in England, the settlers of Virginia reproduced local institutions very much like those of England in the seventeenth century. At first, indeed, close settlements were necessary for defense against Indians; but the population quickly spread beyond the narrow limits of the early plantations, and scattered in agricultural pursuits over the surrounding country. With the increase of population and trade arose the necessity for courts of justice, and the site of the court house was fixed at the original plantation from which the surrounding country had been settled. The counties were the outspreading of towns or plantations, and took their names from them, as in the case of the county of James City. This growth of a settlement into a county is a most curious phase in the development of local institutions, because, as we have seen, the counties in New England, and in England, were formed from the union of smaller communities.[1]

The county in a short time became vested with the few powers of local government that existed. The principal county officer, the lieutenant, was appointed by the governor; he was chief of the militia, and possessed many of those powers which in New England were divided among the officers of the township. A sheriff was also appointed by the governor for each county, from among three persons nominated by the county courts, generally from among themselves. The other county officers were the coroner and constables. Generally, the judges of the courts nominated their own successors, who were appointed by the governor. Court day was a holiday in all the country side, and was to Virginia what the town meeting was to New England. The jurisdiction of the court was limited, and an appeal lay to the governor and council. The county court laid the levy to defray the expenses of roads, buildings, bridges, and salaries of burgesses; and appointed certain officers, as the surveyors of highways, inspectors of tobacco, and collectors of county levies. The court made its own by-laws, and with representatives from the parish could make by-laws for the county. When circumstances arose which the laws had not provided for, the court was empowered to act. The burgesses in the legislature were elected by the counties.

Nearly half a century elapsed while unsuccessful attempts were made to introduce towns with some measure of local power. The need was early felt for a fixed place of export and import, and for the transaction of business in general. The regular attendance upon the weekly religious services was rendered impossible; and among many other inconveniences incident to the scattered population, the want of proper

---

[1] Edward Ingle, Local Institutions of Virginia, Johns Hopkins University Studies, third series. II.-III., page 81.

means for education was keenly felt. But the rivalries of the planters to secure near their own plantations the site of the paper towns; the weakness, and sometimes even the opposition, of the mercantile class, and the increasing importance of the cultivation of tobacco, for a long time rendered such attempts futile. Every large planter had his own "landing" place, was his own factor, and possessed his own artisans. Even Jefferson, the enthusiastic admirer of New England institutions, wrote, "Let our workshops remain in Europe;" for "the mobs of great cities add just so much to the support of pure government, as sores do to the strength of the human body."[1]

Before the Revolution there was not a real city in Virginia. There was the town, for which trustees were appointed by the assembly to attend to the surveying, letting, and selling of the town land, under the direction of the county court; and there were, also, two chartered boroughs, Williamsburg and Norfolk; but the powers of the mayor, aldermen, and council were extremely limited, and almost everything done by them had first to receive the sanction of the central authority in the form of an enabling act of the legislature.

In Virginia, then, the county was the principal, and at first almost the only, organization for purposes of local government; and the dominant idea of the whole system of government was the gradation of power from the governor downward, not, as in New England, upward, from the people. As we have seen, the important county officers were appointed by the governor, and there was a high property qualification for voters. The administration of the county was, indeed, a close corporation, and about the only share the poor white had in the government was to cast his vote for burgess.

Such are the systems of local institutions in New England and Virginia. Their development in the two colonies forms a regular and connected story, and a brief description of them here has been necessary because they are the originals after

[1] Notes on Virginia, page 225.

the pattern of which the institutions of the other States have been modeled. Virginia and New England dominated the continent. The settlers in both were of pure English descent, and had the same political inheritance. The important fact to be borne in mind, which is too seldom realized, is that, in both, the institutions were not, like the territorial boundaries, brand-new and artificial, but have a direct and continuous connection with the past.

The two systems met in a struggle for supremacy in the settlement and organization of the North-west Territory. The State of Illinois, formed from that region, affords us an admirable illustration of the conflict of the two ideas. That State extends north and south four hundred miles, between parallels which include the seaboard States from New Hampshire to North Carolina; and as emigration from the Atlantic to the Western States has always followed parallels of latitude, Illinois was settled in the south by immigrants from Virginia and the neighboring Southern States, and in the north, from New England. When the first constitution was framed in 1818, immigration had been almost exclusively devoted to the southern part of the State, and that instrument consequently bears witness to the origin of its authors. The basis of local organization, as in Virginia, was the county, but the system was marked by a more liberal and democratic spirit. The entire management of each county was placed in a court of three county commissioners. This court was, indeed, modeled after the Virginia county court, but there were two important differences: the commissioners were elected by the people of the county, and, by a process of differentiation, they had no judicial functions, the county judiciary being made a distinct tribunal. A sheriff, coroner, treasurer, surveyor, and recorder were likewise elected in each county. As in Virginia, however, there was no power given to communities within the county to control local affairs.

"But even at this time there had been planted in Illinois, and throughout the whole West, a germ capable, under right conditions, of developing a highly-organized township system.

In dividing and designating the public domain, the Congress of the United States had early adopted the system of survey into bodies six miles square, and had given these divisions the New England name of townships. For purposes of record and sale, each township was divided into thirty-six sections a mile square, and these were further subdivided. Every man held his land by a deed which reminded him that his freehold was part of a township; and there is much even in a name. But, further than this, the United States had given to the people of every township a mile of land, the proceeds of which should be a permanent township school fund. To give effect to this liberal provision, the State enacted a law making the township a body corporate and politic for school purposes, and authorizing the inhabitants to elect school officers and maintain free schools. Here, then, was a rudiment of local government. As the New England townships grew up around the church, so western localism finds its nucleus in the school system. What more natural than that the county election district would soon be made to coincide with the school townships, with the school-house for a voting place? or that justices of the peace, constables, ward supervisors, and overseers of the poor should have their jurisdiction determined by those same township lines?"[1]

After the admission of Missouri as a slave State, under the compromise of 1820, southern emigrants turned to that quarter, while the northern part of Illinois began to be settled by immigrants from New England and New York. A strong sectional bitterness ensued between the northern and southern parts of the State, and the systems of Virginia and New England met fairly in contest for supremacy. The contest was at length compromised in a remarkable manner in the constitution of 1847, which provided that the legislature should enact a general law for the organization of townships to be adopted by any county by a majority vote. One by one the counties

[1] Local Government in Illinois, by Albert Shaw, A. B. Reprinted from the *Fortnightly Review*, in Johns Hopkins University Studies, first series, III., page 10.

of Illinois have taken advantage of the provisions of the law, until at the present time only one-fifth of the two hundred and two counties in the State cling to the old system.

The form of township organization adopted was a modification of the New England system. Each township generally conforms to the boundaries of the congressional or school districts, and possesses very large powers to manage its local affairs. As in New England, the leading feature is the annual town meeting of all the voters for the election of town officers and the transaction of local business.

In Pennsylvania still a third system of local government was developed, wherein neither the county nor the township was the only unit, but what local powers existed were divided between both. This system has likewise had an influence upon the development of local institutions in other States. The history of its growth is not as simple as in the case of New England and Virginia, being complicated by the fact that three different nations for many years contended for the possession of the shores of the Delaware, and it was not till after many compromises that English institutions were finally established there.

The first permanent settlement on the Delaware was Fort Nassau, built by the Dutch West India Company in 1624, near the present site of Gloucester, N. J. While the company was anxious to establish a trading post to secure the valuable fur trade with the Indians, they at the time were so completely taken up with their more lucrative privateering war upon the rich merchant ships of Spain, that for many years the enterprise languished, and, as may be easily imagined, was not favorable to the development of democratic ideas or local government. The powers of the company were in the highest degree despotic, and in many respects were coextensive with those of the States-General themselves. They might, "in the name and authority of the States, make contracts, engagements, and alliances with princes and nations of the countries mentioned," and "also build forts, &c.; appoint and discharge governors, people for war, officers of justice, and other public officers," &c.[1] A general right of approval and superintendence was reserved to the States. In order to forward the prosperity of the colony, the "Charter of Freedoms and Exemptions" was granted by the company. This was a complete feudal constitution, creating a landed aristocracy, and handing the State over to their control. The territory was to be divided into separate principalities, each under the control of a patron—a feudal lord—who was to settle it at his own expense in return for many peculiar privileges.[2] But small success, however, attended these first attempts of the Dutch to effect a permanent settlement, until in 1638 the arrival of a colony from Sweden marks a new era.

The subsequent events upon the Delaware, before the arrival of William Penn, may be divided into three periods: first, the period of Swedish supremacy from 1638, when the first permanent settlement was made, to 1655, when the Swedes were overthrown by the Dutch, under Peter Stuyvesant; secondly, the period of Dutch supremacy, from 1655 to 1664, when the colonies on the Delaware, with the rest of the New Netherlands, were conquered by the English; and, thirdly, the period from 1664, when a large part of the settlements on the Delaware were included in the grant to the Duke of York, to 1681, when the province of Pennsylvania was granted to William Penn.[3]

The first settlement of the Swedes was made at Fort Christina, near the present site of Wilmington, in 1638, by the Swedish West India Company. The powers of that company were very much the same as those of the Dutch company, with the exception that its object was colonization and commerce, and not warfare. In the charter to Henry Hockhammer, a native of Holland, who is said to have actually planted a colony in the vicinity of Fort Christina, it is remarkable that the Swedish company granted much more liberal terms than the Dutch company had previously done.

---

[1] Charter of the West India Company, Hazard's Annals of Pennsylvania, page 9. [2] Hazard's Annals of Pennsylvania, page 22.

[3] Laws of Pennsylvania, 1682–1700. Historical notes.

The land was secured to the settlers as "allodial and hereditary property." They were given the right of administering justice, founding cities, villages, and communities; to make laws and appoint magistrates and officers. Liberal provisions were made for the exercise of religion and the support of education.[1] Of the laws and customs of the Swedes upon the Delaware, however, we have but little record. In the instructions to the Swedish governor, Printz—the most important state document of this period—he is commanded "to decide all controversies according to the laws, customs, and usages of Sweden; to bring to obedience and order, by necessary and convenient means, the mutinous and refractory persons who will not live in peace; and he may punish great offenders, if he finds any, not only by imprisonment and other proportionate punishments, but even with death, according to the crime, if he can seize the criminal; but not otherwise than *according to the ordinances and legal forms*, and after having sufficiently considered and examined the affairs with the most noted persons, such as the most prudent assessors of justice that he can find and consult in the country."[2]

"This—although but a glimpse—is sufficient to show," says Mr. Armstrong in his introduction to the Upland Court Records,[3] "that no special code was prepared for the government of the colony. The laws of the mother country were in ancient times various and conflicting, each province being governed by its own peculiar customs and statutes. About the year 1614 a compilation of these laws was made for the direction of the whole kingdom; deficiencies and doubtful cases being supplied and explained by the aid of the civil law. It must not be forgotten, also, that the period of the independent power of the Swedes was a series of contests with their Dutch neighbors, who claimed an exclusive right to that region, although neither side came to blows for a long time, since they both feared the English, whose encroachments from

---

[1] Hazard's Annals of Pennsylvania, page 53.
[2] Pennsylvania Archives, second series, vol. V., page 764.
[3] Memoirs of Historical Society of Pennsylvania, vol. VII., page 38.

the north and south threatened them both more and more to a much greater extent than they did each other. Surrounded also by Indians, treacherous and uncertain, and being few in numbers, it is natural to suppose that the government was a form of military rule, emanating from the company or its delegated agent, and by no means conducive to the growth of local independence; and that this government, among such a peaceful people as the Swedes, engaged in the cultivation of tobacco and the trade in peltries, was of the simplest kind.

At length the contests between the Dutch and the Swedes culminated in open hostilities, and ended in the conquest of the latter by the Dutch in 1655, under Stuyvesant, the director-general of New Netherlands. This conquest was followed by the establishment of a Dutch government on the Delaware, and the appointment, by degrees, of proper officers for the enforcement of the law and the administration of justice.

The government of New Netherlands, of which the settlements on the Delaware now formed a part, consisted of a director-general and council. The council had the supreme authority to make laws and execute them, and had also jurisdiction over all civil and criminal cases, although distant settlements were allowed their own courts, subject to an appeal.

In this highly-centralized government one of the most important officers was the schout, or fiscaal, who combined many of the duties of a sheriff, district attorney, or prosecuting officer, and acted in many cases for the States-General and the company. He "was charged specially with enforcing and maintaining the placards, laws, ordinances, resolutions, and military regulations of their high mightinesses the States-General, and protecting the rights, domains, and jurisdiction of the company, and executing their orders, as well in as out of court, without favor or respect to individuals. He was bound to superintend all prosecutions and suits, but could not undertake any actions on behalf of the company, except by order of the council; nor arrest nor arraign any person on a criminal charge, except on information previously received, or unless he caught him *in flagrante delicto*. In taking information he was bound to note, as well those points which made for the prisoner, as those which supported the charge against him, and after trial he was to see the proper and faithful execution of the sentence pronounced by the judges, who, in indictments carrying with them loss of life and property, were not to be less than five in number. He was, moreover, especially obliged to attend to the commissaries arriving from the company's outposts, and to vessels arriving from or leaving to Holland, to inspect their papers, and superintend the loading and discharging of their cargoes, so that smuggling may be prevented."[1]

The government on the Delaware was modeled after the manner of the general government at New Amsterdam. A vice-director was appointed, who was instructed "to give orders, and have them observed, in all matters concerning trade, policy, justice, and military," and "to administer law and justice to citizens as well as soldiers."[2] He had a council which was convoked by him, and in case of a tie he had a double vote. In military trials before the council "two sergeants" were added to the board, while in civil suits "two suitable freemen" were added instead of the sergeants. The vice-director was charged "to strictly observe, and have observed, the *published ordinances* against the sale of strong drinks to the Indians; the robbing of gardens and plantations; running about in the country and drinking on or profaning the Sabbath day." In fact, the vice-director and council regulated the most minute affairs of the colonies, such as the enclosing of lots, and the running at large of goats and swine; they tried cases of assault and battery, and had the general regulation of trade.[3]

As the Dutch West India Company was much in debt, especially to the city of Amsterdam, for services rendered in conquering the Swedes upon the Delaware, it ceded to that city, in 1657, a tract of country around Fort Christina or,

---

[1] O'Callahan's History of New York, vol. I., page 102.
[2] Pennsylvania Archives, second series, vol. VII., page 491.
[3] Hazard's Annals of Pennsylvania, pages 209-210.

as it was now called, Fort Casimir, which was known as the city's colony, and was called New Amstel, while the region north was known, by way of distinction, as the company's colony.[1]

It was provided that the city of Amsterdam should hold the country "in the form of a fief," but the sovereign and supreme authority was to remain in the Dutch West India Company. In the "conditions" offered by the city to colonists, subject, of course, to the charter, it was provided that matters of police and the administration of justice were to be regulated as in Amsterdam, "whereof the practice and custom, particularly in regard to descents, shall be adhered to." "A schout," or head of justice, "was to be appointed in the name of their high mightinesses and West India Company by the deputies of Amsterdam, who for this purpose shall give authority to the director by power of attorney. Three burgomasters were also to be appointed by the common burghers from the 'honestest, fittest, and richest,' and five or seven schepens, for which the burghers were to nominate a double number, from which the director, under power of attorney, is to select." The schepens possessed judicial functions to give judgment for all sums under one hundred guilders—afterwards increased to six hundred—and in cases of greater amount, subject to an appeal of the director-general and council of New Netherlands, and in all criminal cases, at first subject to an appeal, which was subsequently removed. When the colony or city of New Amstel, as it was called, should number two hundred families or more, it was to have the right to choose "a common council of XXI. persons," to whom, together with the burgomasters, the government of the city should be intrusted. The common council was a close corporation, since, when "once instituted," it was to possess the authority "thereafter" to fill by election all vacancies in its body, and to it also was to revert the right of annually choosing the burgomasters and the nomination of the double number of schepens. The burgomasters of Amsterdam, however,

[1] Hazard's Annals, page 220.

retained the right to appoint the secretary, messenger, and other inferior officers, and to furnish a schoolmaster, smith, wheelwright, and carpenter.[1] A board of commissioners to manage the affairs of New Amstel, but to reside in Amsterdam, was likewise appointed, and preparations made to increase the colony.

It is interesting to note that these provisons for local government, so far superior to any that had been made, either by the Dutch or the Swedish nation, for the colonies on the Delaware, emanated from the great and enterprising city of Amsterdam. Notwithstanding these liberal provisions, however, a large part of the local affairs of the colony were regulated across the ocean, in Amsterdam. Thus, we learn from the deliberations of the council in that city, that a bridge over the creek, near the fortress of Casimir, is ordered to be built;[2] overseers or inspectors of fences are appointed—an officer which, in New England, it will be remembered, belonged to the township, and in Virginia, to the county; the community are requested to cut palisades to strengthen the fort. Occasionally, however, we have evidence of the more liberal spirit which was beginning to prevail; thus, the "community is summoned at the fort to nominate four persons, out of whom to elect two expert persons as tobacco inspectors;"[3] and upon another occasion "a meeting of the community" was summoned at Fort Casimir to fix the price of skins in the trade with the Indians.[4]

It is not necessary, for this purpose, to go into the details of the Dutch and Swedish rules upon the Delaware, or their mutual influence on each other. Sufficient has been said to give an idea of the two systems. Local government, indeed, can hardly be said to have existed. The administration was principally concentrated in the hands of the officers of the trading companies, either on the Delaware or at home. The acquisition of the country by the English brought about a very different state of affairs.

---

[1] Hazard's Annals, page 221. [2] Hazard's Annals, page 224.
[3] Hazard's Annals, page 225. [4] Hazard's Annals, page 229.

On the 12th of March, 1664, Charles II. granted to the Duke of York a territory comprising within its confines the whole of New Netherlands, and, therefore, including the colonies on the Delaware, without regard to the claim or occupancy of the Dutch, to be held in "free and common socage, and not in capita or by knight's service," in consideration of the annual payment, within ninety days after demand, of forty beaver skins.[1] The duke was given full and absolute power to correct, punish, pardon, govern, and rule; the only qualification to these arbitrary powers being that the "statutes, ordinances, and proceedings be not contrary to, but as near as conveniently may be agreeable to, the laws, statutes, and government of this our Realm of England," and with the reservation of an appeal to the crown. Sir Robert Carre easily reduced the settlements on the Delaware to submission and, with the seat of government at New Amstel, or New Castle, as it was now called, entered into an agreement, "on behalf of his majesty of Great Britain," with the "burgomasters on behalf of themselves, and all the Dutch and Swedes inhabiting the Delaware bay and Delaware river," for the government of the country.[2] By the terms of this agreement the burghers and planters were to be protected in their property upon submission to his majesty's authority; the present magistrates were to be continued in office for the present; "the schout, the burgomaster, sheriff, and other inferior magistrates shall use and exercise their customary power in administration of justice within their precincts for six months, or until his majesty's pleasure be further known;" liberty of conscience was guaranteed, and an oath of allegiance administered.

It is evident by this agreement, and by the transactions of that period, that no attempt was made at once to change violently the officers and government of the conquered people; but it was, nevertheless, the aim of the English to plant the institutions of their own country, in course of time, upon the

[1] Hazard's Annals, 356.
[2] Pennsylvania Archives, vol. V., page 544.

Delaware, and in 1668 several important changes were made to that effect, and for the gradual uprooting of Dutch laws and customs. For the better government of the Delaware, it was ordered by the governor and council at New York that "to prevent all abuses and oppositions in civil matters, so often as complaint is made, the commissioned officer—Captain Carre—call the schout, with Hans Block, Israel Helm, Peter Rambo, Peter Cock, Peter Alricks, or any two of them, as councilors, to advise, hear, and determine by the major vote what is just, equitable, and necessary in the case and cases in question;" and that the same persons likewise might settle difficulties with the Indians. What was still more significant of the approaching change, it was further added "that the laws of the government established by his royal highness be showed and frequently communicated to the said councilors and all others, to the end that being therewith acquainted, the practice of them also in convenient time be established, which conduceth to the public welfare and common justice."

In accordance with these instructions the work of adjusting the government of the Delaware so as to bring it slowly, but steadily, into conformity with the English law progressed systematically year by year, with the slight interruption caused by the temporary suspension of English authority incident to the second conquest of the country by the Dutch in 1673. But progress was naturally slow. For a time the Dutch and Swedes constituted the majority of the population, and English laws and institutions only became gradually possible with an increasing English population. In the meanwhile, as was natural in the case of a conquered population, the government was centralized in the military authorities at New York, or their agents on the Delaware, and the subject population had but little voice in their own affairs. Ordinances for their government were promulgated by the governor and council from time to time as circumstances required, and the governor, as might have been expected, found "the whole frame of government standing at this time still; neither mayor nor alderman elected; the grand assizes likely to be prorogued."[1] Among those ordinances are: "That constables be appointed to keep the king's peace, who shall have staves with the king's arms upon them, as is practiced in the rest of his royal highness's dominions;" and as a condition precedent to the confirmation of land patents, "that each planter shall be obliged to settle upon the land for which they have patents in some convenient time to be appointed for the same; and likewise that they maintain a house lot in the town or towns intended to be erected for their mutual defense to which they shall be nearest related."[2] It is to be noticed that the local office of constable is here revived, and provision made for towns to the constitution of which the constable has been essential from ancient times. It is in military defense that towns first play a practical part. When danger of an Indian outbreak threatens, the inhabitants are ordered "to retire into towns for their better safety and security," and it was mutually ordered by Governor Lovelace and Governor Carteret, of New Jersey, that "the inhabitants at New Castle and parts adjacent upon Delaware river be designated into several companies as the towns and number of men will permit."[3]

The first marked step in the development of local government upon the Delaware, illustrating well the advanced spirit of the English race, was the incorporation of New Castle, which was already recognized as the "strength of the river."[4] At a council held in New York on the 17th of May, 1672, it was ordered that, "for the better government of the town of New Castle for the future, the said town shall be erected into a corporation, by the name of a bailiwick; that is to say, it shall be governed by a bailiff and six assistants, to be first nominated by the governor, and at the expiration of a year four of the six to be out, and four others to be chosen in their places, the bailiff to continue for a year, and then two to be named to succeed, out of whom the governor shall elect

[1] Letter of Governor Lovelace to Captain Carre, at New Castle. Hazard's Annals of Pennsylvania, page 376. [2] Pennsylvania Archives, vol. VII., Historical Notes, page 348. [3] Pennsylvania Archives, vol. VII., Historical Notes, 450. [4] Hazard's Annals of Pennsylvania, page 385.

one. He is to preside in all the courts of the town, and have a double vote. A constable is likewise to be chosen by the bench. The town court shall have power to try all causes of debt or damage to the value of ten pounds without appeal; that the English laws, according to the desire of the inhabitants, be established, both in the town and all plantations upon the Delaware; that the office of schout be converted into a sheriffalty; and the high sheriff's power extend both in the corporation and river; and that he be annually chosen by two being presented to the governor, of whom he will nominate and confirm one."[1]

In 1673 New York and the settlements on the Delaware were, as has been said, conquered by the Dutch, and held for a short time. Such was the brevity of their possession, however, that it is needless to go into the details of the comprehensive government which they forthwith framed for the Delaware, but it is very significant, as marking the progress which local government had already made under English rule, that among other provisions it was ordered that "all cases relating to the police, security, and peace of the inhabitants, also to justice between man and man, shall be finally determined by the magistrates, of each of the aforesaid villages to the amount of and under sixty florins, Beaver, without appeal;" and that "the sheriff and schepens shall have power to conclude on some ordinances for the welfare and peace of the inhabitants of their districts, such as laying out highways, setting of lands and gardens, and in like manner what appertains to agriculture, observance of the Sabbath, erecting churches, school-houses, or similar public works; also, against fighting and wrestling, and such petty offenses, provided such ordinances are not contrary to, but as far as is possible conformable to, the laws of our fatherland and the statutes of this province; and, therefore, all orders of any importance shall, before publication, be presented to the chief magistrate, and his approval thereof requested."[2]

---

[1] Pennsylvania Archives, vol. VII.

[2] Pennsylvania Archives, vol. V., Historical Notes, 452.

At this time, also, three courts of judicature were established on the river, and the inhabitants were ordered to elect by "plurality of votes" eight persons as magistrates for each of the courts. The fact is interesting, not only because it marks the progress which local institutions were making, but also because it shadows forth the limits of the first six counties of Penn's province.[1]

By the treaty of peace between England and Holland, signed the 9th of February, 1674, New York and the Delaware reverted to the Duke of York, and his former grant was reconfirmed to him by the king. The old magistrates were continued in office with one exception. At this time the officers of government on the Delaware were, a schout, or sheriff, a secretary, and five magistrates for New Castle, and five for the river. The policy of gradually establishing English laws was resumed, until, on December 25, 1676, the "convenient" time, already referred to, was held to have arrived; and an ordinance was accordingly promulgated by Governor Andross, declaring "(1.) That the booke of lawes establisht by his Royal Highnesse, and practiced in New Yorke, Long Island, and Dependencies, bee likewise in force and practiced in this river and precincts, except the Constables, Courts, County Rates, and some other things peculiar to Long Island, and the militia as now ordered to remain in ye King, but that a Constable in each place be yearly chosen for the Preservacon of his Maties Peace with all other power as directed by ye Law. (2.) That there be three Courts in ye several parts of the river and bay as formerly To witt one in New

---

[1] The jurisdictions were as follows:—"One court of justice for New Amstel (or New Castle), to which provisionally shall resort the inhabitants dwelling on the east and west banks of Kristina kill unto Boomties Hook, with those of Apoquenamins kill inclusive. One court of justice for the inhabitants of Upland (Chester), to which provisionally shall resort the inhabitants both on the east and west banks of Kristina kill and upwards unto the head of the river. One court of justice for the inhabitants of the Whorekill (Lewiston), to which shall provisionally resort the inhabitants both on the east and west side of Cape Hinlopen unto Boomties Hook aforesaid." (Historical Notes, 453.)

Castle, one above att Uplands (Chester), another below at the Whorekill (Lewiston). (3.) That the said Courts consist of Justices of the Peace whereof three to make a corom and to have the power of a Court of Sessions and decide all matters under twenty pounds without Appeal, in which court the oldest Justice to preside unless otherwise agreed amongst themselves in cases above twenty pounds and for crimes extending to life and Limbs or banishment to admitt Appeale to the Court of Assizes." The courts were to have power to make by-laws or orders, to be of force for one year; they had the sole power to impose fines, and within certain limits fixed by the "Lawes" to regulate fees of officers. It was further provided that there should be a "High Sheriffe for the Toune of New Castle, the River and Bay; and that the said High Sheriffe have power to make an under Sheriffe or Marshall, being a fitt person, and for whom he will be responsible, to be approved by the Court. But the Sheriffe to act as in England, and according to the new practice on Long Island, to act as a principal officer in the execution of the law, but not as a Justice of the Peace or Magistrate." Records of judicial proceedings, orders from the governor, and names of the magistrates and officers were to be kept, in English, by a "fitt person for Clarke," to be "recommended by each Court to the Governor for his Approbacon." All writs, warrants, and proceedings at law were in the king's name, and no rates could be imposed or levies of money made, except in extraordinary emergencies, without the approbation of the governor.

A brief review of the duke's famous Booke of Lawes, so far as they pertain to local government, is necessary. They were not, indeed, ever wholly in force upon the Delaware, but they undoubtedly exercised considerable influence upon the institutions of the State indirectly, and even directly, since many of their provisions were very much admired and imitated by Penn. But the important fact to be noted in regard to them is, that they afforded a far greater degree of local independence than ever obtained upon the Delaware before or afterwards. In fact, they form a singular chapter in the development of local institutions in Pennsylvania, because, as we have seen, under the Swedes and Dutch but a small degree of local independence ever prevailed, while, as we shall see later on, under Penn local divisions within the county had very few local powers, at least in the beginning.

From the caption of the "Lawes" we learn that they "were digested into one volume for the publicke use of the Territories in America under the government of his Royall Highness. Collected out of the severall laws now in force in his Majesty's American Colonyes and Plantations. Published March 1, Anno Domini, 1664, at a General meeting at Hemsted upon Longe Island by virtue of a commission from his Royal Highness James, Duke of Yorke and Albany, given to Colonell Richard Nicolls, Deputy Governor, bearing date the second day of April, 1664." In these "lawes" were revived the ancient English municipal divisions of ridings, towns, and parishes. The riding was an aggregation of towns, chiefly for judicial purposes, but was of small importance in the political organization. In each riding was a court of sessions. Each riding in turn was entitled to have the high sheriff chosen from its jurisdiction. The justices of the last sessions, before the expiration of the office of the then sheriff, presented to the governor three names, out of which he named one to serve as high sheriff for the year ensuing. A marshal was appointed by the sheriff for each riding. A superior general court, called the "court of assizes," was held once a year at New York.

As in New England, however, the town or parish was the principal factor of local organization. By order of the governor and council "the places where the townships upon the river shall be kept be appointed and agreed upon by the schout, commissioners, and the rest of the officers there, according to the proposals sent, as also where the blockhouses and places of defense shall be erected;"[1] and by the Duke's Lawes the bounds of every town were set out within

[1] Hazard's Annals of Pennsylvania.

twelve months after they were granted; and the marks thereof renewed every three years.[1] The jurisdiction of each town was carefully guarded; and it is interesting to note that a special warrant was necessary to cause the arrest of an offender who had escaped within the limits of another town.[2] Upon the seating of each town two town lots were reserved for the governor.[3] Each town kept a registry of marriages, births, and deaths,[4] and had a place of burial.[5] A church was directed by law to be erected in each parish, capable of accommodating two hundred persons.[6] Two church wardens were elected annually by the constable and overseers out of their own number. The church wardens at the opening of each court of sessions delivered in writing a presentment of all misdemeanors committed and not punished during their term, such as swearing, profaneness, Sabbath-breaking, drunkenness, fornication, adultery, and "all such abominable sinnes," and they were empowered to compel the attendance of witnesses.

The town was governed by a constable and board of overseers, consisting at first of eight, and afterwards of four, of the "most able men in each parish." The overseers were elected by the householders for two years, half of the board retiring annually; and the constable was likewise elected from among the retiring overseers. The powers of the constable and overseers were various, and embraced almost all matters of merely local interest. "Whereas in particular Townes," we read in the "Lawes," "many things do arise which concern only themselves and the well-ordering their affairs, as the disposing, Planting, Building, and the like, of their own lands and woods, granting of lotts, election of officers, assessing of Rates, with many other matters of a prudential nature, tending to the Peace and good Government of the Respective Townes, the Constable, by and with the consent of five at least of the overseers for the time being have power to Ordain such and so many peculiar Constitutions as are necessary

---

[1] Lawes, page 13. [2] Lawes, page 9. [3] Page 35. [4] Page 17. [5] Page 14. [6] Page 18.

to the Welfare and Improvement of the Towne; provided they be not of a criminal nature; and that the Penaltyes exceed not twenty shillings for one offence, and that they be not repugnant to the publique Lawes; and if any inhabitant shall neglect or refuse to observe them, the constable and overseers shall have power to levy such fines by distress."[1] The "peculiar constitutions" must be confirmed by the court of sessions within four months after the enacting thereof. As illustrations of the many powers of the constable and overseers, it may be mentioned that they settled disputes concerning fences and improvements of the common lands,[2] and appointed fence viewers for the supervision of such lands; had jurisdiction over unruly servants and children; appointed a register of brands to record every man's particular mark, and see that cattle were properly branded;[3] granted certificates of good character to all liquor dealers and innkeepers who could not, without such certificate, obtain a license from the court of sessions; determined offenses against the liquor and license laws, and received the fines;[4] pursued runaway servants, and protected them from cruel treatment on the part of their masters; and appointed viewers and inspectors of pipe staves, gaugers, and packers.[5]

The constable was the principal executive officer, as in New England. "The constable," in the words of the lawe, "shall whip or punish any one to be punished by order of authority, when there is not any other officer appointed to do it, in their own Towns, unless they can get another person to do it." In the absence of a justice of the peace "every constable shall have full power to make, sign, and put forth pursuits in hue and cryes after Murtherers, Man Slayers, Theves, Robbers, Burglarers, and Other Capital Offenders, as also to Apprehend without warrant such as are overtaken with Drink, Swearing, Sabbath breaking, Vagrant persons or Night Walkers, provided they be taken in the manner, either by the Sight of the Constable or by present information from others, as also to make search for all such persons either on the Sab-

[1] Lawes, 50. [2] Page 15. [3] Page 29. [4] Page 31. [5] Pages 45–47.

bath day or other where there shall be Occasion in all Houses Licenced to sell either Beer or Wine, or any other suspected or disordered places, and those to apprehend and keep in Safe Custody till opportunity Serves to bring them before the next justice of the peace for further Examination." As a badge of office, the constable carried a staff six feet long, with the king's arms on it, provided at the charge of the town. It was his duty, upon the death of any person, to repair to the house of the deceased, with two of the overseers, and inquire after the manner of his death, and in case he had died intestate, to take proper measures to secure the property till administration was granted.

On every page of the "Lawes" we are struck by the predominance of the town; and in nothing more strongly than in the organization of the militia and the collection of taxes. By the militia laws each town was required to provide a sufficient powder magazine; and the inhabitants were compelled to arm themselves properly and attend the military exercises. In each town the overseers and constable sent to the governor the names of three of the "most fit persons" for the offices of captain, lieutenant, and ensigns, who issued commissions. Each town had, once a year, four "training" days; while in each riding, once a year, there was a "general training" of all the towns within the jurisdiction. In the matter of the revenue it was provided that the sheriff should annually direct his warrant to the constable of every town, requiring him to call together the overseers of the town, who were to make a list of all the inhabitants, including male persons, over sixteen years, and a true estimate of all personal and real estate, the rates of persons and cattle being fixed by law. The lists and assessments were returned by the constable to the sheriff, who carefully examined, corrected, and perfected the same, and transmitted them to the governor. The rates were paid to the constable; and "for all peculiars (viz.) such Places as are not yet laid within the boundaries of any town; the said places with the Lands, Persons and Estates thereupon shall be Assessed by the Rates of the Towne next unto it; the measure or Estimation shall be By the Distance of the nearest Meeting House." There were two kinds of tax, both collected in the manner just mentioned; the public charge, the proceeds of which were applied to the maintenance of the general, civil, military, and ecclesiastical authority; and the town rate, for the support of the local government. "When the full amount of the levy could not be obtained, the deficiency was supplied by an extra assessment. Produce was received instead of money in the payment of the town and public taxes. None were exempt from taxation except justices of the peace and indigent persons, and even the justices were subsequently made liable for the town levy. Local taxation was designed chiefly for the support of the poor and the maintenance of parochial churches. The needy and the helpless of every parish were the special charge of the church wardens. They were, doubtless, considered in the light of an ecclesiastical rather than a civil responsibility. Under this *régime*, we see that county government, in the form we know it, did not practically exist. This riding, it is true, came in as a division of the town and the province, but it had little or no significance as a political factor."[1]

While the town or parish thus controlled the principal matters of local concern, the power and influence of the general courts must not be lost sight of. It will be remembered that there were, at the time the Duke's Book of Lawes went into operation, three general courts—at New Castle, at Upland, and at Whorekill. These courts, besides their judicial authority, possessed considerable power of legislation. They could enact "all necessary by-laws or orders to be binding for the space of one whole year,[2] for the administration of local matters within their respective districts. They could make "fitting rates for highways, poor, and other necessaries,"[3] which levy, "for the sake of convenience, generally took the form of a poll-tax; the constable making out the list of

[1] Local Self-Government in Pennsylvania, by E. R. L. Gould, A. B. John Hopkins University Studies, first series, III., page 23.

[2] Hazard's Annals of Pennsylvania, page 427. [3] *Ibid.*, 441.

" 'tydables;' "[1] and for the better management of roads and bridges, the court appointed yearly overseers of highways and viewers of fences;[2] and possessed many other duties and powers for the local government of the province.[3]

An important and radical change in the local institutions of Pennsylvania took place under the proprietor, William Penn. While the tendency of the Duke of York's laws was, as has been seen, to centre local government in the towns, the county under the proprietor became the element of first importance. Indeed, for the first half-century of the province the town had little or no importance or significance as a political division. The county court of general sessions was the real centre of authority, and all local affairs were administered by officers whom it commissioned. For the first few years, indeed, the county courts had almost all local administration in their hands, and appointed the justices, constables, road overseers, &c.[4] With the increase of population, however, a more subdivided local government gradually became necessary, and the township, the borough, and the municipality appeared. The town or any similar subdivision of the county, however, never gained the importance of the township previous to 1682; and the final form which local government assumed in Pennsylvania, as compared with the township system of New England and the county system of Virginia, was one in which the powers of local government were divided between the county and subdivision of the township, borough, or municipality.[5]

The degree and character of local government may be seen by a brief consideration of these three departments of local management embraced under the heads of Rates and Levies, Roads and Bridges, and Poor.

The objects for which the county taxes were raised were "for the support of the poor, building of prisons, or repair-

---

[1] Hazard's Annals of Pennsylvania, page 442. [2] *Ibid.*, 480.

[3] See Records of Court of Upland and Court of New Castle.

[4] Watson's Annals of Philadelphia, vol. I., page 304.

[5] See Local Government in Pennsylvania, by E. R. L. Gould, A. B. Johns Hopkins University Studies in Historical and Political Science, first series, No. III.

ing thereof; paying the salary of members belonging to the assembly, paying for Wolf's Heads, expence of Judges, with many other necessary charges."[1] At first it was the duty of the justices of the court of sessions, with the assistance of the grand jury, to estimate the general county expenses, and to make an assessment upon the basis of the provincial tax to defray them; but in 1696 a much more convenient system was enacted, which provided that six assessors should be annually chosen for each county, to act in conjunction with the justices and grand jury in determining public charges. The county treasurer was appointed by this body. In 1724 a new system was introduced, which, though not unlike the former in its essential features, provided for the election of three commissioners to perform the functions which had previously belonged to the court of sessions, with a few additional duties. "The Revolution did not change the form of local government which had obtained immediately before the year 1776. There was no distinct difference between the administration of the province and of the commonwealth. But in relation to the topic at present under consideration, an advance was made toward the present system in 1779. In that year the assessment board, consisting of the three commissioners and six county assessors, appointed two assistant assessors for each township, to discharge the duties which had hitherto devolved upon the constable in making the returns of taxable inhabitants and property."

In the early provincial times the management of roads and bridges, among the other extensive powers of local government, was vested in the county. All public highways were laid out by order of the governor and council;[2] while private roads, connecting with them, and cartways leading to landing places, were opened up at the instance of the court of quarter sessions, if the viewers had previously made a report upon the projected enterprise. Roads and bridges were made at the expense of the county; but it was not unusual for a

[1] Laws of the Province of Pennsylvania, 1682–1700, page 233.

[2] Colonial Records, I., page 163.

lottery to be established to liquidate the cost of the undertakings. The court named the overseers, and were responsible for the good repair of all highways within their territorial limits. With the gradual subdivision of local government in Pennsylvania, by which the county ceased to be the only factor, the highways were transferred from county to township supervision, together with all financial burdens of their management. The overseers, or supervisors, were thenceforth township officers, and two were elected annually. They were empowered to levy a road tax within certain limits, after having obtained the requisite permission from two justices of the peace.

The act of 1771 embodied the principles of the poor laws of the State as they exist to-day. This act provided for the appointment of two overseers in each township, by the justices of the peace, at a yearly meeting convened for the purpose. These officers could, with the authority of two justices, levy a limited rate on property, and a poll-tax as often as was thought advisable.

This brief sketch of the distribution of powers between the county and township in certain matters of local government is sufficient to give an idea of the Pennsylvania system. The modern system of local government has been developed in accordance with those principles, and does not require much explanation for the present purpose. The county is the leading local unit. The chief authority is vested in three commissioners, elected for a term of three years. Each county has also a treasurer, a surveyor, and three auditors. Judicial and certain other officers do not require mention.

The highest township authority is vested in a board of supervisors. There is also an assessor, two assistant assessors, a town clerk, a treasurer, three auditors, and two overseers of the poor, where the poor are a township charge. "The township has the power to lay certain rates independently of county authority or jurisdiction. For instance, the supervisors are authorized to assess the taxables of their township for a sum not exceeding one cent on the dollar, upon the valuation of their property, to keep the roads, highways, and bridges in good order. It is also the duty of the overseers of the poor, where the poor are in the charge of the township, to make a similar provision for the support of the indigent and helpless, having first obtained the consent of two justices of the peace." These rates, however, can only be laid in accordance with the last adjusted county valuation. Roads and highways lying within the boundaries of a township are under its management. They are controlled by the supervisors, and the expense of their good keeping is borne out of the fund raised by the above-mentioned assessment. The jurisdiction of the county, however, comes in and illustrates the distribution of power, in the case of the opening of a new highway. To open a new highway the court of quarter sessions is petitioned by the inhabitants. The court at once appoints viewers, who inspect the locality and make their report to the court; and if a favorable view is entertained, the road is confirmed and duly opened. Damages are paid by the county.

The poor, as already mentioned, are legally a township charge, though their care is generally placed in the hands of the county commissioners.

While the county was thus made the largest and principal political division in the system of the proprietor, and the existing town with its court was modified into the township under the authority of the county courts, the towns and villages were incorporated into cities and boroughs.[1]

After this brief sketch of the distribution of local powers in Pennsylvania, it will be easy to understand the position of Philadelphia in relation to the county and the State; the character of its early government, the significance of the special legislation relative to it, and the general principles controlling the development of the municipal institutions.

---

[1] Pennsylvania, New Jersey, and Connecticut are the only States possessing borough systems. See Pennsylvania Boroughs, by William P. Holcomb, Johns Hopkins University Studies, fourth series, No. IV.

The Discovery of the first Charter of the City of Philadelphia.

After the completion of this work, and as the sheets were about to be bound, through information derived from Mr. Thomas Cochran, who has rendered valuable assistance and information throughout its prosecution, the authors learned of an old charter in the possession of Colonel Alexander Biddle. Upon calling upon that gentleman the document printed below was discovered, which is undoubtedly a genuine original charter granted in the year 1691. Colonel Biddle states that the charter was found among the papers of his grandfather, Colonel Clement Biddle, the distinguished Revolutionary officer. It is in an excellent state of preservation, and entirely legible; the great seal is unfortunately gone, leaving, however, unmistakable evidence of having been duly attached. It is signed by Thomas Lloyd, deputy governor, and attested by David Lloyd, deputy master of the rolls.

The discovery of this charter confirms the conclusion arrived at, "That there must have been some organized local authority exercised prior to 1701." (See chapter I., pages 4–7.) The evidences of history must of course sustain each other as is here shown: On 6 Mo. 3, 1691[1] (see page 4), "Humphrey Murrey, the present mayor of the city of Philadelphia, appears before the Provincial Council, * * * notice is given to the mayor and aldermen to meet the council" (see page 5). This heretofore isolated reference to Humphrey Murrey as mayor is completely substantiated by this charter which created as ample a city government as did the Charter of 1701. The provisions of this earlier charter are substantially the same as those of 1701, though they have several quaint variances, being fuller in some points and more restricted in others.

It will be remembered that on the occasion of Penn's second visit to this country, he was induced to grant a new charter to the province, and nothing would be more natural than that a new charter should also be granted to the chief city, especially as controversies had arisen as to the right to the ends of the streets, to the use of waste or common land, to the control of Blue An-

[1] This date is erroneously given as May 5, on page 4, chapter I.

chor and Penny Pot Landings, all of which were settled by the Charter of 1701.

A charter regularly issued by the proper authority being produced, bearing date 1691, and containing every intrinsic evidence of being genuine, creating a city with Humphrey Murrey as mayor, and record evidence *aliunde* of Humphrey Murrey acting as mayor in the same year, the mere absence of other evidence does not necessarily show that this charter was treated as a nullity. The careless abandon with which the city of Philadelphia has left its records to survive or perish as chance or accident might dictate, the well-known fact that many records were destroyed during the British occupation, the utter indifference heretofore manifested toward the investigation of its municipal history and the collection and preservation of documents pertaining thereto, all combine to warn against formulating any theory as conclusive which must be based on the absence of complete proofs. It is also to be noted that the printed minutes of the common council under the Charter of 1701 do not go back of 1704, so that it is not at all presumptuous to infer that minutes of a council under the Charter of 1691 might have easily existed down to 1701, and then shared the same fate as the minutes of 1701 and 1702. The Charter of 1701 is substantially a revival of that of 1691, and the concluding sentence of chapter I., page 7, must be transferred and applied to that of 1691, the earlier charter.

On the other hand, however, it is possible that when Penn was deprived of his government in 1692, and Governor Fletcher supplanted him, the city charter may have been considered and treated as a nullity. The fact that the "Clark of the market at philadelphia" held under "Commission from his Excell. Go^{r}. ffletcher" in 1693 (Col. Rec., vol. I., page 343), lends weight to this theory, as this was a corporation office under the Charter. There may also be significance in the silence of Penn regarding it. It is a matter of curiosity and regret that no other allusions direct or incidental have been found bearing upon such an important state paper as the first charter creating the city of Philadelphia, so that for over a century its existence prior to the eighteenth century should have been considered a myth, and it is to be hoped that either here or in England State or family papers, to which we have not had access, may be found throwing new light on this interesting point.

March 10, 1887.

CHARTER.

THIRD MONTH 20TH, 1691.

WILLIAM PENN Propriet'y of the Province of *Pensilvania* *To* all to whom these Prsents shall come sends Greeting &c. *Know Ye* That at the humble petiton of the Inhabitants & Settlers of this Town of Philadelphia being some of the first Adventurers & Purchasers within this Province for their incouragement and for the more imediate & intire Government of the said Town and better Regulaton of Trade therein *I have* by vertue of the Kings Letters Patents under the Great Seal of England erected the said Town into a Burrough *And* by these Prsents Do erect the said Town & Burrough of Philadelphia into a City which said City shall extend the Limits & Bounds as it is layd out between Delaware and Skoolkill *And* do hereby name and constitute Humphrey Morrey to be the prsent Mayor who shall so continue untill another be chosen as is hereinafter directed *And I Do* hereby assigne and name John Delavall to be the present Recorder to do and execute all things which unto the Office of Recorder of the said City doth or may belong *And* I do appoint David LLoyd to be the present Town Clerk Clerk of ye Board and Clerk of the Court & Courts to be holden within the said City and Liberties thereof *And* I do hereby name constitute and appoint Samuel Richardson Griffith Owen Anthony Morris Robert Ewer John Holmes & ffrancis Rawle junr Being the present Justices Citizens and Inhabitants of the said City to be the prsent Six Aldermen of the said City of Philadelphia *And I Do Also* nominate & appoint Samuel Carpenter Thomas Budd John Jones John Otter Charles Sanders Zechariah Whitpaine John Day Philip Richards Alexander Berdsley James ffox Thomas Pascall and Philip James to be the present Twelve Comon Councilmen of the said City *And* I Do by these Presents for me & my heirs & Successors give grant & declare That the said Mayor Recorder Aldermen & Comon Councilmen for the time being and they which hereafter Shall be Mayor Recorder Aldermen and Comon Councilmen within the said City and their Successors for ever hereafter be and Shall be by vertue of these prsents One Body Corporate & Politiq in Deed and by the name of Mayor and Comonalty of Philadelphia in the Province of Pensilvania *And* them by the name of Mayor and Comonalty of the City of Philadelphia One Body Politiq & Corporate in deed & in name I Do for me & my Successors fully create constitute and confirm by these Prsents *And* That by the same name of Mayor and Comonalty of the City of Philadelphia they may have perpetual Succession *And* that they and their Successors by the name of Mayor & Comonalty of the City of Philadelphia be and at all times hereafter shall be persons able & capable in Law To have gett receive and possess Lands Tenements Rents Liberties Jurisdictions ffranchises & Hereditaments to them & their Successors in fee simple or for term of Life Lives years or otherwise And also goods chattels & other things of what nature kind or quality Soever *And* also to give grant let Set & assign the same Lands Tenements hereditaments goods & Chattels and to do and execute all other things about the same by the name aforsyd *And* also that they be and shall be forever hereafter persons able & capable in Law to Sue and be Sued plead & be impleaded answer and be answered unto defend and be defended in all or any the Courts & other places and before any Judges Justices & other persons whatsoever within the said Province & Territorys thereof in all manner of actions suits complaints pleas causes & matters whatsover and of what kind or nature soever *And* that it shall & may be lawful to and for the said Maior & Comonalty of the sd City of Philadelphia and their Successors for ever hereafter to have & use one Comon Seal for the sealing of all businesses touching the sd Corporation *And* the same from time to time at their will and pleasure to change or alter *And* I do for me my heirs & Successors give and by these presents grant full power and authority unto the Mayor Recorder Aldermen & Comon Councilmen of the said City of Philadelphia or any three or more of the Aldermen and Six or more of the Comon Councilmen The Mayor & Recorder for the time being or either of them being present on the first second day of the week in the Second month yearly forever hereafter publickly to meet at a convenient Room or place within the said City to be by them appointed for that purpose and then & there nominate elect & chuse (by the Ballott) out of the Inhabitants of the said City fit & able persons to be in the respective offices & places of Mayor Aldermen & Comon Councilmen *And* that such person who shall be so elected Mayor as aforesaid shall within three daies next after such election take his attestation before the Governor of this Province or his deputy for the time being for his allegiance to the King and Queen & their Successors and lawful obedience to me and my Successors And for the due Execucon of his office And that the Recorder Aldermen & Comon Councilmen and all other officers of the sd City before they or any of them shall be admitted to execute their respective Offices Shall Promise Allegiance to the King & Queen of England and their Successors and lawful obedience to me and my Successors And shall be attested before the Mayor for the tyme being for the due Execucon of their Offices respectively which promises and attestations the Mayor of the said City for the time being is hereby impowered to take & administer accordingly *And* that the Maior Recorder & Aldermen of the sd City for the time being shall be Justices of the Peace and Justices of Oyer and Terminer and are hereby impowered to act within the sd City & Liberties thereof accordingly as fully & amply as any Justice or Justices of the peace or Oyer & Terminer can or may do within the sd Province *And* that they or any three or more of them (whereof the Maior & Recorder of the said City for the time being shall be two) shall & may for ever hereafter have power & authority by vertue of these prsents to hear & determine according to the Laws of this Province & of the Kingdom of England All maner of pleas actons & causes Civil & Criminal whatsoever *Excepting* Treason Murder & Manslaughter within the sd City & Liberties from time to time arising & happening Reserving the Liberty of Appeal according to the King's Letters Patents & laws of this Governmt Hereby also impowering them or any three of them (whereof the Mayor & Recorder for the time being shall be two) with the Town Clerk to hold & keep a Cort of Record quarterly or oftener if they see occasion for the Inquiring hearing & determining of the pleas aforesaid as also for the hearing & Deciding causes in Equity arising in ye sd City *And* I Do by these prsents assign & appoint That the prsent Mayor Recorder & Aldermen herein before named be the prsent Justices of the peace & Oyer & Terminer within the sd City & liberties aforesd *And* That it may be lawfull to & for the sd Mayor & Comonalty and their successors to erect a Gaol or prison & Court house within the sd City *And* that the Mayor and Recorder for the time being shall and by these prsents have power to take Recognizance of debts there according to the Statute of Marchants & of Acton Burnel and to use & affix ye sd Comon Seal thereunto & to all certificates concerning the same *And* That it may be lawfull to & for the Maior of the sd City for the time being forever hereafter to nominate & from time to time appoint the Clerk of the Markett who shall have assise of bread wine Beer wood & other things & do execute & perform all things belonging to the Office of Clerk of the Markett within the sd City *And* I will That the Coroner & Sheriff of the County of Philadelphia for the time being Shall be the Coroner & Sheriff of the sd City & Liberties thereof But that the ffreemen & Inhabitants of the sd City shall from time to time as often as occasion be have equall Liberty with the Inhabitants of the said county to recomend or chuse persons to serve in the respective Capacities of Coroner & Sheriffs for the Said City & County who shall reside within the sd City *And* That the Sherif of the sd City & County for the time being shall be the Water Bayliff who shall & may execute & perform all things belonging to the Office of Water Bayliff upon Delaware River & all other navigable Rivers & Creeks within this Province And in case the Maior of the sd City for the time being shall during the time of his Mayoralty misbehave himself or misgovern in that office I Do hereby impower the Recorder Aldermen & Comon Councilmen or four of the Aldermen and Eight of the Comon Councilmen of the sd City of Philadelphia for the time being to remove such Mayor from his office of Mayoralty and in such case or in case of death of the sd Mayor for the time being That then another ffit person shall within fouer daies next after such death or removall be chosen in maner as is above directed for electing of Maiors in the place of him so dead or removed *And* least there should be a failure of Justice or Government in the sd City in such Intervall I Do hereby appoint That the oldest Alderman for the time being shall take upon him the office of a Maior there & shall Exercise the same till another Mayor be chosen as aforesd And in case of the disability of such oldest Alderman then the next in Seniority shall take upon him the sd office of Maior to exercise the same as aforesd *And* in case the Recorder or any of the Aldermen or Comon Councilmen or any other of the officers of & belonging to the said City for the time being shall misbehave him or themselves in their respective Offices and places they shall be removed and others chosen in their stead in maner following that is to say The Recorder for the tyme being may be removed (for misbehauior) by the Maior and ye major part of the Aldermen and Comon Councilmen respectively and in case of such removal or of the death of the Recorder Then to chuse another fit person Skilled in law to be Recorder there and so to continue during pleasure as aforesd And the Aldermen so misbehaving himself may be removed by the Maior Recorder and major part of the Aldermen and Comon Councilmen *And* in case of such removall or death Then within four dais after to chuse a fitt person or persons to supply such vancancys *And* the Comon Councilmen Town Clerk Constables Clerk of the Markett and other Officers for neglect or misbehauior shall be removed & others chosen as is directed in ye case of Aldermen *And* I do also for me and my successors by these prsents grant to the said Maior & Comonalty & their Successors That if any of the Citizens of the sd City shall be hereafter elected nominated & chosen to the office of Mayor Aldermen or Comon Councilmen as aforesaid and having notice of his or their sd electon shall refuse to undertake & exercise that office to which he is so chosen That then & so often It Shall and may be lawfull for the Maior and Recorder Aldermen & Comon Councilmen or the major part of the Aldermen and Comon Councilmen for the time being according to their discreton to impose such moderate ffines upon Such refusers so as the Mayors ffine exceed not ten pounds The Alderman five pounds and Comon Councilman four pounds and other Officers proportonately To be levyed by distresse & Sale by warrt under the Comon Seal or by other lawfull waies To the use of the sd Corporaton *And* in Such Cases It shall be lawfull to chuse others to supply the defects of such refusers in maner as is above direct for Electons *And* That it shall and may be lawfull to and for the Mayor Recorder and one of the Aldermen for the time being from time to time so often as they shall find occasion to sumon a Comon Council of the said City *And* that no Assembly or meeting of the said Citizens shall be deemed and accounted a Comon Council unless the said Maior and Recorder and at least three of the Aldermen for the time being and fouer of the Comon Councilmen be present *And* also That the said Mayor Recorder Aldermen & Comon Councilmen for the time being from time to time at their Comon Council shall have power to admitt such & so many ffreemen into their Corporaton & Society as they shall think fitt *And* to make and they may make Ordain Constitute & establish such and so many good and reasonable Laws Ordinances & Constitutons (not repugnant to the Laws of England or of this Government) as to the greatest part of them at such Comon Councils assembled whereof the Mayor & Recorder or in their absence four of the Aldermen for time being to be alwaies some shall seem necessary & convenient for the good Government of the said City *And* the same Laws Ordinances Orders & Constitutons so made to be putt in use and operaton accordingly by the proper Officers of the said City *And* at their pleasure to revoke alter and make anew as occasion shall require *And* also to impose such mulcts & amerciaments upon the breakers of such Laws & Ordinances as to them in their discreton shall be thought reasonable To be levyed as above is directed in case of ffines to the use of the said Corporaton without rendring any account thereof to me my heirs & Successors with power to the Comon Council aforesd to mitigate remitt or Release such ffines and mulcts upon the submission of the parties *And* I do further grant to the said Mayor and Comonalty of the said City of Philadelphia That they and their successors shall and may forever hereafter hold & keep within the said City in every week of the year Two markett daies The one upon the fourth day of the week and the other upon the seventh day of the week in the place already appointed or in such other place as they shall think convenient *And* also three ffaires there in every year The first of them to begin on the Sixteenth day of the Third month yearly and so to be held in & about the markett place and continue for that Sixteenth day & two dayes next following The next to be kept at the Center of the said City on the thirtieth & one and one & thirtieth daies of the Sixth Month yearly *And* third of the said ffaires to be held in or about the markett place on the Sixteenth Seventeenth

& Eighteenth daies of the Ninth Month yearly Hereby giving and granting That this present Charter or Grant Shall in all Courts of Law and Equity be construed and taken most favorably and beneficially for the said Corporaton *Given* under the Broad Seal of the said Province *Witnes* Thomas LLoyd Deputy Governor of the said Province of Pensilvania with the advice and assent of the Provincial Council at Philadelphia the Twentieth day of the Third Month in the third year of the Raign of *William* and *Mary* King and Queen of England Anoqe Dni One Thousand six hundred ninety and one.

Tho: lloyd
Depty Gov^{rr}.

Recorded in the Office of Rolls & Publiq Registry at Philadelphia the 29th day of the third month 1691. Ex^{d} pr Da. lLoyd Deput. } Patent Book A.

(Place where seal was affixed.)

[Endorsed: "Philadelphia City Charter."]

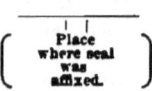

PHILADELPHIA
1681–1887.

A HISTORY OF MUNICIPAL DEVELOPMENT.

CHAPTER I.

EARLY GOVERNMENT.
1681–1701.

Authority of the Proprietor.

Section 1. When Penn landed on the shores of the Delaware, in 1682, he came armed with *quasi* regal power, and found English institutions and laws engrafted on and modified somewhat by Dutch and Swedish customs; but his beloved city was settled on almost virgin soil, and presented a white page for legislation. The site, after having been twice purchased from the Swedes and Indians, was laid out under William Markham by Thomas Holme. The land which was to form the province of Pennsylvania and its territories passed into the hands of the Proprietor by Royal charter and deed of confirmation from the Duke of York, and the colony formed one of the group of three of proprietary governments. By Section X. of the Royal charter Penn was authorized "to divide the country into towns, hundreds, and counties, and to erect and incorporate towns into boroughs, and boroughs into cities, and to make and constitute fairs and markets therein."

The scheme of government entered into between Penn and the adventurers, or proposed settlers, contemplated the foundation of a city, and an allotment of city lots was made to each original purchaser of land in the province. This town or city was laid out, as we see, by Penn's agent Markham before Penn's arrival, and received the name of Philadelphia. The province was also divided into three counties, Philadelphia, Chester, and Bucks, which, together with the three lower counties of the territories (Delaware), Kent, Sussex, and New Castle, made up the division of Penn's domain. The county was the unit of government.

Sec. 2. Under the Duke of York we find that the township was the political unit, though not, perhaps, in the integrity established in New England; but, under Penn, we must, from the beginning of his rule, look to the county as the unit. In the absence of complete records (between 1681 and 1701) regarding many details of administration in Philadelphia this fact, if kept in mind, will save us from embarrassment, and enable us to predicate certain conclusions with reasonable assurance, which otherwise we could hardly infer with certainty. Especially true is this in fixing the date of the birth of Philadelphia as a municipal entity. By Penn's Frame, Section X., it is provided that the Governor and Provincial Council shall at all times settle and order the situation of all cities, ports, and market towns in every county. (Duke of York's Laws, page 95.)

The boundaries of Philadelphia were determined as follows: From what is now Vine street on the north, to what is now South street on the south, along the Delaware river, nearly a mile in front or breadth on said river, and westward about two miles to the river Schuylkill.

Division of Subject.

Sec. 3. The life of the city government of Philadelphia naturally presents itself for treatment under five sharply defined periods:

I. The first period covers twenty-one years, from 1681 to 1701, being the infant era of the town prior to its incorporation by William Penn.

II. The second period stretches from its municipal birth, seventy-five years, to the Revolution, and on through the Revolution to the passage of the act of 1789; the thirteen years between 1776 and 1789 being an era of suspended municipal life.

III. The third period reaches from 1789 to 1854, and records the life of what is now called the old city. For a little over half a century the city grew rapidly under the legislative charter of 1789, with the divers acts amendatory thereof and supplementary thereto, up to consolidation. In an analytic point of view, this period is of the greatest importance, for in it the organic law and the policy of Philadelphia as a modern municipality are crystallized.

IV. From 1854 to 1887 the consolidated city and county of Philadelphia has staggered under a patchwork of outgrown laws and ordinances, customs, and practices, often resulting in legislative and executive maladministration.

V. The Reform Charter or Bullitt Bill. The changes by it effected in the organic law of the municipality.

While the term charter is used with reference to acts of the legislature incorporating the city, or materially amending or altering such incorporating acts, it should be stated that such use of the term is not, legally speaking, correct. A charter ordinarily implies the granting of vested rights without reservation of the power of revoking or altering the rights and privileges so granted at the pleasure of the grantor. All acts incorporating towns and cities by the legislature are made with a reservation of the power to alter, repeal, or amend. The incorporation of a town is simply the delegation by the sovereign people of certain local administrative functions to the inhabitants of the locality.

Organized Government Prior to 1701.

Sec. 4. When Penn arrived at Philadelphia most of the people were living in caves in the banks, but a number of houses were soon erected; and in the minutes of the Provincial Council and Acts of Assembly it is constantly spoken of as "the town of Philadelphia," or the "city of Philadelphia;" but obviously these terms may have had no significance apart from the designation of a more thickly settled spot laid out and surveyed for a town and established as a port and market.

On the other hand, Acrelius in his New Sweden, page 112, published in 1712, speaks of Philadelphia as receiving its first charter in 1682, and its so-called liberties as extending three English miles beyond the city between the rivers; but this is mere dictum, and most probably refers to Penn's charter of that date to the colonists. On 26th 5 mo., 1684, the following minute appears on the record of the P. C. "Thos. Lloyd, Thos. Holme, Wm. Haigue appointed to draw up a charter of Philadelphia, to be made a Borough, consisting of a Mayor and six Aldermen, and to call to y^r^ assistance any of ye Council." There is no record that this committee ever acted. Prior to this, in 1684, a bill passed second reading in the Council providing for 3 members of ye Council and 6 for the Assembly from "ye city of Philadelphia;" but there is no record of a third reading or co-ordinate action of the Assembly, and evidence is wanting as to any members sitting for the city as distinct from the county. Whether the town or city was really made a borough, as thus indicated, is not clearly shown; but there is undoubtedly evidence of some sort of a government existing in 1691, but how organized or granted does not appear. The minutes of the Provincial Council are lost or destroyed for that year and 1692; but the Recorder's office, in Deed-book H, No. 7, page 92, shows in the nature of perpetuated testimony the proceedings of the citizens of Philadelphia, in 1753, to secure the dedication of the Blue Anchor landing for public use forever. These proceedings recite the minutes of the Provincial Council of May 5th, 1691, as follows: "Present, Thomas Lloyd, Dept. Governor and six Councilors: Humphrey Murrey, the present Mayor of the city of Philadelphia, on behalf of the said city moves the Governor and Council to lay out the end of the street near the Blue Anchor."[1]

[1] See article by A. & P., in Penn. Hist. Mag. for April, 1886, page 61.

Whereupon it is ordered that "the said Mayor and the Aldermen of Philadelphia have notice to attend the Governor and Council about the 8th hour in order to view the said landing."

This protest and proceedings, antiquated and forgotten as they are, have considerable historical value. 1st. Taken in connection with the delegation to the committee, in 1684, of the duty of drawing up a charter for Philadelphia to be made a borough, and the assertion of Penn, that he had created the town a borough, they seem to indicate that some charter may have been given of such purport; at least they may be taken as evidence that some sort of organization existed among the citizens, whether formally delegated by the proprietary power or assumed by the citizens. The absence of any other even remote or incidental allusion to any such town organization would lead to the deduction, either that it was fugitive in its existence, or at least of very limited functions, since it has left no lasting impress of any influence on the history of its times. 2d. The proceedings of that time, while primitive in one sense, were very formal in all creative details of organization, the power of the Proprietor being so ample and unquestioned. 3d. The expression of protest on the part of the citizens to the alleged unwarranted assumption of power by the corporation on this occasion, manifested in 1753, the time when these old records were exhumed and re-recorded in formal and elaborated shape in the deed-book, took shape in the assembling of something as analogous to a town meeting as anything which we have in the history of the city. The citizens assembled in mass meeting, headed by the Guardians of the Poor, City Warden, Members of the Legislature, and Assessors, and prominent citizens; every dignitary, saving the titular officials of the corporation, *i. e.*, Mayor, Recorder, Common Councilmen, and Aldermen.

The question involved here came before the Supreme Court of Pennsylvania, in the Penny Pot Landing case, 16 Pa. St., 79, although it was not necessary for the court to decide on the point whether Philadelphia was actually chartered as a town or borough prior to the charter of 1701. This record, taken with the minute of May 26th, 1684, and Penn's statement in the charter, "I have by virtue of the King's Letters Patent * * erected the said town into a borrough, and do, by these presents, erect the said town & borrough into a city," while it does not give us very satisfactory information as to the character of the putative organization, is as conclusive, as it is slight, of the existence of some such organization.

From the weight of the evidence, then, as recorded, we can safely conclude that there must have been some local authority exercised prior to 1701; but the interest thereof is purely historical, for the traces which it has left are vague and shadowy. There was hardly room and no imperative demand in the nature of things for any clearly outlined municipal life or influence apart from the autonomy of the county. The county judges appointed by Penn, and assisted by the grand juries, provided for the limited local administration; they laid and collected the taxes of the county, laid out roads other than the king's highways, which fell to the Council, and for the rest, the general laws and actions of the Council provided the meagre legislation necessary to the primitive wants of a people to whom governmental and legislative action came as a public tax or duty, to be avoided rather than sought. There were no contracts or corporations in those days to make a seat in councils or legislature a profitable vocation. The good Quaker had his land to clear, his houses to build, his merchandise to sell. All officers held their commissions direct from the Proprietor during his life. The township and town meeting had no existence as we see them in New England. The Provincial Council had wide powers, jointly with the Proprietor when present, representing him when absent. It sat as a Court of Appeals, an Orphans' Court, a Privy Council, a Senate. It proposed all bills to the lower house; tried old women for witchcraft, and young men for drunkenness; passed regulations to punish negroes who disturbed the peace by gadding about the streets; took cognizance of defective drains, gradings, market regulations, the size of bakers' loaves, and divers other kindred minutiæ, which, in New England, would have been the province of the town meeting. Finally, we must conclude that such organization as existed must have been of fugitive existence, or of very limited scope. The charter of 1701 was not the evolution of any customs or growth of institutions of the infant town; it was a new creation, flowing from the sovereign pleasure of the Proprietor. It was his creature.

SEAL OF PHILADELPHIA IN 1683.

CHAPTER II.

PENN'S CHARTER. A MEDIÆVAL CORPORATION.

1701–1789.

AUTHORITY TO INCORPORATE.

SECTION 1. The first charter incorporating Philadelphia as a city was granted by the Proprietor, William Penn, in 1701, by virtue of the authority given him in the royal charter of the province "to erect and incorporate Towns into Borroughs, and Borroughs into Citties, and to make & constitute ffaires and markets therein, with all other convenient privileges and imunities according to the meritt of the inhabitants & the ffitness of the places."[1] The charter of 1701, therefore, differs from the subsequent charters in this important particular, that the former was created by the grant of the Proprietor, while the latter were created by act of legislature. While the legislature as the sovereign authority may grant such powers as it chooses, the king or his delegated agent, the Proprietor, was restricted in many ways. He could not incorporate a community without its consent; and while he might confer the usual powers of a municipality, he could not confer extraordinary powers out of the course of the common law, as power to punish by forfeiture or imprisonment, or an exclusive right of trading.[2]

A CLOSE CORPORATION CONSTITUTED.

SEC. 2. In accordance with these principles the charter granted by Penn resembled in its outlines the typical constitution of an English town, such as prevailed from the close of the middle ages to the Municipal Reform Act of 1835.[3] A close corporation is constituted, under the name of the

---

[1] Lowber's Ordinances, page 2. [2] Dillon, 2d ed., vol. 1, page 108.

[3] Stubb's Constitutional History of England, vol. 3, page 560.

"Mayor and Commonalty of the City of Philadelphia," consisting of a mayor, a recorder, eight aldermen, and twelve common councilmen,[1] and possessing the five usual powers of a legal corporation. The first corporate officers were appointed in the charter. The mayor was elected annually from the aldermen, by at least five of the aldermen and nine of the common councilmen, the mayor or recorder being present. The recorder, aldermen, and common councilmen held office for life. The corporation might add to their number from time to time as occasion required. The important characteristic of such a charter, from which many local consequences followed, was that, strictly speaking, the corporation proper was not the place or inhabitants, but a close, self-elected corporate body, existing, as it were, independently of the community in which it was constituted, and possessing certain powers to govern the inhabitants.

Origin of Close Municipal Corporations.

Sec. 3. This constitution was reached by the boroughs of England after many years, in consequence of the dislike on the part of the authorities of popular elections, and, more especially, in consequence of the intrigues of the crown to control the elections of the burgesses in Parliament. The franchise of returning members to Parliament was granted to a great number of towns about the time of Edward the First; and from that time they obtained great political importance. At first, to strengthen itself against the barons, the crown encouraged popular elections, until, perceiving it had raised a more formidable opponent to its power, it began to assume a different policy and to endeavor to secure the return of its own creatures by discouraging popular elections of the municipal magistrates, and by raising a sort of burgher aristocracy. In Queen Elizabeth's reign the judges, upon the application of the Privy Council, determined that from usage within time of memory a by-law may be presumed restraining to a select body the right of election of the principal corporators, though

[1] Charter of 1701.

vested by the ancient constitution in the general assembly of the freemen. In the reign of King James they went still farther, and determined that the king could by his charter incorporate the people of a town in the form of select classes and commonalty, and vest in the whole corporation the right of sending representatives to Parliament, *restraining the exercise of that right to the select classes;* and this was the form of all the new corporations. "These doctrines," says Willcock, "with more consideration of precedent than principle have been carried in modern decisions to an extreme subversion of an ancient law, and established the opinion that the franchise of electing corporators can be surrendered by the commonalty, not only for themselves but also for their successors."[1]

Charles I. was dethroned by the power of corporate representation, then at its height, while the Protector, unable to cope with the same, expelled it from the House. In the reign of Charles II. the famous proceedings of *quo warranto* to repeal the charters of the obnoxious corporations on pretense of forfeiture were brought. Judgment was given against London, and the charter forfeited. Such consternation was spread among the other towns that most of them let judgment go against them by default, or surrendered their charters, and secured new charters in return. Although the old charters were restored in the succeeding reign, the select classes, unwilling to relinquish their power, and supported by the royal party and the decisions of the courts, retained thus in their grasp the municipal power, and by this means prevented the restoration of popular elections until the Municipal Reform Act of 1835.

The charter of Philadelphia was granted during the reign of Charles II., subsequently to the *quo warranto* proceedings already referred to. This was the period at which the liberties of the boroughs were most oppressed, and the crown most active in attempting to restrain popular elections. The decisions of the courts concerning the boroughs were made by partisan judges controlled by the crown, and are to be

[1] Willcock on Corporations, page 5.

received with great caution. Such was the fallen state of their ancient privileges that Willcock in his book on boroughs exclaims, "This, called the Augustan age, should have rather derived its name from Heliogabalus!"[1] Granted in such a period, it is not surprising to find the first charter of Philadelphia marked by many illiberal features compared with the modern ideas of municipal privileges.

Integral Parts.

Sec. 4. The mayor, recorder, aldermen, and common councilmen composed what was known to the writers of the day as the integral parts of the corporation; that is to say, strictly speaking, the existence of the single members and a majority of the select classes was essential to the existence of the corporation. Hence, at common law, during a vacancy in the office of mayor no valid corporate act could be done except to elect another, since without a mayor the corporate body was incomplete; and no corporate meeting was complete to transact any business whatever unless the mayor and recorder and a certain number of the aldermen and common councilmen were present.[2]

The Mayor.

Sec. 5. The mayor was the head of the corporation, and at common law, as well as by the charter, his presence was essential to the dispatch of corporate business. It was the duty of the mayor, together with the recorder and at least three of the aldermen, to summon a common council or corporate meeting as they saw occasion.[2] This privilege of the mayor to call a corporate meeting was also his at common law; and so far was it supported by the court that it was determined that however obstinate or interested in his motion the mayor might be in refusing to convene a meeting, it not only could not be convened by anybody else, but to do so and to transact business was an indictable offense. The doctrine was sustained on grounds that give a fair idea of the position

[1] Willcock, page 5. [2] Charter of Philadelphia.

of the mayor; that if the presence of the mayor were not necessary there would be no corporate superiority in the office; and the very purpose of creating such an office was to prevent the confusion that would follow from leaving it in the power of any corporator to call together the assembly at pleasure.[1] It was also the duty of the mayor to preside and propose business or acquiesce in the proposal of another;[2] but the mayor, unlike the mayors of modern municipalities, had, neither by the charter nor at common law, a veto or casting vote.

On the ground that a municipal corporation had a right to the service of all its members in those offices to which they were capable of being elected, it was provided in accordance with the common law that any citizen elected to the office of mayor, alderman, or common councilman and refusing to serve was liable to a fine.[3] Yet such was the expense and labor incident to the office of mayor that frequently the person so elected preferred to pay the fine rather than accept the office. At the expiration of his year of office it was the custom for the mayor to give an expensive banquet to the members of the corporation,—a custom which many of the later mayors abandoned, and instead presented the city with an amount of money equivalent to the cost of the banquet.[4] At first no salary was paid to the mayor; and with the growth of the city the difficulty of getting a proper person to accept the office increased. At length, in 1747, a salary of one hundred pounds a year was granted to the mayor; and although three years afterward this salary was abolished, it was subsequently revived for a time.[5]

As already mentioned, the mayor was elected annually from among the aldermen by any five or more of the aldermen and nine or more of the common councilmen, the mayor or recorder being present. Within three days after his election the mayor was to be presented before the governor of the

---

[1] Willcock, page 29. [2] *Ibid.*, page 103. [3] Charter

[4] Min. C. C., page 463. See, also, page 511, and several other cases.

[5] Min. C. C., 1704–1776, pages 480, 485, 511, 666.

province and subscribe the declaration and profession of his Christian belief, and take the oath for the due execution of his office. In case of the misconduct of the mayor he might be removed by the recorder, at least five aldermen and nine common councilmen; and in case of such removal or of the death of the mayor, then another person was to be chosen within five days; and in the interval the eldest alderman was to act as mayor.[1] Besides his duties under the charter the mayor had from time to time additional duties imposed upon him by the common council. Thus he is appointed city treasurer (page 322, Minutes); he is ordered once in every month to inspect the bread bakers, and to seize and dispose of all bread found deficient in weight, according to law (Min. C. C., page 9 [1704]).

THE RECORDER.

SEC. 6. The recorder was next in importance to the mayor. The duties of this ancient office are described in Bohun's Privilegia Londini,[2] where it is said that the recorder was one "skillful in the laws and customs of the city;" and was "chief assistant to the Lord Mayor and aldermen, for their better direction for administering the law and justice, and taketh place in all their councils & in courts before any man that hath not been maier. And being the mouth of the city he learnedly delivers the sentences and judgements of their court." His qualifications are thus set down in the book called *Liber Albus:* "He shall be one of the most skillful and virtuous apprentices of the law in the whole kingdom. He is to sit on the right hand of the maier in recording pleas and passing judgements, & by him records & processes had before the maier at St. Martins le Grand are to be recorded by word of mouth before the Justices assigned there to correct errors. The maier & aldermen have therefore used commonly to set forth all the customs & business touching the city before the King & his Council as also in the King's Court by Mr. Recorder as a chief man endued with wisdom and eminent for eloquence."

[1] Charter of Philadelphia. [2] Bohun's Privilegia Londini, page 63.

The recorder was elected by the corporation, and held his office for life. He was admitted by taking the usual oaths before the mayor. He might be removed by the mayor and two-thirds of the aldermen and common councilmen respectively.[1]

ALDERMEN.

SEC. 7. The aldermen held their office for life at common law and by the charter. They did not represent any particular ward or precinct of the city, as in London or in Philadelphia in later time. The important distinction between them and the common councilmen was the judicial power of the former; and this leads us to a consideration of the judicial functions of the mayor, recorder, and aldermen, which constituted a large and peculiar part of their powers in the municipalities of the day.

JUDICIAL FUNCTIONS.

SEC. 8. The mayor, recorder, and aldermen were appointed by the charter justices of the peace and justices of *oyer* and *terminer*. This usage of appointing municipal magistrates justices of the peace by charter began at some period much earlier than the reign of Richard II., and produced an essential change in their character.[2]

They were given civil and criminal jurisdiction within the city and liberties. As to the criminal jurisdiction, any four of them, of whom the mayor and recorder must be two, had full jurisdiction over all felonies and misdemeanors; for which purpose they were, together with the city sheriff and town clerk, to hold a court of record quarterly or oftener. They were in this court also given authority, upon their own view or after legal procedure, to cause the removal of all nuisances and encroachments in the streets of the city, and punish the parties concerned according to the law.

The mayor and recorder were furthermore created to be of the quorum of the justices of the county courts, quarter sessions, oyer and terminer, and gaol delivery in the county of

[1] Charter of Philadelphia. [2] Report of Eng. Munc. Cor., page 17.

Philadelphia, and had full power to award process, bind to the peace, or commit to prison, not only in all cases arising within the city, but even in the body of the county. They were also to cause calendars to be made of prisoners, which, together with all recognizances and examinations taken before them for or concerning any matter or cause not determinable by them, were to be returned to the justices of the county before whom they were cognizable.

As to the civil jurisdiction it was provided that the mayor and recorder should have power to take recognizance of debts according to the statute of merchants and of acton burnel;[1] and to use and affix the common seal thereupon, and to all certificates concerning the same.[2]

Common Councilmen.

Sec. 9. The remaining integral part of the corporation to be considered—the common councilmen—held office like the aldermen, for life. They did not represent any particular ward or district. The aldermen and common councilmen were qualified by taking the usual oaths before the mayor.[2] This taking of the proper oaths of office, and the entry thereof in the corporation books, was called admission, and was necessary before any one elected to the freedom or a corporate office could enter upon the enjoyment of them, he being considered a mere usurper without admission.[3] The aldermen and councilmen might be removed for misconduct by the mayor, recorder, and nine of the aldermen and common councilmen.[4]

The common councilmen were not recognized by the common law as a select body, and consequently their office is not noticed as to its duration or duty. Indeed, they may be said to be the faint vestige of the ancient liberties once enjoyed by the freemen of boroughs. Boroughs existed in England from the earliest period. The burgesses were the permanent free inhabitants, performing their duties and en-

[1] Acton Burnel, 11 Edw. I.; Stat. at Large by Keble, 351; 1 Ashmead, 395, case of John *vs.* Furey. See, also, Beck *vs.* City, 5 Harris, 104.
[2] Charter of Philadelphia. [3] Willcock, § 555–6, 575. [4] Charter.

joying their privileges as the free inhabitant householders, paying scot and bearing lot, presented, sworn, and enrolled in the court leet.[1]

Incorporation of Boroughs.

The first charters of municipal incorporation were granted by Henry VI., and superinduced upon the original character of burgesses that of corporators also. "In ancient times little difference was made between a populous town that was gildated or incorporated and one that was not gildated or incorporated." There was a general analogy as to perpetual succession, payment of aid, talliages, common fines, &c. The towns were incorporated for their greater advantage, "*emendationem burgi.*" "There were several advantages which a corporate town had above a town not incorporated. The incorporation fitted the townsmen for a stricter union among themselves, a more orderly and steady government, and for a more advantageous course of commerce."[2] The corporation then consisted of a head or heads, one or more definite classes, and an indefinite class consisting of the general body of those entitled to the freedom. The common council or corporate meeting consisted of the definite classes and as many of the indefinite class as chose to attend without any other qualification than that of being freemen, and such a common council was incident to all corporations of common right unless otherwise regulated by charter.[3] This indefinite body was usually known as the commonalty, and was the class for whose advantage municipal corporations were obviously intended. When, however, the number of freemen was very great, their presence at the corporate assemblies would be found very inconvenient, and their votes would generally outnumber those of the select classes; for which reason in the prescriptive corporations in England there generally existed a common council to represent them, consisting

[1] Merewether & Stephens, Hist. of Boroughs, page v., introduction.
[2] Firma Burgi, by Thomas Madox, London, 1726.
[3] Willcock, § 1, 764.

in some cases, notably in the case of London, of a certain number of the common freemen periodically elected by the remainder. This right of election, however, was not, as already mentioned, long retained, and the common council became a select, definite class, and as much independent of the rest of the freemen as any of the other definite classes. While the trivial affairs of the corporation alone were to be managed, and the right of returning members to Parliament was regarded rather as an inconvenience than a privilege, the supineness of the commonalty in general permitted the administration of corporate affairs, and, among others, the right of election of their officers, to devolve upon the select classes. To this want of importance those usurpations attributed to by-laws had their origin, and secured its first legal sanction in the famous case of corporations,[1]—a case expressly prepared in the Privy Council and submitted to the judges, as the basis for those successful attempts already noticed by successive sovereigns against the liberties of the boroughs.

The Common Council.

Sec. 10. The assembly of the integral parts of the corporation in a corporate meeting for the transaction of business was called the Common Council. It was convened from time to time by the mayor, recorder, and at least three of the aldermen, and besides these the presence of at least nine of the common councilmen was necessary.[2] The corporate assembly being duly convened, it was not necessary that there should be a majority of any of the select classes in favor of any measure, but the votes of the mayor, recorder, aldermen, and common councilmen who sat together as one body were all of equal account, and all questions were determined by a vote of the whole assembly. Besides having the power to add to their own number from time to time, the common council might admit as many freemen "into their corporation and society" as they saw fit.[2] They might make all such laws and ordinances as were necessary and convenient

[1] Case of Corporations, 4 Rep., 77 b. [2] Charter of Philadelphia.

for the government of the city, and execute them through the proper officers. They might also impose, at their discretion, fines for the violation of such ordinances to be levied by distress and sale, by warrant under the common seal, or by other means to the use of the corporation.

The procedure of the common council was simple. There were no committees, in the modern acceptation of the word. When a public necessity arose requiring legislation, it was "ordered" by councils that an ordinance be drawn for the purpose, and a committee consisting of a few of the aldermen was appointed to draw it and report at a subsequent meeting. Frequently a second committee would be appointed to act on the report of the first. The ordinances were published—if they were published at all—upon single broadsides. There was no accurate record kept of them, and they remained in the greatest confusion. That but few of them are extant to-day is not surprising, from the record in the Minutes of the Common Council: "Alderman Coxe proposed that there has lately appeared a necessity for putting into Execution some of the Ordinances of the Corporation, particularly the last made relating to the Cording of Wood, brought for sale into this city, and as the city Ordinances are dispersed among several members of the Corporation, a Committee be appointed to collect and lay them before this Board." Page 657.

Charter Officers.

Sec. 11. A few offices were regulated by the charter, the incumbents of which were not members of the corporation. A town clerk was elected by the corporation, who was also "Clerk of the peace and Clerk of the Court and Courts." A clerk of the market was appointed by the mayor to "have assize of bread, wine, beer, wood, and other things; and to do, execute, and perform all things belonging to the clerk of the market,"[1] such as acting as regulator of weights and measures and "searchers and packers of flour and bread."[1] The coroner and sheriff of the county were also to act for the

[1] Minutes Common Council, page 58.

city; but the inhabitants of the city were to have equal liberty with the inhabitants of the county to elect sheriffs and coroners who should reside within the city. The sheriff was constituted water bailiff upon the Delaware river and all other navigable streams in the province. As water bailiff it was his duty to preserve the river from all encroachments, and exercise a general control over the fisheries.[1]

By the act of 1705 [An Act for regulating elections of Sheriffs and Coroners: passed 1705, chapter 16, repealed 13th September, 1785, M. S. Laws] the freeholders were to elect two persons for sheriff and two for coroner, to be presented to the governor, who selected one respectively for each office.

The Freemen.

Sec. 12. While the corporation proper, in its strict legal sense, is composed of the integral parts already described, there remains yet another class which once were likewise an integral part of the corporation, and still in a larger sense and for many purposes are to be considered as still forming a part, viz., inhabitants entitled to the freedom, and enjoying, in consequence of the incorporation of the city, certain franchises and privileges. The freedom was gained by acquiring certain qualifications or by purchase. The qualifications were, that the freeman should be a free denizen of the province, twenty-one years of age, and a resident of the city, possessed of a freehold estate therein, or a resident for two years in the city, having personal property worth fifty pounds.[2] Women as well as men might be admitted to the freedom.[3] The price of the freedom by purchase varied from time to time and in different cases. One James Bingham paid £3 2s. 6d.; Samuel Savage, £1 2s. 6d. Besides possessing a qualification essential to holding municipal offices, the freemen possessed many privileges, some of which date far back in the history of boroughs. Among them were certain customs,

[1] Bohun's Privilegia Londini. [2] Charter of Philadelphia.
[3] Minutes Common Council, page 21.

called customs against common right, since they were in restriction of the general rights under the common law, the most usual of which were the customs that none but freemen should sell by retail or practice any trade or occupation, and that nothing shall be sold by a foreigner to a foreigner within the city. Such customs had their origin in the early importance of towns and their almost exclusive possession of commerce, with the assumed authority of establishing rules for their own government anterior to the charters of freedom.[1] To preserve this venerable privilege to the freemen of the city it was ordered by the common council, as early as 1705, that an ordinance be drawn by the recorder and one of the aldermen "for restraining those that are not admitted freemen of this city to keep open shops or be master workmen.[2] While the privileges of the freemen were thus extended and protected, the same suspicion of strangers, and the importance attributed to local residence and respectability, existed that are found as far back as 691, when Witred, the Saxon king of the inhabitants of Kent, provided in his code, "If one be found wandering about not proclaiming his ware by acclamation or by the blowing of a horn (the usual method in those times of giving public notice), he was to be taken for a thief and slain."[3] To this law, which was repealed by Ina, is probably to be traced the principle upon which notice was required to be given before any person could become a settled inhabitant of a place; and a further illustration is afforded by the ordinance of the common council passed in 1705, that bonds should be taken from all strangers entering the city for saving the town harmless from charges during seven years.

Miscellaneous Provisions.

Sec. 13. A few miscellaneous provisions of the charter of 1701 remain to be considered. The limits of the city were to extend between the Delaware and Schuylkill as originally laid out. The streets also were forever to continue according

---

[1] Willcock, page 4. [2] Minutes Common Council, page 34.
[3] Merewether & Stephens, page 15.

to the original plan, and the corporation had consequently no power to alter them. The ends of the streets upon the Delaware river were to remain for the free use of the inhabitants of the city, and the corporation might improve them and erect wharves into the river.

The corporation were empowered to erect a gaol and court-house within the city. They were also empowered to hold two market days every week, and two fairs annually. The form of proclamation for opening these fairs is rather quaint and characteristic of the period.

"Form of the Proclamation of the Fairs.[1]

"O Yes and Silence is commanded while the Fair proclaiming upon Pain of Imprisonment.

"A. B. Esq., Mayor of the City of Philadelphia, doth hereby, in the King's Name strictly charge and command all persons trading and negotiating within this Fair to keep the King's peace.

"And that no person or persons whatsoever presume to set up any Booth or Stall for the vending of strong Liquors within this Fair.

"And that no Person or Persons presume to bear or carry any unlawful Weapons to the Terrour or Annoyance of his Majesty's Subjects, or to gallop or strain Horses within the Built Parts of this City.

"And if any person shall receive any Hurt or Injury from Another let him repair to the Mayor, here present, and his wrongs shall be redressed. This Fair to continue Three Days and no longer. God save the King."

Toward the close of the period these fairs became regarded as a nuisance. The assembly was petitioned to abolish them, since, with the increase of stores, they were no longer needed, and, as it was alleged, they "debauched the morals of the people and facilitated the commission of thefts and other crimes."[2] It was a question of doubt whether the assembly

[1] Min. of C. C., page 569. [2] *Ibid.*, page 803.

had the power to lay down a chartered institution, so they were permitted to continue until the Revolution put an end to the fairs and charter together.

PHILADELPHIA MADE A PORT.

The city was constituted a port under the name of the "Port of Philadelphia,"[1] to extend into all the streams and places in the province, and to have such wharves and landing places as the corporation deemed proper, with the approbation of the chief officers of the king's custom. Certain vacant lands in the city were declared common of pasture until taken up by improvements.

Finally it was provided, contrary to the general principle of the law, that the charter should be construed and taken most favorably and beneficially for the corporation.

EARLY NECESSITY OF ACTS OF LEGISLATURE.

SEC. 14. Modeled after the corrupted constitution of the old English borough, and in a period most unfavorable to municipal privileges, it is not suprising that the powers granted in the charter were soon found to be extremely insufficient for the rapidly growing city. As early as 1706, but five years after the grant of the charter, it is ordered by the common council that a new charter be drawn, containing "such privileges as the present charter is deficient in,"[2] to be sent to the proprietor for his concurrence.[2] Nothing came of this

---

[1] Penn was given in his charter "full and absolute powre and authoritie to make, erect & constitute within the said province and the Isles and Isletts aforesaid, such and soe many Seaports, Harbours, Creeks, Havens, Keyes and other places, for discharge and unlading of goods & merchandise out of the Shipps, boates and other vessells and Lading them in such and soe many places, and with such rights, Jurisdictions, liberties and privileges unto the said ports belonging, as to him or them, shall seem most expedient, and that all and singular the shipps, boates and other vessels which shall come for merchandize & trade unto the said province,or out of the same shall depart shall be laden or unladen only att such ports as shall be erected & constituted by the said Wm. Penn, &c." Also power to lay reasonable duties at the ports and to have and enjoy the same.

[2] Min. C. C., page 36.

attempt, however; and in 1710 it was resolved to make application to the assembly for the passage of an act empowering the corporation "to make Ordinances & By-Laws for the better Support, Rule & Government of this City;"[1] and two bills were accordingly prepared for the purpose by the recorder, which were rejected by the assembly.[2] In the following year the recorder was ordered to prepare an act to be laid before the assembly, confirming the city charter and granting the much-needed power to raise money for the maintenance of the streets, wharves, and other public departments.[3]

The inability to raise sufficient revenue for the current expenses was one of the earliest and most urgently felt deficiencies in the powers of the corporation, and afforded a good illustration of how ill adapted the antiquated system was to the necessities of a modern municipality. By the common law the power of taxation of the borough, if it can be said to have existed at all, was of the most restricted character; nor could the king or proprietor grant such a power, that being confined to the sovereign authority of Parliament alone.[4] By a by-law a talliage might indeed be levied on the municipality to compel each member to furnish his proportionate share toward the necessary expense to which the corporation was liable, such as the expense of keeping up beacons and watch towers in the Cinque Ports and ancient towns; the expense of erecting courts for the reception of the judges; or the expense of renewing the charter.[5] Except, however, inasmuch as all the members were liable to such general charges on the corporation, the levy of any tax was illegal, and a by-law pretending to effect it void.[6] Such antiquated and jealously restricted powers were ill fitted to bear the support of street, police, poor, and other departments which fall within the scope of modern municipalities.

[1] Min. C. C., page 72. [2] *Ibid.*, page 73. [3] *Ibid.*, page 77.
[4] Willcock, § 326. [5] *Ibid.*, § 318. [6] *Ibid.*, § 326.
[7] See Guide Book "Philadelphia in 1824," where it is stated that no power of taxation whatever existed under the charter of 1701. The book is in the Phila. Hist. Soc.

In 1704 the common council made a primitive enough attempt to levy a tax, by ordering that every inhabitant keeping cows over two years old should pay twelve pence per annum for each cow, "towards the Buying and keeping of the Town Bull;"[1] but the cow-tax seems to have been insufficient for that purpose, as the mayor two years afterwards liberally advances the money necessary for "the repair of the fframe of the Town Bull."[2] A small duty was also paid from time to time upon wood landed at the public wharves,[3] which in later times was farmed out for a term of years.[4] The main sources of revenue, however, were from fines, fees, freedoms, city property, and lotteries.

Fines.

Fines furnished a large part of the city revenue. They were levied upon persons refusing to accept office, and for the non-attendance of members of the common council;[5] and they constituted the penalty for many violations of the laws and ordinances. Some cases of fines are curious. One person is fined, "he being very poor, and his wife like to be a charge upon the town;"[6] and, after the sheriff's commissions were deducted, one Laughton McClane's fine, "for kissing of Osborne's wife," amounted to £24 5s. 0d.,—a very large sum for those days.[7] The fines, indeed, were frequently severe; and although the corporation was frequently appealed to by the offender, who meanwhile lay in the gaol, to remit or abate them, such were the urgent necessities of the city that they seldom consented, although occasionally they allowed a certain number of days' grace, or took a note for part of the fine.[8]

Other Sources of Revenue.

Among the fees which added to the revenues of the corporation may be mentioned the bench fees, and the charges in the indentures of apprentices, and goods sold at public sale

[1] Min. C. C., page 20. [2] *Ibid.*, page 43. [3] *Ibid.*, page 43; 326.
[4] *Ibid.*, 497. [5] *Ibid.*, page 3, page 60. [6] Min. C. C., page 106.
[7] Christopher Marshall's Diary, page 287. [8] Min. C. C., page 47.

under the court house. The purchase of the freedom formed a variable source of revenue, at times amounting to little and then again being considerable.[1]

The rents from the wharves, market stalls, and other public property became yearly more valuable with the growth of the city.[2] The principle is laid down by many modern writers on municipal questions, that markets belong to that class which are not proper subjects of municipal control, but should be left to private enterprise.[3] The control of markets, however, as incident to the control of local trade in general, was a leading principle of the old borough organization; and after this local control ceased to be of the same importance, the possession of the markets was valued as affording a substantial addition to the meagre revenues. Thus when the common council of Philadelphia finds that stalls have been erected in the street in front of the court house by private persons, who derived a profitable rent therefrom, they take steps to pave the street, and erect stalls of their own.[4] In addition to these regular sources of income lotteries for raising money for the use of the city were occasionally sanctioned by the corporation; and sometimes tickets would be taken for which the city treasurer gave notes in behalf of the corporation, payable in case of any loss.[5]

But all these sources of revenue became annually more and more insufficient; and, although the corporation performed some most remarkable feats of financiering, the condition of the treasury grew more and more desperate; so that when the governor granted a license to a person who had suffered misfortune to solicit the charity of the inhabitants, the common council immediately became alarmed, and ordered that, whereas "the Charge of this City occasioned by the Repairs of the Wharfs, Maintenance of the Poor, & other Incidents, laying Hard on the Inhabitants, that the Mayor, Recorder & Alderman Hill do wait on the Governour & request him that he would be pleased to give the Magistrates of this City a Hear-

---

[1] Min. C. C., pages 112, 144, 209. [2] *Ibid.*, pages 49, 105.
[3] Dillon, Munc. Law. [4] Min. C. C., 360–363. [5] *Ibid.*, 493, 504, 583.

ing in ffavour of ye Inhabitants before he Grants any person Such a lycence for ye ffutur."[1]

Financial Difficulties.

The financiering of the corporation is extremely curious and amusing. Loans were of course speedily resorted to. It is interesting to note one of the earliest and simplest loans made by the city in an ordinance of 1706, providing that any citizen who would advance money for repairing the wharves, bridges, and streets should be repaid out of the first money raised by the city, or might have the same discounted in their taxes; but there is no mention of interest being allowed.[2] When the common council desired to build a new market house they unselfishly resolved that the money should be raised by contribution from the aldermen and common councilmen, the former paying double the amount of the latter; one-half of the subscription might be paid in money, the other half in goods. Other citizens were invited to join the subscription; the loan to be repaid with interest out of the rent of the stalls.[3] This method of raising money by subscription was not infrequently adopted.[4] In 1720 money to defray the expenses of new market stalls was raised by subscriptions of one hundred pounds each from four of the aldermen. The mayor for the corporation, under the seal of the city, gave a distinct obligation to each; the loans were to be repaid with interest out of the profits of the stalls; and copies of the minutes of common council in the matter were ordered to be drawn and signed by the mayor, under the city seal, and delivered to the aldermen who advanced the money.[5]

The corporation finding itself plunged in debt and the accounts in the greatest confusion, a committee is appointed after much difficulty to settle them, which, after still further delays, reports a settlement, showing a deficit against the city of £42. After full debate the city treasurer is ordered to pay the proceeds of the sale of the old prison to

---

[1] Min. C. C., page 141, and page 158. [2] *Ibid.*, page 38. [3] *Ibid.*, page 64.
[4] Min. C. C., page 87. [5] *Ibid.*, pages 178, 189, 190.

the treasurer of the city and county for joint use thereof; the mayor is ordered to take up the bonds given by a former mayor for money borrowed to build the market stalls and bring them to the next meeting; and also to secure £300 lent by the assembly to the corporation for discharging the market-stall debt, and another £300 lent for bridges and wharves, and to give bond therefor to the loan office of the province. The city treasurer is then directed to pay the mayor and two aldermen, who are appointed a committee to repair the wharves and bridges, £100 of the £300 loaned for the purpose, while the mayor is directed to pay off nine obligations amounting to £282 8s. 9d. A floating debt of £60 odd and a bonded interest-bearing debt of £600 was thus created.[1] Loans by the assembly to the city were not uncommon during this period.[2] In 1730 £1000 was loaned for an almshouse.[3] Occasionally the corporation resorted to other expedients. Thus the market at Second and Lombard was built, with permission of the corporation, by individuals who were to hold the same until the principal and interest were repaid them; although the corporation retained the control and direction of the markets, and reserved the right to take possession at any time on payment of the amount still due.[4]

The bad management of the corporation added to the financial difficulties; continual compromises were resorted to with officials who petitioned for arrears of salary unpaid for several years—the said officials being earnestly requested to consider "the infancy and small income of the corporation."[5] Promissory notes were taken for fines and frequently paid in goods, and sometimes remained several years in the hands of successive sheriffs without any account;[6] rents were long in arrears and collected with difficulty; subscriptions and advances on the part of members of the corporation were made to be repaid out of the uncertain revenues of the future; and a general scheme of personal debts and promises existed, illustrated by the order of the common council that "William

---

[1] Min. C. C., page 339. [2] *Ibid.*, pages 242–3. [3] *Ibid.*, page 305.
[4] Min. C. C., page 446. [5] *Ibid.*, pages 110–144. [6] *Ibid.*, page 604.

Fishbourn pay the sum of Ten Pounds to William Carter towards finishing the Market Wharf in this City, when John Budd pays the money he received from Thomas Oakley, one of the collectors of the tax for building wharfs."[1]

Act of 1712, Granting Power of Taxation.

Sec. 15. The corporation, as already mentioned, never succeeded in obtaining either from the proprietor or the legislature the powers of taxation they so urgently required; but at length the necessities of the city became so great that another plan was adopted by the legislature similar to that followed in England. In England it had long been customary not to rely on the corporation for the government of the town; but additional powers of municipal government were granted from time to time by local acts of Parliament for various purposes, not to the officers of the corporation, but to trustees or commissioners distinct from and largely independent of them; and while the former had the nominal government the efficient duties and responsibilities were transferred to the latter.[2] A similar course was followed by the assembly in the case of Philadelphia, and exercised a most important influence upon the development of the city government.

The first act of this character was passed in 1712, and is the basis of subsequent legislation for the period. The cause of its passage was the great necessity of providing means to pay the public debt and defray the expenses of building a workhouse of correction, building and repairing the public wharves, paving and regulating the streets, and providing suitable markets.[3] Six assessors were to be chosen annually by the voters of the city, who, in conjunction with the mayor, recorder, and aldermen, annually, at the general sessions of the peace, or oftener if necessary, were to calculate the amount

[1] Min. C. C., page 103. There was a "Provincial Tax" laid upon the property of the corporation, page 647.

[2] Rep. of Munc. Cor., page 17.

[3] An act for raising money on the Inhabitants of the City of Philadelphia for the Publick Use and Benefit. 1712. Bradford's Laws, page 102. Chap. 176, MS. Laws.

of the public debt and what sums were necessary for repairing the streets and for the other purposes already mentioned. This act of 1712 provided for the first municipal officers created by the people, and was the basis of the revenue legislation of the period, and is interesting as recognizing the right of the people to control taxation. They were to appropriate certain sums to each item, and within six weeks afterward lay the rate. The constables were to make returns of the names and estates of persons in their respective wards; and the assessment being duly laid was signed by five assessors and allowed by the mayor, recorder, and two aldermen, under their hands and seals. The assessments were to be made after the manner of the county basis, but were not to exceed two pence on the pound, or four shillings *per capita*. The assessment being made by the mayor, recorder, aldermen, and assessors conjointly, a characteristic distribution of power is then made. The assessors appointed the collectors and the treasurer; while the disbursements by the treasurer were made on the order of the mayor, recorder, and four of the aldermen, and his accounts were to be annually audited by the mayor, recorder, aldermen, and assessors, and before any citizens who chose to be present. The collectors turned in all sums received to the treasurer, and gave notice of the day of appeal. Upon the neglect to elect assessors, the mayor, recorder, and aldermen acted with the grand inquest.

HIGHWAYS.

SEC. 16. One of the most urgent reasons demanding the passage of this act was the condition of the streets. As early as 1700 an act was passed authorizing the governor and four of the council to nominate commissioners to regulate the streets and water-courses of the towns of the province; and with the consent of at least two justices of the peace to levy and collect assessments on property-owners.[1] The charter incorporating the city, however, limited the powers of the

[1] Act for Regulating Streets, wharves & watercourses in the citys & towns of this province, 1700. 1 MS. Laws, 103.

county magistracy. By a law of the province, copied from an ancient English law, the inhabitants might be compelled to furnish labor for the repair of the highways; but, as money was much more necessary than labor, it was ordered by the common council, in 1711, that the old law be strictly enforced, and at the same time providing that instead of a day's labor any person might pay 1s. 6d.[1] Even after the passage of the act of 1712 the streets continued in a wretched condition, and received little attention at the hands of the corporation. Many of the inhabitants in 1718 voluntarily paved "from ye kennel to the middle of the streets before their respective tenements with pebble stones;"[2] and as the pavements were greatly injured by the heavy weights carried over them, the common council passed an ordinance to prevent carters and others from carrying such heavy loads.[2] A subsequent ordinance for the same purpose regulated the number of horses that might be driven in one team, the weight of the load, and the character of the wheels.[3] Some years later an ordinance was passed compelling property-owners to pitch and pave in front of their lots, under penalty of having it done at their expense by the corporation.[4]

Two serious defects existed in the system introduced by the act of 1712. The first was the absence of any head or responsibility among the mayor, recorder, aldermen, and assessors, together with the inevitable jealousies and conflict, and the consequent difficulty of securing united action. Complaints began to be made about 1739 that great difficulty existed in getting the mayor, recorder, and aldermen to act as frequently as necessary in conjunction with the assessors, thereby occasioning great delay in the affairs of the city, and even a direct loss of revenue by the delay in the adjustment of the accounts and the due collection of the taxes, some of which were many years in arrears, while many persons even refused to pay anything, and seem to have been, from some defect in the powers of the municipal authorities, practically out of

[1] Min. C. C., page 80. [2] *Ibid.*, page 155. 1718.
[3] *Ibid.*, page 172. 1719. [4] *Ibid.*, 364–368. 1736.

reach of the law. The assembly was consequently petitioned by several of the inhabitants to grant a highly characteristic remedy,—the erection of still another board by electing commissioners to act with the assessors, as in the county. The corporation resisted the attempt as a great infringement on the privileges granted them by the charter, while at the same time they denied that things were as bad as they were represented. Such a bill was actually passed by the assembly, but the corporation succeeded in persuading the governor not to sign it.[1] The circumstance is interesting, however, not only as showing the bad working of the complex system, but as showing the gradual growth of that distrust and dislike of the corporation on the part of the citizens, which, as will be seen, reached such a height at the termination of the charter.

The second defect in the system was the absence of any definite executive officer to superintend the department of highways. A futile attempt was made in 1762 by an act[2] directing the mayor, recorder, aldermen, and assessors annually to appoint one or more supervisors, and to contract with them for the proper care of the streets for a year, at the same time imposing a penalty for neglect on the part of the supervisor. The plan, however, did not prove at all satisfactory, and a month later the act was repealed, and another, "An act for regulating, pitching, paving and cleaning the highways, streets, water-courses and common sewers within the inhabited and settled parts of the city of Philadelphia, and for raising money to defray expenses,"[3] passed, making provisions, with elaborate detail, for regulating, pitching, paving, and cleaning highways, streets, water-courses, and common sewers within the settled part of the city. Besides the assessors, still another board, of six commissioners, was created. One change in this new board is noticeable, namely, that the term of office was lengthened,

[1] Min. C. C., page 389. 1739.

[2] An act for opening & better amending & keeping in repair the public Roads & Highways within this Province. Passed 2/17/62. MS. Laws, chapter 479.

[3] Chap. 480, MS. Laws.

two commissioners being elected annually; but, apart from this, there is small improvement in the new system. The commissioners were to meet and consult respecting the best methods of paving and cleaning the streets, and building and repairing the drains and sewers, and to contract for work and materials. They were then to consult with the mayor, recorder, and aldermen as to what streets should be first paved; while the mayor, recorder, and aldermen, with four of the regulators, were to have general control of the streets and sewers and water-courses. They had no power, however, to build them upon private property without the permission of at least four commissioners and the assessment and payment of damages to the owner; while, on the other hand, although the commissioners were given power to contract for cleaning the streets, they were obliged to do so at such time as the mayor, recorder, and aldermen might direct. Such was the nice balance of authority among municipal officers which characterized the legislation of the age.

The details of this act may be briefly stated. Property-owners were directed to sweep the sidewalks every Friday; and a penalty was imposed for throwing rubbish or ashes into the streets. Public scavengers were appointed by the commissioners to collect such rubbish and ashes once a week, and were to be paid extra when the dirt was not incident to ordinary housekeeping. In the absence of the landlord the tenant was responsible for taxes levied under the act, to be deducted from the rent. Owners were to pave the footways, and allowance was to be made to such as had already done so.

While the commissioners co-operated with the mayor, recorder, and aldermen in the management of the streets, they co-operated with the assessors in matters of taxation. The commissioners were authorized to receive from the managers of certain lotteries organized for paving the streets such sums as had been realized. With a majority of the assessors they were to meet annually to determine the amount necessary to be raised. The constables were to make returns of property and taxables, and no assessment was to exceed 3d. on the pound. The commissioners and assessors together appointed a clerk, while the assessors alone appointed the collectors, and had jurisdiction over appeals. The collectors paid all moneys to a treasurer appointed by the commissioners, who gave a bond and paid out money on the order of four of the commissioners.

Between 1762 and 1767 several acts concerning streets were passed supplementary in various ways to the act already described.[1]

In 1769 an act was passed continuing the act of 1762, which was near expiring, having been passed only for seven years.

Chapter 554, February 21, 1767, was an amendment having relation to the weight of loads and the number of horses to any one wagon. Chapter 833, April 5, 1779, was an act to amend act for regulation of wagons and the supplement and further supplement to said act. Chapter 838, September 30, 1779, continues the act of 1769 and increases the assessment from 3d. to 9d. for two years. Chapter 889, March 18, 1780, directs the apportioning of taxes to be laid for the watch, streets, &c., conformably to the State tax. Baily, 343.

---

[1] Chap. 485—MS. Laws, March 4, 1763.

Supplement to an act entitled an act for regulating, pitching, and paving and cleansing the highways, streets, lanes, and alleys, and for regulating, making, and amending the water-courses and common sewers within inhabited and settled parts of the city of Philadelphia, and for raising of money to defray the expenses thereof, provides for certain loans to be created by the commissioners—the three pence assessment having proved insufficient.

Chapter 503—MS. Laws, 30th September, 1763.

An act to enable commissioners to settle accounts of the managers and to sue for and recover from several persons such sums of money as are now due and unpaid on account of the several lotteries set up and drawn for the paving of the streets.

Chapter 524—February 15, 1765.

An act to fill up the dock between Walnut and Third streets.

Chapter 537—February 8, 1766.

An act regulating width of fellies, and the number of horses attached to one wagon.

CHARACTERISTICS OF ABOVE LEGISLATION.

The legislation of this period affords a most forcible illustration of the prevalent ideas of municipal government. The original corporation, without powers of taxation, distrusted by the people and jealous of its prerogatives, was speedily found inadequate to the needs of a modern municipality; and resort was had to new boards which, at least, had the advantage of being elected by the people. The streets, however, were but ill managed, even for those provincial days, by the mayor, recorder, aldermen, commissioners, and assessors, with their cumbersome machinery and intricate distribution of powers. The next branch of municipal government to be treated—police—shows the same features.

The commissioners, with the mayor, recorder, and any two aldermen, might regulate the depth of all wells dug for privies.

Any person building any encroachment in a fifty-foot street or upwards,—porch, cellar, &c.,—extending beyond the distance of four feet three inches, liable to fine.

Signs projecting into the street also forbidden.

For the subsequent history of act of 1769 see note in Smith's Laws, vol. 1, page 511.

POLICE.

SEC. 17. The modern policeman is a creature of statute; the conservator of the peace of old time being the constable. The first watchman was appointed in 1700 by the provincial council, and had the whole care of the city within his charge. It was his duty to go through the town at night ringing a bell, to cry out the time of night and the state of the weather, and to inform the constables of any disorder or fires. In 1704 it was ordered by the common council that the city be divided into ten precincts, and that an equal number of watchmen be assigned to each constable therein.[1] In the same year the city was divided into ten wards. The consta-

[1] Min. C. C., page 8, 1704. *Ibid.*, page 14.

ble was the principal officer of the watch. The watch was not a permanent body of paid men, but every able-bodied housekeeper was supposed to take his turn at the watch or furnish a substitute.[1] In 1711 the constables were ordered to furnish the mayor with a list of all persons within their respective wards, in order that the night watch might be better regulated.[2] The system, however, was onerous and unsatisfactory. In 1743 the grand jury in their presentment complained that it was a much greater expense than necessary, and bore hard upon the poor. The common council voted that a stated watch to be paid for by the city would be most effectual, and application was made to the assembly for authority to establish it, but without any immediate result.[3] In case of riots it was ordered that the members of the corporation should immediately repair to the mayor's house and bring such inhabitants as they could to suppress it.[4] At length, in 1749, the complaint concerning the want of a "sufficient & regular Watch" culminated. It was complained that the watch was weak and insufficient, and that the housekeepers refused to pay watch money upon the pretense that they would attend the watch duty when warned, but frequently neglected to do so. The common council was unanimously of the opinion that the only effectual way to remedy the evil was to obtain an act of assembly for raising money by tax for supporting a "regular & stated Watch as is done in London." Such application, however, requiring time, and there being need of immediate action, the constables were ordered to report to the mayor, the morning after the night watch, the names of all persons who had been warned by him to attend, with the names of those who had attended, in order that the delinquents might be compelled to perform their duties.[5] Soon afterward the grand jury again

[1] See Westcott, vol. 3. 1777. By custom or ordinance the citizens of London were all in turn bound to do watch duty or to find a substitute. See Privilegia Londini, pages 138–384. Watchmen and constables in Philadelphia carried pointed staves. Min. C. C., page 35.

[2] Min. C. C., page 81. [3] *Ibid.*, page 422. [4] *Ibid.*, page 405.

[5] *Ibid.*, page 512.

presented at the sessions the weakness and insecurity of the watch; and the common council again resolved to apply to the assembly for powers to raise the necessary money by taxation.

At length, in 1750,[1] an act was passed "for the better regulating the nightly Watch within the City of Philadelphia, & for enlightening the streets, lanes, and alleys of the said city, and for raising money on the inhabitants of the said city, and for defraying the necessary expenses thereof;" granting the much-needed powers, not to the corporation, but, as in the case of the highways, to a board composed of six wardens, two to be annually elected. They were to erect a sufficient number of lamps throughout the city, and contract with persons for the lighting, trimming, snuffing, and general maintenance of the same. They were annually to appoint and pay as many watchmen as they deemed proper. In conjunction with the mayor, recorder, and four aldermen they were to fix stands throughout the city at which the watchmen were to be posted, and to have general control of the watch. The constables and watchmen were supplied with copies of the rules and regulations. The constables reported regularly at the court house and had general superintendence of the watchmen. Neglect or violation of the police rules of the mayor, recorder, aldermen, and watchmen was punished by fine.

In conjunction with the city assessors the wardens were to meet annually and estimate the amount required for the year. Returns of taxable property were made by the constables. The assessors and wardens appointed a clerk. The assessors alone appointed the collectors, while the wardens entertained appeals, and granted the warrants authorizing the collectors to distrain and sell for arrears of taxes. The wardens and assessors elected a treasurer, who gave a bond. In case of the failure to elect wardens they were to be appointed by the mayor, recorder, and aldermen, to serve until an election should be held.

---

[1] MS. Laws, chapter 389.

WATER.

SEC. 18. The water supply during this period was by means of pumps. They were originally erected and owned by private persons, but their great importance led to various ordinances for their regulation.

In 1713 it was ordered by the common council that the place where a pump was to be driven should be first viewed by the mayor, recorder, and at least three aldermen; and the owner of the pump was authorized to charge rent from the neighbors using it.[1] Two years later another step was taken toward the control of the water supply by the city in an ordinance providing that the owners of pumps should hold the same of the corporation for the term of twenty-one years under the annual rent of one shilling.[2] When pumps became a common nuisance, or for any other cause, they might be removed by the corporation.

In 1756 the general control of the pumps was placed in the hands of the wardens, with power to sink new wells and buy up private pumps; and in the following year the wardens were empowered to assess such householders as used the public pumps.[3]

POOR.

SEC. 19. The care of the poor was one of the earliest matters requiring the grant of additional power by the legislature. An idea of the inadequate provision made for the poor is given in the record of the common council where the mayor, pursuant to an order of common council to "treat with the overseers of the poor," reports that he has done so, and "for a present supply to the poor (they having no money in their hands), paid them out of his pocket the sum of £3 16s. 8d., which is to be repaid out of the first money raised" (Min. C. C. 1704, page 17). By the act of 1705 the mayor, recorder, and aldermen, or in the counties the justices of the

---

[1] Min. C. C., page 48. 1713. [2] *Ibid.*, page 105. 1715.

[3] Chapter 411, MS., vol. VIII., page 108, Sept. 15, 1756; chapter 418, Jan. 18, 1757.

peace, were empowered to appoint overseers of the poor. The overseers were authorized to lay an assessment of one penny per pound on all real and personal estate, and four shillings per head upon all freemen not otherwise rated. The assessment was to receive the approval of the mayor, recorder, and aldermen, and to them an appeal lay. The overseers settled their accounts annually before the mayor, recorder, and aldermen, and at the same time returned the names of the proper number of persons to succeed them in office. Any one refusing to accept the office was punishable by fine.[1] By a subsequent act, the rate was raised to three pence per pound and nine pence per head;[2] and the mayor, recorder, and two aldermen were empowered to appoint a superintendent of the Philadelphia almshouse, and make proper regulations therefor.

Nevertheless, in 1740, it appears that there were many poor in the city whom the overseers were unable to provide for, and certain members of the corporation are appointed for the different wards to join with the rest of the inhabitants in raising contributions for such purpose.[3] Nine years later an act was passed to incorporate the overseers, and to empower them to hold real estate to the extent of £800 yearly value, and all personal property whatsoever.[4] The heavy charges incident to the support of the poor very early brought about the partial union of Philadelphia with several of the outlying districts. In 1766 Philadelphia was consolidated with the district of Southwark, the townships of Moyamensing and Passyunk and the Northern Liberties.[5] All persons con-

---

[1] An act for the relief of the poor, chapter 154, MS. Laws, passed 1705, repealed 9th March, 1771, supplied.

[2] A supplement to the several acts of assembly of this Province for the relief of the poor. MS. Laws, vol. VII., page 70. 29th March, 1735, repealed.

[3] Min. C. C., page 397. 1740.

[4] Chapter 379. An act for amending the laws relating to the poor. MS. Laws, vol. VII., 255. 19th August, 1749, repealed.

[5] Chapter 534. An act for the better employment, relief, and support of the poor within the city of Philadelphia, the district of Southwark, the townships of Moyamensing and Passyunk and the Northern Liberties. MS. L., vol. XI., page 7.

tributing out of charity £10 were incorporated under the name of the "Contributors to the relief and employment of the poor in the city of Philadelphia." They were to meet annually and elect twelve managers to have control of the finances and buildings, and one other person as treasurer. The corporation might hold real estate not exceeding the yearly value of £1000, and personalty in any amount. The managers appointed all the subordinate officers; had general management of the almshouse and house of employment; and had power to make all necessary rules and regulations, which were to receive the approval of the speaker of the assembly, chief justice, and attorney-general of the province.

As soon as the contributors had raised £1500, the mayor, recorder, and aldermen were authorized to borrow £2000, to be given them, for which the present almshouse grounds were to be mortgaged; and when the contributors had got up their building the old grounds were to be sold, the mortgage discharged, and the residue paid to the contributors. Inasmuch as this old almshouse property belonged to Philadelphia, it was further provided that the districts, townships, and liberties should within five years make up to the city a sum equal to one-quarter of what they sold for. The managers were empowered to borrow a sum not exceeding £1000 at six per cent., giving certificates which might be transferred on being endorsed. In case enough money was not raised by these means, the overseers were empowered to lay a tax in the usual manner, and were to pay all money received by them to the treasurer. The managers were to erect an almshouse and house of employment for all able-bodied paupers, disorderly persons, rogues, &c.

Finally, by the act of 1771,[1] the mayor, recorder, and two of the aldermen were empowered annually to appoint twelve overseers of the poor for the city (and a smaller number for the townships, districts, and liberties) out of the requisite number of names, to be returned by the overseer

[1] Chapter 635, act for the relief of the poor, March 9, 1771. Smith, vol. 1, page 332.

going out of office. The mayor, recorder, and any two of the aldermen might, upon complaint, made by the managers elected by the contributors to the house of employment, that money is wanting for the support of the poor, issue their warrant to the overseers, requiring them to levy and collect the amount necessary. Appeals from the assessments of the overseers lay to the magistrates at the next quarter sessions. The managers of the almshouse and house of employment, with the consent of the overseers of the poor and of two or more of the magistrates, might apprentice all poor orphans—males under twenty-one; females under eighteen. No person could be entered in the house of employment without an order from two magistrates. The overseers were to render an annual account to three of the magistrates, the mayor or recorder being one. Any person refusing to accept the office of overseer was liable to a fine of £20. The overseers were incorporated and empowered to hold property, real and personal, not exceeding the yearly value of £500. A legal residence was gained by filling an office, paying taxes, having a lease of the yearly value of £10, being seized of freehold estate, and residing therein a year, or, if hired or bound, by residence of a year. Persons lately arrived from Europe gained a settlement by residence for a year. The act makes elaborate provision for the control of the poor, and embodies the system of this period.

Fire.

Sec. 20. While the danger of fire continually threatened the city, the early precautions against it were extremely primitive. The great danger came from chimneys; and in 1701 an act was passed imposing a fine upon any one in the city who permitted his chimney to catch fire,[1] to be re-

[1] An act to prevent accidents that may happen by fire in the towns of Bristol, Philadelphia, Germantown, Darby, Chester, New Castle, and Lewis, within this government. 1701. Chapter 54, MS. Laws.

Note.—A similar act for Philadelphia and New Castle was passed in 1696. (See Westcott, page 1883.)

covered before a justice of the peace on the testimony of two credible witnesses. It was also provided that every householder should keep in his house a swab, at least twelve feet long, and two leather buckets, to be always ready in case of fire, under penalty of ten shillings; and, as a further precaution, all persons were prohibited from smoking tobacco in the streets by day or night, or to keep more than six pounds of gunpowder in any house within forty perches of a dwelling. Fines were to be paid to the justices of the peace for the purchase of leather buckets, hooks, and other instruments; and the justices were empowered forthwith to procure six good, sufficient hooks for pulling down houses in case of fire. From time to time throughout the period acts were passed by the legislature regulating chimneys, prohibiting the firing of guns, and other details, but there was no organization by that body of a fire department.

The corporation, however, made repeated efforts to obtain the proper facilities in case of fire. By an ordinance passed in 1708 the constables and beadle were directed to notify a magistrate upon discovering any chimney on fire;[1] and three years later the mayor or recorder, with two of the aldermen, were given authority to manage and direct at all fires;[2] and buckets, hooks, and engines were ordered to be provided. In 1718 an engine was bought for £50;[3] and some years afterward a person was hired, at an annual salary of three pounds, to keep the city engine in repair and make monthly trials of it. This apparatus soon proved inadequate; and in 1730 three engines, two hundred leather buckets, twenty ladders, and twenty-five hooks, with axes, were purchased.[4] In order that the expense might not fall too heavily on the inhabitants it was proposed that a subscription be raised for the purpose; and it was ordered that a tax of two pence per pound and eight shillings per head be immediately laid on the inhabitants. One of the new engines was made in Philadelphia, while the other two were procured in Lon-

---

[1] Min. C. C., page 57. 1708. [2] *Ibid.*, page 79. 1711.
[3] Min. C. C., 1718, page 157. [4] *Ibid.*, 1730, page 297.

don.[1] One of the engines was housed in a corner of the great meeting-house yard, corner of High and Second streets; the other, at the corner of one Francis Jones' lot, at Front and Walnut; and the old engine in a corner of the Baptist meeting yard, in Second street near Arch.[2] The buckets were hung in the court house.

The formation of fire companies was from time to time suggested;[3] and at length, in 1736, the Union Fire Company was established, mainly through the efforts of Benjamin Franklin.[4] The constitution of this company furnished the model for all others in Philadelphia till long after the period under discussion. The company was an association for mutual assistance. Each member agreed to furnish, at his own expense, six leather buckets and two stout linen bags, each marked with his name and the name of the company, which he was to bring to every fire. The buckets were for carrying water to extinguish the flames, and the bags were to receive and hold property which was in danger, to save it from the risk of theft. The members pledged themselves to repair to any place in danger, upon an alarm of fire, with their apparatus. Some were to superintend the use of the water, others were to stand at the doors of the houses in danger, and to protect the property from theft. On an alarm of fire at night it was agreed that lights should be placed in the windows of houses of members near the fire, "in order to prevent confusion, and to enable their friends to give them more speedy and effectual assistance." The number of members was limited to thirty. Eight meetings were held annually. At each meeting there was a supper, costing three shillings. Members who came late were fined one shilling. Members who did not come at all were fined four shillings. There was a treasurer, but no president, of the company. Each member served in turn during a month as clerk, in which time he notified his associates of the meeting, inspected their buckets and bags, and when they were not in good order re-

---

[1] Min. C. C., 1730, page 307. [2] *Ibid.*, page 307.

[3] *Pennsylvania Gazette*, December, 1733. [4] Westcott, page 1884.

ported the fact to the company. Engines and buckets were the only available apparatus, as pumps were few and the supply of water scant.

In 1738 the Fellowship Fire Company, with thirty-five members, was formed; in 1742 the Hand-in-Hand, and in 1743 the Heart-in-Hand, were established; and in 1747 still a fifth company was established, named the Friendship Fire Company; and several other companies were from time to time established.

PARTY-WALLS.

SEC. 21. The regulation of party-walls early demanded the attention of the legislature in consequence of the rapidity of building operations in the city. In 1721 an act was passed which in its principal features is in force at the present day. By this act the mayor and commonalty of the city, in common council assembled, were empowered to appoint two persons as surveyors or regulators of party-walls.[2] No person could lay the foundation of any building or party-wall within the city before making application to the regulators. Upon such application the regulators had full powers to enter upon the land of any person in order to set out the foundations and regulate the thickness of the walls to be built. The foundations were to be laid equally upon the adjacent lands; and the first builder was entitled to be reimbursed one moiety for so much of the wall as might be used by a subsequent builder, to be estimated by the regulators. A penalty of £5 was imposed on any person who built without making application as aforesaid; one-half to go to the prosecutor or informer, the other to the city. An appeal from the decision of the regulators lay to the mayor and commonalty at the next common council, and their decision was conclusively binding on all parties. The regulators were paid a

---

[1] See Westcott, page 1884, who probably got his account from the *Pennsylvania Gazette* for December 7, 1736, which see.

[2] "An act for regulating party-walls," February 24, 1721, chapter 242, Smith, page 214. Full title of act: "An act for regulating party-walls, buildings, and partition fences in the city of Philadelphia."

fee of three shillings. They were given power also to regulate partition fences within the city.

As the corporation was alone empowered to appoint regulators, the provisions of the act of course became ineffective on the dissolution of the corporation at the Revolution. It was therefore amended and rendered effectual by a new act, by which the power of appointing the surveyors and regulators was vested in any four or more of the justices of the peace of the city and county of Philadelphia; appeals from the orders of the regulators were directed to be made to the court of common pleas; the penalty on laying the foundation of a party-wall before it was adjusted and marked out by the regulators was raised to £10, to be recoverable within ten months. The regulators and justices, on appeal, were directed to keep records of their orders, &c. The regulators were paid by fees, and they were empowered, at all reasonable hours, to enter on any lot in the city, in order to perform their duties; and the streets which had been opened by private persons and dedicated to public use, or which had been laid out by the executive in pursuance of law, were declared to be highways. The act likewise declared, that no length of possession of any part of a public street or way within the city, should be available as a bar to prevent the removal of a nuisance.[1] By the same act it was provided that no vaults were to be dug under the street without first obtaining leave from four justices of the peace and a majority of the regulators, and that within three months, iron grates of a specified size should be placed over all vaults where grates of a different kind had been previously placed. The twelfth section of the act, which empowered the commissioners to remove all trees from the streets, was subsequently repealed.[2] The legal principles involved in these acts were very early considered by the courts, and it was decided to be no justification, on an indictment for a nuisance by intruding on the public property, that the public was benefited.[3]

[1] Act April 15, 1782, 2 Smith, 48. [2] Act September 20, 1782, 2 Smith, 54. [3] Respublica *vs.* Caldwell, 1 Dallas, 150.

The claim for reimbursement of the moiety of the cost of a party-wall it was decided is not a lien upon the land, but only a personal charge against the builder of the second house.[1]

On an appeal from an order of the regulators of Southwark, the court observed that a feigned issue to try the controverted question can only determine whether the regulators have done right or not; it cannot determine the title, which must be settled by an action of ejectment.[2]

It was also decided that the regulation of a lot by regulators, under the act of *March* 9th, 1771, from which no appeal is entered to the common pleas, is conclusive as to the foundations and party-walls of buildings erected conformably thereto, but not so as to the lines of the lot on which there are no buildings.[3]

The constitutionality of the act authorizing the corporation of Philadelphia to prevent the erection of wooden buildings in certain parts of the city was affirmed in the MS. reports of the Supreme Court.[4] It should also be noted that a general act making provisions on this subject for counties had been passed as early as 1700.[5]

The building acts in England were principally directed to the preservation of dwellings from fire, and the main cause of these arose from the great fire of London in 1666. The act of 1721 was partially modeled after 6 Anne, c. 31, and 7 Anne, c. 17, but was superior to these in its common sense; the act of 1721, as has been seen, was revived and amended by the act of 1782.[6]

---

[1] Ingles *vs.* Bringhurst, 1 Dallas, 341.

[2] Wells *et al. vs.* Fox, 1 Dallas, 308.

[3] Godshall *vs.* Marian, 1 Binney, 352.

[4] Act for regulating party-walls and buildings in Philadelphia, passed in 1710. MS. Laws, chapter 178. Repealed February 20, 1713, and subsequently supplied in 1721. See 1 Smith's Laws, 124.

[5] Act 1700, 1 Smith's Laws, page 14.

[6] Act April 15, 1782, 2 Smith, 48. For provisions of these acts see The Harmony Fire Company *vs.* Trustees of the Fire Association, 11 Casey, 496. Similar laws were enacted for the district of Southwark, March 26, 1762, and the southern part of the Northern Liberties of the city of Philadelphia, March 9, 1771. See 1 Hall & Sellers, pages 101, 293, 390.

Such legislation was very early found necessary in consequence of the plan of the city. The city, as laid out by Penn, was a parallelogram two miles long east and west, and one broad north and south. The distance between the streets made very deep lots, whether fronting on the east and west or north and south, and in the division of city property led to narrow fronts with great depth, and to the erection of back buildings, a style peculiar to Philadelphia. The regulation of party-walls so as to secure the largest inner front to dwellings became, therefore, a matter of vital importance.[1]

City Officers.

SEC. 22. Besides the city officers already mentioned there were a number of minor officers that only require cursory mention. The town crier proclaimed the public notices,[2] and had from time to time various duties assigned to him, such as making a list of the inhabitants keeping cows, &c.[3] The beadle, together with the constables, gave notice to the inhabitants of an election for representative;[4] he collected the cow-tax; summoned persons to appear before the common council;[5] and executed other trivial duties. There was a wood-corder, who was paid so many pence per cord;[6] a wharfinger, to collect the wharf fees;[7] an inspector of water-courses, to be paid a fee of 1d. per foot by the owner;[8] a vendue master, appointed by the governor.[9] It seems that the vendue master injured the trade of the small shopkeepers, and it was, therefore, ordered by the common council that the vendue master should sell no goods under 40s. except wearing apparel, second-hand goods, and such other articles as are specified in the act regulating vendues.[10] There was an officer for measuring salt and sealing measures, and an officer for measuring wheat;[11] a clerk of the common council;[12] a public

---

1 *Vollmer's Appeal.* For a full history of English and Pennsylvania legislation on party-walls, 61 Pa. St. Rep., 125.

2 Min. C. C., page 9. 3 *Ibid.*, page 18. 4 *Ibid.*, page 30.
5 *Ibid.*, page 184. 6 *Ibid.*, page 34. 7 *Ibid.*, page 109.
8 *Ibid.*, page 145. 9 *Ibid.*, page 302. 10 *Ibid.*, page 411.
11 *Ibid.*, page 359. 12 *Ibid.*, page 457.

whipper, at a salary of £10 per annum; and other minor officers not necessary to mention.

A large part of the executive duties of the city were transacted by boards or committees of councils. These committees were not standing committees, and had but little resemblance to the committees of more modern times. They were merely a certain number of the members of the corporation to whom from time to time, as convenience dictated, certain matters were assigned to be attended to. Thus a certain number of aldermen were appointed overseers of wharves and other public works;[1] their duty being to have general superintendence of those branches. Upon one occasion one of the aldermen was appointed city treasurer to receive all moneys and pay out the same as the common council should direct;[2] at another time the mayor was elected treasurer;[3] there was no regular city treasurer for a long time; certain aldermen were appointed regulators of highways,[4] and were directed from time to time to view certain public works and report thereon;[5] three aldermen were appointed commissioners of property;[6] in 1737 the surveyor-general of the province was appointed one of the regulators of the streets, and he was to receive a salary therefor.[7]

After the manner of boroughs in England, Philadelphia was given representatives in the legislative district from the county in 1705.[8] The number of representatives was increased from time to time. In 1779 the city had five representatives; the county, nine.[9] It is interesting to note that the citizens of Philadelphia voted not only for their own burgesses, but also for the representatives from the county at large.[10]

The freeholders of each ward elected two justices of the

---

[1] Min. C. C., page 23. [2] *Ibid.*, page 22. [3] *Ibid.*, page 322.
[4] *Ibid.*, pages 99, 170, 326, 414, and 500. [5] *Ibid.*, page 181.
[6] *Ibid.*, page 215. [7] *Ibid.*, page 369.
[8] Chapter 137. 1705—An act to regulate the number of members of the assembly, and their method of election.
[9] Chapter 836. September 24, 1779. Smith, vol. 1, 286.
[10] See broadsides and election tickets in Penn. Hist. Soc.

peace.[1] Finally, the port wardens remain to be mentioned. The number of port wardens varied from time to time, being generally seven. They appointed a clerk and had a seal; they licensed pilots and made general rules and regulations affecting the port, which were enforced by fines.

Ferries.

Sec. 23. By the royal charter Penn was given "the free and undisturbed use and continuance in and passage into and out of all and singular Ports, harbours, Bayes, waters, Rivers, Isles, and Inletts belonging unto or leading to and from the Country or Islands aforesaid; and all the soyle, lands, fields, woods, underwoods, mountains, hills, fenns, Isles, Lakes, rivers, waters, Rivuletts, Bays and Inletts, scituate or being within or belonging unto the Limitts and Bounds aforesaid."[2] Upon this provision, and others similar in the charter, was based the claim of the proprietor to exclusive power over ferries. In the original charter of Philadelphia the corporation was not granted any such power over the ferries; and, as they increased in importance with the expansion of the city, they were a frequent source of contention between the provincial government, the corporation, and individuals. A power to a municipal corporation to establish and regulate ferries within its limits does not give it an exclusive power, and consequently does not authorize it to delegate an exclusive privilege to others.[3] The corporation endeavored to obtain a general grant of powers over ferries, but never succeeded. In several instances the right to certain ferries was vested in the corporation; in others it was vested directly in individuals by the assembly.

Markets.

As already mentioned, the markets were a substantial source of revenue. The markets were built in the centre of the

[1] Smith, chapter 728, 2/5, 1777.
[2] Also all fisheries therein. Charter of Penna.
[3] Dillon on Mun. Cor. See Westcott, 2436.

streets. In some cases this called forth loud protests from the property-holders, who correctly maintained that the corporation had no right to use the streets for such purpose.[1]

Courts.

Sec. 24. We have seen that the mayor, recorder, and aldermen were vested with ample jurisdiction in all criminal matters,—jurisdiction as extensive as that of the quarter sessions and oyer and terminer. This court so established was known as the mayor's court. They had also jurisdiction in the city and county as justices of the peace. The mayor's court had jurisdiction in civil matters arising out of actions burnel and staple. By divers early acts justices of the peace were given summary and final jurisdiction in all civil controversies not exceeding 40s., except in matters of rent and contracts for real estate. It would appear that the corporation by ordinance set up a special court for the same purpose, holden by certain of the aldermen, to which were incident certain large fees. In 1704 a "Petition from ye Inhabitants of Phila. ag^st^ ye Court for Tryals under 40s.,"[2] was presented "To the Hon^eble^ John Evans, Esq., Governor of the Province of Pennsylvania and Counties of New Castle, Kent & Sussex on Delaware," asking for relief from said court. This petition is so quaintly worded, and is so indicative of the times, that we cannot forbear setting it out in full, especially as we do not think it has ever been printed :—

"The Humble Petition of Diverse poor Inhabitants of the City and County of Philadelphia

"Humbly Sheweth, That Whereas by an Act of General Assembly of this government It is Enacted to this effect (vizt) That any Justice of the peace upon complaint made may Issue his warrant to the Constable to Bring the Defendant to answer the Plaintiffe of all debts under forty shillings and such Justice may give Judgment thereupon

[1] See Broadside Phila. Library, Folio No. 99, 2/58.
[2] Penn. Hist. Soc., Penn Papers. Vol. of Mis. Papers. City Lots, &c.

and grant Execucon against the goods and in default of goods against the Body of such Defendant the fees whereof were usually about and seldom Exceeding three shillings. But now so may it please your honour that about six months since by an act or ordinance of Common Councill The Mayor Recorder Aldermen and Comon Council of the City of Philadelphia have taken upon them to erect and by Publick Proclamation to make known that they had Erected Ordained and Constituted a Court for the Determining of Debts under forty shillings and had appointed officers of the same Court and Established large ffees (a list whereof is herewith presented most humbly to your honour) and since the publication of the same Ordinance they have in pursuance thereof kept the same Court & Compelled divers of your peticoners to pay the same extravagant ffees and some of your Peticoners not having money to pay their Creditors the several sums due and the said Extravagant ffees they have been kept in the Comon Gaol several weeks and until they did find a person to sell themselves unto for a Term of Years to pay the same and Redeem their bodies to the great Ruine and Destruction of themselves and families.

"May it therefore please Your honour in your usual and wonted Mercy Clemency and Goodness The premises wholly to consider and deliver Your Peticoners and all other the poor distressed Inhabitants of this City out of the Jaws of that pernicious devouring and Extravagant Court by taking such methods as to your honours wisdom and conduct shall seem most just and meet and your distressed Peticoners and their poor ffamilies shall ever most heartily pray as in all humble Duty bound for your honours health and prosperity."

This petition, or other motives, induced the assembly to grant relief, for an act was passed[1] repealing all ordinances of councils as to collection of debts under 40s., and making the jurisdiction of the justices of the peace exclusive and final. Executions could issue against the person in default of any assets.

[1] Act of May 28, 1715, chapter 211, Smith's Laws.

Miscellaneous Ordinances.

Sec. 25. The ordinances for this period are with few exceptions lost, and there is nothing left to indicate their character, except a few titles scattered about in different records. Among these titles may be mentioned, in order to convey an idea of the character of the municipal legislation, "An ordinance to restrain the number of dogs and prevent their running at large;"[1] "An ordinance to encourage the building of a public slaughter-house,"[2] and of a burial ground;[3] prohibiting galloping horses and all fast driving;[4] an ordinance "grounded upon a law of this province," for "the Ascertaining the Dimensions of Casks & for true Packing of Meat for Transportation;"[5] "regulating the price of victuals & for the better settling of the markets;"[6] requiring the sellers of meat and grain under the court house to open the mouths of the sacks "that the inhabitants may see what they buy;"[7] regulating the wages of carters, draymen & porters;[8] authorizing James Henderson to be a chimney sweeper & employ assistants;[9] to prevent "frequent & tumultuous meetings of the Negro Slaves, especially on Sundays, Gaming, cursing, swearing, & Committing many other Disorders to the Great Terror & Disgust of the Inhabitants of the City;"[10] an ordinance for regulating the cording of wood; providing for public entertainment to prominent officials;[11] "for preventing Frauds & Abuse in the Measuring of Salt, Flaxseed, wheat & other Grain imported & brought by water into the harbor of this city;"[12] and finally, inasmuch as the Recorder reported that "certain persons had lately taken upon them to act Plays in the City & as he was informed, intended to make a frequent Practice thereof; which it was to be feared would be attended by very mischievous Effects, such as the encouraging of Idleness & drawing great Sums of Money from weak & inconsiderate People who are apt to be fond of such kinds of Entertainments tho' the performances be ever so mean & contemptible;"

[1] Min. C. C., page 37. [2] Page 34. [3] Page 46. [4] Page 57. [5] Page 81. [6] Page 86. [7] Page 101. [8] Page 164. [9] Page 188. [10] Page 314. [11] Page 334–337. [12] Page 373.

therefore an ordinance was unanimously passed requesting the Magistrates to send for the actors and bind them to their good behavior or to deal with them by such other means as they should judge proper.[1]

The Revolution.

Sec. 26. The corporation of the mayor and commonalty of the city of Philadelphia came to an end at the Revolution.[2] The last records of the corporation bear date February, 1776. Committees of correspondence, which had been formed June 18, 1774, were organized into the committees of safety June

[1] Page 523.

[2] It is curious to note that amidst all the flurry and intense excitement of the approaching revolution there is no other reference or remote allusion thereto, save the following answer to a communication from selectmen of Boston, nine years before the storm burst. Its cautiously-worded, nicely-balanced sentences might well have emanated from the Quaker yearly meeting, in point of substance and style.

"Answer to a letter from the selectmen of Boston, a draft presented, which was adopted.

"Phila. Dec. 22d, 1767.

"Gentlemen:—We were favored with your letter of the 9th of November last, and thankfully acknowledge your kind intentions of communicating to us the votes of your Town Meeting of the 28th October, which, however, you omitted to enclose, but we take for granted are the same as inserted in your public papers. We desire that you will be assured of our having a due regard to the general interest of the colonies, which we conceive cannot be more effectually served than by diffusing a spirit of Industry and Frugality. But, however the particular circumstances of your place may require public measures to be taken for that purpose, we do not see the expediency of adopting them here, more especially in the present critical situation of American Affairs. Yet, altho' we cannot on this occasion think the steps you have taken altogether suitable to our circumstances, we shall always wish to see, and endeavor by every expedient to promote the general Union of the Colonies, so essential to the preservation of their Liberties.

"Signed at a Common Council
"By order of the Board

"ISAAC JONES,
"*Mayor.*"

"To Joseph Jackson, Samuel Sewall, John Ruddock, John Hancock, Wm. Phillips, Timo. Shewell, John Rouce, Esqs., Selectmen of Boston." Min. C. C., page 725.

30, 1775. Congress passed the resolution recommending the colonies to form proper governments suited to the times. In the autumn of 1776 the convention met to form a state government, and sent delegates to Congress. On September 3 an ordinance was passed appointing justices of the peace, under authority of the people. On September 28 it completed its work, and the declaration of rights and the constitution of the State of Pennsylvania were promulgated.

The first state legislature met in January, and promptly passed an act authorizing and enjoining all constables, overseers of the poor, supervisors of highways, and the wardens and street commissioners of Philadelphia, to exercise the functions of their respective offices until their successors were appointed.[1]

Soon after, an act was passed directing the election of justices of the peace for Philadelphia by wards.[2] The act of March 14, 1777, is very important.[3] It recites the various acts creating certain officers, and duties to be performed by the designated officials in conjunction with the mayor, recorder, and aldermen of the corporation, and states, "Whereas by change in the government this power in the mayor, recorder, and aldermen has ceased, whereby the aforesaid acts of assembly cannot be put into force according to the true intent and meaning thereof, &c.," and enacts that the coordinate powers of the mayor, recorder, and aldermen are vested in three justices of the peace.

After the occupation of the city by the British the city was under military rule; and even after the patriot army resumed possession, martial law and military government still prevailed, and the municipal affairs got on as best they could, under the meagre skeleton of government left from the wreck of the old corporation. This machinery was found very defective long before any practical remedy was applied in the shape of a new charter, which did not come till 1789, some time after the war. The confusion and imminent dangers of revolution do not account for this long delay of legislative

[1] Baily's Laws, page 5. [2] Baily, page 14. [3] Baily, page 37.

action. The citizens of Philadelphia could doubtless have had a new charter from the legislature as early as 1777 had they desired one; as in that year an act was passed to renew the charter of the borough of Lancaster, which, having been granted by the proprietor, was deemed canceled by the war. In fact, the old corporation of Philadelphia had turned out so inefficient, and had so excited the jealousy and dislike of the people, that there was a general distrust about creating another one.

SUMMARY.

SEC. 27. As early as 1773 this feeling was very strong among the citizens, and gave vent, among other things, through a broadside entitled "An address to my fellow-citizens—Friends to Liberty & Enemies to despotism," signed Andrew Marvel,[1] in which he makes fourteen charges against the corporation, the last of which is that "As the Corporation have in divers Instances exceeded Powers granted by charter, query whether by a proper application to the Crown their charter may not be dissolved;" and concludes, "Long have the inhabitants of this city seen with concern the Inconveniences of the Corporation Charter & as they have exceeded the powers granted to them by charter in many Instances, ought we not in Justice to ourselves & our Posterity, make use of this favorable Opportunity to lay the Ax to the root of this unprofitable tree & apply to the Crown for a dissolution of the charter?" While the abuses in Philadelphia were never as extensive as in the towns and boroughs of England, they were sufficient to afford ample cause for the universal complaints of the citizens. The condition of the revenues has already been noticed, and many of the other departments were in an equal state of confusion. The minute distribution of authority, and the constant distrust and jealousy between the corporation and the various boards and commissions, was a principal cause of the disordered condition of affairs. For this reason the streets were continually in want

[1] See Folio of Broadsides in Phila. Library, 992/59.

of repairs. For many years, indeed, the surplus money was applied for that purpose, but to expend it required the authority of the mayor, recorder, and aldermen, the assessors, and, in many cases, the final consent of the common council. The magistrates and assessors were hampered by the necessity of calling a meeting of the common council every time an exigency arose, however trivial, involving any outlay of money. With the idea of making a more simple system, the funds were placed by a resolution of the board under the control of the mayor, recorder, and any three aldermen, with the assessors.[1]

Upon one occasion the Water street drawbridge urgently required repair. It was proposed by the common council to lay a tax for the erection of a substantial stone bridge. The magistrates and assessors held a conference. The assessors refused to agree to the levy of a tax unless they were satisfied that there were not sufficient funds in the hands of the corporation for the purpose. The common council in reply declared that they were not obliged to apply the funds of the corporation for the erection of a bridge, "the act of assembly expressly directing that the magistrates of the city, in conjunction with the assessors, should from time to time lay a tax on the inhabitants of the city for such like purposes;" and that the claim of the assessors to inspect the funds of the corporation was without foundation. Compromise appearing impossible, the matter was postponed, and a committee was appointed by the common council "to agree with some person to put up a fence to prevent any danger to people passing that way."[2]

The business of the common council was conducted without system, and, in consequence of the absence of officers possessing adequate executive authority, the time was largely frittered away in trivial matters which never should have reached it. The petition of some person convicted of a petty misdemeanor, begging the remission of his fine which he was unable to pay, required the corporation to deliberate thereon

[1] Min. C. C., 1760. [2] *Ibid.*, 746-7-8.

with all the integral parts present, and either to enforce justice by letting the offender remain in gaol, or perhaps transact a financial arrangement with him by taking his note or bond therefor, or easily getting rid of him by releasing him on condition he left the province, or, if occasion existed, enlisted in a regiment. Every time a wharf, a ferry, or a market stall was rented or needed repairing, the whole corporation was similarly called in. The pettiest accounts were solemnly audited in full council. The few executive officers were, as a rule, elected by the common council, while the remaining executive duties were sometimes performed by committees appointed for each occasion; but even these committees were unable to act until they had reported to the common council, who sometimes appointed a second committee to act upon the report.

But the leading defect that went to the root of the abuses incident to the system, and explains the distrust and dislike of the citizens at large for the municipal government, was that the municipal government consisted, as previously noticed, of a corporate body, existing independently of the community. The corporation came to look upon itself, and was so considered by the inhabitants, as a separate and exclusive body; and while it had powers and privileges within the city, in many cases all identity of interest was lost.[1] A similar defect existed in nearly all the boroughs of England before the Municipal Reform Act of 1835, although there it was vastly increased in consequence of the importance which the privilege of electing members of Parliament conferred upon the governing bodies of municipal corporations. It is interesting to note the extent of the abuses in consequence of this cause. The rewards for political services which were thus brought within the reach of the ruling corporators caused them to hold the franchise of electing burgesses as the principal object of their institution. To this cause, rather

[1] Exactly similar defects prevailed in the municipal corporations in England before the Reform Act of 1835. See Rep. of Mun. Corp. Com., page 33, Introduction.

than to the desire of monopolizing the petty perquisites of municipal authority, may be referred the custom of keeping the number of corporators as low as possible. "Hence," says the Report of the Municipal Commission, "a great number of Corporations have been preserved solely as political engines, and the towns to which they belong derive no benefit, but suffer much injury, from their existence. To maintain the political ascendancy of a party, or the political influence of a family, has been the one end and object for which the powers intrusted to a numerous class of these bodies have been exercised. This object has been systematically pursued in the admission of freemen, resident or non-resident, in the selection of municipal functionaries for the council and the magistracy; in the appointment of subordinate officers and the local police; in the administration of charities intrusted to municipal authorities; in the expenditure and management of the corporate revenues. These most flagrant abuses have arisen from this perversion of municipal privileges to political objects."[1] Admission to the corporate body was sought with a view to the lucrative exercise of the elective franchise, while elections to municipal offices became a trial of strength between political parties.[2]

Offices were treated as matters of patronage, and many useless offices were in existence, while salaries were divided among candidates. Carelessness and extravagance in the administration of municipal funds, and an exclusive distribution of patronage among friends and partisans, prevailed. The funds were wasted in public dinners and in supporting useless officers.

Public works were built extravagantly, and there was no system of public contracts and adequate estimates. Abuses arose sometimes from neglect of municipal officials, but more frequently from political reasons.

Being self-elected, and holding office for life, it was inevitable that the common council should feel unchecked by any feeling of responsibility; and the discharge of their functions

---

[1] Report M. C. Commission, page 34. [2] *Ibid.*, pages 34, 35.

was rendered difficult by the dislike and suspicion which the manner of their election inevitably entailed upon them. The inhabitants at large possessed very imperfect knowledge of the proceedings of the corporation; the ordinances which were passed, as well as those repealed, were often unpublished, or were printed upon loose broadsides, and a complete collection of ordinances was scarcely possessed, even by the corporation itself. Great ignorance prevailed concerning the provisions of ordinances, and of the acts of legislature, and of the powers granted by the charter, and all were naturally violated with impunity.

Not the least defect was the absence of executive officers; and an inherent vice was that the officers appointed by the charter for particular functions were regarded as a necessary part of the legislative body. This notion originated in times when the separation of constitutional authority was not understood, and when legislative, judicial, and executive functions were confounded.

The union, likewise, of the functions of mayor and magistrate, and even more especially of alderman and magistrate, was one of questionable expediency, and caused frequent complaints on the part of the citizens; and the same may be said of the union of other officers, such as treasurer and mayor.

That the public property should be mismanaged, was an inevitable result of the system. There was an inevitable tendency for the corporation to consider the public property as held by them as trustees for the community at large. From this idea the transition was not difficult to the idea that the property of the corporation was held for the benefit of the corporation as distinct from the community with which it was locally connected; and from this idea the final transition was also easy to the opinion that individual corporators might justifiably derive a personal benefit from that property. Thus while it is almost a maxim of modern legislative assemblies of any kind, that their individual members shall not profit in any manner from the public property under their control, the members of the common council of Philadelphia, as in all similarly constituted municipal corporations of the age, were continually making profitable contracts with individual members concerning the public property. Thus the mayor and aldermen took leases for a term of years of the various public wharves of the city.[1]

[1] 1720. Min. C. C., page 174.

SEAL OF PHILADELPHIA IN 1701.

CHAPTER III.

CHARTER OF 1789 TO ACT OF CONSOLIDATION.

THE OLD CITY.

CAUSES LEADING TO ACT OF 1789.

SECTION 1. The friction caused by the anomalous existence of a close corporation, alluded to in the last chapter, resulted in a feeling of hostile criticism, widely felt and clearly evidenced by many incidents of the time, and it was greatly intensified by the fervid acceptance of the democratic idea naturally pronounced during the revolutionary era. To this feeling may be attributed directly the thirteen years' period of suspended municipal existence from 1776–1789. The distrust and suspicion of a municipal charter, felt by the citizens, were evidences of a *post-mortem* protest against the idea of an autocratic government, rather than attributable to the memory of any actual tyranny or injustice suffered by the people from the manner in which the old corporation exercised the trust and powers vested in it by the Proprietor.

All proprietary charters fell with the Revolution. There was, however, no indisposition on the part of the legislature to renew or re-create them when so desired by the parties in interest. Amidst the hurry and pressing claims of a war period we find the assembly, as early as 1777, renewing the charter of the ancient borough of Lancaster.[1]

As time went on, the evils arising from lack of systematic government became so imminent that the memories of past grievances vanished before present necessities; and in 1783 a petition[2] largely signed by citizens was presented to the legislature and referred to the city members. As a result of this petition we have the second charter of Philadelphia, passed on the eleventh day of March, 1789.[3]

---

[1] Act June 19, 1777, 1 Smith, 446.

[2] See original petition in possession of the Hist. Soc. of Pa.

[3] 2 Smith, 462.

A MODERN MUNICIPAL CORPORATION.

SEC. 2. The Revolution of 1776 was followed by no more radical change in state and national affairs than that which it introduced in the municipal history of Philadelphia.

The legislative charter of 1789 created a modern municipality, in sharp contradistinction to the mediæval character of the proprietary charter. The city affairs during the interregnum had been but poorly attended to under the various legislative commissions; and the failure of the administration of municipal affairs is most forcibly set out in the preamble to the act of March 11th, 1789: "Whereas the administration of government in the City of Philadelphia is in its present form inadequate to the suppression of vice and immorality, to the advancement of the public health and order, and to the promotion of trade, industry, and happiness: And in order to provide against the evils occasioned thereby, it is necessary to invest the inhabitants thereof with more speedy, vigorous, and effective powers of government than are at present established, * * * Be it enacted, &c., * * * That the inhabitants of the City of Philadelphia, as the same extends and is laid out between the rivers Delaware and Schuylkill, be, and they and their successors forever are, hereby constituted a corporation and body politic, in fact and in law, by the name and style of The Mayor, Aldermen and Citizens of Philadelphia."

The usual corporate powers were granted. Fifteen aldermen were to be elected septennially by the freeholders, and thirty common councilmen triennially by the freemen. The mayor was elected by the aldermen from their own number; the recorder, by the mayor and aldermen from the freemen of the city. The mayor, recorder, and aldermen and common councilmen in common council granted power to make and enforce ordinances necessary and convenient for the government of the city, which were to be published and recorded.

The mayor's court was continued; and the aldermen's court,

consisting of three aldermen, to be chosen and appointed by the mayor and recorder, was established to meet four times a year, "for hearing and determining all matters and things by this act made cognizable therein, &c." The duties, powers, contracts, and property of the city, wardens, and street commissioners were transferred to the corporation. Records of the city court were to be surrendered to the mayor's court; all rights, property, &c. of the old city corporation were vested in the new one. No assembly or meeting was to be deemed or accounted a common council unless the mayor or recorder, and at least eight aldermen and sixteen common councilmen, were present. The corporation was required to publish its accounts annually.

Such were the substantial provisions of the act of 1789, though the full text embodies some other important details which may be considered declaratory of the general powers conferred.

A radical change effected by this act, which is the fundamental distinction between the mediæval and modern corporation, is the total abolition of the privileged class and of every vestige of a close corporation.

The government is made essentially representative, and the administration of all local affairs is fully placed in the hands of the people through their duly-elected servants.

The citizens elected the aldermen and common councilmen. The aldermen elected the mayor from among their own number. The mayor appointed the clerk of the market; and such officers as councils might think requisite for the ordering of affairs were to be created and appointed as councils should direct.

Amendments to the Charter of 1789.

Sec. 3. While the essential features of this era were fixed by the act of 1789, its charter was changed and modified in many important particulars by various supplementary acts.[1]

[1] Act December 9, 1789; April 2, 1790; March 8, 1792; April 4, 1796; April 11, 1799; February 18, 1805.

Some of these enactments only made changes in matters of minor detail; others were so far-reaching as to be fairly entitled to the name of amendments. The act of 1790 explicitly recognizes the intent of the act of 1789 to abolish the office of assessors as created under the act of 1712, and empowers the corporation "to assess and levy taxes for lighting, watching, pitching, paving, and cleaning the streets, and to make all necessary ordinances both for raising the tax and for conduct of the work."

A step in the direction of a double house is to be noted in the provision, as to the majority necessary to pass an ordinance contained in section 4 of this act: "That the consent and approbation of the mayor or recorder, and a majority of the aldermen, and also of the common councilmen, who shall from time to time be present, and in common council assembled, shall be necessary to the making, &c. of all ordinances."

The act of 1792 authorizes the corporation to accept resignations of its members, and to issue writs for elections to fill vacancies.

The act of April 4th, 1796, passed "on prayer of many citizens, to render the charter more conformable to the frame of government of this Commonwealth," made these important changes:—

1. Qualified electors of representatives are to elect twenty persons qualified to serve in the house of representatives to be members of common council for one year.

2. Said freemen are to elect twelve members eligible as senators to be members of select council for three years.

3. The whole legislative power of the corporation shall be exclusively vested in said select and common councils, who shall perform all legislative acts as separate and distinct bodies. The appointment of recorder and aldermen was vested in the Governor, and their tenure of office limited by life or good behavior; their powers, duties, and privileges remained the same as before, exclusive of participation in legislative duties.

The mayor was to be elected *viva voce* at a joint meeting of councils from among the aldermen for the term of one year. He now ceased to be a member of common council; his duty was to promulgate the laws and ordinances, and to pay special attention to the due execution and fulfillment of the same, but he was given no veto power.

The act of 1799 was confirmatory and declaratory. It provided, "That freemen were not disqualified by interest from being witnesses for the city, or serving as jurors."

Powers of Appointment given the Mayor.

The mayor was to appoint all officers of the corporation "who shall be created by ordinance of councils, excepting only the treasurer of the corporation, and the clerks, messengers, and doorkeepers of councils."

By the act of 1800 the city was divided into fourteen wards. The act of March 25th, 1805, vested in councils all and every power of regulating markets. The act of 1839, June 21, makes the election of mayor to be by the citizens at large, and amends the act of 1799 so as to transfer the power of appointment of the city officers created by councils from the mayor to councils.

Every act of assembly directly affecting the city is, in a measure, an addition to or modification of its charter. The statute books are crowded with such acts during this period; but the acts above cited are those which may be fairly construed as forming its organic law. Such other legislation as may be pertinent to illustrate our subject will be treated of under special heads, where it can be most appropriately marshaled.

The Mayor.

Sec. 4. During this period there were repeated changes and modifications affecting the mayor, both as to his general duties and method of election. Under the charter he was elected by the aldermen from among their own number.

When councils were divided, some seven years later, into two bodies, his election from the same class devolved upon them.[1] This course was followed for thirty-six years, when councils were authorized to select him from the body of freeholders,[2] and thirteen years later his election from the people by the people was enacted.[3] His appointing powers were proportionally very great after 1799; for by that act he was authorized to appoint all the officers created by the ordinance of councils; by the charter he was to appoint the clerks of the market. The act of assembly, in making the office of mayor elective by the electors of Philadelphia, also vested in councils the powers to provide by ordinance for the election or appointment of all officers then appointed by the mayor.

Up to the passage of the act of 1796 he was a component part of common councils, the meetings of which were to be called either by him or the recorder, and the consent of one or the other was necessary to the enactment of an ordinance. He had the same judicial duties as heretofore; and among his general duties may be enumerated the publication and enforcement of the ordinances, direction and supervision of the duties and accounts of the city treasurer and commissioners, and drawing of orders on the city treasurer for payment of city debts.[4]

He was certainly a paid official after 1796, and received a fixed salary of $1000;[5] before that date he was probably dependent on the fees of the office. In 1805 his salary was raised to $2000, and in 1835 to $3000.[6]

Recorder, Aldermen, and City Courts.

Sec. 5. The supplement of 1796 divested the recorder and aldermen, as well as the mayor, of all connection with legislative duties, but left their other powers and functions unimpaired.

---

[1] Act 1796. [2] Act April 10, 1826. [3] June 10, 1839.
[4] § 5, Act April 4, 1796. Ord. September 9, 1796.
[5] Ord. March 9, 1797.
[6] Ord. December 20, 1805. Ord. December 24, 1835.

The mayor, recorder, and aldermen had jurisdiction, through the county, of justices of the peace, to hear and determine, subject to appeal, all actions of debt for breach of ordinance and consideration of claims not exceeding $100.[1] They had also summary jurisdiction in amounts not exceeding 40s. The mayor's court[2] had the powers of the quarter sessions, oyer and terminer, &c. The mayor or recorder and three aldermen constituted a quorum. A writ of error lay to the supreme court.

By the same charter was created a court known as the aldermen's court; a quorum to consist of three aldermen, to be appointed by the mayor and recorder, to sit four times a year, having original jurisdiction in civil matters in controversies between 40s. and £10, and an appeal lay from the mayor or aldermen to the aldermen's court.[3]

By the act of 1796 the recorder and aldermen were made appointees of the governor, and their functions made strictly judicial. The recorder received a salary of $500 from the state treasury.

Councils.

Sec. 6. Under the charter of 1789 councils consisted of the mayor, recorder, aldermen, and common councilmen. Meetings were called by the mayor or recorder; it sat as one body; but, in order to make a valid ordinance, the consent of the mayor or recorder, and a majority of the aldermen, and also of the common councilmen present, was necessary.[4] The act to alter and amend the several acts incorporating the city made the most radical changes in the government of the city, and especially affected the constitution of the councils. The bicameral system was introduced; though the members of both houses were elected on a general ticket and did not represent particular wards. The meetings were made public, and the whole legislative power of the corporation was vested in select

[1] Acts of April 15, 1835; April 5, 1849. [2] § 20, act 1789.

[3] § 25 act 1789 repealed by act March 28, 1804, 6 Smith, 339. See act March 26, 1810. [4] Act April 2, 1790, 2 Dall., 654.

and common councils, of which the mayor, recorder, and aldermen ceased to form part. The new councils elected their respective presidents, who signed all ordinances; a duty heretofore performed by the mayor and corporation clerk. They had power under the charter to provide for the election or appointment of all necessary agents or officers.

This duty was performed by councils until 1799,[1] when the appointment of all officers created by ordinance of councils was vested in the mayor, excepting the city treasurer, who was invariably elected by councils. The mayor, as we have seen, exercised the appointing power down to 1839, when he was divested of the general power of appointment, which was again conferred upon councils. The duty of electing the mayor devolved upon councils down to 1839, as has been set out above.

Corporation Offices created by Ordinance. Freemen, Citizens, &c.

Sec. 7. The elections of officers, as we see by the acts of 1789–1796, vested the power of election of the aldermen in freeholders, and that of councilmen in the freemen of the city; but there does not appear any prescribed qualification to constitute a freeman; and after the act of 1796 the electoral qualification was defined by the right to vote for state senators and representatives. We may therefore infer that state citizenship carried with it the freedom of the city, when coupled with residence therein.

Very early it was deemed necessary by the legislature to declare that no freeman shall be disqualified as a witness or juror in litigation arising out of corporate matters, paupers only excepted. The very idea of a modern municipality carried with it, as the central thought, the idea of incorporation of a place and its inhabitants, for the purpose of local administration and government. The mediæval charter was, in theory and practice, a grant of certain governing rights, privileges, and franchises from the crown to a privileged class. The

[1] April 11, 1799, 4 Dall., 482.

commonalty may have been named among the grantees; but they were the patient ass, upon whose back the burden was to be laid, with no voice as to choice of drivers. In the modern municipality the rights and duties of citizenship follow from existent residence; they can neither be assumed nor laid aside by present choice or refusal. Popular sovereignty, as expressed by the voice of the legislature, may impose such duties as to its wisdom seem fitting and expedient. That the residents of a place shall have a controlling voice in the execution of these duties, and the appointing of the agents and officers, is a well-grounded principle of our institutions; but the manner in which this voice shall be exercised is always within the control of the legislature, to be by it modified and changed, as to it from time to time may seem most advisable.

Charter Officers.

The charter officers have already been enumerated, but it may not be amiss to recapitulate them here. They are the mayor, aldermen, recorder, select and common councilmen, and clerks of the markets. There were to be also "such other officers, and at such salaries as the councils shall direct, to be appointed by councils or the mayor." This list, as subsequently made out, included constables and policemen, clerks and messengers, city treasurer, solicitor, city commissioners, superintendents of various departments, and other minor officers. There may be also mentioned here a class of legislative officers to be appointed through corporate agency, such as regulators, guardians of the poor, port wardens, and board of health.

City Treasurer.

The importance of this officer, and everything connected with his appointment and conduct, was always recognized. All through this third period he was elected by councils. The very first ordinance passed by councils, on May 27, 1789, was an ordinance for ascertaining the duty and pay of the treasurer of the corporation, which remained in force for nine years. He was subsequently elected by councils, at a joint meeting, for a term of one year,[1] subject to removal at their pleasure.

His duty was to keep a list of rentals of city property, notify the mayor of neglect of tenants to pay; to receive all moneys, and keep distinct accounts of moneys arising from different sources; to pay checks drawn by the mayor, and to deliver to the mayor accounts of receipts and disbursements every three months; his books to be subject to inspection by the mayor; he was to report delinquent tax-collectors, and generally to account to, and advise, the mayor, councils, and city commissioners of the financial status. His salary, in 1811, was fixed at $2000.

City Commissioners.

Sec. 8. In the last chapter was shown the necessity, arising from the narrow limits and construction of the proprietary charter, for legislative assistance, and the result of this necessity in the creation of the various legislative commissions of assessors, street commissioners, and wardens. This defective power to administer the most pressing internal affairs was cured by the charter of 1789.[2] The powers and duties of the street commissioners and wardens were conferred on the corporation. The importance of the powers and duties thus conferred is evidenced by the fact that it received the attention of councils in its second ordinance, vesting in commissioners certain powers for lighting, watching, paving, and watering the city, and for raising money to defray the expenses thereof.[3] These provisions were extended by ordinance two years later, and again supplied in six years. And we find the purport of these creations clearly set out in the ordinance of May 22, 1797,[4] which supersedes all former enactments.

---

[1] Ord. May 27, 1789; Ord. April 14, 1797; Act April 11, 1799; Act of 1802. [2] § xxv.

[3] Ord. May 30, 1789; Ord. June 3, 1791. [4] Ord. May 22, 1797.

The creation, powers, and duties of this board are of significance, as registering the trend of the municipal theory, as applied to executive functions, and from the fact that the great proportion of executive duties was imposed on and concentrated in it. In it were combined the duties and powers of the assessors, street commissioners, and wardens, with a view to obtaining a more intelligent and effective service, by reason of this very concentration. The commissioners were not elected directly by the people, but were appointed through their representative agents, the officers of the corporation. There could no longer remain, therefore, any clashing or jealousy, as between officers of the people who were compelled to act with the corporation officers in a complex system; all were now officers of the corporation, and the corporation was the body of the freemen. Let us see how they were appointed, and what were their duties. Prior to 1799[1] councils, by concurrent resolution, were to appoint not less than three nor more than five discreet citizens, by the name of city commissioners, who were to employ a clerk to attend in their office and keep their accounts. Their duties were numerous: to let the real estate for terms not exceeding one year, unless with consent of councils; to invite proposals therefor by advertisement; to let market stalls; to repair and superintend the real property; to prevent and remove nuisances in the streets; to cause wells to be dug and pumps and lamps set up, and to regulate the same; to appoint a superintendent of nightly watch; to provide for lighting and watching the city; to contract for repairs of public pavements; to repair unpaved streets; to contract for pitching, paving, and cleaning streets; to cause footways and private causeways to be paved at expense of owners, conforming to the regulations of the mayor, aldermen, and regulators in paving; to assess whatever sum might be laid by councils; to appoint collectors, &c., to examine and approve all accounts for work done, and report to the mayor, who made an order on the treasurer, when satisfied as to legality and correctness. When the appropriation

[1] Ord. May 22, 1789, Lowber, 136–147.

was exhausted for any particular item, no further order was to be drawn without action of councils. They were to present annually to councils a full account of their transactions, and keep separate and distinct accounts of the several objects under their superintendence.[1]

By act of 1799[2] they were made appointees of the mayor. By ordinance of 29th August, 1839, the appointment of the president of the board and three commissioners was again vested in councils.

The elaboration of their duties was the subject of frequent municipal legislation in regard to manner of performance of public work, their appointment, salaries, method of keeping accounts, reports and auditing of same, limitation of expenditures, supervision by highway committee, granting of building permits, and licenses to omnibuses, &c.[3]

Highways.

Sec. 9. The care of the highways of a state or town is a topic of the first importance to its citizens, and is a crucial test of executive efficiency. The defects in their creation and repair are open and palpable, and their condition may be taken as a fair index of the thoroughness and integrity of all public work. If the work which has to stand the test of daily use, which is, perforce, examined daily by thousands of eyes, is badly and corruptly done, *a fortiori* we may expect to find similar and greater deficiencies in other works which are not so patent to every observer. Of course, this is to be modified somewhat by the character of the time and climate, the fortunes and demands of the place and people; but, as a general rule, the proposition stands good.

It seems to be the curse of our municipal system that the

---

[1] Ord. February 20, 1800, Lowber, page 172. [2] Act April 11, 1799, Lowber, page 95.

[3] Ord. December 23, 1813, L. & M., 41; Ord. December 22, 1814, L. & M., 42; Ord. December 24, 1818, L. & M., 43; Ord. December 16, 1819, L. & M., 44; Ord. April 29, 1823, Digest of 1851, 137; Ord. June 12, 1828, *Ibid.*, 161; Ord. December 10, 1829, *Ibid.*, 165; Ord. August 29, 1839; Ord. January 16, 1840.

character of our public work deteriorates in ratio to its increasing magnitude, and the growing wealth and necessities of the cities. It is not the purpose of this work to indulge in any doctrinaire theory on social or political science; its effort is limited to the recital of the history of a single municipality, and the indication of such obvious results, be they defects or virtues, which are clearly deducible from undisputed premises. Many evils as obvious as the sunrise, and apparently as regular in their appearance, are the direct and inevitable products of a vicious system, and not the result of the particular inefficiency and dishonesty of the governing class of the day. Individual honesty and competency, or dishonesty and inefficiency, are equally accidents which do not affect the net result in the long run.

Ultimate Control of Highways vested in the General Public.

In the consideration of the subject of highways and streets for this period, and in fact for every period, one principle must never be lost sight of, and that is this, streets and public squares belong, when once dedicated or opened according to law, to the general rather than the local public.[1] The municipality holds them in trust for this general public. The name may be changed, but the idea is well expressed in the old title of the king's highway. The crowded avenue of the metropolis, the shady, sandy street of the village, the lonely mountain road were all alike the king's highway, and all alike belonged to that people whose sovereignty was personified at one time by the king, and now by the commonwealth. This principle is not theoretical alone, but in its applications intimately connected with the multitudinous interests dependent upon the control of the highways. The modern municipality is, as we have seen, entirely a creature of the legislature, called into being to regulate and administer matters peculiar to the place incorporated, and not common to the state; but the legislature has the power to, and in point of

[1] Com. *vs.* Rush, 14 Pa. St., 186. Reading *vs.* Com., 1 Jones, 106.

fact does, impose on its creature the exercise of certain state powers and duties within its defined limits. Local as, at first blush, may seem the control of highways, it speedily leads us up to the *Ultima Thule* of sovereignty vested in the legislature. That body may say to a city: You shall have the power and duty to control the streets, to pave, repair, and keep them fit for travel; but except by our express consent ye have no other power over them; ye cannot grant permits to obstruct them with markets, to allow them to be covered with railroad tracks, to be encroached upon by buildings; ye cannot open them; ye cannot close them, except as we dictate; our wisdom alone has the power of a sovereign over the king's highways.[1]

Keeping in view, then, this thought, that the highways of a state, including streets in cities, are under the primary and paramount control of the legislature, and that all municipal powers are derived from the legislature, we must examine not only the charter of the city but the pamphlet laws, year by year, if we would come to a correct understanding of the subject of streets and highways at any one time or period.[2] This same doctrine applies to public parks or squares. The whole question of highways touches on and arises out of the right of eminent domain, conspicuously a sovereign right vested only in the commonwealth. The only possible limitation to the power of the legislature to control and regulate streets and highways must be found in the constitution, and where that instrument is silent the control is indeed paramount.

Beginning with the charter itself, we find the duties and powers of the city wardens and street commissioners vested in the corporation, with power to make the necessary ordinances.[3] An illustration of the paramount and primary con-

---

[1] Coms. *vs.* Gosler, 12 Pa. St., 318. Stormfeltz *vs.* Co., 13 *Ibid.*, 555. Mercer *vs.* R. R. Co., 36 *Ibid.*, 99. R. R. Co. *vs.* Phila., 47 *Ibid.*, 314. O'Connor *vs.* Pittsburgh, 18 *Ibid.*, 187. Trenton R. R. Case, 6 Wharton, 25. Reading *vs.* Com., 11 Pa. St., 196. Suber's Road, 28 *Ibid.*, 199.

[2] Sharrett's Road Case, 8 Barr, 89. R. R. *vs.* Dusquennes, 46 Pa. St., 223. Road Case, 14 S. & R., 447. Road in Easton, 3 R., 195. Newville Road, 8 W., 172. Road in Milton, 40 Pa. St., 300.

[3] Act March 11, 1789, 2 Smith, 462.

trol of the legislature is evidenced in the act[1] which vested in the court of quarter sessions of Philadelphia county the right, on petition, to appoint twelve freeholders, who, with the county commissioners, are to open streets, lanes, and alleys, the damages to be paid by the *county* treasurer; the mayor then to cause streets to be opened. Councils were to make ordinances for graveling or paving, and owners were to pave footways. That councils soon busied themselves about their duties in regard to the streets is evidenced by the passage of the second ordinance,[2] vesting in commissioners certain powers for lighting, paving, watching, and watering the city, and for raising money to defray the expense thereof. This ordinance was repealed and supplied in two years;[3] and, finally, six years later, by the ordinance creating the city commissioners[4] and prescribing their duties, a settled policy was adopted.

Duty of City Commissioners as to Streets.

It was made the duty of the city commissioners to repair unpaved streets, to cause streets to be cleaned, to see that footways and private cartways were paved, and to conform to the regulations of the mayor, aldermen, and recorder. Subsequent municipal legislation[5] provided for the appointment of two persons to survey and regulate, with respect to ascents and descents, all principal streets, and to make a draft of the same, and deposit it in the city commissioners' office. We see here the origin of the survey department. The surveyors and commissioners were next required to regulate the streets according to the survey.[6] Where unpaved cartways were regulated the owners were required to pave the footways with some hard substance. The regulators were to determine the width of footways, and enter their regulations in a book of records.[7]

---

[1] Act of March 25, 1805, 7 Bioren, 469. [2] Ord. May 30, 1789.
[3] Ord. June 3, 1791. [4] Ord. May 22, 1797, Lowber's Digest, 136.
[5] Ord. March 9, 1804, Lowber's Digest, page 187. Ord. March 3, 1806, L., 195. Ord. August 6, 1814. [6] Ord. July 13, 1809, Lowber, page 195.
[7] Ord. October 1, 1811, Lowber, page 256.

Duty of City Commissioners as to Street-Cleaning, &c.

The commissioners, in addition to enforcing other requirements from the street-cleaning contractors, were directed by councils[1] to prescribe that the streets be scraped at least once a week, and, when required, twice, or oftener. In case of default the work was to be done by the commissioners at the expense of the contractor.

At this time the streets were cleaned by contract.[2] Convicts were employed on the streets under the act of 1786, but the practice was abandoned early in 1789.

Streets Cleaned by the City Itself.

In 1826 the corporation undertook to do its own street-cleaning, dividing the city into the northern and southern districts, over each of which was appointed a superintendent. These superintendents were to hire men, purchase horses and carts; to render an account in writing to the mayor, and deliver up property when required; to cleanse all streets once a week, and Market, Broad, and Second streets semi-weekly, and furnish monthly accounts to the city clerk. The street dirt was sold at auction.[3]

In 1832 there seemed to be great fear as to the sanatory condition of the city. A sanatory board of three from select and five from common council was constituted, who, with the mayor and recorder, directed all measures for cleansing the city, and controlled the funds. The city was divided into eight districts, with eight superintendents for cleansing purposes. A loan of $30,000 for the sanatory fund was made.[4] And in October[5] of same year an additional appropriation of $2000 was made.[6]

Ordinances were passed from time to time fixing the width of the footways on different streets. In 1818 the state

---

[1] Ord. February 23, 1821. [2] Ord. March 9, 1818. Ord., page 104.
[3] Ord. March 23, 1826, page 1826; March 8, 1827.
[4] Ord. June 18, 1832, page 450. [5] Ord. October 4, 1832.
[6] Repealed by Ord. of December 31, 1834.

house and square were sold to the city;[1] and in this year an act was passed vesting the swamp between Society and Budd's Hill, fronting on Front and Spruce streets (originally granted to the corporation by Penn for harbor and dock purposes[2]), in the corporation, freed and discharged from the use stated in the charter.[3] This is significant as illustrating the necessity of legislative action to change the nature and right of property in streets and land originally dedicated for public use, or a particular purpose. From time to time ordinances were passed authorizing the construction of culverts or sewers.

The standing committee of councils for cleaning the streets was instituted by ordinance of August 28, 1834.

About this time the legislature authorized[4] councils "to direct curbing and paving of footways, and if owners neglect, then the commissioners were to do it, expense to be a lien on ground until paid." Under the will of Stephen Girard Delaware avenue was laid out, and Water street improved;[5] in 1835, $50,000 of the income of the Girard estate was appropriated therefor; and during 1835 and 1836 frequent ordinances[6] were passed, providing for the extension of Delaware avenue, and awarding Girard income for the purpose, and the city solicitor was directed to institute proceedings to ascertain the damages.

Joint Committee on Highways.

In 1835[7] the joint committee on highways, consisting of members from select and from common council, appeared among the standing committees. Its duties were to have charge of paving and repairing streets, building and repairing culverts, to grant permission to make openings into same, to appoint a superintendent of railroads,[8] previously appointed

---

[1] Act March 11, 1816. Act March 23, 1818. [2] Charter of 1701.
[3] Act February 25, 1818. [4] Act April 10, 1826, P. L., 326. Act April 23, 1829, P. L., 301. Act April 16, 1838. Act April 15, 1850.
[5] Act of March 24, 1832. Ord. of February 27, 1834.
[6] Ord. February 12, 1835; Ord. March 26, 1835; Ord. April 30, 1835; Ord. April 7, 1836; Ord. May 5, 1836; Ord. May 19, 1836; Ord. September 22, 1836. [7] Ord. October 1, 1835. [8] Ord. February 27, 1834.

by the mayor, and, in conjunction with the regulators, to fix the regulation of streets not heretofore regulated. They were authorized to make contracts for the use of railroads, and to have general supervision of the streets.

The city was authorized to construct a railroad and bridge to connect with the Columbia Railroad, and to collect tolls therefrom.[1]

The importance of system in the regulation of the city was early and fully recognized, and divers provisions made therefor by ordinance. The mayor was to appoint two persons to regulate the ascents and descents, and the persons so appointed made a draft of all the principal streets to be kept in a book for that purpose.[2] They were to fix line-stones at central places below the level of the ground, and deposit in the commissioners' office a draft of their regulations.[3]

The streets were to be regulated by the surveyors according to the draft or book prepared by them for the purpose.[4] In 1814 an important ordinance was passed,[5] authorizing the mayor to appoint three city regulators or surveyors, two of whom should be practical surveyors, one of whom should be the recording surveyor, and, in addition to his other duties, keep the records of the city in eight large books, one for each district into which the city was divided for the purpose.

Provisions were made for the future making and preservation of these drafts or records, and a diagram of every lot surveyed by the surveyors was to be filed in the office and entered on the books; every footway thereafter paved or repaved to descend at the rate of half an inch a foot. A standard rod was ordered to be prepared and kept, stakes were to be driven to show height of curbstone, and the names of owners of lots were to be noted. It will be observed that elements of the present very complete survey department, afterward somewhat elaborated and perfected by experience, are present.

---

[1] Act March 21, 1831, P. L., 194; act April 10, 1849, P. L., 642.
[2] Ord. May 9, 1804. [3] Ord. March 3, 1806; Ord. June 18, 1807.
[4] Ord. July 13, 1808. [5] Ord. August 6, 1814; May 21, 1818.

Paving Material Used.

The paving material used during this period was confined almost entirely to the historic and much-abused cobble stones, these useful articles being brought down the river in scows from the Delaware rapids, and when well laid in properly graded and graveled beds they make, perhaps, the most enduring of modern pavements. During the period paving was, on the whole, very well done, as can be remembered by many of our older citizens; though the heavy drivers were swung by good Whig voters, under a Whig administration. The old city was also famous, both at home and abroad, as being the cleanest city in America; and both the street-cleaning and street-paving of the day stand out in sharp contrast with present results. But it must be remembered that the compact limits of the city proper, amounting to two square miles, presented a territory which it was child's play to control and supervise, as compared with the one hundred and twenty-nine square miles of the city and county of to-day. The elements which entered into the city government under the proprietary, the legislative charter and consolidation remain pretty much the same, though their combinations and effects may and did vary.

When a system of government, which was conceived for a provincial town, is carried, somewhat modified, into the concerns of a comparatively small city, and still further into those great and complex affairs of a widely extended territory and immensely increased population, the inherent defects thereof, which are toned down and counteracted by other influences in the smaller community, such as the watchful attention generally accompanying the feeling of personal interest and responsibility, more or less felt by each individual of that small community, become glaring and patent defects when that personality is lost in the atmosphere of a metropolis. This, in a nut-shell, is the history and experience not alone of Philadelphia but of all of our great municipalities, many of which have grown to man's estate to find their free development hampered by the insufficient swaddling-bands of infancy. No student of municipal history, either at home or abroad, can fail to be struck with wonder when noting how heavily weighted has been the prosperity of our cities by a system of government in many respects inherently inadequate, inharmonious, complex, and even vicious.

Public Squares.

Sec. 10. The origin of the five public squares was described in the last chapter. For over a century they were designated, when spoken of by their location, as Centre Square, North-east Square, &c. It was not until 1825 that they received their present names by ordinance,[1] and were christened as follows: "Centre Square; Penn Square, after William Penn, the founder of the State of Pennsylvania. The square in the north-western section, Logan Square, after James Logan, one of the early settlers of the State, secretary to William Penn, and founder of the Loganian Library. The square in the south-west section, Rittenhouse Square, after David Rittenhouse, the enlightened philosopher. The square in the south-east section, Washington Square, after George Washington, the father of his country. The square in the north-east section, Franklin Square, after Dr. Benjamin Franklin, the philosopher and statesman. The square bounded by Chestnut and Walnut and Delaware Fifth and Sixth streets, Independence Square."

Control of the Squares—Practical and Legal.

The care and control of these squares had gone with that of the other city property, and for a long time the authority of the corporation to make such temporary disposition of them as it saw fit was unquestioned. They were rented for cultivation and pasture in the earlier times; and Washington Square had been used as a potter's field in yellow-fever times. Had the question been raised, it may be seriously ques-

[1] Ord. May 19, 1825.

tioned whether the corporation had the right to divert them from their dedicated purpose of parks or squares; but in the earlier days, when space was ample and the country as near as Broad street, it did not matter much to the people, while the more utilitarian diversions answered a pressing want. It may be asserted safely, that the paramount authority over parks and squares dedicated to the public or acquired by right of eminent domain vests in the legislature, though the municipality may make police regulations.

With the important change in the administration of affairs culminating in the formulation of a set of standing committees, prescribed by ordinance in 1835,[1] the public squares were put under the care of the commissioner of city property, under direction of the committee on city property.

The title to Washington and Independence Squares is in the city by right of purchase; the title to the other squares remained in the proprietor, but was held by him for public uses and passed to the commonwealth. A most complete treatment of city squares, as far as their titles are concerned, may be found in Land Titles in Philadelphia,[2] a most excellent work, in which Mr. Lawrence Lewis, of Philadelphia, has treated his subject in an exhaustive and scholarly manner. We commend our readers to it for complete information on that branch of the subject.

However, all the squares by this period were subject to the easement of remaining open to the public use. Centre Square was occupied by the city water works early in the century, these being removed by ordinance only when the Fairmount works were built.[3] Centre Square was intersected by streets, Market and Broad, after 1826; although this intersection was clearly unauthorized by legislature, and, therefore, *ultra vires.*

Washington Square was used as a potter's field, and rented out as a pasture up to 1773, being the legal property of the city.[4] This purchase did not change its original dedication to public uses.

---

[1] Ord. October 1, 1835. [2] Lewis on Original Land Titles in Philadelphia, page 135. [3] Ord. November 26, 1826. [4] Ex. Rec., 683.

Franklin Square has given rise to important litigation, in which the question of the effect of the legal consequences of a public dedication was learnedly expounded by court and counsel. John Alburger *et al.*, trustees for the German Congregation, were indicted, in 1834, for a nuisance in erecting certain structures on a part of the then Franklin Square. They justified under title of a patent from Thomas Penn, granted in 1741. Sergeant, J., decided, in an elaborate opinion, that the square had been dedicated to public use by the original proprietor; that the act of Thomas Penn, in 1741, in attempting to sell a portion of it, was without authority, and passed no title.[1]

State House Square has an entirely different history. It was first purchased on behalf of the province in 1730,[2] and by act of assembly the title was vested in certain trustees, for the use of the representatives of the freemen of the province.[3]

Two lots carved out of this square were vested, one in the city, and one in the county,[4] to be used for public buildings. The act of March 10, 1812,[5] authorized councils "to take care of the State House Yard, and to pass ordinances for the preservation of order and decorum therein."

Four years later[6] the square was sold to the city, excepting the city and county lots, and the Philosophical Society's lot, for $70,000, under certain building restrictions, which were removed in 1847.[7] In 1834 iron railings were directed to be placed around Franklin and Washington Squares.[8]

In 1821 it was provided by the legislature that no streets should be laid out by the quarter sessions over the public squares or State House Yard.[9]

---

[1] Com. *vs.* Alburger, 1 Wharton, 469. Runy *vs.* Shoneberger, 1 Watts, 23. [2] Deed-book H, No. 15, page 112, &c.

[3] Acts March 20, 1735–6; February 17, 1762; May 14, 1762; February 28, 1780.

[4] Act February 17, 1762; March 29, 1787; March 11, 1789.

[5] 5 Smith's Laws, 313. [6] Act March 11, 1816, 6 Smith's Laws, 340. Deed-book M. R., No. 20, page 241. [7] Act March 16, 1847, P. L., page 471.

[8] Ord. February 27, 1834. [9] Act March 7, 1821.

But councils from time to time did authorize the use of certain portions of these squares for public streets.[1]

In 1838[2] the saying "that coming events cast their shadows before them" was exemplified by an act authorizing the authorities of Philadelphia to erect a city hall on Penn Square, at the expense of the city. No action, however, was taken under this act.

Dogs and smoking were prohibited in the public squares.[3] One of the mayors, it is said, was arrested for smoking in the square, and paid his fine.

City Property.

Sec. 11. The property of the city which, under the charter government, was in charge of the wardens, was vested in the new city by the act of 1789, and by the corporation placed in the control of the city commissioners,[4] who were to let and superintend the real property of the city, such as the general real estate, markets, docks, wharves, &c. They also had charge of the wells, pumps, and lamps. It was their duty to advertise for proposals before leasing.

Later, in 1835,[5] the mayor was authorized to appoint a commissioner of city property, who, under the direction of the committee on city property, "shall personally superintend the preservation, repairing, and improvement of the real estate, market-houses, wharves, and landings belonging to the corporation, also the public squares, and shall also collect the rents, excepting those of the Girard estates, and with the city commissioners shall superintend the prosecution of public works." It was his duty to certify correctness of all claims for material or labor for work under his charge, to lease stands for fish, &c. The ordinance creating the general standing committees conferred on the committee of city property the charge of all real estate property. The committee

---

[1] Ord. May 11, 1826; March 27, 1817; February 13, 1834; August 60, 1838.

[2] Act April 16, 1838, P. L., 626. [3] Ords. June 18, 1840; May 24, 1849.

[4] Ord. of May 22, 1797. [5] Ord. October 1, 1835.

appointed the commissioner, and to him were delegated the executive duties as stated above. They had by ordinance the appointment of several other minor officers, and had assigned them from time to time certain special duties, such as constructing railroads and bridges, charge of public clocks, &c. The city treasurer received the money due the city, and held the railroad stocks owned by the corporation. The committee of finance had the general supervision of the fiscal concerns of the city, and the investment of moneys accruing to the sinking fund. The important portion of city property represented by the Girard estate was placed in the possession and control of a separate board, and will be treated of under the head of City Trusts. By divers acts of legislature the action of the corporation in building the market-houses in the streets, and extensions thereof, was sanctioned; and full authority to regulate[1] and rent the same was conferred upon and exercised by councils in numerous ordinances. The corporate powers are fully discussed and sustained by the supreme court.[2] The power of the city to own the market-houses, and rent the same, has been always fully recognized.[2] Under the legislative charter the care of the wharves was placed with the city commissioners. By act of 1805[3] the power over the Schuylkill wharves was granted, and by an earlier act[4] the control of the Delaware wharves was vested in the port wardens. The city, being in possession and control of the wharves within its limits, is bound to keep them in proper condition.[5]

City Trusts. Early Bequests.

Sec. 12. There have been from time to time, outside of the varied munificent eleemosynary bequests for which the

---

[1] Act February 12, 1795; March 27, 1795. See 2 Smith, pages 68, 272, 331, 479.

[2] Mayor *vs.* Davis, 6 S. & R., 269; Wartman *vs.* City, 9 Casey, 202; Woelpper *vs.* City, 2 Wright, 203.

Act March 25, 1805, 4 Smith, 232.

Act of March 29, 1803, 4 Smith, page 67, and Supplement, page 186. Wardens *vs.* City, 6 Wr., 209. [5] City *vs.* Grier, 10 H., 54.

citizens of Philadelphia are famous, numerous bequests or legacies to the corporation direct for public charities.

Franklin's Bequest.

Under the will of Dr. Franklin £1000 were bequeathed to the corporation, in trust, to loan the same in sums not exceeding £60, to assist young married artificers in setting up business. The testator fancied that the increments of this fund judiciously farmed out would at the end of a century amount to £131,000. Thirty-one thousand pounds were then to be devoted to general municipal improvements, and the use of the principal, of £100,000, continued as at first directed. At the end of the second century this would amount, so he calculated, to £4,061,000, which was to be divided between the city and the State. It is needless to state that the sanguine expectation of the scientific statesman has not been realized. The fund, however, is still in existence, and the principal amounts to $73,321.83.[1]

Legacies of John Bleakley *et al.*

By the will of John Bleakley, in 1802, the city received £1000 as a fund to procure fuel for the poor, and another £1000 as a fund to relieve the necessities of the poor placed in the hospital during the yellow fever. Eliz. Kirkpatrick left $2278.59, which was added to the fund for the purchase of fuel for the poor.

John Scott, of Edinburgh, in 1816, left $3000 to the city to be applied to the same purpose as the Franklin legacy; also, the sum of $4000 to be distributed among deserving men and women who make useful inventions. This distribution was confided by the city to the managers of the Franklin Institute.[2]

---

[1] See interesting report on this fund, Journal of C. C., 1836–7, appendix, page 45. The kindred bequest of £1000 made by Dr. Franklin to the city of Boston would appear to have been better managed; for on February 1, 1886, its accumulations foot up to $315,207.54. See annual report of (Boston) city auditor for 1885–86, page 317.

[2] Ord. September 9, 1841.

Elias Boudinot, in 1821, devises certain real estate to the corporation, the rents, issues, and profits to be applied in aid of the fund for supplying the poor with fuel.

In 1825 the city received the residuary estate of James Wills, to be applied in the erection of the Wills Hospital for relief of the indigent blind and lame. Paul Beck, in 1845, bequeaths an annual ground-rent of the yearly value of $500, which was added to the soup fund.[1]

STANDING COMMITTEE.

The standing committee on legacies and trusts, consisting of four members from each branch of councils, was created in 1835,[2] and was entrusted with charge of all legacies and trusts confided to the city, except the Girard estate. Upon this committee was also imposed the duty of visiting annually the fire engine and hose companies, and reporting to councils on their condition.[3]

GIRARD TRUST.

SEC. 13. The most valuable bequest ever left to the city of Philadelphia, and up to that time one of the most considerable ever left to any municipality, is the well-known Girard estate. No citizen of Philadelphia, or commentator on either her local or municipal history, can avoid a willing tribute to the generous Frenchman who so dearly loved his adopted home. To no one, since the time of Penn, does the Quaker City owe a greater debt of gratitude; for no one, since the time of her illustrious founder and lawgiver, has left such a far-reaching and beneficent stamp on her streets and institutions. The fame of his wisely-guarded munificence is national. The record of the legal contest which arose over it has passed into history as a *cause célèbre*. In his great argument as counsel for the city, Horace Binney evolved his beautiful definition of a charitable gift: "Whatever is given for the love of God, or the love of your neighbor, in the catholic and

[1] Ord. April 24, 1845. [2] Ord. October 1, 1835. [3] Ord. May 21, 1840.

universal sense—given from these motives, and to these ends —free from the taint of every consideration that is personal, private, or selfish."[1]

Any elaborate description of this remarkable man, or the details of his still more remarkable gift, is beyond the scope of this work.[2] Such features, however, as have taken a place in the municipal life must be touched on.

The whole estate amounted to $7,500,000. Of this sum $321,000 was left to his family, friends, and sundry minor charities; $300,000 to the State of Pennsylvania; two hundred and eighty thousand acres of land in Louisiana to the cities of New Orleans and Philadelphia; subsequently lost to the legatees under the ruling of the courts; $500,000 to the city of Philadelphia for the improvement of its Delaware water front and all the residue of the estate to the city in trust for the following purposes:—

(1.) To erect, improve, and maintain a college for poor white orphan boys; (2.) To establish a better police system; and, (3.) To improve the city of Philadelphia and diminish taxation.[3]

The execution of the provisions of the will required legislative aid and sanction, which was obtained in the act "authorizing the mayor, aldermen, and citizens of Philadelphia to make certain improvements and execute certain trusts under the will of Stephen Girard."[4] About the time of the completion of the college, the guardians of the poor were authorized to bind poor children to the city for admission;[5] and by ordinance of the same year councils were to elect sixteen citizens as directors, who should have general charge of the college.[6]

In pursuance of the authority in them vested by the act of 1832, councils provided, by ordinance,[7] for a board of nine directors, from citizens, to be elected for three years. After-

[1] Vidal *vs.* Girard's Exrs., 2 Howard, 128. Approved by the S. C. of Pa., Price *vs.* Maxwell, 4 Casey, 35.

[2] See "The Life and Character of Stephen Girard," by H. A. Ingram, LL. B., of the Philadelphia Bar. [3] Will of Girard.

[4] Act March 24, 1832, P. L., 184. [5] Act February 27, 1847, P. L., 178.

[6] Ord. May 27, 1847. [7] Ord. September 15, 1832, page 454.

ward, by further ordinance,[1] for a special standing committee of eight commissioners, four to be chosen annually from and by each branch of councils, who, with the mayor, constituted the board of commissioners of the Girard estate, to have charge of the estate, with power to lease and rent the real estate, and appoint an agent of farms. Leases were to be executed by the mayor. By ordinance in same year the special standing committee was made one of the joint standing committees of councils.[2] This policy was reaffirmed and established by the general ordinance,[3] entitled "Ordinance for auditing and controlling the expenditures of the city."

They had charge of any property coming to the college students.[4] It was made their duty to report to councils, at the time of making their annual estimates, what repairs, &c. were necessary.[5] The affairs of this trust have been administered, on the whole, with prudence and honesty, and the benefits inuring to the city have been of course immense.

Steam Railroads.

Sec. 14. The paramount control of the streets being vested in the legislature, it follows that the use of them for laying down the tracks of either steam or passenger railroads must be granted by that body, either in special instances or by delegation of general powers.

The question of street railways did not arise prior to consolidation, but steam railroads began in this period to be a feature. The city herself went into the business, and, by authority of the legislature,[6] constructed a bridge and railroad to connect with the Columbia, also branches to the Schuylkill Railroad, and charged toll thereon.

Subsequently it was authorized to regulate tolls[7] on its railroad, and to build a railroad to connect with the Inclined Plane Railroad.[8]

[1] Ord. January 10, 1833, Digest 1851, page 191. [2] Ord. November 21, 1833. [3] Ord. October 1, 1835. [4] Ord. September 13, 1849.
[5] Ord. November 22, 1849, Digest 1851, page 345.
[6] Act March 21, 1831, P. L., 194. [7] Act August 2, 1842, P. L., 452.
[8] Act April 10, 1849, P. L., 642.

Superintendent of Railways.

The office of superintendent of railways was created by ordinance, and the appointment at first vested in the mayor.[1]

His duties were to receive the tolls and keep the road in repair.[2] The cars in the city were drawn by horses and mules. In 1839 the appointment of the superintendent of railroads was transferred to the committee on public highways,[3] who were empowered to make contracts for the use of the railroads, and to grant permission to make turnouts from them, and to approve the route of the Schuylkill Railroad.

Subscription to Railroad Stock.

Upon the advent of the Schuylkill and Pennsylvania Railroads the city was authorized to subscribe to their stock. This raises a very important question, as the power to do so is considered in the books as the most noted of the extra-municipal powers conferred upon municipal corporations. Dillon in his work on municipal corporations[4] says: "While a long, unbroken line of authorities support this power, its exercise is to be deprecated, and the soundness of the principle, viewed as one of constitutional law, is doubted, and in the light of experience this invention to aid private enterprises has proved itself baneful to the last degree." Fortunately, this authority is now denied in Pennsylvania by the Constitution. By the act incorporating the Pennsylvania Railroad[5] the corporation was authorized to subscribe for its stock, and to borrow money to pay for the same; it was to have a director for every ten thousand shares to represent its stock. The certificates of loan for the payment of the stock subscription were exempted from tax, except for State purposes. The city did by ordinance prescribe for subscription to fifty thousand shares, and for loans to meet the necessary payments. The city took also fifty shares in the Schuylkill Railroad Company.

---

[1] Ord. February 27, 1834.

[2] Ord. January 11, 1838; Ord. December 20, 1838.

[3] Ord. August 29, 1839. [4] Page 144. [5] March 27, 1848, P. L., 272.

Fire Department.

Sec. 15. To any one who is familiar with life in Philadelphia, even twenty years ago, the volunteer fire department stands out in bold relief; all classes of citizens belonged to the various engine companies, which were at once the protection and terror of the city. Many a stirring story could be told by gentlemen in the prime of life about the contests of their younger days, when "Moyamensing Hose" boys would fight the flames, or the "Good Will," with equal alacrity; but all this kind of reminiscence, full of color as it is, belongs to local history, and not to the part played by the corporation. We have seen the rude machinery employed during our first century, and find that it continued into this period. The Second-street market-houses furnished accommodation to some of the hand engines, and was furnished with a cupola and alarm-bell.[1]

Volunteer Fire Companies.

The engine companies were private volunteer associations; they were required to obtain from the watering committee permits to use the hydrant water.[2] This committee was authorized to distribute an annual appropriation among the companies of $2000, according to their necessities. In this appropriation was included the Philadelphia society for protection of movable property in time of fire,[3] a forerunner of the insurance patrol. The spirit of rivalry among the bold and daring men who composed the companies, naturally led, in the absence of systematic discipline, into many dangerous street fights, which forced councils to pass the following ordinance :—[4]

Ordinance regulating the same.

"Whereas certain irregularities and frequent violations of the public peace have taken place under the present organiza-

[1] Ord. August 16, 1804, Duane, page 250.
[2] Ord. August 10, 1809, Lowber & Miller, page 74.
[3] Ord. August 2, 1811, Lowber, page 25. Ord. May 17, 1813, L. & M., page 75. [4] Ord. May 21, 1840, Digest 1851, 247.

tion of the fire department of the city; and whereas the respectability of the department and the moral character of the city require more efficient measures to maintain the same," &c.; the appropriation, then amounting to $8700, was placed under the control of the committee on legacies and trusts, to distribute the same in sums not exceeding $300, as said committee shall assign and councils approve. It was made the duty of this committee to visit the different companies, inspect their apparatus and inquire into their condition and conduct, and report thereon to councils. Riots and outrages being still perpetrated by the fire companies, councils declared the need of concentrated action between the city and districts, which were divided into three districts:—southern district, consisting of Southwark, Moyamensing, adjoining districts, and adjacent townships; middle district, Philadelphia and West Philadelphia; northern district, Northern Liberties, Spring Garden, and adjoining townships.[1]

The city companies were not to pass into adjoining districts unless so requested by authorized persons. The use of fire plugs was regulated, and minors were forbidden to join companies; each hose carriage was directed to carry eight hundred feet of hose; the companies were required to make annual reports to councils and to present two persons to councils, from whom councils should appoint one from each company, to form a board, which, under direction of councils, had general supervision of fires; the mayor had the power of removal, and penalty was provided for riotous and disorderly conduct. It was provided that no company could receive appropriation without certificate from the board of engineers;[2] the station-house bells were to be rung by the nightly watch, to indicate direction of fires from the state house.[3]

The authority of the legislature was finally invoked to prohibit rioting at fires, and to provide methods of forming new companies, subject to the approval of the court.

The appointment of the board of engineers was finally

[1] Ord. January 4, 1844, page 864.

[2] Ord. April 24, 1845; Ord. March 26, 1846. [3] Act March 7, 1848.

intrusted to the committee on legacies and trusts, and in 1850 $10,000 was appropriated, to be distributed among sufferers from a recent fire, and $570 for distribution among disabled firemen.

The prevention of fire is clearly an object within the scope of municipal authority without express grant under the general power to make police regulations and by-laws; and the corporation is, therefore, authorized to make appropriations for the purpose of purchase of engines, and for the repair thereof, whether they belong to it or are purchased partly by private subscription.

WATER DEPARTMENT.

SEC. 16. We have seen how the water supply of the city, for over a century, was confined to pumps and wells, despite the fact that it lay between two broad rivers; but very speedily after the renewed incorporation the prompt introduction of a copious supply of wholesome water was deemed essential. A petition, signed by hundreds of citizens, pressed the matter on the attention of councils, urging its probable efficiency in moderating, if not preventing, the yellow fever, and the immense loss already experienced from fire. Councils appointed a committee to investigate the various schemes proposed, and early in 1799 passed an ordinance[1] authorizing a loan for the purpose, of $150,000, to be taken by subscription, and pledging the entire revenue of the city property, except the tolls of the Market-street bridge, for its payment; all subscribers to have free water-rights for three years, these water-rights being transferable; commissioners were appointed to receive subscriptions; preference in supply was to be given to subscribers; the emoluments arising from the water works were to be applied, in the first instance, to defraying expense of superintendence, repairs, and improvements, and in the second instance to redemption of aforesaid capital stock, and thereafter to the improvement of the city and alleviation of taxes on its inhabitants. It was made the duty of the city commissioners

[1] Ord. February 7, 1799, Lowber, 160; Ord. May 7, 1801, Lowber, 178.

to aid the special commissioners in carrying into execution all and every of their requisitions. A further loan of $50,000 was authorized in 1799,[1] in anticipation of taxes. Again, in 1805,[2] a further loan of $35,000 was authorized, and new commissioners were appointed. Among the names of the commissioners appear the names of Edward Tilghman, Jared Ingersoll, Stephen Girard, Levi Hollingsworth, Jacob Shoemaker, which are enough to assure us of the intelligent execution of the duties imposed, and the work was pressed with great vigor.

By the plan adopted water was brought by a tunnel from the Schuylkill to Centre Square, where it was forced into a reservoir, or stand pipe, and thence distributed through the city. The water works began delivering water on the 27th January, 1801, to the great joy of our forefathers. The first cost was about $220,360. The regulations for distribution of water[3] prescribed penalties for injuring the pipes or wasting the water, regulated use and sale for manufactures, as well as the use of fire-plugs; and prescribed that no one should introduce a ferrule without a permit from the watering committee. It would appear that the watering committee of four members from each branch of councils was the first of the recognized standing committees; it was appointed annually and was in existence prior to 1806, probably from 1801 or 1802. It was made the duty of the superintendent of the water works, among his other duties, to prevent waste and examine ferrules. He was at first appointed by the mayor along with other city officers. The water-rents were collected by tax collectors from lists furnished by the water committee. The mayor and water committee were formally invested with the power to conduct the water works, to purchase supplies, and distribute the water, and for these purposes to employ such agents as they might deem proper, not exceeding appropriations, and to report to councils from time to time. The rates were then ordered to

---

[1] Ord. August 5, 1799, Lowber, page 164.
[2] Ord. March 13, 1805, Lowber, page 193.
[3] Ord. May 7, 1801; March 15, 1805.

be paid in advance, the pipes to be disconnected upon delinquency, and the commissioners for distribution of the water were discontinued.[1] Many ordinances were passed from time to time relative to waste, injury to pipes, nuisances, making connections and disconnections, which fell within the recognized limit of municipal power, and have therefore no special significance worthy of comment in a work of this kind.

CENTRE SQUARE WATER WORKS.

The water works and reservoir situated at the head of Chestnut street on the Schuylkill, having their distributing point at Centre Square, had not been in operation for ten years, when it became obvious that the site had been badly chosen, and no permanent supply of water could be expected from there. Popular agitation was instituted in the newspapers of the day. The watering committee considered many plans, and finally decided on locating on Morris Hill, now known as Fairmount, where work was begun in 1812. To conduct the water to the city, the streets of Penn township had to be traversed, and to do this legislative aid was necessary. In consequence an act was passed[2] authorizing the corporation to use the streets of Penn township and district of Spring Garden at its own proper expense for laying and repairing its water works. Penalties were prescribed for injuring the dam or throwing any nuisance into the water works. These new works were finished and started in 1815. In October, 1835, the watering committee appears in the list of joint standing committees, its general duties are re-enacted, and it is authorized to appoint the superintendent and register, and such laborers and workmen as they may deem necessary. For a time the city supplied water to the inhabitants of the neighboring districts. The register made out duplicate lists of the water-rents due by the districts, and furnished the city treasurer with a copy. Loans amounting to $281,000 were authorized for the purchase of grounds and erection of new reservoirs in 1848. The duty

---

[1] Ord. April 1, 1809; L., 225. [2] February 16, 1813, 6 Smith, page 22.

of collecting water-rent was first imposed on city commissioners and water commissioners; afterwards, until 1822,[1] the water-rents were collected by the tax collectors, on lists furnished by water committee; these collections were made in the same manner as city taxes; weekly returns were made of proceeds of collection to the treasurer, and annually written reports to the water committee of all delinquents. In 1822[2] the mayor was authorized to appoint one or more collectors of water-rents, who collected upon lists furnished by register; they paid over to the treasurer and made returns of delinquents as before. In 1839 the appointment of these collectors was placed in the hands of the watering committee.[3] The rate at first was fixed at five dollars for private houses, that for manufacturers to be a matter for agreement. In 1806 the fixing of the rates for all classes was vested in the water committee who contracted for the same; in 1814 the rates were made payable in advance.[4]

The validity of the ordinance authorizing a tax for erection of the water works was called in question. It was argued that it was an attempted exercise of alleged delegated legislative power, such as was not intended by the framers of the Constitution. The court, however, were unanimously of opinion that the ordinance of March 29, 1799, was valid.[5]

Gas Works.

Sec. 17. We have seen how the lighting, watching, watering of the city was originally vested in the wardens, a legislative commission independent in great measure of the corporation. With the erection of the new city the powers and duties of assessors, wardens, and street commissioners passed to it, and were consolidated in the city commissioners, who had, among other duties, charge of the erection and maintenance of the public lamps, as has been set out in the consideration of the duties of the city commissioners.

---

[1] Ord. May 7, 1801; March 15, 1806. [2] Ord. December 26, 1822.
[3] Ord. August 29, 1839. [4] Ord. April 28, 1814.
[5] Stiles *vs.* Jones, 3 Yeates, 491.

The use of gas for illuminating purposes had been made in Philadelphia as far back as 1796, and in 1803 J. C. Humfrey made a proposition to councils to light the city with gas,[1] and in 1817 the petition was renewed by James McMurtrie. Both offers were rejected. In 1825 an effort was made to induce the legislature to incorporate the Philadelphia Gas Light Company, which was opposed and defeated by influence of councils. Applications were again made in 1825 and 1826, and were favorably reported by committee, and in 1827 common council approved the project but it was defeated in select council. The application was renewed and refused in 1828, and in 1830 a public meeting was called to urge the matter on councils. Common council was again ready, but was blocked by the other branch. In 1831 another petition showed the successful use of gas in other cities in Europe and the United States. In 1833 a committee of councils again reported favorably. Many ridiculous protests were made by intelligent citizens; much evidence was collected and publicly discussed. The matter dragged on till 1834, when councils sent an expert to Europe to examine the practical workings of gas lighting, and finally, in 1835, councils passed the ordinance for the construction and management of the Philadelphia Gas Works. The prominent feature it has played in the economy and politics of the city warrants a careful outline of its history, especially as the question of its disposal is a living one at this moment.

The ordinance of 1835[2] is the groundwork of our present system. A subscription of $100,000 was authorized for the purpose of constructing gas works. Certificates of stock were to be granted, subject to the right of the corporation, at any time councils may deem it expedient, to take possession of the works and convert the stock into a loan redeemable in twenty years, and carrying interest at six per cent., with a certificate for the subscriber's share of the profits; councils to elect by ballot twelve citizens as trustees, six to be elected by common and six by select council, the term to be three years, and the first

[1] See S. & W., page 643. [2] March 21, 1835, Digest 1851, page 135.

set to be selected by lot so that four should retire each year, and each branch should thereafter elect two trustees each year. The trustees were to construct and manage the works, and report annually to councils; moneys arising from the manufacture and sale of gas to be paid into the city treasury and placed to the credit of the gas works, and paid out on requisition of trustees; dividends were to be declared semi-annually out of the receipts after deducting all expenses; gas was to be furnished the city at half price for three hundred lamps; the city was not liable for any contracts in excess of the subscriptions; the trustees were to prepare and submit to councils regulations under which gas was to be furnished to consumers; the city rented to the trustees the ground owned by the corporation at Schuylkill Front and Filbert at a rental of $500. In 1841[1] the city exercised its option to become the owner of the gas works, and directed the mayor to issue a loan, payable in 1861, to take up the stock. In the same year[2] another loan of $125,000 was authorized for the extension of the gas works, redeemable in 1866, to bear interest at five per cent.; the faith of the city, the buildings, apparatus, pipes, &c., fixtures, income, and profits of the gas works were pledged for prompt payment of interest and ultimate reimbursement; the trustees were to set apart all net profits to form a sinking fund; trustees were to make annual statements to councils; the price of gas was not to be reduced till loan be paid. That, for further security of said loanholders, it was therein stipulated that the said works shall be controlled and managed by a board of trustees elected as heretofore, who shall have the control and management of works and sinking fund; no funds or profits to be thereafter paid into the city treasury, but applied and appropriated as therein directed until principal and interest of loans be paid; the receipts applicable to sinking fund were to be invested either in gas or city loans. One month later the trustees were authorized to distribute $48,000 among the stockholders in exchange for a release;[3] and in

[1] Ord. June 3, 1841, Digest 1851, page 260.
[2] Ord. June 17, 1841, D. 51, page 260. [3] Ord. July 1, 1841, page 261.

September the time for executing these releases was extended.[1]

Several ordinances[2] creating new loans for extension of the gas works were passed, with provisions for sinking fund, and adding to the number of city lamps at half price. The trustees were required to furnish city commissioners with a list of streets opened to lay pipe, and repay them for expense of repairing said streets.[3] In 1849 a committee on gas was added to the joint committees, to consist of two members from each branch, to perform all duties to be assigned from time to time.[4] The legislature, in 1851, passed several acts, one authorizing the corporation to lay pipes in the county, to conduct the gas from works which might be built outside the city.[5] These works were not to be located in Moyamensing or Southwark,[6] and no pipes were to be laid therein east of Broad street without consent of the commissioners, and no works were to be erected or pipes laid in any incorporated district north of Vine street, nor were any pipes to be laid for the introduction of gas without the consent of the districts through which the same passed. The summary of the history of the gas legislation of the city may be stated as follows: The property invested in the gas works is in the city which possesses all the muniments of title, but its control and management is placed in a *quasi*-independent department, consisting of twelve trustees, whose power and responsibility could not be discharged pending the payment of outstanding loans, such complete control by the trustees being a part of the security of the holders of loans created prior to 1850.

Education.

Sec. 18. As early as 1809 the legislature of Pennsylvania passed an act to provide for the education of the poor, which

[1] Ord. September 9, 1841, page 262.

[2] December 22, 1836, page 222; February 8, 1838, page 229; January 14, 1841, page 252; January 28, 1841, page 255; June 17, 1841, page 260; May 25, 1848, page 329; March 15, 1849, page 335; January 10, 1850, page 346. [3] Ord. January 19, 1843. [4] Ord. December 6, 1849.

[5] Act April 8, 1851, P. L., page 384. [6] Act April 14, 1851, page 577.

was the foundation of our public school system.[1] It was, however, shortly repealed and supplied by the act of 1812.[2] Six years later the assembly passed another act, reciting that the provisions of the law towards establishing public schools had proved unsatisfactory, and for remedy thereof, it enacted[3] that the city and county be one school district, to be known as the first school district, to be divided into convenient sections: First, the city; second, districts of Kensington and Northern Liberties; third, Southwark, Moyamensing, and Passayunk; fourth, Penn township. The councils and commissioners were to appoint school directors, *i. e.*, the city twenty-four, and the districts a proportionate number, who were to elect one from each six, to form a board of controllers. The system of public education is a child of the state; municipal control of its administration is a proper imposition of a general duty, in a special locality, upon local authorities. For a history of the cause the inquirer would do well to consult a special authority.[4]

Police.

Sec. 19. After the legislative charter the control of the police force fell to the city commissioners. The police power is one of those which are inherent in a municipal corporation, and in fact is a primary object of its existence. The exercise of this power or duty may be divided very properly for convenience of treatment into two distinct branches.

1st. The preservation of the public peace or safety by means of a constabulary, watch or police force.

2d. The enactment of police regulations.

These police regulations may be as varied and numerous as the peculiar demands of a particular locality require. Their enactment, of course, is an exercise of the legislative function; their enforcement comes within the strict line of executive duty.

---

[1] Act April 4, 1809, 5 Smith, 73 and 74.

[2] Act March 13, 1812, 5 Smith, 378.

[3] Act March 3, 1818, 7 S., 53. Act January 23, 1821.

[4] See Wickersham's History of Education in Pennsylvania, 1885.

The general scope of the exercise of this function by our municipality can, perhaps, be more clearly treated in a separate section, and this one will therefore be confined to the development of the legal history and autonomy of the police force.

Constables and Watch.

The constable and watch were officers well known to the common law, and, as we have seen, our fathers naturally turned to them when the city was first incorporated. The police officer is a creature of modern legislation, and his powers and duties must be sought for in the statutes which create him, and in those statutes we find the limits of his powers and duties. The lack of adequate protection of the peace was one of the moving causes both of the charter of 1789 and 1854. During the Revolution there was practically no police protection to the city apart from the military, and even after the act of 1789 was passed the same radically inadequate system continued as existed under the charter government. The police force, if we may use the term, consisted of the high constables, the constables, the watch, and the superintendent of the watch; the two former appointed by the mayor, the latter by the city commissioners. The constables had their common-law powers. The ordinance of 1789, creating city commissioners and the several ordinances supplementary thereto, placed the appointment and regulation of the watch in their hands, where it remained till 1833, subject to removal by the mayor for misconduct. The first decided step to be noted in this period is that the city commissioners were to appoint a superintendent of the nightly watch, and *hire* and employ a sufficient number of able-bodied men to light and watch the city at fixed wages, prescribe rules for their government, and dismiss them when they thought proper.[1]

This was certainly an improvement. A paid, regulated, and to some degree disciplined body of men were substituted for the unreliable and forced service imposed on the citizens

---

[1] Ord. May 22, 1797, Lowber, page 141.

as a public duty. In 1810 an act was passed providing for the election annually of two constables from each ward, from whom the mayor should appoint one.[1] Together with the high constables they seem to have been the reliance during the day for the maintenance of the public peace and obedience to the ordinances; it was also their duty to attend the mayor's court, for which they received a dollar a day.[2]

The High Constable.

The office of high constable was provided for in 1798;[3] he was appointed annually by the mayor, and the enumeration of his duties falls quaintly upon the ear of to-day: "He shall take rank and precedence among the officers of the city next before the constables, and shall carry in his hands to distinguish him a short mace, and constables and citizens are enjoined to assist him in the execution of his office when thereunto reasonably required by him."

His particular duty was "to walk through the streets, lanes, and alleys of the city, daily, with his mace in his hand, taking such rounds that in a reasonable time he should visit all parts of the city; he was to examine and, if necessary, apprehend vagrants, beggars, and disorderly persons, give information to the mayor of breach of ordinances and cause obedience to the same, and do all such things as the mayor, recorder, or aldermen should require touching the ordinances, regulations, and policy of the city." He was also register of chimney sweeps, and his salary was $700; and if he did his duty he doubtless earned it, as the city grew bigger and more wicked.

The mayor was authorized to appoint another high constable and to apportion the duties;[4] and as the necessities still increased, to raise the number by two more.[5] In 1814 a fur-

---

[1] Act January 30th, 1810, Lowber, page 116.
[2] Ord. October 3, 1804, Lowber, page 191.
[3] Ord. March 29, 1798, Lowber, 149.
[4] Ord. March 28, 1811, Lowber, 243.
[5] Ord. December 23, 1830, page 417.

ther attempt at system was made; a permanent stationary watch was located at Centre Square engine house from sunset till eleven P. M., when all people disorderly or other, it seems, were presumed to be in bed.[1]

A captain and a lieutenant were substituted for the superintendent, by appointment of the mayor, who were required to give bond.[2] Some particularity has been observed in regard to the functions of constables and watch, because up to 1830 the sole reliance of the city was placed upon the constables by day and the watch by night. In that year, however, we find an ordinance[3] entitled "Ordinance providing for appointment of additional police officers." In substance it provides that the mayor should appoint twelve able-bodied, discreet persons, of good moral character * * who shall be styled officers of the general city police; they shall be subject to the orders of the mayor as well by day as by night, and shall perform the duties now performed by the "silent watch." They as well as the watch were removable at pleasure of the mayor. The silent watch was abolished.

The term of silent watch probably has reference to the nightly patrol which the mayor was authorized to employ when he deemed the measure expedient for the protection of the city.[4] They were evidently distinct from the regular nightly watch employed by the city commissioners to light and watch the city, who were wont to call the hour as they went the rounds with such comments as they thought might be of interest to the wakeful citizen. This custom of calling the hours was of very ancient date, and observed in the English and German Fatherlands. Westcott mentions the legend which every well-regulated Philadelphian, who had a grandmother, has heard from her of the cry of the German watchman, "Oh, past dree oh clock, unt a cloudy morning, unt Cornwalist ish daken!"

---

[1] Ord. March 3, 1814, L. & M., 232.
[2] Ord. December 16, 1819, L. & M., 232.
[3] Ord. December 30, 1830, Ord. page 415.
[4] Ord. December 14, 1816, Ord. page 78.

Will of Girard.

The will of Stephen Girard left a bequest for the improvement of the police. The time was ripe for a new effort to obtain a better force. A committee of councils was appointed to investigate the subject. These special commissioners made a report condemning the then system,[1] and in the same year an ordinance was passed making somewhat elaborate provisions:[2] The city was divided into four districts; each district into three divisions; the force to consist of a captain and one lieutenant for each district, one inspector for each section, twenty-four policemen, and one hundred and twenty watchmen, all to be appointed by the mayor, and to be subject to his orders or those of the recorder. The police served by day, the watch by night, and had the same powers as constables at common law. A clerk of police was established; four additional policemen were to attend at the mayor's office for special duties. This ordinance supplied and repealed all former police ordinances. It did not seem to be satisfactory, for it was repealed and supplied two years later,[3] when the city was divided into four watch districts; the mayor was to appoint one captain, eight silent watchmen, and thirty-five watchmen for each district, removable at pleasure, to have the power of constables and that vested by law in the watch of the city; the mayor was to appoint four special constables; and to divide the city into beats, and procure the necessary watch-houses. Half the expenses were to be paid by the Girard estate and half by the city. The captains of the watch had the care and distribution of the oil for the city lamps. In this year the joint committee on police was established as a standing committee to perform the duties of the committee on "lighting and watching," and to have general supervision of all fiscal matters connected with the police. The following year[4] the city was divided for care by day into four dis-

[1] Poulson's Police History, page 7. [2] Ord. 26 December, 1833.
[3] Ord. January 1, 1835, Ord. 537. Amended by Ord. of February 15, 1844, Ord. 874.
[4] Ord. September 1, 1836, Ord. page 600.

tricts, one for each high constable, who were forbidden to be absent from the city without leave.

The condition of the police force at this time was deplorably inefficient when called upon to suppress any riotous disturbance. An occasion arose on May 15th, 1838, when a mob attacked and burned Pennsylvania Hall at Sixth and Haines. The mayor at the head of the entire police force stood by without an effort to disperse the mob. The report of the police committee made after an investigation is simply an admission that there was no police force of sufficient discipline to disperse a mob or protect private property in face of any popular excitement, which in this case arose from the strong pro-slavery feeling of the mass of Philadelphians.

Another effort was made in 1841,[2] by the erection of a special department under the mayor for the more effectual prevention and detection of crime; the officers consisted of a first and second lieutenant, and a special constable, aided by the clerk of police, who was appointed by the committee on police; records were to be kept, and policemen from the general force could be assigned for duty under them. The four high constables were continued, and in place of the silent watch there were to be twelve night policemen and one captain thereof, and ten day policemen with power of constables. The general supervision and control was vested in the mayor.

The mayor in the following year was authorized to employ special policemen upon any emergency he might deem necessary.[3]

Impotence of the Police.

In 1844 Philadelphia reaped the whirlwind in the shape of riots from the wind sown at the burning of Pennsylvania Hall. The absolute impotence of the police force and the civil arm served to invite very serious disturbances at any moment

[1] See Report of the Police Committee of Councils, Journals of Councils, 1838. [2] Ord. December 23, 1841, Ord. page 767.

[3] January 20, 1842, Ord. page 771.

when the populace might be moved by any strongly-felt prejudice or passion. The provocation arose from the disturbance known as the Native American Riots. With the merits of that controversy we have nothing to do, and in truth any disturbers of the peace can have no merits in the eyes of the police department. While the laws are defied, no extenuating circumstance or legitimate provocation can be recognized by the authorities. The history of these riots would be instructive as illustrating the inefficiency of the police of the day, but such an account is precluded by the limits of our work. Suffice it to say, that a meeting of Native Americans was disturbed in Kensington. A stormy mass meeting was held next day in Independence Square, and adjourned to the meeting place of the previous day. A shot was fired, a street fight ensued, several persons were killed and wounded, and buildings burned. The militia were called out and at first refused to respond, and the excitement spread to the city. The Governor came to town, and ordered out the militia under Generals Patterson and Cadwalader. St. Augustine's Church was burned, other Catholic churches were threatened, several street fights between the mob and the soldiery occurred, the blood of citizens was shed on both sides; all of which could have been prevented by a decently organized and disciplined police force.

There were far more dangerous elements smouldering into flame, and a more dangerous class of the community ready to burst out into riot, arson, and bloodshed in 1876, when they were kept in subjection and under control by the determined attitude and good discipline of Mayor Stokley and his police.

Attempts at Improvement.

The experience and lesson of 1844 incited the legislature to action, and an act was passed[1] requiring the city and districts to keep a police force of one for every one hundred and fifty taxables, and in the same year the mayor was authorized

[1] Act April 12, 1845. P. L., 380.

to appoint lieutenants of the night police, and in June an ordinance was made in obedience to the act of assembly,[1] in which the mayor was made the superintendent of the force. A very full ordinance remodeling with extended detail the whole police system was passed three years later,[2] repealing all former police ordinances, except so much of ordinance of 1841 as related to the detective force. It retains the four districts, divides the force into day and night police; prescribes station houses for each district; makes the mayor superintendent, with general powers of appointment and division of beats; retains the four high constables, appointed by the mayor; and authorizes him to appoint private policemen at request of owners of public places. He was also to appoint[3] a superintendent and fifty-seven lamplighters. The police were then first required to appear in uniform when on duty; the requirements of the act of 1845 are met, and other police ordinances repealed by title and date. This ordinance remained in force but two years, and gave place to the ordinance of 1850.[4]

Marshal's Bill.

The next step was the most important one of the period.[5] It was the passage of the marshal's police bill by the legislature, providing that the city and districts be made one police district under a marshal, to be elected by the voters for three years and was vested with all the police powers of the mayor. The city was divided into four sub-districts; the outlying districts were also each to be a sub-district; the commissioners and councils elected a lieutenant for each sub-district, and sent in three times the number of names of policemen for each district on the basis of one for each one hundred and fifty taxables, from which the marshal selected his force. The marshal and lieutenants formed a police board and made all necessary regulations. The force had power to act in any part of the city or districts. The marshal or

[1] Ord. June 19, 1845, Ord. 919.
[2] March 16, 1848, Ord. 1061.
[3] Ord. August 31, 1848.
[4] Ord. December 5, 1850.
[5] Act May 3, 1850, P. L. 1850.

one or more lieutenants were to be present at all fires. The mayor, aldermen, and judges were to have the power of justices of the peace throughout the district. Special duties and powers were conferred on the marshal in case of riots; and on his certificate, in writing, requiring assistance, the major-general was enjoined to assist him with the military until notified that their assistance was no longer needed. After proclamation the marshal, police, and other persons were to be held harmless in case of killing. The requisition of the marshal was to be held conclusive evidence that the service of the military was necessary.

Councils speedily passed an ordinance[1] to carry this act into effect, and it remained in force until after the consolidation, with some minor modifications regarding the police board under the provisions of an act passed in the same year.[2]

Summary.

At the risk of seeming tedious we have traced with somewhat minute care the course of police legislation during this period, and have omitted mention of no important act or ordinance; so important seemed this branch of municipal duty, and so slowly did the public mind work in the attainment of even an approximately efficient service.

Prior to the act of 1850, the disjointed system of separate forces for a closely-settled territory, divided by arbitrary lines over which the constable or watch were unauthorized to step in enforcing the law, offered a premium to every description of offenders; the Northern Liberties or Southwark presenting a more available temporary haven to the escaping malefactor than does Canada to offenders of the present day.

Poor.

Sec. 20. The foundation poor act of this period was that of 1803,[3] entitled "An act for the consolidation and amend-

[1] Ord. November 7, 1850.
[2] Act May 3, 1850, P. L., 666.
[3] Act March 29, 1803, 4 Smith, 50.

ment of the laws as far as they respect the poor of the city of Philadelphia, the district of Southwark, and the township of the Northern Liberties," which were thereby made one poor district, and a corporation created by the name of the "Guardians of the Poor of the City of Philadelphia, District of Southwark, and the Township of Northern Liberties." The city, through councils, was to appoint sixteen substantial housekeepers guardians, and the two districts, six each, to be elected annually. The guardians elected eight managers, four from the city, two from Southwark, and two from Northern Liberties, to have charge of the house of employment. The managers, with the consent of four aldermen and two commissioners of the respective district, might lay a tax, not to exceed one dollar per hundred on property, or three dollars per head, according to the county assessment. The collectors of the poor tax were appointed by the guardians and managers, and paid the same to a treasurer appointed by guardians from their own number. Powers of relief were granted to two guardians in cases of emergency; the qualifications for admission and settlement were defined, the immigration of paupers was forbidden, and summary powers of removal with right of appeal to the mayor's court granted to two aldermen or justices of the peace. The managers were authorized to make rules for government of paupers, and the guardians to sue for fines due under this act. Auditors of the treasurer's account were appointed, one by the mayor's court to represent the city, and two by the quarter sessions to represent the two districts.

By a supplement passed two years later,[1] it was provided that all moneys levied and collected for the use of this poor district should be under control of the guardians, and the rules, regulations, and restrictions of every department, respecting the poor, should be prescribed by this board. By a further supplement the guardians were directed to be chosen by the city and districts at the same day and hour.[2]

A further supplement, by which the above details and others were either re-enacted or modified, was passed three years

[1] Act April 10, 1805, 4 Smith, 247. [2] Act March 24, 1809, 5 Smith, 38.

later.[1] By this act the number of guardians for the city was reduced to ten, for Southwark four, and for Northern Liberties six. Managers of the alsmhouse were given power to examine the poor residents under oath, touching their place of legal settlement, and on refusal to answer to commit to prison, and had power in all cases appertaining to their office to receive and execute such warrants of arrest as might be issued by any alderman or justice.

An act was passed to provide for the education of the poor gratis.[2] This, with its further supplements or amendments,[3] although touching on the poor, is more properly treated under the head of education. The necessity for the better care of the diseased poor soon became apparent, and was provided for by act of assembly.[4] In 1821, by act of assembly,[5] commissioners were appointed to investigate the cause and extent of pauperism in Philadelphia, and in the same year a dog tax was laid for the benefit of the poor of Philadelphia county,[6] and in 1828[7] the Philadelphia poor district was remodeled to include the city, district of Southwark, township of Penn, Northern Liberties, and Kensington. The guardians were constituted a corporation with powers substantially as before. The care of the poor, therefore, while not made strictly a municipal duty, has ever been recognized as a local duty and burden, and local authorities have been wont to examine critically into the rightful imposition of the burden in each individual case. The right of settlement, which carried with it a claim to be supported, has always been more or less strictly guarded; in the old country the parish was the unit of charge, with us the township, though the administration of the poor department has generally been vested in county functionaries, and the miserable pauper who could not show a legal settlement was liable to be tossed about between contending townships, each anxious to avoid the responsibility

---

[1] Act March 31, 1812, 5 Smith, 391.
[2] April 4, 1809, 5 S., 73.
[3] March 31, 1812, 5 Smith, 378.
[4] Act January 30, 1816, P. L., 35.
[5] April 4, 1821, P. L., 192.
[6] February 15, 1821, P. L., 38.
[7] Act March 5, 1828, P. L., 162.

of being a foster mother. It is to be observed that as far as the action of the corporation is concerned, its duties ended with the election of its quota of guardians and it had no visitorial powers, the board of guardians being a creature of the legislature, a separate corporation, and a law unto itself. Hence we find no ordinances relative to the management of the poor, or affecting the duties of the guardians.

Port Wardens.

Sec. 21. The board of wardens of the city of Philadelphia was constituted and its powers and duties defined by various acts of assembly, beginning with the act of 29th March, 1803, and extending down through a series of half a hundred acts to that of 14th May, 1861.[1] The first act passed during this period on this subject was one entitled "An act to reduce the expenses of the port wardens of Philadelphia."[2] This was supplied two years later,[3] amended by act of April 22, 1794, extended March 21, 1797, amended and continued April 5, 1797, continued April 9, 1799, all of which acts were repealed and supplied by the act above mentioned, March 29, 1803, which was recognized by Justice Woodward as the foundation act of the Philadelphia port wardens. By this act a board of wardens was created to consist of a master warden and six assistants, four from Philadelphia, one from Northern Liberties, and one from Southwark, to be appointed by the Governor. They were to pass regulations for the management of the port, collect certain dues, pay surplus into state treasury, and receive deficit therefrom. It was for them to grant licenses for extension of wharves, and to grant licenses to pilots. This act was amended and supplied by divers acts extending over half a century.[4] By these acts the board came to be constituted as follows: A master warden appointed by the Governor, and thirteen wardens elected

---

[1] Board of Wardens *vs.* City of Philadelphia, 6 W., 216.

[2] April 13, 1791, L. B. IV., page 209. [3] Act April 11, 1793, L. B. V., 157.

[4] March 25, 1805; February 7, 1818; April 24, 1843; February 4, 1846; April 6, 1850; April 28, 1851; February 18, 1853; April 15, 1853.

by the city and adjoining municipal districts having river frontage on one or other of the rivers, of which great public highways they were made custodians; no encroachment was to be made into the tideway without their license. Their accounts were to be settled like public accounts, and any surplus received by them was to be paid into the state treasury. The share in their creation and management imposed on the city was limited to the appointments of the wardens, and was an instance of the imposition of a general duty upon local authorities for the general good, and was entirely ministerial, and carried with it no further power of control of the board of wardens, who continued as a body independent of municipal control. Up to the date of consolidation the limit of their action was based entirely on legislative control. An appeal from the decision of the board of wardens lay to the county courts. As we have heretofore noted, the ultimate control of public highways is in the sovereign, the state; the care of its highways, when they become streets, it vested more or less completely in the local authorities; but the portion of the great water highways of the rivers Delaware and Schuylkill, where they become the port of Philadelphia, it kept under its immediate control, through its own agents, the port wardens. It gave them jurisdiction to license pilots; to control the mooring of vessels; to prescribe the wharf lines; to license the erection of wharves and buildings below low-water mark, and to keep the navigable waters of the city for ever open and free from obstruction. Their power was to be executed for the benefit of the public at large; but the wisdom of the legislature, recognizing the more immediate interests of the city corporation, vested in it the naming of the persons who were to exercise these large legislative powers affecting so nearly local and municipal interests.

GAOLS AND PRISONS.

SEC. 22. Under the old city, by reason of there being city and county courts, there must needs be city and county prisons.[1] The old gaol at Third and Market streets having become insufficient, the legislature, in 1773, erected the county commissioners into a body politic, and authorized them to sell the old gaol, and borrow money to purchase land and build a new one, any deficiency to be met by a county tax.[2] The title to this and other public buildings was vested in the state a few years later.[3]

The new prison was erected on a lot situated at the southeast corner of Sixth and Walnut, extending in depth to Locust street along Sixth, and in front on Walnut street half way to Fifth, upon ground bought from the Proprietary.[4] It was large and massive, and was provided with dungeon cells that would have done credit to a feudal castle.

In 1803,[5] a new prison was provided for on Arch street, and in 1831[6] both were directed to be sold and proceeds applied to the erection of the Moyamensing county prison; the Walnut-street property sold for $229,000.99. There were about sixty executions from this prison in twenty-five years, which were mainly public displays, and often conducted at Centre Square. The management of prisons in those days was extremely bad; they were crowded and filthy, the nest and home of cholera and yellow fever, and societies were organized for the relief of the suffering prisoners. The control and management of the prison was given to inspectors who were elected by the city and districts.[7]

The inspectors had power to provide for and regulate the convicts with the approbation of the mayor[8] and two aldermen and two judges of the supreme court.

They were to make such orders for the regulation and cleanliness of the debtors' apartment as should be approved by the mayor of the city and the president of common pleas;[9] they

---

[1] Charter of 1701. [2] Act February 26, 1773, 1 Smith, 403.

[3] Act February 28, 1780, 1 Smith, 487

[4] For description, see account of Walnut-street prison, *United States Gazette* for October, 1835. [5] Act April 2, 1803. [6] Act March 30, 1831.

[7] See act April 5, 1790, 2 Smith, page 535–539.

[8] Act September 23, 1791, 3 Smith, 45.

[9] Act April 4, 1792, 3 Smith, 78.

could inflict solitary confinement;[1] they provided necessaries for every description of prisoners, separated and classed them.[2] By a later act, all powers vested in the mayor, aldermen, and justices were to be exercised exclusively by the inspectors.

By act of 1809,[3] the inspectors were elected by councils, and commissioners of districts of Northern Liberties and Southwark.

By act of 1835[4] twelve inspectors of the county prison were appointed; four by the mayor and aldermen, four by judges of the quarter sessions, four by the judges of the district court. A sufficient sketch has thus been given to show the autonomy of prison management and to class the municipal duties imposed relative thereto among the delegated powers relating to state or general duties.

Board of Health.

Sec. 23. The end to be obtained by the establishment of a board of health has to do with a kind of oversight, falling strictly within the line of police regulations. While the inherent powers of the corporation might have been sufficient to meet the requirements of the case, yet, either from the intimate concern which the general public must have in the preservation of the health of its ports or from the apathy of local authorities the state and federal authorities have from time to time exercised themselves in the preservation of the health of seaports.

As early as 1774[5] an act was passed to prevent infectious diseases being brought into the province. Twenty years later this act was revived, amended, and supplied,[6] and the act of April 22, 1794,[7] was passed to establish a health office in Philadelphia.[8]

---

[1] Act April 22, 1794, 3 Smith, 189. [2] Act April 18, 1795, 3 Smith, 247.
[3] February 3, 1809, 5 Smith, 11. [4] Act April 14, 1835, P. L., 232.
[5] January 22, 1774, MS. Laws, chapter 689.
[6] September 5, 1793, Law Book V., 177. February 8, 1794, Law Book V., 184. March 11, 1794, Law Book V., 189. [7] Law Book V.
[8] Amended act April 17, 1795, L. B. V., 450. Act April 9, 1799, L. B. VI. 432.

The board of health was established and incorporated by that name in act of 1806.[1] It consisted of five citizens, three from Philadelphia, one from Northern Liberties, one from Southwark, to be appointed by the Governor. Its powers and duties are laid down in the text of the act, with considerable minuteness, and it repealed all other health laws. By it the Governor appointed one port physician, one lazaretto physician, and one quarantine master, all to be under the control of the board. Their expenses were met by a county tax.

By act of 1818,[2] the appointment of the members of the board of health, eleven in number, was vested in councils and the district commissioners. By act of 1849,[3] the term of service of the board of health, still appointed as before, six from the city and four from each incorporated district, was made three years, and was arranged by lot, so that six should go out of office every year. It is thus to be observed that the direct concern of the municipality with these four important departments, *i. e.*, prisons, poor, port wardens, and board of health, was limited to the nomination of the members, who then became *quasi*-independent bodies, amenable only to state authority. Their funds came from the state, and to the state their accounts were made.

FINANCE.

SEC. 24. If any comment were needed as to the immense importance of the methods of municipal finance, it would be supplied by the imperative manner in which they confront one in consideration of every department of the city government, and by the difficulty always experienced in getting the worth of one hundred cents out of a dollar in the expenditure of public funds. It is, moreover, a subject which, beyond all others, is likely to lead astray both the doctrinaire philosopher and the city father. No topic is more delusive,

[1] Act March 17, 1806, 4 Smith, 303; amended by act March 31, 1812, 5 Smith, 373.

[2] January 29, 1818, 7 Smith, page 5. [3] April 5, 1849, P. L., 346.

and none with which the average American citizen, whether his own experience has been limited to the handling of a few hundred dollars or a million, feels better able to grapple. The financial record of the city of Philadelphia is hardly one of which her people can be proud, and yet it only illustrates the experience of all our great cities. The various evils, which must thrust themselves on the attention of every intelligent student, were the result of a generally accepted theory inherently vicious in itself. Under the old charter there was no power to levy a tax. We have seen how this want was supplied, in part, by the act of 1789. The property of the old corporation was transferred to the new, and the power of estimating and raising taxes so far as respects the lighting, watching, watering, paving, and cleaning the streets was conferred by act of 1790. The right to collect fines for breach of ordinances was of course continued.

Sources of Revenue.

The sources of revenue then consisted of:—

1. Income from city property, such as wharves, ferries, markets, &c.
2. Receipts from fines.
3. The amount raised by taxation.

In time the receipts from gas and water became an appreciable item, and fines and licenses amounted to a considerable sum. Still the main source of all municipal revenue must ever be taxation; and a large sum raised from citizens does not imply necessarily either oppression or extravagance. People will be satisfied to pay a round sum in taxes if it is so expended as to increase the value of the city property, and if they have reasonable assurance that the money is wisely and honestly spent.

Methods of Appropriation.

We find very early councils making annual appropriations for the necessities of the coming year. In 1797 the appropriations foot up to $138,715, and in the same year the mayor is authorized to borrow money in anticipation of the taxes of the present year, and this course is pursued for a series of years, showing a poor idea of economical financiering, to borrow money for current expenses when the power existed to have an adequately well-filled treasury. For instance, the ordinance authorizing this loan in 1797, was passed in September, when the taxes should have been well in, the main reason being assigned that taxes could not be collected "because many citizens were at their country houses." It is to be observed that taxes were not made a lien then, nor does any penalty appear to have been imposed for delay in paying them. They were collected by suit. See Digest of 1851, title Collection of Taxes. These loans were considered of a temporary character, and were ordered to be paid forthwith. In the year 1800, the appropriation ordinance may be taken as a fair sample.[1] The mayor was authorized to borrow in anticipation a sum not exceeding $10,000.

This was applied as follows:—

To meet the deficiency of the tax of 1799,	$1,315 44
Interest on water loan,	4,200 00
Interest on debts due the banks,	1,200 00
Purchase of paving stones and repair of old pavements,	1,600 00
Repairs to unpaved streets, &c., paving intersections,	2,400 00
For cleansing city,	11,250 00
Cleansing and repairing sewers and docks,	1,850 00
Lighting and watching the city,	18,000 00
Repairs of pumps and wells,	2,500 00
Regulating streets,	400 00
Centre Square improvements,	1,650 00
Salaries of city commissioners and clerk,	2,800 00
Expenses of city commissioners and clerk,	100 00
Salaries to mayor, recorder, high constable, clerks and messengers of councils,	3,000 00
Pay of constables for patrolling streets on the Sabbath day,	156 00
Incidental expenses of councils,	600 00
Residuary fund for preventing and removing nuisances,	4,478 56
	$57,500 00

[1] Ord. February 20, 1800; Duane, page 205.

This sum the city commissioners were directed to raise by tax on the estates, real and personal, and on the professions of persons within the city, agreeably to the last county assessment. By the same ordinance the following appropriations were made out of the receipts to arise from the income from city property:—

Reimbursement from tax fund to corporate fund, 1799, . .	$165 92
Other advances by citizens, ...	360 00
Salaries of clerks of markets, ...	1,200 00
Menial service in markets, ...	560 00
Repairs, &c., ...	700 00
Meeting contract engagements for maintenance of two steam engines, ...	8,000 00
	$10,985 92

The city commissioners were directed to open and keep distinct accounts of the several objects under their superintendence, and in their certificates to the mayor clearly to designate each object for which payment was asked. The treasurer was also to keep separate accounts of the appropriations.

We have given this detailed statement of the appropriation bill for the year, that we might start square with the century. From it we have the following summary:—

City rental, at least	$10,985 75
Tax levy, ...	57,500 00
Total expenditure, ...	78,485 75
Water loan, ...	70,000 00
Floating debt, ...	4,000 00

Seven years later the fiscal ordinances make instructive reading.[1]

The appropriations foot up to	$106,000 00
The floating debt has risen from $4000 to	40,200 00
The water loan to	210,000 00
The amount fixed to be raised by tax is	80,000 00
The corporate income is rated at	13,000 00
Of which there is to be carried to the sinking fund, . . .	5,000 00

[1] Ord. March 12, 1807; Ord. March 26, 1807; Ord. March 26, 1807; Lowber, pages 206–214.

The Credit System.

We can notice here the advent of the future financial policy in § 3 of ordinance of March 12, 1807: "Whereas, in the demands for the city service for the present year there is to the amount of $18,000 for objects which are permanent improvements of, or additions to, the city property, and not of ordinary or common expense, and which ought, therefore, to be provided for *by money borrowed rather than by a tax on the citizens.* And whereas it is advisable to transfer the debts owing by the city to the banks to the funded debt of the city," &c., it is enacted that the mayor borrow on loan $50,000, at six per cent., payable in 1830, to be applied, first, to paying the item of $18,000; next, to payment of part of bank debts, the balance thereof to be paid by the city treasurer out of receipt from delinquent taxes of 1802. A sum of $5000 per annum was directed to be carried to the sinking fund out of the income of the corporate estate. It may be of interest to look at the class of expenditures called permanent improvements, which councils so glibly class among the objects which should be *"paid for by money borrowed and not by a tax on citizens."*

Repairs of engines and engine-houses, ...	$9,000
Purchase of gravel lots, ...	4,155
Distributing Schuylkill water and repairing pipes, ...	4,855
	$18,000

To say nothing of the principle, this classification is certainly elastic enough to provide posterity with an excellent debt for things which perished in the using.

Budget for 1827.

Let us now step forward twenty years and audit the accounts for 1827.[1]

The budget foots up	$230,380 09
The city boasts a funded debt, at six per cent., of	600,000 00
" " " " " at five per cent., of . . .	991,000 00
Her floating debt was	95,100 00

[1] Ord. April 26, 1827; Ord. page 330.

Status for 1853.

By 1853, the year before consolidation, the annual expenditure had reached [1]	$1,005,732 83
Of this the interest on the debt amounted to	473,191 00
Which, at six per cent., indicates a debt of	7,886,511 10

To meet this the interest to be received from railroad companies is appropriated, and the city commissioners are authorized and required to levy forthwith a tax of fifty-eight cents on the hundred dollars on real estate, pleasure carriages, and horses, according to last county assessment, and also to levy on the freemen a tax of $7000.

Increase of Debt Inevitable.

This increase of debt was inevitable, despite the sinking fund, when we consider the latitude allowed to the class of so-called permanent improvements. The floating debt grew up mainly out of the deficiencies in the yearly appropriation. The funded debt was composed of the following principal items: The water loans, begun in 1799; the gas loans, begun in 1841; loans for subscription to railroad stock, and sundry other so-called permanent improvements, which come more or less properly under their alleged classification, such as a loan to improve High street,[2] to complete Ninth-street sewer,[3] for purchase of State House Square,[4] extending market-house.[5]

Right to Borrow Money and the Right to Subscribe to Railroads.

The right to borrow money to carry out the inherent powers, and to effect the express ends of a municipal corporation belongs to such corporation at common law, and is only to be precluded by the statute or organic law. It remained undoubted during this period. The right to subscribe to stock of public enterprises, while it might be open to serious doubt

[1] Ord. April 1, 1853; Ord. page 1344.
[2] Ord. October 1, 1808. [3] Ord. September 29, 1810.
[4] Ord. April 11, 1816. [5] Ord. March 29, 1821.

if a question of first impression either before the legislature or as one of sound constitutional construction, was very early conceded in this country to be within the grant of the legislature. It could not, however, be exercised without the general or special grant of that body. As early as 1818[1] the city subscribed to the stock of the Schuylkill Navigation Company, but no loan was authorized, the treasurer being directed to pay for the same in cash. In 1848 the city was authorized[2] to subscribe to the capital stock of the Pennsylvania Railroad to the extent of five per cent. of the assessed value of the property, subject to taxation for state and county purposes; by several ordinances councils authorized subscription to fifty thousand shares, and directed a loan amounting to two and a half millions to pay for the same. This stock then became an asset of the sinking fund. A like power was granted in regard to the stock of the Schuylkill Railroad.[3] Two years later came legislative authority to subscribe to the stock of Hempfield Railroad Company,[4] and the stock of the Philadelphia, Easton and Water Gap Railroad Company;[5] it was attempted to enjoin the action of the mayor and citizens by a bill in equity, filed by W. P. Sharpless *et al.*;[6] this brought the matter fully before the supreme court. The case was elaborately argued on the basis of the authority of the legislature to confer the authority on the municipality to subscribe to the stock of a railroad company. The injunction was denied, and the court sustained the power of the legislature. Each of the judges who sat delivered a separate opinion; that of the learned chief justice, Black, is so profound and exhaustive on the whole subject that we are not surprised that this case has taken its place as the leading case which has been uniformly followed in the United States in a long line of unbroken decisions. The learned judge stated, "That it was beyond all comparison the most important case which had ever been in that court since the foundation of the

---

[1] Ord. June 11, 1818. [2] Act March 27, 1848, P. L., 272.
[3] Ord. March 14, 1850, Digest 1851, page 351. [4] Act April 9, 1853.
[5] Act May 6, 1852. [6] Sharpless *vs.* Mayor, 9 Harris, 147.

government." His opinion is a masterly treatise on the branch of constitutional law applicable "to the powers necessary for a branch of the legislature of a free state." He further said he decided the case as one of first impression, as due to the immense magnitude of the issues at stake. As a comprehensive exposition of the law of the subject, this decision is in every way worthy of one of Pennsylvania's greatest jurists; and, as such, while he expounded the law as it was, unterrified by that "appalling reverse of the picture," we can listen with greatest deference to these significant words taken from his opinion: "It may be conceded that the power of piling up these enormous public burdens, either on the whole people or on a portion of them, ought not to exist in any department of a free government; and, if our fathers had foreseen the fatal degeneracy of their sons, it can scarcely be doubted that some restriction on it would have been imposed." His words are the words of wisdom, though it may be doubted whether the compliment to the wisdom of our fathers is very much deserved, when we examine into their financial policy.

Folly of the System.

The evidence all goes to show that our venerated fathers took very kindly to the policy of paying for all classes of improvements "*by money borrowed, rather than by a tax on the citizens*," *i. e.* themselves. Even a fool can vie with Hamilton, if his drafts on the future are not protested, by the ingenious device of closing the popular eye by that will-o'-the-wisp called a sinking fund.

It is simply astounding, when the record is dispassionately examined, to realize the great folly exhibited by our fathers,—men wise, prudent, and honest in the conduct of their own affairs,—when they come to the conduct of the public funds, and cut every Gordian knot by supinely throwing themselves, a fearful incubus, on the future, with its equal necessities.

Origin of the Sinking Fund.

The delusive idea of the sinking fund, doubtless borrowed from Pitt's English fiasco, was inaugurated by the ordinance of March 12, 1807.[1] Certain sums were to be carried annually to the sinking fund with a view of meeting the obligations when they became due; the theory was that the sums so carried would with interest compounded aggregate to the amounts of the various loans when and as they became due. The proceeds of the sinking fund were to be invested in the purchase of said loans in open market, at or below par. The annual appropriation for this purpose was $5000, from 1807 to 1811, when it was made $7000.[2] The practice, however, was, that while the wisdom of the fathers with one hand transferred $5000 to the fund, they yearly found new objects which *should be provided for with money borrowed rather than by a tax on themselves*, and with the other hand they either borrowed from the market or even the sinking fund itself a loan of $10,000, and blandly referred the public to the sinking fund, which was supposed to be a panacea for all financial ills. When a loan came due that they could not pay they were not troubled, but simply gave certificates of a new loan. The country was new, the faith of the people in themselves and their future was rightly boundless, and they easily permitted any occasional qualm to be salved by high-sounding ordinances about transfers to the sinking fund, and a spendthrift and specious system of book-keeping, and the pleasant fiction that the sinking fund was an actual practical security for the public debt. The touchstone of the fallacy is seen in the facts of history; the sinking fund did not sink; the debt increased with gigantic strides; the real collateral was the increased earning power of the city and the increased capacity for tax-bearing. There could be no hope of ever paying the debt, or of putting it on the high road to payment, till the city earned more than it spent; or, to put

---

[1] Lowber, page 202.

[2] Ord. February 28, 1811, Lowber, page 240.

it in municipal language, till it raised more by taxes than it spent and borrowed each year.

Appropriations were made to the fund from time to time from the corporate estate, all of which was pledged to the payment of the debt as well as the public faith. The sales of any real or corporate estate were to go to its credit, as well as the stocks of railroads. The finance committee was to invest all moneys accruing thereto[1] in the city debt.[2]

The first water loan was made as early as 1799, and the first gas loan guaranteed by the city was in 1836.

Subjects of Taxation.

An effort was made to impose a tax on offices, posts of profit, professions, occupations, pleasure carriages, and horses. The preamble to the ordinance set out: "Whereas, by the system of taxation established in Philadelphia, an undue proportion of the public contribution is levied on real estate, and whereas it is just that the burthen of taxation should be as equally and impartially laid as circumstances will permit, and duly apportioned among the citizens, so that each should contribute to the support of the various objects of the public police in proportion to his ability," &c., therefore provision was made for levying a tax on the above-recited objects.[3] This ordinance, however, was not effective, and was considered obsolete in 1812,[4] and was formally repealed in 1828.[5]

The ordinary subjects of taxation during the period were the persons of citizens, legally taxable, and their estates, real and personal, taxes being laid agreeably to the last county assessment.[6]

The form used in the enacting clauses was as follows: "That the city commissioners be and they are hereby authorized and required to levy on the estates, real and personal, within

[1] Ord. December 22, 1842, page 273.
[2] Digest of 1851, page 308.
[3] Ord. March 26, 1806, Lowber, 199.
[4] See note Lowber, page 199.
[5] Ord. April 10, 1828, Ord. page 353.
[6] Ord. February 28, 1811, Lowber, page 243.

the city of Philadelphia, a tax for city purposes of — cents on every one hundred dollars and —— thousands of personal taxes."

In 1838 and thereafter the appropriation ordinance began as follows: "That the following sums be and the same are hereby appropriated to the several standing committees for conducting the affairs of the corporation," &c.—here follow the specific appropriations, and then the enacting clause directing the city commissioners to levy the tax as before, and fixing the rate each year.

Collection of Taxes.

Collectors of taxes were first appointed by the city commissioners,[1] afterward by the mayor,[2] and finally by the committee on finance.[3] The tax was laid by councils, and levied by the commissioners agreeably to the last county assessment; duplicate lists of taxables were furnished the collectors;[4] they gave sureties and paid over weekly to the city treasurer; they were authorized, upon warrant of the mayor, recorder, and aldermen, to collect delinquent taxes by distress and sale. The city treasurer inspected their duplicate lists.[5]

Taxes made a Lien.

City and county taxes were made a lien on real estate in 1824,[6] to be registered when unpaid by April of following year. By this act taxes became a lien from date of assessment.[7] The tax to remain a lien had to be registered before July 1st,[8] and in 1846 an act was passed directing methods of recovery,[9] the treasurer having power to enforce payment of registered taxes.

The treasurer was to demand and receive all moneys of the

[1] Ord. March 29, 1797.
[2] Ord. April 2, 1811.
[3] Ord. August 29, 1843.
[4] Ord. March 29, 1797.
[5] Ord. March 26, 1806.
[6] Act February 3, 1824.
[7] Parker's Appeal, 8 W. & S., 449; Shaw *vs.* Quinn, 12 W. & S., 299.
[8] Act April 16, 1845, P. L., 486.
[9] Act March 11, 1846, P. L., 114.

corporation;[1] to keep distinct accounts;[1] to present quarterly accounts of receipts and disbursements;[2] to examine tax lists and report delinquent tax collectors;[3] to preserve countersigned duplicates of receipts;[4] to exhibit same to committee of accounts and finance, and to city commissioners, and to render account of proceedings of sinking fund;[5] to open, number, and keep distinct accounts corresponding with those kept by the city clerk, and to keep such other accounts as may be necessary; and he was forbidden to pay out any money except upon requisition of a committee and warrant of the mayor,[5] and to pay any requisition unless the amount be to the credit of specified item of appropriation.[6]

While it has been deemed impossible to give a complete abstract of the fiscal legislation of the city, yet whatever citations have been made are accurate, and it is believed that they give the reader a clear idea of the general history of this department without misleading him in any important particular.

Power of Committees of Councils.

Sec. 25. If there is one thing in the history of this period which stands out more clearly defined than any other, it is the trend of the policy exercised by councils of vesting more and more the executive duties in the hands of committees of their own body, thus confounding the true theory of republican policy, which should tend to keep the line between these two arms of government sharply defined. The full fruition of this course of action was to be realized and reaped in our own day, but the policy and precedent had been fully crystallized before the consolidation.

No one can dispute the obvious necessity of every legislative body acting more or less by committees; the time of the

---

[1] Ord. April 14, 1797. [2] Ord. August 5, 1799.
[3] Ord. February 20, 1800.
[4] Ord. June 11, 1806; December 10, 1829.
[5] Ord. October 1, 1835, Digest 1851, page 211.
[6] Ord. April 10, 1851, Digest 1851, page 376.

whole body would otherwise be frittered away in discussion of trifling details. But all history teaches us that the constant tendency of all legislative bodies is to absorb, when unchecked, executive and even judicial functions. We see this every day at Washington, and the integrity of our political system demands that it be jealously watched and sternly checked.

The national and state legislatures can be controlled only by the fundamental law of the land as formulated in our respective constitutions. The action of the municipal council is likewise to be controlled by the common law and the charter acts. It is simply a creature of the legislature, and theoretically easily controlled when the wisdom and action of the legislature can be invoked to restrain general powers unwisely used.

Under Penn's charter we see councils appointing special committees from time to time, and very early in this period councils appointed standing committees for certain specific purposes. Early after the charter of 1701 we see councils performing certain functions through committees: committee to audit accounts of the treasurer, committee on wharves and property, &c. These committees became more or less permanent or standing committees. The standing watering committee is spoken of as in existence in 1806, and was probably organized by motion or resolution as early as 1802 or 1803. It took some time for the full development of the system, and not till 1833 do we find the joint standing committees recognized by a general and permanent ordinance.[1] This ordinance enumerates them, ten in number: 1st. Watering committee. 2d. Finance. 3d. Delaware wharves. 4th. Schuylkill wharves. 5th. On fire companies. 6th. Public squares. 7th. Accounts. 8th. Markets. 9th. City hall and state house. 10th. Lighting and watching. But the system is fully defined and crystallized two years later.[2] Its purposes are set out as follows: "That, for the purpose

[1] Ord. December 6, 1833, page 504.
[2] Ord. October 1, 1835, Digest 1851, page 211.

of auditing and controlling the expenditures of the city, and giving necessary direction to the officers of the corporation for the prosecution of the public works, the following joint standing committees, to consist of four members of each council, shall be appointed by the respective presidents thereof, annually, on the organization thereof: 1. A watering committee. 2. Finance. 3. Police. 4. Highways. 5. On cleansing the city. 6. City property. 7. Legacies and trusts. 8. Commissioners of Girard College. 9. Building of Girard College." The chairmen of 1, 5, 6, and 8 to be members of select council; of the others, to be members of common council. The register of the water department acted as clerk of the watering committee; the assistant clerk of councils acted as clerk of all other committees, except 8 and 9.

By the above ordinance, and that of February 25, 1839, these committees were forbidden to exceed their appropriation or transfer any part of an appropriation from one object to another. Their powers and duties included the general supervision and control of the subjects to them respectively committed. They were to present to councils, annually, an estimate of the amount required for the public service in the ensuing year in their departments, and examine all claims against the corporation for work done and materials furnished, and, when satisfied, issued requisitions on the mayor for amounts thereof.

When the mayor was made elective by the people, by a curious coincidence he was stripped of most of his appointing power;[1] it was given directly to councils or the committees of councils, the committees coming in for the following share:—

Collectors of taxes by committee on finance.

Collectors of water-rents by committee on water.

The commissioner of city property and superintendent of state-house steeple by committee on city property.

Superintendent of railroads by committee on highways.

Clerk of police by committee on police.

The library committee of two from each branch had charge

---

[1] Ord. August 29, 1839, Digest 1851, 242.

of the preservation and increase of the books, papers, and documents belonging to councils.[1] But, when the present clerk of councils went into office, he found the department despoiled of books, papers, and manuscripts of every kind. The city of Philadelphia does not own a complete set of its own printed ordinances. Members of councils were constituted a visitation committee of Girard College, to be divided into four sub-committees, which should be on duty two months each to visit the college and report to standing committee or councils.[2] A committee on gas was created in 1846 to supervise the department of gas.[3]

WATER COMMITTEE.

As early as 1806[4] we find mention of a joint committee, consisting of four members from each branch, called the watering committee. It gave permits to connect with the pipes, and permits to fire companies to use the plugs. In 1809 it was with the mayor invested with general powers to conduct the works, purchase materials, &c., and employ necessary agents.[5] It also furnished the collectors with a list of water-rents, appointed the register,[6] and in 1833 was directed to appoint the collectors of water-rent; in 1835[7] it was placed among the general joint standing committees to be appointed annually, and formally recognized by a permanent ordinance. Its powers were therein defined to include all powers necessary for conducting the works, distributing water, regulating same, purchase of materials, and appointment of superintendent, register, agents, and workmen.

THE CLEANSING COMMITTEE.

As organized by the ordinances of 1834 and 1835, this committee had general supervision over the cleansing of the

[1] September 28, 1843, Digest 1851, page 280.
[2] Ord. November 9, 1848, Digest 1851, page 331.
[3] Ord. December 6, 1846, Digest 1851, page 340.
[4] Lowber, page 197. [5] Ord. April, 1809, L., 236.
[6] Ord. January 21, 1821. [7] Ord. October 1, 1835.

city, theretofore placed in the superintendents for cleansing the streets, and in 1840 it was authorized to contract for the cleansing of the whole of the public highways, lanes, and alleys.

The Highway Committee.

To this committee was given general supervision of the streets, the charge of paving, repairing, grading, building, and repairing culverts, the granting of permission to make openings into same, the appointment of the superintendent of railroads; it was authorized, in conjunction with the surveyor and regulator, to fix the regulation of streets not theretofore established, and to make contracts for the use of railroads.

Other Committees.

The control of the Girard estate was placed in a distinct committee, and the balance of legacies and trusts in the hands of a committee of that name.

The committee on police succeeded the committee on lighting and watching, had general supervision of all fiscal matters connected therewith, and the appointment of the clerk of police.

Finance Committee.

The committee on finance was then, as it is now, the most important committee of councils. Its duties are elaborately laid down in the ordinance of 1835, but for our present purpose may be summarized in a few lines. It had general supervision and control of the fiscal concerns of the city, invested moneys of the sinking fund, made requisition for payment of interest and salaries, reported to councils how and what taxes should be levied, audited the accounts of the city commissioner, treasurer, and clerk; performed the duties of the previous committee on accounts, appointed and commissioned collectors of taxes, and examined and reported on estimates of all other committees.

Summary.

It is instructive to note the changes which took place in the scheme of executive government in this short period. After experiencing the evils of independent boards of commissioners, power having been given the corporation to regulate its public work as from time to time expediency might dictate, it concentrated all the heretofore scattered executive duties in one executive board, the city commissioners. With a wise recognition of the value of a responsible and effective chief magistrate, the appointment of all city officers was vested in the mayor; but, as time went on, nearly all discretionary power was finally taken from the commissioners and vested in the respective committees, the mayor was stripped of all appointing power, and such appointment vested in councils and its committees. While we can only conjecture the motives for this change, it is a fair presumption that it arose from the massing of the details of business, so that in the absence of any well-digested system, the city fathers turned naturally to the apparently easiest method of dividing these duties among committees of their own bodies. The fundamental principles of sound policy being thus violated by the confounding of executive and legislative functions, it is not surprising that the result was weighted with very great detriment to the city. An immense business like that of a city must necessarily be very complex, but it should and must be conducted on a practical scientific basis, if the best attainable results are to be hoped for; and such approximately best results cannot be obtained under the faulty system of executive government by committees. It is simply a spectacle of uncorrelated forces. Friction and extravagance might readily be expected from such divided responsibility, and the answer of history does not disappoint this expectation.

Police Regulations.

Sec. 26. The police regulations and general municipal legislation of this period require brief notice as illustrating the extent of the municipal power and the character of the times. Awning rails were to be six feet four inches high, under penalty of a fine of one dollar.[1] Bake-houses were to be built of brick, under penalty of a fine to be used for the repair of the fire engines and the purchase of leather buckets.[2] As a further precaution against fire, it was enacted that no person should keep a stack of hay within one hundred feet of any building. The corporation was given power by act of assembly to regulate the rates and prices of wagoners, carters, draymen, porters, wood sawyers and chimney sweepers.[3]

In view of the increasing traffic on the street, and in order to secure the responsibility of porters and draymen, it was provided by ordinance that all hackney coaches, carts, drays, &c., used for hire should be numbered in conspicuous letters; a registry was to be kept by the city clerk of the names and places of abode of the owners of such vehicles and of the numbers of the vehicles under the several heads, and a certificate was issued to the owner on the payment of a fee; no carriages or wagons were to stand in any parts of the streets, except such as were fixed by the city commissioners.[4]

Barrows and handcarts above a certain size were not allowed on the pavements[5] except during certain hours of the night;[6] wheel-barrows and handcarts used for hire were to be registered by the city clerk and have a number affixed; they were not to be driven or carried faster than a walking pace, and were to be kept within three feet of the curbstone; they were to stand at certain stands fixed by the city commissioners, and were not to carry loads exceeding five feet in width.[7] Owners of such barrows, or any person using the same, upon violation of the provisions of the ordinance were liable for any damage that might happen by reason of any misconduct, as well as to certain penalties.

---

[1] Ord. January 18, 1790, Digest 1851, page 53.

[2] 1730–31, Digest 1851, page 13. [3] Act of April 2, 1790, 2 Dallas, page 795.

[4] Ord. April 16, 1812, Digest 1851, page 92.

[5] Ord. October 1, 1811, Digest 51, page 91. See Ord. March 12, 1846, *Ibid.*, 299. [6] Ord. July 2, 1846, Digest 1851, page 302.

[7] Ord. February 25, 1819, Digest 1851, page 120.

By act of legislature a penalty was imposed for the adulteration of flour used in bread;[1] and the clerk of the market of any borough or town was empowered to weigh all butter and seize the same if found deficient in weight. By a subsequent act all bread was to be sold by weight.[2]

BROKERS.

By the act incorporating the city[3] the corporation was empowered to license and regulate brokers; and in 1827 an ordinance was passed for the regulation of pawnbrokers.[4] The mayor was empowered to grant licenses to pawnbrokers, and every person so licensed was to give bond with two securities.

BUILDINGS.

In 1831 the corporation was authorized to pass ordinances regulating the thickness of walls, and prohibiting the construction of walls not composed of incombustible materials,[5] and to declare all buildings the walls whereof were not wholly composed of incombustible materials to be nuisances. Any building declared by ordinance to be a nuisance might be removed by the corporation. Any person being damaged by such removal might petition the court of quarter sessions, who thereupon appointed a jury of twelve freeholders to assess the damages. Soon after the grant of this power wooden, framed, and brick-framed buildings were declared by ordinances to be a nuisance and were prohibited;[6] and any person constructing such a building or employed therefor was liable to a heavy fine, and likewise for neglecting to remove the same on conviction; and it was made the duty of the city commissioners, high constable, and ward constables to give notice to the mayor or one of the aldermen of violations of the ordinance. Building materials were not to be

[1] Act March 18, 1775, 1 Smith, page 425.
[2] Act April 1, 1797, 3 Smith, page 294.
[3] March 11, 1789, 2 Dallas, page 654.
[4] July 9, 1821, Digest 1851, page 126.
[5] Act March 24, 1832, P. L., 1831-2, page 176.
[6] Ord. June 8, 1832, Digest 1857, page 189.

placed in the gutters to obstruct the flow of water;[1] and application for permission to occupy the streets with building materials was made to the city commissioners.[2]

Carriages and Horses.

By act of legislature for the protection of the street paving various provisions were made regulating the felloes of wheels, weight of loads, and the general traffic on highways.[3] By ordinance it was provided that no carriage or other vehicle should remain in a street over two hours;[4] drivers were to keep to the right; and no second vehicle was to enter a street not wide enough for two; and many other regulations of carriages, sleighs, and horses.[5]

Cellar Doors and Signs.

The encroachment of buildings upon the streets was early a matter of great complaint. In 1769 it was provided that no cellar door, porch, or step in a street fifty feet wide or over should extend beyond four feet three inches into such street;[6] and in 1838 the councils were given power to regulate the whole matters of projections and incumbrances in the streets.[7]

Chimney Sweepers.

The chimney sweeper was at an early date relied upon as a means of preventing fire. In 1787 an act[8] was passed requiring them to be registered and numbered, and to have a certificate. They were to wear their numbers on their hats, and were to attend within forty-eight hours' notice. The office of register of chimney sweepers was established, which

---

1 Ord. June 18, 1849, Digest 1851, page 341.
2 Ord. February 14, 1850, Digest 1851, page 349.
3 Act February 18, 1769, 1 Smith, 284.
4 Ord. January 18, 1790, Digest 1851, page 53.
5 Ord. January 14, 1790, Digest 1851, page 57.
6 Act February 18, 1769, 1 Smith, 284.
7 Act April 16, 1838, P. L. 1837–38, page 626.
8 Act September 29, 1787, 2 Smith, 432.

was afterward abolished, and the duties transferred to the high constable.[1]

SEC. 27. An idea of the character of the government of the city for this period will be best given by the following summary of the principal officials, and the method of appointment or election :—

By councils.

Agent of the Girard estates.
Appraiser of tavern licenses.
City commissioners.
City clerk.
City regulators and surveyors.
City solicitor.
City treasurer.
Directors of Girard College.
Directors Pennsylvania Railroad.
Directors public schools.
Guardians of the poor.
Lieutenants of the marshal's police.
Managers of the Wills Hospital.
Members of the board of health.
President of the board of city commissioners.
Treasurer of the Girard fund.
Trustees of the gas works.
Trustees of the ice boat.
Vaccine physicians.
Wardens of the port.
Nomination of policemen to the marshal.

By committees of councils.

City carpenter.
Clerk of the tobacco warehouse.
Clerk of the police.
Commissioner of city property.

[1] Ord. March 29, 1798, Digest 1851, page 72.

Collector of taxes.
Collector of water-rents.
Inspector of tobacco.
Register of watering committee.
Secretary of the commissioners of the Girard estate.
Superintendent of the Girard farms.
Superintendent water works.
Superintendent railroads.
Superintendent Statehouse steeple.
Superintendent permanent bridge.
Watchman of permanent bridge.

By the directors of Girard College.

President of the Girard College.
Recording secretary.
Matron.
Matron's assistant.
Steward.
Four governesses for every one hundred pupils.
Visiting physicians.
Janitor and gardeners.
Prefects (2).
Instructor in French and Spanish.
Instructor in natural history and physiology.
Instructor in drawing and writing.
Instructor in English and mathematics.
Principal teachers (2).
First assistant teachers (2).
Second assistant teachers (3).
Dentist.
Assistant teacher in principal department.

By the mayor.

Clerks of the markets.
Watchmen of the markets (4).
Collectors of vaccine cases.

Lieutenant of police.
Special constables (4).
High constables (4.)
Captain of night police (4).
Turnkeys for station houses.
Night policemen.
Day policemen.
Watchman of city hall.
Turnkey of city hall.
Superintendent of lamp-lighters.

By the managers of Wills Hospital.

Steward.

By the city commissioners.

A messenger.

By the city treasurer.

A messenger.

By the citizens.

Mayor.
Members of select and common councils.

City Carpenter.

A city carpenter was annually appointed by the committee on city property who was to perform such duties incident to his office as were required by the several committees of councils or the city commissioners, and received a fixed salary.[1]

City Clerk.

The office of city clerk was established in 1811.[2] At first he was annually appointed by the mayor, but was subse-

[1] Ord. December 22, 1842, Digest 1851, page 272.
[2] Ord. June 28, 1811, Digest 1851, page 90.

quently elected by councils.[1] He gave a bond and had the custody of all books, papers, records, and documents belonging to the city, except those belonging to the treasurer's office.[1] He was to pay to the city treasurer weekly all moneys received by him belonging to the city, and was to countersign the orders drawn by the mayor on the treasurer, and to keep a book and enter all orders under proper heads.[2] At first he also filled the duties of clerk of the watering committee, but subsequently his duties were completely separated from any connection with the watering committee.[3] He transmitted an annual account to councils of all moneys received and paid by him, which was printed.[4] He made account of the taxes on the Girard estate;[5] registered hacks, wagons, drays, carts, &c., and granted certificates therefor.[6] He published quarterly the list of cases deposited in his office by the vaccine physicians.[7] It was his duty to keep accurate and distinct accounts for the several standing committees, and an account for expenses authorized by councils. He was to issue and countersign all warrants on the city treasurer for the payment of money, and transmit the same to the mayor for his signature, with the requisition in which the warrant was founded; and was to perform all the duties of an accountant for the standing and special committees of council.[8]

Clerks of Councils.

There was a clerk for select and one for common councils. The clerk of select councils acted as secretary to the committees on finance, on city property, and on legacies and trusts,

---

[1] Ord. August 29, 1839, Digest 1851, page 243.

[2] Ord. December 24, 1818, Digest 1851, page 118.

[3] Ord. January 25, 1821, Digest 1851, page 124.

[4] Ord. December 10, 1829, Digest 1851, page 165.

[5] Ord. September 19, 1833, Digest 1851, page 196.

[6] Ord. April 16, 1812, Digest 1851, page 93; see, also, Ord. April 1, 1841, Digest 1851, page 256; also, pages 265, 258, and 263.

[7] Ord. January 2, 1830, Digest 1851, page 167.

[8] Ord. October 1, 1835, Digest 1851, page 211. The city treasurer kept similar account. See *ibid.*

while the clerk of common councils acted as secretary to the committees on police, on public highways, and on cleansing the city. They had joint control of the library of councils, and prepared the journal of ordinances for publication. They were paid a salary.[1] They delivered certificates of election to all officers elected by councils.

Clerks of the Market.

By the act incorporating the city[2] the mayor was authorized to appoint one or more clerks of the markets, who were to have assize of bread, wine, beer, wood, and other things within the city. By an act previous to the Revolution it was made his duty to seize all butter found deficient in weight.[3] It was further the duty of the clerks of the market to attend during market hours and to enforce the rules and ordinances made relative thereto; to weigh all bread, butter, lard, and other provisions sold by mass purporting to be of a certain weight, and to test all scales and measures. They gave bond for the faithful performance of their duties. An appeal from the decision of the clerk of the market lay to the mayor; and penalties were recovered before the mayor, recorder, or any alderman.[4] The clerks of the market were still further empowered to visit all provision stores, to enforce the ordinance prohibiting the sale of stale and unwholesome provisions.[5]

Clerk of the Police.

A clerk of the police was appointed by the committee on police.[6] The committee on police placed in the hands of this clerk such sums as were necessary for the payment of lieutenants of police, high constables, captains of the watch,

---

[1] Ord. December 23, 1841, Digest 1851, page 265.

[2] March 11, 1789, 2 Dallas, 654. [3] Act March 18, 1775, 1 Smith, 425.

[4] An ordinance relating to markets, December 22, 1831, Digest 1851, page 174.

[5] Ord. August 2, 1849, Digest 1851, page 342.

[6] Ord. August 29, 1839, Digest 1851, page 243. See this ordinance for a list of the city officers and methods of appointment.

watchmen, and all other employés of the police department.[1] The clerk gave a bond. In case of the inability of the mayor, by reason of sickness or absence, to draw warrants upon the city treasurer, the warrants were signed by the president of common council, and the absence or inability of the mayor was certified on the back of such warrants by the clerk of police.[2]

Collectors of City Taxes.

Collectors of city taxes were appointed by the committee on finance.[3] It was their duty to collect all taxes and to report all delinquents. In case of delinquents the mayor, recorder, and any three aldermen issued a warrant, under their hands and seals, authorizing the collectors to distrain.[4] They made weekly accounts to the city treasurer, and gave bond.[5] They were paid a commission of four per cent. on all moneys collected before January 1, and three per cent. on all collected thereafter.[6]

Collectors of Water-Rents.

Collectors of water-rents were appointed by the watering committee.[7] They were paid a commission not exceeding four per cent.,[8] and gave bond.

Review of the Third Period—1789–1854.

The records of the period treated of above are of the first importance in the consideration of the municipal affairs of Philadelphia. In it we have noted the advent of Philadelphia as a modern American municipality. The entire personality, if we may use the term, of the city is changed; it

---

[1] Ord. January 5, 1843, Digest 1851, page 273.
[2] Ord. January 18, 1849, Digest 1851, page 334.
[3] Ord. August 29, 1839, Digest 1851, page 343.
[4] Ord. March 9, 1797, Digest 1851, page 64.
[5] Ord. May 3, 1821, Digest 1851, page 125.
[6] Ord. January 18, 1838, Digest 1851, page 229.
[7] Ord. Dec. 5, 1839, Digest 1851, page 244.
[8] Ord. Dec. 26, 1822. Collectors of water-rents originally appointed by the mayor. See *ibid.*

becomes the creature of the legislature, and every vestige of a close corporation is swept away. The city is now the place, and its inhabitants, and all freemen, have a voice in the election of the municipal government.

Throughout the period are manifest the ebb and flow of two distinct lines of policy. Starting out with a remembrance of the evils of divided authority, and with a well-expressed effort toward concentration of executive power and responsibility illustrated by the large powers of the city commissioners and mayor, we find in the latter half of the period a steady reversal of this policy indicated by the absorption of all branches of executive supervision and control by the various committees of council. The mayor also is, step by step, shorn of his various powers and duties as executive, until he is relegated to the position of being simply chief of police and the figure-head of the corporation. The responsibility is scattered through a dozen committees, whose personnel change from year to year, and the executive wheels are found running by a complex system which could not fail of disastrous results even then, and still more so when carried over into the operations of the immensely extended consolidated city and county.

SEAL OF PHILADELPHIA IN 1789.

CHAPTER IV.

THE CITY AFTER CONSOLIDATION.

1854–1887.

Causes Leading to Consolidation.

Section 1. The country adjacent to the city but beyond its prescribed limits, especially that along the Delaware known as the Liberties, very naturally soon began to be densely settled, to assume an urban appearance, and to experience the necessities incident to urban life. This territory, at first divided into townships, soon outgrew their limited machinery, and by successive acts was divided and incorporated as districts and placed in charge of commissioners elected by the citizens. As time went by, the city and the more adjacent of these districts became so intimately connected, especially in the matters of police, making and repairing streets, education, care of the poor, control of the port, public health, &c., that by the middle of this century many active and influential citizens, conceiving that the general good would be conserved by a consolidated government, agitated the question and secured the passage of the act of February 2, 1854, known as the consolidation act. The history of this act has been well told by the Hon. Eli K. Price, who was sent to the senate as a popular candidate, especially to secure its passage. To this book the reader is referred for any extended history of this important event.[1]

Necessity for Consolidation.

The necessity for some sort of consolidation may be summed up in a sentence. The city and contiguous territory had practically become one city, with a common future and common wants, and their adequate development was crippled by

[1] History of the Consolidation of the City of Philadelphia.

the multiplicity and jealousy of the many existing governing bodies acting independently of each other. Police, gas, water, highways, poor, education, and public improvements imperatively demanded a homogeneous system and a firm, controlling hand. That the police system was weak was shown by the negro riots of 1835 and 1838, by the labor riots of 1843, and by the Native American riots of 1844. The poor, the port, board of health, &c. had all been placed under legislative commissions acting for the city districts, boroughs, and townships, thus recognizing and foreshadowing consolidation. There were, in fact, "ten corporations, or separately organized bodies, mostly emanating from the ten municipal corporations, overlapping and intertwined with them, and exercising each a share of the local government in and about Philadelphia, the extent of whose powers and doings was generally unknown to the citizens. "To these excrescent bodies must be added the county commissioners, ten municipal corporations, six boroughs, and thirteen townships, and we have forty corporate or *quasi*-corporate bodies to manage the affairs of the smallest county in the State; and, with the help of them all, it was undoubtedly the worst governed, from the number of limited territorial divisions and incongruous powers and conflicting interests of these various governing and executive institutions."[1]

History of the Act.

Sec. 2. These evils being recognized, the question of consolidation was agitated for ten years before it was effected. A town meeting was called by many well-known citizens, an executive committee was appointed and continued by a similar meeting in 1850. This committee addressed the legislature by memorial in 1851; and in 1853 the friends of the act met, nominated and elected Eli K. Price for the senate, and also candidates for the house, to secure the passage of the act. The act was passed January 30, 1854, and carried to

[1] Price on Consolidation, page 53.

Erie, where Governor Bigler was, and received his signature February 2. The cause of haste was the reckless disposition of the city and districts to forestall the act by wholesale increase of the debts. The passage of the act was made the occasion of elaborate festivities,[1] and the overwhelming majority for it in the legislature testified the widely-felt recognition of the necessities which called it into being. Notwithstanding the diligence exercised in securing the approval of the act, its passage having been for some time a foregone conclusion, the old city and districts vied with each other in the reckless increase of debt. Within thirty days they added four and a half millions to the burden to be assumed by the new city, which started with $17,108,343.79. The cash assets handed over footed up to something over a million. The first mayor under consolidation was Robert T. Conrad, the Whig nominee, elected over Richard Vaux, Democrat, by the intervention of the Know-nothing party.

Municipal Bodies Consolidated.

Sec. 3. The act of February 2, 1854, incorporating the "City of Philadelphia," provided that the city of Philadelphia, as limited by the act of 1789, should be enlarged so as to include the territory constituting the county of Philadelphia. It thus abolished the old city, the incorporated districts, and all townships and boroughs contained therein, which included the following corporations or *quasi*-municipal bodies and territories:—

1. The old city of Philadelphia.
2. Nine incorporated districts: Southwark, Northern Liberties, Kensington, Spring Garden, Moyamensing, Penn, Richmond, West Philadelphia, and Belmont.
3. Six boroughs: Germantown, Frankford, Manayunk, White Hall, Bridesburg, and Aramingo.
4. Thirteen townships: Passyunk, Blockley, Kingsessing, Roxborough, Germantown, Bristol, Oxford, Lower Dublin,

[1] See North American and U. S. Gazette for March 13, 1854.

Moreland, Northern Liberties (unincorporated), Byberry, Delaware, and Penn.[1]

All franchises, rights, duties, property, assets, debts, and liabilities of all these corporations and governments were transferred to the new corporation. While the city was thus consolidated to include the whole county, the identity of the county was not lost; and it was expressly provided that the machinery of the county government should continue.

Sketch of the Incorporated Districts.

Sec. 4. The preceding chapters have been exclusively devoted to tracing the municipal development of the old city of Philadelphia. A sketch, therefore, of the other component parts of the new city seems desirable, though it must of necessity be very brief.

Southwark.

In course of time the city ran over its original boundaries, and a peculiar condition of affairs was the result. The first act of assembly that indicates the existence of a dense population in the territory lying south of the city was passed March 26, 1762; the preamble to which sets forth that "there is a certain tract of land adjoining to and bounded by the south side of the city, beginning," &c. (giving the boundaries of the district of Southwark), "in which the owners and possessors thereof have erected, at a very great expense, a large number of houses, messuages, wharves, stores, and other buildings, and have, by agreement among themselves, continued the several streets of the city running north and south through part of said improved ground; and have in like manner opened cross streets running east and west, which streets not being confirmed by legal authority, ill-disposed persons have frequently committed nuisances therein. For remedy thereof said tract of land shall be called the district

[1] Sec. 6, act of 1854.

of Southwark." The said streets are declared public highways, and all nuisances committed therein are punishable according to law in the county court of quarter sessions of Philadelphia county. Provisions were made for the surveying, laying out, and opening of streets, and for the regulation of footways. Three surveyors or regulators of the streets were to be annually elected by the citizens, who had also authority over party-walls. By the same act three assessors and three supervisors were to be annually elected. The supervisors, together with the assessors, were to levy a rate not exceeding three pence in the pound on real and personal property, as near the county assessment as possible, for the purpose of repairing and maintaining the streets.

With the increase of the district new machinery of government became necessary. By act of April 15, 1782, certain trustees were empowered to hold land for the use of a public landing. By act of September 20, 1782, certain commissioners were empowered to purchase public landings in the district and raise a fund therefor.

The district continued to increase rapidly. "Whereas the district of Southwark has become populous, and the freeholders thereof are daily erecting buildings and making improvement thereon; but, for want of a public and general regulation of the streets, lanes, and alleys, they are irregularly placed, and there is danger that in time they will become a heap of confused buildings, without order or design, unless a remedy be speedily applied; and whereas it is highly necessary that every town, or part of a town, should have a direct and convenient communication with the country in order to an easy exchange of the necessaries of life with each other, and there is no road from the district of Southwark to the surrounding country but what is circuitous and inconvenient;" therefore, five commissioners are appointed, with full power to lay out streets, "laying the same at or as near to right angles with each other as the nature of the place and a reasonable conformity to the streets, lanes, and alleys already established and built upon will admit."

A subsequent act[1] gave the supervisors control over pumps in the district; empowered them to regulate water-courses; to pave and place posts in streets; and to appropriate money for watering and lighting the district.

Finally, the improvements in the district became so great that it became necessary for the legislature again to interpose; and by the act of April 18, 1794,[2] to constitute the inhabitants of the district of Southwark and their successors a corporation by the name of "The commissioners and inhabitants of the district of Southwark," fifteen commissioners were to be elected, who must be citizens eligible as members of the house of representatives. The five persons receiving the highest number of votes to serve for three years; the five having the next highest to serve for two, and the remaining five for one; five to be elected annually thereafter.

The commissioners were granted power to make such ordinances, not inconsistent with the constitution and laws of the Commonwealth, as were necessary and convenient for the purpose of ascertaining the toll and rates of wharfage of goods brought to public landings; for directing the conduct of all persons concerned in "buying, selling, or acting on any part of the estate belonging to the said district;" for fixing the compensation of officers appointed by the commissioners; for lighting, watching, watering, pitching, paving, repairing, and cleansing the streets; for preventing nuisances therein; and the same to enforce by proper officers, under such penalties as they might prescribe; and to alter and revoke the same.

All violations of ordinances could be tried by the court of quarter sessions of the peace for the county of Philadelphia. Ordinances were to be published in two papers, and recorded with the master of the rolls. The commissioners were to appoint regulators of party-walls, and to build a sewer under South street, and make such other improvements as they deemed necessary.

The commissioners were further empowered to lay and

---

[1] Act October 4, 1788, 2 Smith, 455. [2] 3 Smith, 130.

assess all the taxes previously laid and assessed by the assessors, supervisors, or commissioners, and also annually to levy an additional rate, not exceeding five shillings, on every one hundred pounds on real and personal property. The surveyors, assessors, supervisors, trustees, and commissioners established under previous acts were abolished.

Such in brief is the development of the southern section of Philadelphia. The growth of the city southward over its limits caused the necessity for some kind of government for the district. This necessity first was felt in the case of the streets, and supervisors and assessors were appointed. Subsequently it became necessary, for the commercial good of the district, to hold certain water fronts, and accordingly a board of trustees was created for the purpose. The district still continued to increase rapidly, and a board of commissioners was created to whom additional powers were from time to time given. Finally, when the locality grew to be a city in itself, it was erected into a corporation, with fifteen commissioners, who possessed all the legislative and executive powers of unit government.

For different purposes from time to time Southwark, like the other outlying districts, was united to Philadelphia, foreshadowing the final consolidation which was to take place. In 1828 it elected guardians of the poor in conjunction with Penn township and the Northern Liberties,[1] as we have seen. In conjunction with the same districts, and with Moyamensing, they elected members of a board of health.[2] In the same way they elected inspectors for the prison of the city and county of Philadelphia.[3]

NORTHERN LIBERTIES.

SEC. 5. The term "Liberties" was applied by the proprietor Penn to a certain tract of land lying north and west of the city. They were called Northern, Western, and

[1] Act of March 5, 1828, Digest 1851, page 156.
[2] Act of January 29, 1818, 7 Smith, page 5.
[3] Act of February 23, 1809, Lowber, page 114.

Eastern, according to their situation. The soil contained within these bounds was called "liberty land," or "free lots," because the proprietor gave the first purchasers of land in the colony, according to the extent of their purchase, a portion of land within these limits free of cost.

By the "concessions," dated July 11, 1681, it was agreed between Penn and the first purchasers "that a certain quantity of land or ground plot shall be laid out for a large town." By a special order to his commissioners, dated October 14, 1681, Penn ordered them "to lay out *ten thousand* acres for a *great town.*" The town was subsequently laid out, and, as appears by the original draft, included the city and Liberties of Philadelphia.[1] In October, 1682, Penn arrived from England, and the "great town" was divided into two parts, which were called the City and Liberties of Philadelphia. The city contained about 1820 acres; the Liberties, about 16,236.[2]

The opening of streets or roads in a new settlement is the first feature in the history of its improvement. As the city of Philadelphia increased many roads or streets immediately north of it were laid out and opened by the property-owners by common consent. Most of these were afterwards opened by public authority, and the courses and width regulated. Among the earliest acts of the provincial assembly were those which authorized the courts as established to open roads and highways. The county records show the dates of the opening of the streets by order of court; and indicate the growth of improvement.[3] No particular mode of regulation as to the heights, ascents, or descents of streets, or as to the erection of buildings, was established until the act of March 9, 1771, which provided for the appointment of regulators by the county commissioners for this purpose. The preamble of many of the early acts pertaining to the Northern Liberties are remarkable for the descriptions of the rapid march of improvements.

---

[1] 2 Smith's Laws, page 105. Proud's Hist. of Penna.

[2] Preface to digest of acts and ordinances for the district of N. L.

[3] See notes to streets, &c. in digest of acts and ordinances of the district for a full list of streets opened by order of court.

The period at which the Northern Liberties began to assume an importance from its increase in size, and the necessity of a systematic government for the comfort of its inhabitants, may be fixed about 1791. By the act of March 30, 1791, although no corporation was established, the first step was taken toward the adoption of a system of regulations calculated to answer the wants of the inhabitants. The preamble recites that, "Whereas the inhabitants of that part of the township of the Northern Liberties of the city of Philadelphia which lies between the middle of Fourth street and the river Delaware, and between Vine street and Pegg's run, have by their petition to the legislature represented that from the increase of population, buildings, and improvements great inconveniences are sustained, which are likely to increase from the want of proper regulation in respect to *lighting and watching these streets by night, and supporting at a common charge a suitable number of pumps* within the said division of the Northern Liberties," &c. By this act three commissioners were elected by the inhabitants. They had power to levy a tax for the purpose of lighting, watching, and establishing pumps. They received a compensation of five shillings for each day engaged in the public service.

In 1795 the population of the Northern Liberties had so increased as to require the division of the whole township into two districts, for the purpose of electing assessors and inspectors for each district. By act of April 17, 1795, a very important act, the governor was authorized to appoint regulators to survey and regulate the streets, water-courses, &c. of the township south of Shackamaxon creek, &c. Their report was duly made, and formed the basis of the subsequent street regulations of the district. By the same act provision was made for paving the footways, which were placed under the direction of three justices of the peace. Up to this time, as appears by act of April 4, 1796, the public landings or wharves within the township of the Northern Liberties were vested in the commissioners of the county of Philadelphia, who by that act were continued in that jurisdiction.

By act of 1796 the first attempt was made to establish a systematic police. It, among other things, authorized the appointment of a high constable for the township. In 1798, however, the law was repealed, and provision made for the appointment of an additional number of constables. By act of February 12, 1801, further provision was made for the regulation of the streets, and the supervisors of roads were ordered to pave passageways across the streets and the gutters.

It was, however, soon found that it was impracticable in a section so rapidly increasing to devise any system to answer the purposes of health, cleanliness, and comfort to the inhabitants, unless through the medium of a corporation. Accordingly, in 1803, the legislature passed an act incorporating certain parts of this region. To this several supplementary acts were added; and on March 16, 1819, the final act of incorporation was passed, repealing all previous acts inconsistent with its provisions. This act incorporated the inhabitants of that part of the township of the Northern Liberties "lying between the middle of Sixth street and the river Delaware and between Vine street and Cohocksink creek."

Twenty-one commissioners were to be elected; seven annually, to hold office for three years. The board of commissioners when assembled together for that purpose had full power and authority to make such ordinances as were necessary for the welfare of the district, and to appoint proper officers to enforce the same and fix their salaries. Violations of ordinances were tried by the district court of the city and county of Philadelphia. The commissioners did not receive any compensation.

The board of commissioners were granted full power annually to lay a rate not exceeding seventy-five cents in every one hundred dollars clear value of all real and personal estate as ascertained by the last county assessment.

By the act of March 7, 1840, a mayor was elected annually by the citizens, and vacancies in the office of mayor were filled by board of commissioners.

The mayor was given power to hear actions for penalties, fines, or forfeitures; and to have "the same power within the said district in all matters and things connected with the police as largely and amply as is now exercised by the mayor of the city of Philadelphia." The commissioners were authorized to make all such police regulations, and to prescribe by ordinances such duties and rules for the mayor as they chose. The mayor was paid a salary of $500.

MOYAMENSING.

SEC. 6. The first act in relation to Moyamensing was passed March 26, 1808. As in the case of the other districts, it was the necessity for proper regulations for the streets and buildings[1] that first called for grant of local powers. Three commissioners were appointed, who were to employ a surveyor and survey the streets. Three street regulators were to be chosen, who, with the supervisors, were to regulate the streets, direct the paving of footways on the application of a certain number of freeholders, and levy a tax not exceeding ten cents on the hundred for sinking wells and mending pumps. They were also to ascertain and fix the line of party-walls, &c.

Five years afterward the act of March 12, 1812, was passed, incorporating "the commissioners and inhabitants of the Township of Moyamensing." Subsequently various acts were passed, enlarging and extending the powers of the corporation, the most important of which was the act of April 5, 1848.

SPRING GARDEN.

SEC. 7. By act of March 22, 1813,[2] a portion of Penn township, described in the act, was incorporated under the title of "The Commissioners of the district of Spring Garden." The powers of this corporation were vested in a board of twelve commissioners, four to be elected annually by the qualified electors of the district. The commissioners

---

[1] See preamble to act. [2] P. L., chap. 106, page 136.

did not receive a salary. As in the other districts, they possessed the legislative and executive powers of government. They appointed regulators; a treasurer of the district, who was not to be a member of the board; surveyors; and other officers. They had control of the streets and pumps. They might lay a tax not exceeding one per cent. on the real and personal property, according to the county assessment. They published their accounts annually, and kept minutes of the proceedings. By the act of March 8, 1815, provision was made for the election of two constables, one of whom was to be appointed by the court of quarter sessions.

As already noticed, Spring Garden was included in the provisions of the act providing for the consolidation of the poor laws, "so far as they respect the poor of the city," &c. Real estate was made subject to lien for municipal claims;[1] and by the same act provision was made for a superintendent of police. A few years later the commissioners were authorized to enact laws for the good government of pawnbrokers;[2] and in the same year they were empowered to erect a market-house and town hall; to elect one inspector of prisons; to introduce wholesome water; to lay pipes, collect water-rents, &c.[3] The act of 1827 enlarged the territory formerly included in the district;[4] and numerous other acts were passed from time to time, either enlarging the powers already granted to the commissioners or more explicitly defining the manner in which those already granted should be exercised.

Other Districts.

Sec. 8. The remaining districts were—Kensington, Penn, Richmond, West Philadelphia, and Belmont. The character, however, of the development of the districts around Philadelphia, included in the consolidation is now understood, and further details of the others is unnecessary. Of the remaining districts Kensington was created March 6, 1820; Penn,

---

[1] Act March 3, 1818, P. L., 136. [2] Act March 8, 1823, P. L., 62.
[3] P. L., 100. [4] Act of March 2, 1827, P. L., 65; April 23, 1829, P. L., 26.

February 26, 1844; Richmond, February 27, 1847; West Philadelphia, April 3, 1851; and Belmont, April 4, 1853.

The Boroughs Consolidated.

Sec. 9. It has been noted that the proprietor had original power to create boroughs.[1] Prior to the Revolution the proprietors erected four boroughs: Germantown, 1689; Chester, 1701; Bristol, in 1720; and Lancaster, in 1742. After the Revolution the erection of boroughs was the subject of special acts of assembly till the passage of the general borough act in 1834,[2] when the courts of quarter sessions were given power to incorporate towns or villages into boroughs. This act was followed by the still more important act of 1851.[3] Boroughs, even after this act, were sometimes created or had special powers conferred by special acts. It is not necessary here to go further into the general powers of boroughs; although it is interesting to note that they are an institution which has survived in this country only, in the States of New Jersey and Pennsylvania.[4]

The boroughs included in Philadelphia by the act of consolidation were six in number: Germantown, Frankford, Manayunk, Bridesburg, White Hall, and Aramingo.

Germantown.

The curious charter of Germantown, at first known as German township, incorporated Francis Daniel Pastorius and others under the title of "The Baliffe Burgesses and Commonalty of German Towne." It created a bailiff, four burgesses, six committeemen, and granted them power to hold a court and market; to admit citizens; to impose fines and make ordinances.[5] The corporation began by limiting membership after the old English fashion. The original court records are in possession of the Historical Society of Pennsylvania, and are very quaint and interesting.

[1] Sec. X., royal charter. [2] Act April 1, 1834, P. L., 183. [3] P. L., 320.
[4] Johns Hopkins University Studies, IV. series, No. 4.
[5] Pennsylvania Archives, vol. I., page 111.

The Germans objected to paying county taxes, alleging they were exempt by reason of their keeping up their own roads and bridges; but this position was untenable, and was promptly disallowed by the provincial council. The corporation lapsed in 1707 by reason of failure to elect officers, and the territory became known as a township. In 1769 the records of the old borough court were ordered to be filed in the recorder's office.[1] In 1834 it was enacted that the voters of a portion of the township should be authorized to elect commissioners, to regulate sidewalks, and to levy a tax for certain local purposes.[2] Eight years later the township was divided into two wards.[3]

Between that time and 1846 it was constituted a borough under the general borough act of 1835, and the borough of Germantown was made the subject of legislation.[4] An act passed in 1848, provided that the ancient records be handed over to "the present borough to which of right they appertain."[5] There are numerous other acts relating to the borough of Germantown, extending down to the time of consolidation.

FRANKFORD.

Frankford was incorporated March 7, 1800. By the act of that year the "town of Frankford in the county of Philadelphia" was erected into a borough. Two burgesses were annually elected by the freemen; the one having the highest number of votes to be chief burgess; and also five suitable persons as "assistants to advise with and aid the said burgesses in the execution of the authority hereby given them;" and one person as constable.

The burgesses and assistants passed ordinances and appointed regulators of party-walls. It is to be noted, however, that the burgesses and assistants lacked the important power over streets given to the commissioners of the

[1] Act February 18, 1769, 1 Smith's Laws, page 283.
[2] Act April 5, 1834, P. L., 185. [3] Act February 8, 1842, P. L., 5.
[4] Act of March 7, 1846, P. L., 185. Act March 6, 1847, P. L., 240.
[5] Act April 10, 1848, P. L., 467.

incorporated districts; it being provided "that so long as the borough of Frankford shall continue to be and remain a part of the township of Oxford, the powers and duties of the supervisors of the highways, overseers of the poor, and constables therein" should remain unaltered. Subsequent acts were passed increasing the powers of the burgesses.

Remaining Boroughs.

Manayunk was made a borough between 1839 and 1841, since which date the legislations affecting it have been voluminous. Bridesburg was incorporated as a borough in 1848. White Hall followed, as a borough, the next year. Aramingo makes its appearance the following year.

Townships.

Sec. 10. There remains for consideration one other class of municipal organizations represented in consolidated Philadelphia, and that is—The Township. It seems a curious fact that there is so little to be discovered about the history of this numerous and ancient political division of the Commonwealth; but the result of a diligent and painstaking search of all sources of information has been but meagre.

The charter[1] granted the proprietor, authorizing him to erect townes, hundreds, and counties, is the foundation of that division of the county known as The Township, though the term is sometimes used indiscriminately with borough.[2]

It was a part of Penn's original plan that his province should be laid out into townships of five thousand to ten thousand acres;[3] and though this plan was not long pursued, the subdivision of townships continued from the earliest date to the provisions for their more definite creation by the act of 1803,[4] which was substantially incorporated in the revised code of 1834;[5] and further provision was made whereby they

[1] Sec. X. [2] Road in Milton, 4 Wr., 300.
[3] 2 Sm. L., 140; XII. Haz. Reg., 342; Lewis on Land Titles, page 76.
[4] P. L., 439. [5] P. L., 538.

assumed a corporate existence, and liability to suit through their supervisors.[1] Much obscurity covers the history of the creation of the oldest townships, and it is impossible to ascertain with certainty whether their origin is due to the fiat of the proprietor or to the allotment of his surveyor, the only evidence of which is the map of said surveyor,[2] or the general acceptance of the name and boundaries of the township arising from custom or usage. Sometimes they appear to be first acknowledged as townships by the appointment of officers for them.[3] In early times they appear to have exercised a *quasi*-legislative authority, though by what warrant is a difficult question.[4] After the act of 1834, authorizing the creation, alteration, and division of townships, their powers became better defined and more fully understood, and though the lowest order of municipal government they are fully recognized as belonging to that class.[5]

By the act of 1803 the court of quarter sessions of the respective counties was authorized to lay out and define townships upon petition of the inhabitants; but before that act, as early as 1726, we find in the records of the quarter sessions the assumption by courts of the power to record and erect townships.[6] But there is no legislative authority for such jurisdiction, and it was probably resorted to as a matter of convenience, as it is by no means universal, and does not seem to have been followed in many, nay most, of the early cases; the practice of referring to the courts was probably borrowed from that in vogue in the lower counties (Delaware).

[1] Rep. Coms. of 1834, pages 9, 155.

[2] Futhey's Hist. Chester Co., 155–6.

[3] Smith's Hist. Del. Co., 156–173–388, &c.

[4] *Ibid.*, page 183; Annals of Harrisburg, page 92.

[5] Com. *vs.* McWilliams, 1 Jones, 66.

[6] Petition to erect by bounds the township of Providence; Road Records, Phila. Co., 1729, vol II., page 166; petition to have Limerick township recorded, vol. II., page 137 (1726). See, also, vol. II., page 138; vol. II., page 186; vol. III., 51.

The petition of inhabitants of Skippack and Perkiomen asking to have the bounds certainly marked, saying they "have been at charge to have the said Township Regularly Layed out by a Surveyor." (1725.) Vol. II.

The townships taken into the city were thirteen in number, as named above in section 3.

SEC. 11. Apart from the obvious need for a consolidated government with greater concentration of the executive powers the act of 1854 does not mark any radical departures in the organic law like those brought about by the act of 1789 and its supplements. Great as was the change in conditions it was the result of the increase of territory, the abolition of the intimately connected yet independent districts and boroughs, &c., rather than of any change in the theory of government. The framers of the act of 1854 doubtless went as far as they were justified in doing by the state of public sentiment at that time; but they attempted to attain certain results by machinery which had proved itself defective, and to this extent they failed. The need for concentration of powers, and for the divorce of legislative and executive powers and duties, was recognized, and an attempt was made to meet this. Many improvements in matters of detail were, however, made, and certain new and useful offices created, notably those of city controller and receiver of taxes. The changes effected by the act of consolidation, and the practices which grew up under it, will be best considered under the various heads treated of in the following sections:—

THE MAYOR.

SEC. 12. After the consolidation the status of the mayor was not essentially different from that which we find in the latter part of the third period. By the act of 1854 he was elected by a plurality vote of the citizens for two years, increased afterwards to three years; he must be thirty years of age, and beside the ordinary powers as the nominal executive, he was given like power with the sheriff in keeping the peace; could make requisition for the military; might dismiss all police officers save the marshal; was obliged to make at least one annual message as to the condition of the city, and recommend the adoption of necessary measures; he was required to be vigilant and active in causing the laws and ordinances to be obeyed, and to this end the marshal and police were placed at his orders. He was given a veto power subject to a two-thirds vote of councils. In the event of his absence, or a vacancy in his office, councils appointed or elected.[1] He had the powers of a justice of the peace, and could take acknowledgment of deeds, &c.[2] He was required to register the amount of appropriations, and to withhold his signature for all new constructions and redemption of tolls till the payment of accruing debt and interest and necessary and ordinary expenses were provided for;[3] but this limitation was modified by the act of 1864, placing this class of appropriations on a footing with others, subject only to the general veto power.[4]

The act of 1856 provided that, at the expiration of the term of the then marshal of police, all his powers not subordinate to the mayor should be vested in the mayor; while all his subordinate duties were to be performed by a chief of police to be appointed by the mayor. The mayor was prohibited from sitting as a committing magistrate;[5] but this power was restored to him by the act of 1860;[6] and by the same act he was empowered to appoint one of the aldermen to sit as a committing magistrate at the police station. He appointed, with the approval of select council, all police officers; made all police rules and regulations, subject to the approval of councils; and located the station-houses, which were under his control.[7] Councils could pass an ordinance over the mayor's veto only by acting within five days,[8] by a two-thirds vote in each branch.[8] All fees collected by the mayor were paid into the treasury,[9] and his salary was fixed by councils.

---

[1] Act February 2, 1854, P. L., 35. [2] Act January 9, 1817, 6 Smith, 395.
[3] Act April 21, 1855, section 21, P. L., 264.
[4] Act March 31, 1864, section 1, P. L., 305. [5] Act May 3, 1856, P. L., 567.
[6] Act of March 28, 1860, P. L., 318.
[7] Act of February 2, 1854; ord. of November 15, 1855; act of May 3, 1856, P. L., 567.
[8] Act May 23, 1874, P. L., 232. [9] Act of July 8, 1874, P. L., 277.

Prior to 1854 his salary could have been changed during any given term; and it was decided by the supreme court, that in the absence of constitutional provision or legislative action, the salary of the mayor, or other city officer, could be changed during his term of office.[1] The question came up on the reduction by councils of the salary of Mayor Barker in 1816, during his term of office. The court took the view that services rendered by public officers do not partake of the nature of contracts. Since the act of 1854 it cannot be increased or diminished during a term.

General Powers of the Mayor.

Among the mayor's general powers the following may be noted: He was the custodian of the ballot-boxes;[2] was a commissioner of the sinking fund;[3] drew warrants for moneys of sinking fund;[4] granted licenses for sale of gunpowder; had jurisdiction of the claims of pilots; appointed the fire marshal, and directed him to enter buildings; issued subpœnas to witnesses knowing cause of fire;[5] appointed inspectors of steam engines;[6] contracted with the gas trustees for lighting the city;[7] and made leases of coal land of the Girard estate.[8]

Miscellaneous Police Powers.

The mayor had power to grant licenses for places of amusement;[9] to close such places for violation of law;[10] to detail policemen as dog-catchers;[11] to commit vagrants to the house of correction[12] or county prison;[13] to issue search warrants for gunpowder kept contrary to law;[14] to grant licenses[15] for storing petroleum; to issue search warrants for petroleum im-

[1] Com. *vs.* Bacon, 6 S. & R., 322. [2] Act May 1, 1861, P. L., 577.
[3] Ord. May 7, 1857, page 188. [4] Ord. January 29, 1855, page 33.
[5] Act April 20, 1864, P. L., 516. [6] Act April 18, 1856, P. L., 401.
[7] Ord. February 16, 1856, page 17. [8] Res. December 26, 1841, page 341.
[9] Act May 22, 1879, P. L., 144. [10] *Ibid.*
[11] Ord. October 2, 1855, page 213. [12] Act June 2, 1871, P. L., 1301.
[13] Act April 14, 1835, P. L., 232. [14] Act March 20, 1856, P. L., 137.
[15] Act March 2, 1865, P. L., 262.

properly stored; to license pawnbrokers;[1] to appoint measurer of paving stones;[2] to cause the forfeiture of the licenses of passenger railroads in case of collision caused by their negligence.[3]

The mayor of the city, being charged with the conservation of property therein, is justified in abating a nuisance whereby the lives, health, and property of citizens are endangered and the public safety imperiled. This power was strictly enforced about the time of the Centennial, when Mayor Stokley tore down certain wooden buildings erected in close proximity to the Centennial Exhibition buildings.[4] The mayor's court was not continued by the act of consolidation.

Impeachment.

He was said to be liable to be impeached for malfeasance in office; the articles being presented by common council and tried in select. Such action has only been taken once in two hundred years.[5] Its legality was questioned.

Judicial Officers.

RECORDER.

Sec. 13. The powers of the recorder remained unchanged until the passage of the last recorder's bill.[6] By that act, in addition to the duties then assigned by law in conjunction with the State treasurer, he appointed three citizens, and the treasurer two, "who shall be appraisers of mercantile taxes." Appeal lay to the recorder and appraisers, who adjusted suits for tavern or mercantile licenses brought before the recorder. He was paid by fees, and the receipts of the office were enormous. By the act of May 29, 1883, P. L., 48, this ancient office was entirely abolished. Prior to the passage of this act David H. Lane, the then incumbent, was removed from office by Governor Pattison. The recorder being a judicial

---

[1] Ord January 19, 1856, page 5. [2] Act April 5, 1859, P. L., 360.
[3] Ord. July 7, 1857, page 250. [4] Fields *vs.* Stokley, 11 W. N. C., 344.
[5] See Impeachment of Mayor Smith, Journal of C. C. for 1886.
[6] Act April 18, 1878, P. L., 26.

officer, the right to so remove without approval of the senate was contested; but the supreme court held that, as an appointee of the governor, he could be removed at the pleasure of the appointing power.[1]

ALDERMEN.

SEC. 14. By the act of 1854[2] the office of alderman was continued, but the office made elective. Two were to be elected in each ward; though additional aldermen might be elected in each ward when required by a majority of citizens. They had the powers of justices of the peace. A list of taxable persons was to be furnished to the aldermen,[3] who were to receive the personal taxes,[4] give public notices of unpaid taxes, and pay over their receipts to the receiver of taxes. It was made their duty to report to the city controller, on the first of each month, all money received by them payable to the city, and to pay the same to the treasurer.[5] Councils elected annually one alderman to be police magistrate for each police district.[6]

MAGISTRATES.

SEC. 15. By virtue of the constitution of 1874 the aldermen were supplanted by magistrates, one being elected for every thirty thousand inhabitants on a general ticket at the city election, each voter voting for two-thirds the number to to be elected.[7] Each magistrate presides in a court not of record. They have civil jurisdiction over debts not exceeding $100; are *ex officio* justice of peace; and they have the same powers and exercise the same jurisdiction, civil and criminal, as that theretofore exercised by aldermen. In all civil cases appeal and *certiorari* lie to the common pleas. No

[1] Commonwealth *vs.* Lane, 7 Out., 481.
[2] Act February 2, 1854, P. L., 35. [3] Ord. July 27, 1854, page 35.
[4] Act April 17, 1866, P. L., 969. [5] Act May 13, 1856, P. L., 573.
[6] Ord. November 15, 1855, page 249.
[7] Const., act V., section 12, P. L. of 1874, page 15; act February 5, 1875, P. L., 56.

federal officer is eligible to the office of mayor, recorder, or alderman.[1]

Councils—Their Powers and Limitations.

ENCROACHMENT OF COUNCILS.

Sec. 16. In the modern municipal corporation there is no feature more important than the functions of the municipal legislature. The great trouble and defect of the past was due to the fact that the lines of executive and legislative action were not always clearly defined, whereby arose corrupt and extravagant expenditure of the public funds, political abuses and incompetent and bad administration of affairs.

It must be conceded that the part to be played in a city government by councils must always be paramount. Its members come directly from the people, and, unless Democratic government is a failure, it must also be admitted that they fairly represent the tone of thought and policy which the people tolerate, even if the better portion do not always approve the character of their representatives, and the methods by which they are elected. The remedy as to the personnel is always within the potential control of the citizens. The end, therefore, which statesmen should keep in view, is the moulding of the machinery of municipal government on such a scientific basis as will render a business-like conduct of affairs possible. The changes that are effected in the government of the city by the Bullitt bill, which are looked upon by the present generation as somewhat new and startling, are, in point of fact, in great measure only a restoration of the greatly diminished power of the executive, as will be pointed out more clearly in the next chapter.

The reader who has followed us thus far cannot have failed to notice how the constant trend of policy from 1835 down to the consolidation was toward an absorption of executive powers by councils, either directly by the main body or by the standing committees. It must be conceded also that large

[1] Act May 15, 1874, P. L., 186.

powers of supervision must be always left to the legislature, and that the scheme under which the people's money is raised and spent should be constantly submitted to the people's representatives; but the chief lesson taught by the past is that intelligent control of the executive departments has been conspicuous chiefly from its absence.

Powers of Councils under Consolidation.

By the act of consolidation[1] the legislative powers of the city are still vested in a select and common council. The select council consists of one member from each ward, who had the same qualifications as those required by the constitution for members of the senate. The term was originally two years; that of the first members, however, being arranged so that the seats of one-half the members became vacant each year; later this was modified, so that one-third of the members were elected each year for three years.[2] Common councilmen were to be elected by the citizens of the respective wards for a term of one year. They required the qualifications of members of the assembly. The term has now been changed to two years;[3] one-half are elected each year on the ratio of one for each 2000[4] taxable inhabitants. Councils organized in separate chambers, and elected a president and necessary officers. The officers of the old councils who held over had the right to organize the meeting whereat the credentials of members-elect were received, and this right could be enforced in equity. The old and new members then completed the organization by the election of officers. Alleged frauds did not affect the right to organize; but the attempt to organize one of the city councils in the interest of a particular party, by illegal action of the clerk at the organization in calling the names of persons not duly elected, could be prevented by injunction.[5]

[1] Act February 2, 1854, P. L., 35.
[2] Act March 21, 1861, P. L., 165. Act May 23, 1874, P. L., 231.
[3] Com. *vs.* Henszey, 32 P. F. S., 103. [4] Act March 20, 1874, P. L., 465.
[5] Kerr *vs.* Trego, 11 Wr., 292.

No member of the legislature, nor any one holding office under the State, shall be eligible as a member of councils.[1] Members shall not hold any office or employment in the choice of councils during the term for which they have been elected, nor any city or county office in the choice of the people while serving as a member.[2] A member is required to live in his ward. Any member may resign;[3] and in case of a vacancy the same shall be filled at the next municipal election for the unexpired term.[4] Councils and their committees are required to sit with open doors.[5]

All elections made by councils are by *viva voce*[6] vote. The provisions against the acceptance of any direct or indirect reward, inducement or bribe by any member are very stringent.[7]

Qualification of Members.

Councils are the judge of the qualification of a member;[8] but they are not a legislature with the constitutional privileges and immunities of legislators; and while councils may refuse a seat to members whom they consider disqualified, their neglect or refusal so to do does not prevent judicial inquiry, and the judicial power to oust a usurping officer, or one holding over unlawfully.[9]

Contested Elections.

Contested elections were formerly decided by councils, but they are now heard and decided by the common pleas,[10] and the lower court is the judge of the facts, and no appeal lies to the supreme court on the merits.[11]

---

[1] Act of February 2, 1854, P. L., 35. [2] Act March 11, 1869, P. L., 317.
[3] Act April 21, 1864, P. L., 638. [4] Act May 20, 1864, P. L., 912.
[5] Act February 2, 1854, page 35.
[6] Ord. July 21, 1856, page 184. [7] Act May 23, 1874, P. L., 233.
[8] Act of February 2, 1854. Case of David Mouatt, J. of C. C., 1885.
[9] Commonwealth *vs.* Allen, 20 P. F. S., 465; Commonwealth *vs.* Henszey, 32 P. F. S., 103.
[10] Act May 23, 1874, P. L., 231.
[11] Carpenter *vs.* Conway, 10 W. N. C., 169, and 11 W. N. C., 163.

Fundamental Powers.

The provisions of the sixteenth section of the charter of 1789[1] are still in force, giving councils full power and authority to make such laws and ordinances as shall be necessary and convenient for the government and welfare of the city, and the same to enforce, revoke, and alter. The general act following the new constitution[2] provided that the legislative power of every city should be vested in the councils. In general terms it may be said that a municipal corporation derives all its powers from its charter, and from it the duties, obligations, and liabilities of its officers are to be determined.[3] By the common law of Pennsylvania every municipal corporation has power to make by-laws and establish ordinances, to promote the general welfare and preserve the peace of the town or city.[4]

But in proceedings on a by-law, if based on special authority, it must appear that that special authority was strictly pursued;[5] and whenever a municipal corporation engages in things not public in their nature, it acts as a private individual, it no longer legislates but contracts, and is as much bound by its engagements as is a private individual. It is not within the power of the legislature to authorize the violation of such a contract.[6] Though these large general powers are granted by the legislature, that body has seen fit from time to time to particularize certain powers or duties, and to impose certain restrictions, which it will be well to notice very briefly. It was made the duty of councils to provide by ordinance for the establishment and regulation of all the departments indicated by the act of 1854; *i. e.*, law, police, finance, surveys, highways, health, water, gas, fire, poor, city property, and such others as might from time to time be needful, and through the mayor and proper committees maintain a supervision of each department for the exposure and correction

---

[1] Act March 11, 1789, 2 Smith, 467. [2] Act May 23, 1874, P. L., 231.
[3] Graffin *vs.* Commonwealth, 3 P. & W., 502.
[4] Wartman *vs.* City, 9 C., 203. [5] Coms. *vs.* Neill, 3 Y., 55.
[6] Savings Fund *vs.* City, 7 C., 175.

of all evils and abuses, and for that purpose they could require the production of books and papers and the attendance of witnesses; but no member or members, whether as committee or otherwise, could make any disbursement of moneys, or audit accounts, or perform any executive duty.[1] The heads of departments were elected by councils, and these in turn appointed their subordinate assistants, subject to the approval of select council. They fixed the compensation and prescribed the duties of all officers, and filled all vacancies in city offices till the next city election.[2]

No salary could be reduced or increased during a term;[3] and members of councils could receive no remuneration, direct or indirect. Officers elected under act of 1854 might be impeached by common and tried by select council.[4]

Standing Committees.

For the purpose of supervising the operations of the different departments, and of assisting councils in the consideration of subjects brought before them, the following joint standing committees were appointed by the respective presidents of councils annually, on the organization of councils:—

I. Committee on finance.

II. Committee on department of water.

III. Committee on department of gas works.

IV. Committee on department of highways, bridges, and sewers.

V. Committee on department of city property and public grounds.

VI. Committee on department of police.

VII. Committee on department of fire.

VIII. Committee on department of prisons.

IX. Committee on department of schools.

X. Committee on department of surveys and regulations.

---

[1] Act 1854, section 50.

[2] Act 1854, section 50; act May 20, 1864, P. L., 912.

[3] Act 1854, section 47. This does not apply to salaries fixed by ordinance. Baldwin *vs.* Phila., 10 W. N., 558. [4] Act 1854, section 45.

XI. Committee on railroads.

XII. Committee to compare bills.

XIII. Committee on law.[1]

These committees held stated meetings at such times as a majority determined. They were charged with the general supervision of their departments, and were to perform no executive act, but simply to report to councils. Various other committees were added, such as a committee on cash account of treasurer; to supervise disbursements of clerks of councils; on wharves and landings; house of correction; boiler inspection; police and fire alarms; on navigation of rivers Delaware and Schuylkill.[2]

The clerks of councils were to be elected annually; keep the journals; deliver same to the mayor; inform the mayor and heads of departments of action upon nominations made by them; sign certificates of councils as well as bills; have charge of the library, and care of the printing, stationery, and ordinary expenses of councils.

The duty of councils, upon organization, to meet and appoint the heads of departments at the time and for the terms fixed by law, was a mandatory one, and could be enforced by *mandamus.*[3] They were also required to prescribe by ordinance the number, duties, and compensation of officers and employés of each branch, and were forbidden to allow any extra compensation except by a two-thirds vote of each branch.[4]

A much-needed power was conferred on councils very recently by an "act authorizing councils of cities of the first class to issue subpœnas and to take testimony of witnesses concerning the management and accounts of any of the departments of said city, or of any other matter which may be subject to their supervision; also, providing for the compulsory production of books and papers, and a mode of compelling the attendance of witnesses by attachment for contempt.[5]

[1] Act July 3, 1854, P. L., 20. [2] West's Digest, pages 99 and 100.
[3] Lamb *vs.* Lynd, 8 Wr., 336. [4] Act May 23, 1874, P. L., 24.
[5] Act May 17, 1883, P. L., page 32.

Powers Relating to Finances.

The general outline of the power and duties of councils was quite clearly defined. They fixed the tax rate and levied all taxes; taxes were to be voted so as to show how much was raised for respective objects.[1] In making appropriations they were required to state the items of expenditure under separate and distinct heads for which such appropriations were made.[2] They were also required annually to publish a list of receipts and disbursements;[3] provide how purchases should be made,[4] and what officers should draw warrants;[5] fix salaries of all officers elected by the people;[6] and regulate salary of mayor.[7] The control of councils over all departments in the matter of disbursement of money, as well for work done and materials furnished as for the salaries and wages of officers and employés, was settled by the supreme court.[8] No debt or contract was binding on the city unless authorized by councils.[9] Councils had power to make appropriations for contingent expenses, and for civic entertainments.[10]

Police Powers of Councils.

Under the head of enumerated police power councils had the powers of the old police board; were empowered to provide for the inspection of milk;[11] to pass ordinances for good government of all oyster saloons and pawnbrokers;[12] to provide for paving streets,[13] cleaning docks at expense of owners;[14] for inspection of tobacco.[15] They were granted power, also, to pro-

[1] Act 1854, section 39; act August 25, 1864, P. L., 1030.
[2] Act April 21, 1855, Digest of 1856, page 55; act May 13, 1856, P. L., 568.
[3] Act May 18, 1875, P. L., 17. [4] Act May 13, 1856, section 26, P. L., 568.
[5] Act April 21, 1858, section 5, P. L., 386.
[6] Act May 23, 1874, P. L., 24; Baldwin *vs.* Phila., 10 W. N. C., 558.
[7] Act June 8, 1874, P. L., 277.
[8] City *vs.* Flanigen, 11 Wr., 21; City *vs.* Johnson, 11 Wr., 382; Bladen *vs.* City, 10 Sm., 464. [9] Act April 21, 1858, P. L., 386.
[10] Tatham *vs.* City, 2 W. N. C., 564.
[11] Act May 20, 1864, P. L., 912. [12] Act April 23, 1874, P. L., 235.
[13] Act 1854, sec. 40. [14] Act May 13, 1856, P. L., 567; act April 22, 1858, P. L., 449. [15] Act April 21, 1855, P. L., 264.

vide by rule for the use of highways by omnibus lines;[1] to fix wharf lines, regulate the construction of wharves, and provide for the appointment and regulation of pilots;[2] have control over passenger railways;[3] create a home guard;[4] and prohibit erection of wooden buildings.[5]

The power of the city to collect a license tax from street railway companies was necessarily found in the general police powers.[6] The passenger railway companies were required by law to keep the streets in repair, and in the event of their refusal so to do city could do so.[7]

Miscellaneous Powers of Councils.

Councils were authorized to alter and regulate curb lines, and to make a uniform width for footways;[8] to have exclusive control and direction of the opening, widening, narrowing, vacating, and changing grades of all streets;[9] and to contract with railroad companies as to change of routes and grades.[10]

Ordinances were required to be printed in book form and advertised.[11] By the act of 1854 councils had power to extend the operation of the laws then in force within the city, police or municipal districts, over the whole enlarged limit, and to declare what laws became obsolete by that act, or the extension of other laws.[12] They were also empowered to modify the duties of or abolish any offices or departments, and transfer the duties to other offices or departments.[13]

All ordinances of the city or districts were to remain in force till repealed.[14] An action of debt is the remedy for a breach of ordinances.

---

[1] Com. *vs.* Baldwin, 9 W. N. C., 233. [2] Act 1854.
[3] Digest of 1860, pages 247–253. [4] Act May 16, 1861, P. L., 762.
[5] Respub. *vs.* Duquet, 2 Y., 493.
[6] Act April 15, 1850; act April 11, 1868, P. L., 849; R. W. Co. *vs.* City, 2 W., 432. [7] R. W. Co. *vs.* City, 2 W. N. C., 639.
[8] Act April 28, 1873, P. L., 854.
[9] Act May 23, 1874, P. L., 235; act June 8, 1881, P. L., 68.
[10] Act June 9, 1874, P. L., 282. [11] Act March 21, 1866, P. L., 262.
[12] Edwards *vs.* City, 28 S., 61; Fell *vs.* Phila., 31 S., 73.
[13] Act May 19, 1874, P. L., 218. [14] Act of February 2, 1854, P. L., 44.

Methods of Procedure.

Ordinances were passed by bill, and no bill could be so altered or amended as to change its original purpose. No bill could be considered unless referred to a committee, returned therefrom and printed; and no bill could be passed containing more than one subject, which should be clearly expressed in the title. Each bill was required to be read at length, all amendments printed, and no bill could become a law on the day it was introduced or reported. The yeas and nays were required always to be called,[1] and the names of persons voting entered on the journal. No amendments by one branch could be concurred in by the other, except by a majority of the members elected, taken by yeas and nays. The report of a committee of conference could be adopted only by a majority of members. Such in outline were the powers and duties of councils. It had been clearly intended by the act of 1854 that the councils of Philadelphia should confine themselves to their legislative duties; and they were specially prohibited by section 50 of the consolidation act from performing any executive duties whatever, whether as committees or as councils. This injunction was disregarded in practice. Councils usurped all powers, legislative, executive, and visitorial. The executive arm of government was the system of "government by committees."

Without going into details, it is sufficient to say that the system was thoroughly and inherently bad. As an attempt at organization it was ill-fitted in principle and outgrown in practice. It was contrary to the theory of scientific government, against the weight of experience, and in bold defiance of common sense. It resulted not only in defective executive administration, but also in mal-administration, confusion, and extravagance.

City Commissioners.

Under the consolidation the former duties of the city commissioners were transferred to the department of highways.

[1] Act May 23, 1874, P. L., 231.

The title, however, with other duties was continued. Three commissioners were elected by the people to succeed the county commissioners, and were charged with all duties relating to assessors and assessments, the selection and drawing of jurors, and the oversight of elections and election officers, and all other duties of county commissioners not otherwise provided for by that act.[1] With the treasurer and receiver of taxes they formed a board of revision of taxes, and performed the duty of a county board of revision. They also for awhile appointed places for holding elections, and furnished the papers lists of taxables.

Early in 1855 the new department of city commissioners was duly organized by ordinance of councils. It was made the duty of these officers to issue their precept to the assessors; to publish a statement of the assessments; to sit with the board of revision; to draw the jurors, and perform all duties as to elections theretofore appertaining to county commissioners; to draw warrants for payment of all county officers; and to perform such other duties as councils should from time to time call upon them to perform.[2] Three years later they were required to give bonds;[3] and, in case of removal of any assessor by death or resignation, were authorized to fill the place till next general election.[4] All licenses for the sale of intoxicating liquors were obtained from them.[5] By the new constitution of 1874 the commissioners were made county officers; their salaries were fixed by the legislature, and the governor given the power to fill any vacancy in their ranks; and by the act of same year certain deliberative and discretionary powers were conferred upon them.[6] All duties of county commissioners by the general act of 1874 were imposed on the city commissioners of Philadelphia.[7] The duties thus imposed pertained to elections.

---

[1] Act February 2, 1854.
[2] Ord. February 12, 1855, Digest of 1856, page 127.
[3] Act April 21, 1858, P. L., 386. [4] Act March 26, 1859, P. L., 262.
[5] Act April 10, 1864, P. L., 318.
[6] Act May 23, 1874, P. L., 230; act March 31, 1876, P. L., 17.
[7] Act June 4, 1874, P. L., 42.

The commissioners having once exercised their discretionary powers, such exercise of discretion, whether right or wrong, cannot be reviewed or reversed by the courts on *mandamus.*[1]

LAW DEPARTMENT.

SEC. 17. The early law officer of the city was, as has been seen, the recorder, who not only exercised certain judicial functions, but was also the adviser and mouthpiece of the city, and appeared in court when the city was a party to a suit.

In a case[2] heard on a *certiorari* from the mayor's court to the supreme court, involving a judgment upon the ordinance of November 26, 1792, imposing "a penalty on hucksters who within the limits of the city buy provisions before ten o'clock, A. M., on market days," exception was taken, "that the ordinance was contrary to the constitution"; Wilcox, the recorder, appeared for the city, and contended for the power of the city to enact the ordinance. In the same year the recorder again appears for the city, in the case of Carlisle *vs.* Baker,[3] touching the power of the city to pass certain other ordinances. A few years later the mayor was empowered to appoint a solicitor or attorney, whose duty it was to draw up all papers, to prosecute and defend all suits, and, when required, to furnish his opinion to the mayor or councils. He was removable at the pleasure of the mayor, and received a salary of $500.[4] His office was abolished by ordinance of December 28, 1815, but re-established two years later,[5] when he was directed to exhibit quarterly to the city commissioners his accounts for professional services rendered. In 1831 he again became a salaried officer, drawing $1000 annually. In 1842, with other officers, he became an appointee of councils, and so continued until the consolidation.[6]

---

[1] Senior *vs.* Douglas, 14 W. N. C., 455; Douglas *vs.* Commonwealth, 16 W. N. C., 476. [2] Detwiler *vs.* Smith, 2 Dallas, 237. [3] 1 Yeates, 471.
[4] Ord. February 27, 1801, Poulson's Ords., page 53.
[5] Ord. April 10, 1817, L. & M., 1.
[6] Act of June 21, 1839, P. L., 373; ord. of December 22, 1842, page 795.

By section 15 of that act councils were directed to establish a law department, and to prescribe the number of assistants to the city solicitor, who was to be elected by the voters for the term of two years. By ordinance[1] of same year the law department was duly established and placed under control of the city solicitor. He was required to give bond, and directed to make return of moneys received to the city controller, and pay the same to the treasurer monthly. His duties were such as appertained to his office as the law officer of the city. In his office were deposited and preserved all title papers, bonds, notes, and contracts belonging to the city, and such others as councils directed. He was authorized to appoint, with consent of select council, four assistants. He was also to perform all duties imposed on him by councils. Heads of departments were to furnish him with a statement of all claims originating in their departments; sureties of contractors were to be approved by him;[2] and notice was to be given him of all meetings of viewers to lay out streets;[3] and the commissioners and treasurer were to report to him any person delinquent in making returns of moneys and accounts; he was to enter satisfaction on bonds and mortgages when accounts had been properly audited by the proper departments; and he was required to furnish councils annually with a copy of all laws relative to Philadelphia. He was to advise the committee on law of all suits against the city,[4] and was forbidden to compromise any suit without authority from councils. In 1873 his term was extended to three years. In 1881 his salary was increased to $15,000, and his fees were directed to be paid into the city treasury; he was required to draw all contracts and bonds in which the city was interested, and the number of his assistants was increased.

City Treasurer.

Sec. 18. By the act of consolidation the treasurer was elected by the voters for a term of two years, afterwards

[1] Ord. August 22, 1854, page 74. [2] Act April 21, 1855, page 264.
[3] Act May 13, 1856, page 567. [4] Ord. June 29, 1868, page 280.

increased to three. He was to give bond in such amount as councils required; and any vacancy was to be filled by councils. He was to keep itemized accounts of the city's funds; he received and paid all moneys; he could not exceed appropriations; his accounts could be inspected by any citizen; while his cash account was to be audited by the committee on cash account.

Speedily after the passage of the act of 1854 the department of city treasury was organized by councils, and the treasurer's duties prescribed in detail.[1] His security was fixed at $100,000; he was to take an oath; to deposit public moneys as required by councils; to verify his accounts once a week; to pay all warrants properly drawn and countersigned by the proper committee; to keep his accounts in the form of accounts current, and keep separate trust accounts.

The city treasurer was a member of the board of revision. He was given four clerks and a salary of $3500.[2] He received and paid the State tax.[3] He issued licenses to hawkers of foreign fruit.[4]

The credit system was clearly presented, when he was authorized to endorse on warrants, when there was no money to meet the same, "This warrant shall bear interest from this date at six per cent.," the limit of time to be indicated by the finance committee.[5] A slight restraint on this system was attempted by resolution in 1868,[6] by which he was required when in funds to advertise the number of warrants he was ready to pay, and interest should then cease. In 1874, by a very important act of legislature, he was forbidden to pay out of the treasury any money except on appropriation by councils, upon warrants signed by the proper officer.[7] In 1872 the banks for deposit were indicated by councils,[8] and by ordinance of 1872 the limit of

[1] Ord. July 27, 1854, page 32. [2] Ord. July 25, 1854, page 29.
[3] Act May 18, 1857, P. L., 570. [4] Act April 24, 1857, P. L., 301.
[5] Ord. March 1, 1861, page 59.
[6] Resolution Oct. 9, 1868; ordinances 1868, page 388.
[7] Act May 23, 1874, P. L., 233.
[8] Ord. October 24, 1873, page 475; March 18, 1872, page 97.

deposit was made $300,000. In 1882 the funds of the city were directed to be deposited with the different banks in the ratio of their capital.[1]

The treasurer was required to make to the controller daily returns of the cash received, and monthly of the preceding month. He was to deposit with the fiscal agent of the city a sufficient amount to meet the interest on the public debt, and to apply all other money promptly to the payment of warrants. In 1873 his term was extended to three years.[2]

By the constitution of 1874 the city treasurer was made a county officer; and vacancies in his office were consequently filled by the governor.

City Controller.

Sec. 19. The office of city controller was created by the act of consolidation. He was elected by the citizens for two years, this term being subsequently increased to three years. It was his duty to scrutinize, audit, and publish the accounts of the city and of the trusts; to countersign all warrants on the treasury to prevent appropriations from being overdrawn; and to perform all duties of the former county auditors.[3]

The duties of county auditors are set out in the act of April 15, 1834,[4] as follows :—

"The auditors of each county shall have power to issue subpœnas to obtain the attendance of the officers whose accounts they are required to adjust * * *and to compel their attendance by attachment* in like manner and to the same extent as any court of common pleas of this State may or can do in cases depending before them; and, also, *to compel, in like manner, the production of all books, vouchers, and papers relative to such accounts.* * * If any person appearing before such auditors for examination shall refuse to take such oath or affirmation, or after having been sworn or affirmed *shall refuse to make answer to such questions as shall*

[1] Ord. June 22, 1882, page 230.
[2] Act August 12, 1873, P. L., 1874, page 432.
[3] Ord. November 6, 1862, page 376. [4] Section 50, P. L., 545.

be put to him by the auditors touching the public accounts, or the official conduct of such public officers, or any of them, such person so refusing *may be committed by the auditors to the county jail by warrant, under their hands and seals*, directed to the sheriff or any constable of the county, setting forth particularly the cause of such commitment, until he shall submit to be sworn or affirmed, or to make answers to such questions, or be otherwise legally discharged." It has been questioned whether the conferring upon the city controller of "all the powers of the county auditors" applied to all offices and departments whose accounts it was made his duty to examine, or whether it was limited in application to the examination of the accounts of such officers as were previously audited by the county auditors. While the broad, common-sense interpretation is in favor of extending these powers of the controller to all the offices and departments whose accounts it was made his duty to examine, yet, as the statute is penal in its nature, a doubt can be raised. The question arose in the investigation into the alleged mal-appropriation of receipts by Mayor Smith, and hampered the city controller.

The city controller was, in a word, to superintend the fiscal concerns of the city, and to make reports thereon at such times as councils might direct.[1] The department of city controller was promptly organized by ordinances which prescribed in detail his duties.[2] Many additional powers and duties were conferred by subsequent ordinances.[3] He was given general charge of the finances, countersigned all warrants, kept separate accounts, examined accounts of outgoing officers, and received from other departments a weekly list of all warrants drawn by them. He supervised the accounts of all officers who managed the city's moneys, and might call for an account at any time. He audited all bills against the city; was forbidden to pass any bill for objects not authorized by law, or which were in excess of the appropriation; he was empowered

[1] Act February 2, 1854.
[2] Ord. July 25, 1854, page 29; ord. November 6, 1862, page 376.
[3] See Digest of 1868, pages 84–87.

to put persons presenting bills on oath as to their accuracy, and was made one of the commissioners of the sinking fund. He was afterward forbidden to countersign bills unless endorsed by appropriate committee.[1] He registered all warrants and took receipts for them. This reform was introduced by Controller Page in 1882, and had it been enforced prior to that time the almshouse frauds would have been impossible.

By the act of June 11, 1879, all the departments, trusts, commissioners, boards of the government of the city, were required to make their annual estimates of expenses and receipts for the following year to the city controller, who thereupon was directed to make his own estimate, according to the provisions of the act, of the money required for the government of the city, and to make report thereon to councils before the first day of September.[2] It was also his duty to make an annual report to councils, under oath, with an estimate of the city's expenses, and any financial suggestions which to him seemed proper; to report delinquents to the city solicitor, and an account of the city claims as furnished him by the latter officer to councils.

The Controller a County Officer.

By the constitution of 1874, article XIV., section 1, and of the act of March 31, 1876,[3] section 17, the city controller was made a county officer; and by the act of May 15, 1874,[4] the governor was authorized to fill a vacancy occurring in such offices, with the consent of the senate. This question, however, as to whether the controller was a city or county officer, was the subject of a heated controversy in 1883. Robert E. Pattison, the then incumbent, was elected governor, and immediately appointed S. Davis Page to fill the unexpired term made vacant by his election. City councils, however, claimed the right to fill the vacancy as a city office,

---

[1] See West's Digest, pages 63–74. [2] See act June 11, 1879, P. L., 130.
[3] P. L., 13. [4] P. L., 205.

and elected William M. Taggart as city controller. Mr. Taggart assumed the functions of the office so far as to take the oath and present bond for approval; but, being refused admission and recognition by the chief clerk in possession of the office, he opened an office for himself. Learned counsel gave directly opposite opinions; while the city solicitor advised councils that they had the right to fill the vacancy. The matter was speedily brought by the attorney-general before the courts by *quo warranto* issued against the appointee of councils. The supreme court, affirming the decision of court of common pleas, No. 3, held, that councils had no authority to fill a vacancy in the office; that the facts that in the act of June 11, 1879, P. L., 130, the controller is referred to as city controller, and that several ordinances passed since the act of 1876 imposed duties on him as city controller, do not change his status as a county officer.[1]

This decision is of great moment, for it fixes the status of several important officers as constitutional officers; *i. e.*, city controller, city treasurer, and city commissioners, all of whom act in dual capacities as city and county officers.

It has also been settled that the controller is not merely a ministerial officer, but is vested with discretionary and judicial powers.[2] It was held by Peirce, J., in Commonwealth *vs.* Page, in refusing a *mandamus* seeking to review the exercise of his discretion by Controller Page, "That the office of controller is one of highest importance to the welfare of the city, and he requires and is clothed by law with great powers of judgment or discretion. If these powers be unfaithfully or weakly administered the interest of the city may be greatly prejudiced, and she may become the prey of reckless and dishonest spoliators of her treasury. It is the duty of the court to uphold the controller in the exercise of his powers."[3]

An important restriction was imposed in 1878,[4] when he

---

[1] Taggart *vs.* Commonwealth, 6 Out., 354.
[2] Runkle *vs.* Commonwealth, 10 W. N. C., 213.
[3] 13 W. N. C., 532, Controller *vs.* Com., 18 W. N. C., 157.
[4] Ord. December 21, 1878, page 239.

was forbidden to countersign any warrant for materials or supplies unless said warrant be presented by the payee accompanied by the bill. In the same year an ordinance was introduced in common council by Mr. S. Davis Page, entitled "An ordinance to systematize and arrange a better mode of keeping the accounts in the several departments of the city," which was duly passed. To it the present complete efficiency of the system of the controller's office is largely due. The sub-committee to whom it was referred claimed in their report that this ordinance met the necessity, long felt, of having all receipts and disbursements of the city's moneys and condition of contracts on behalf of the city directly under the eye of the officer selected by the people, for the very purpose of supervising the accounts of the various city officials and employés, and which imperatively demanded that such a system should be adopted as would make it obligatory upon all departments to make constant reports to the city controller of all such matters.[1]

The powers of the controller are very great. He is intended, as his name implies, to control the immense financial concerns of this great city. All accounts of the departments culminate in his office, and are checked and verified there. He is the guardian of the city's treasury, and the efficient and honest administration of his office, or the reverse, is felt to the remotest branch of the city government. His salary, which is fixed by act of legislature, cannot be touched by councils.

HIGHWAYS.

SEC. 20. The department of highways was enumerated in the list of departments that councils by section 50 of the act of 1854 were directed to organize; and in the same year was passed an ordinance establishing the department of "Highways, Bridges, Sewers, and Cleansing of the City." This department was in charge of a chief commissioner and six commissioners, and the number of supervisors was defined

[1] Journal of C. C., vol. 2, 1878, page 1059.

for each ward; it was charged with the execution of all ordinances of councils affecting the department. The chief commissioner and commissioners were annually elected by councils; the surveyors were appointed by the mayor from a list of three times the required number furnished him by the respective councilmen from each ward; some wards had one, others five supervisors, according to the territory covered; the supervisors had the immediate charge of the work in their wards under the commissioners, and these again were responsible to the chief. There was also in this department a superintendent of city railways. The chief made bi-weekly returns of moneys received by him to the controller and paid the same to the city treasurer. From this department issued all licenses for omnibuses, cabs, &c.

Powers of Highway Committee.

By the twentieth section of the ordinance "The joint standing committee of councils shall have supervision over all matters appertaining to this department, and it shall be the duty of the chief to submit all contracts, plans, &c., together with all accounts, bills, &c., for work or labor done, which may appertain to this department, to the said committee for their inspection, before any action shall be had thereon." The paramount control of councils over the executive departments of the government is shown by this section, and it is typical of the complete assumption of executive powers immediately made and continually exercised by councils in regard to every department.[1]

Department Reorganized.

The next year the legislature made some changes. The chief and commissioners constituted a board, of which the chief was to be president, for the transaction of the business of the department; the board were to nominate three supervisors to the mayor for each district, from which he

[1] Ord. August 29, 1854, page 65.

appointed one; it was made the duty of the board to notify the city solicitor of all violations of the building line; and they were forbidden to enter into any contract unless with the previous consent of councils.[1] In the same year the number of supervisors was increased, and the number of commissioners reduced to four.[2]

Opening of Streets.

The subject of opening and laying out streets is one involving much technical learning, and hardly comes within a treatise on municipal history. Concisely stated, the general rule of law is as follows: The municipal authorities and the county courts having jurisdiction in any city of the Commonwealth have exclusive direction and control of the opening, widening, narrowing, vacating, and changing grades of all streets, alleys, and highways within the limits of the said city.[3] The regulation of travel on the streets is, of course, a subject for exclusive control of councils under its general inherent powers, as well as by statute.[4] Regularly, streets are opened by a petition to the quarter sessions, who refer it to a jury of view; but summary powers were also conferred upon councils, providing that when they shall deem the public exigency to demand it they may by ordinance order any street to be opened on the city plan, giving three months' notice to the owners, whereupon the latter might petition the court for a jury of view to assess the damages.[5] The purpose of this act was, of course, intended for special cases, requiring immediate and speedy action, where there was an urgent want or need that could not without prejudice to the interests of the public be subjected to the delay incident to petition to the quarter sessions. The courts have held, however, "That councils are the exclusive judges of the public exigency, and when they have decided that a case is a proper

[1] Act April 21, 1855, Digest 1856, page 55; ord. December 23, 1874, page 431. [2] Ord. July 31, 1855, Digest of 1856, page 582.

[3] Act June 8, 1881, P. L., 68.

[4] See title Regulation of Travel, West's Digest, page 186.

[5] Act April 21, 1855, Digest of 1856, page 57.

one for their affirmative action, there is no review of their action."[1] The jurisdiction of the highway committee has consequently become very often practically concurrent with that of the quarter sessions as to the opening of streets.

Cleansing the City.

In 1866 the city was divided into the northern and southern districts for cleaning purposes. The mayor, on his own information or that of the inspector or committee, might annul contracts on default of the contractor. There was a chief inspector of streets, whose duty it was to overlook and supervise the work of the contractors, and report to the committee on street-cleaning any default. All disputes were to be determined by the mayor.[2] Later, the chief commissioner was made *ex officio* superintendent of street-cleaning;[3] the number of districts was increased, and the mayor authorized to advertise for proposals; all paved streets, &c. were to be cleansed once a week, and the mayor was again given power to annul contracts.[4]

Department again Reorganized.

In 1874 the organization of the department was again defined as the department of highways, bridges, and sewers, and was constituted as follows: One chief commissioner, six commissioners; one superintendent of city railroads; chief clerk, assistant clerk; license clerk, one assistant license clerk; one miscellaneous clerk; one messenger; twelve superintendents; and such other officers as might thereafter be created. The building and repairing of all bridges, culverts, sewers, and inlets; the opening and grading, curbing, paving, repaving, and repairing of all streets, roads, lanes, and alleys, and other highways, were placed under the control of the chief,[5] who was elected by councils for three years;[6] he again appointed

[1] Sower *vs.* City, 11 Casey, 231. [2] Ord. April 6, 1866, page 118.
[3] Ord. March 7, 1868, page 104. [4] Ord. May 30, 1868, page 214.
[5] Ord. December 23, 1874, page 431.
[6] Ord. December 12, 1876, page 302.

the commissioners and superintendents, subject to approval of select councils.

It was made the duty of the chief to require contractors to enter security for all work awarded to them by the department sufficient to guarantee to the city the faithful performance of such work.[1]

Licenses Issued by Highway Department.

The following licenses were to be issued by the highway department: Building licenses;[2] for wagons, carts, barrows;[3] for omnibuses;[4] licenses to remove cobble stones;[5] and licenses to construct vaults under the sidewalks.[6]

Sewers.

By the act of 1866 councils were given power to fix the charges for culverts.[7] By the act of 1855 the charges for culverts and pipes had been fixed at seventy-five cents per lineal foot.[8] Permits for opening into culverts were granted by the highway department; all drains were to be constructed in accordance with plans furnished by the surveyors of the district, under supervision of the commissioners of highways, and an annual rent was charged[9] until within a few years.

Paving.

The paving of cartways of the public is done at the expense of the owners of the ground fronting thereon, but the repairing thereof is done at the expense of the city.[10] There are many ordinances as to the requirements of paving and repaving, which it is impossible to enter upon here in detail.

---

[1] Act March 28, 1872, P. L., 609. [2] Ord. May 3, 1855, page 144.
[3] Ord. March 1, 1855, page 84. [4] Ord. May 10, 1855, page 157.
[5] Ord. February 28, 1860, page 96. [6] Ord. November 12, 1855, page 246.
[7] Act March 30, 1866, P. L., 354; act of April 8, 1868, P. L., 324.
[8] Act April 21, 1855, Digest 1856, page 53. [9] Ord. May 3, 1855, Digest 1856, page 583. See, also, act March 27, 1865, P. L., 791; act April 10, 1867, P. L., 111; ord. December 23, 1874, page 431. [10] Sec. 40, act 1854; ord. May 3, 1855, page 140; May 23, 1874.

Strictly speaking, streets could not be paved until the chief inquired from the engineer and surveyors what drainage was required, and paving could not be done until the sewer was completed,[1] and the gas and water pipes were supposed to be laid before the pavement is put down; but it was not infrequently the case that a street would be first paved, then opened for water mains, repaved to be reopened for gas mains, repaved, and finally torn up for culverts, and again repaved.

Streets were to be paved on petition of a majority of owners presented to councils;[2] and the footways were also paved on petition of a majority of the owners.[3]

Street Law.

The cases of what might be called street law, touching upon its varied phases of road juries and damages, claims for paving, cleaning, repairing, &c., are so numerous that their proper consideration would involve a work equal in volume to this book; but these controversies mainly involve the nice distinctions and complications incident to the application of well-known principles of law to the infinite complications arising from slightly different states of fact. They are of interest rather to the lawyer, contractor, and city officers than the general student of municipal history. The general principles, so far as they affect municipal law, are simple, and have been pointed out in the last chapter. It may be, however, not without advantage to summarize them here.

A street or alley in an incorporated town is synonymous with a road.[4] The dedication of a street or landing will be intended for the public use and not for part of the public.[5] The city has no power to open a street without paying or giving security to the owners for damages, nor has it power to construct a culvert in a street not opened, though laid out.[6]

---

[1] Res. June 14, 1873, page 306. [2] Ord. December 23, 1874, page 431; act May 23, 1874. [3] Act April 10, 1826, P. L., 336; act March 22, 1865, P. L., 562. [4] Sharrett's Road, 8 Barr, 89.

[5] Penny Pot Landing, 4 Harris, 79. [6] Wistar *vs.* City, 30 Smith, 505.

No usage, however long continued, will justify an encroachment upon a highway.[1] Statutes of limitation do not run against the public, nor will lapse of time change the nature of a nuisance.[2] Streets and roads are public highways, under control of cities and towns, subject to the paramount authority of the Commonwealth. Whatever authority may be supposed to be necessary to lay down a railroad upon a street, there can be no doubt of the authority of the city, under its general powers, to remove the rails and clear the streets when it becomes necessary or convenient for the government and welfare of the city, in the judgment of councils. The sixteenth section of the charter of 1789 is full to this purpose; and the consolidation act continues the powers of the old city, subject to the paramount authority of the Commonwealth. The regulation and control of the streets, which are the great highways of the city, belong to the city government. This authority is clearly within the wide domain of power granted by the acts of 1789 and 1854.[3] The legislature may confer upon a municipal corporation the power of assessing the cost of local improvements upon the properties benefited;[4] but this, as it is a species of taxation, will be best considered under that head. A power to pave conferred by act of assembly implies a power to repair and repave.[5]

In England a highway is the property of the king, as *parens patriæ*, or universal trustee. In Pennsylvania it is the property of the people, not of a particular district, but of the whole State, who, constituting as they do the sovereign, may dispose of it by their representatives as they see fit. Highways, therefore, being universally the property of the State, are subject to its absolute direction and control. An exclusive right of ferriage across a navigable stream which is a public highway is granted only by it. The right of passage by land or water is a franchise which she holds in trust

[1] City's Appeal, 28 Smith, 33.
[2] Commonwealth *vs.* Miltenberger, 7 W., 450.
[3] Southwark Railroad Company *vs.* City, 11 Wr., 314.
[4] Hammett *vs.* Philadelphia, 15 Smith, 146.
[5] Wistar *vs.* Philadelphia, 30 S., 505.

for all her citizens, but over which she wields despotic sway. Similar principles are applicable to streets in an incorporated town. The regulation of streets is given to a corporation only for corporate purposes, and subject to the paramount authority of the State in respect to its general and more extended uses.[1] Ordinances in relation to use of streets must be reasonable.[2]

SURVEY DEPARTMENT.

SEC. 21. Closely allied to the highway department is the department of surveys. By the act of consolidation councils were to appoint a competent number of surveyors and regulators to perform the duty required by law. The duties of such officers were to extend over a convenient limit to be prescribed by councils; they were to continue in office during good behavior, and kept records of their regulations; they were organized into a board, under a head, for purposes relating to surveys, the planning of the city, the building of bridges, the construction of sewers, and grading of highways, as councils ordained by ordinance. The board were to hear appeals, and decide upon all questions of party-walls. Surveys already made were not to be altered unless by resolution of councils approved by the court.

The department was duly established by ordinance,[3] and entitled the department of city surveyors and regulators. It consisted of a chief engineer and surveyor, who was the president of the department, and twelve city surveyors, who, with the president, constituted the board. The city was divided into twelve districts. The board held two meetings every month; the chief and surveyors were directed to prepare a full, minute, and accurate survey of the whole city, showing the horizontal curvatures, and designating how the same should be graded and leveled, so as most beneficially to accomplish the drainage and sewerage of the whole city. The chief had

---

[1] The Phil. & Trenton R. R., 6 W., 25.
[2] Northern Liberties *vs.* Gas Co., 2 J., 318.
[3] Ord. November 9, 1854, page 130.

superintendence of all surveys and regulations as authorized by acts of assembly and ordinances of the several districts, or such as should be thereafter enacted by the councils. He was required to submit to the committee on surveys all plans, drafts, specifications, and other documents as they might require for examination, and report to said committee all applications for new streets, passages, surveys, and other improvements. He furnished the chief commissioner of highways with all plans and specifications for laying out, grading, and regulating streets, public ways, &c., and for bridges, culverts, and other improvements, to be done under direction of the committee.

The executive duties in each district were imposed on the surveyor of the district, subject to the supervision of the chief engineer. The chief engineer and surveyors were to be appointed by councils in joint meeting. By the supplement of the following year the surveyors were made elective by the voters of their respective districts, who were each to elect one surveyor of five years' standing for a term of five years. These constituted a board, and elected a chief surveyor. All public plans or town plots were to be deposited in the survey office, and it was directed that the survey of the city be completed and the plans filed. The board, under direction of councils, had authority to alter the lines and regulate the grades of streets laid out on the city plan, but not opened, subject to the approval of the court of quarter sessions, as in the case where the plans were originally submitted for approval.[1] When paving had been done by authority of councils the account was to be presented to the district surveyor, whose duty it was to assess the same against the several owners in proportion to their fronts, and make out duplicate bills and deliver the same to the supervisor of highways.[2] The department was soon afterward reorganized, the chief engineer remaining its head, with former powers; he was also required to sign plans, surveys, &c., furnish highway department with plans

[1] Act April 21, 1855, P. L., 264.
[2] Ord. May 3, 1855, page 140.

for laying streets and bridges, and to direct regulations and grades; certified copies of surveys and plans were to be kept in the department; the executive duty in each district was imposed upon the surveyor, under control of the chief; each district surveyor was ordered to keep an accurate record of surveys and adjustments of party-walls, and to furnish a copy to the chief; surveys of lots were to be made before a building was commenced, and no curbing set or streets regulated unless by regulation of surveyors.[1]

All drains were to be constructed according to plans furnished by surveyor of the district.[2] No railroad company whose road terminated in Philadelphia could construct that part of the road which extended into the city without submitting the plans to the board of surveys, which had power to conform the same as far as was possible to the general plan and regulation of the city.[3]

Vacancy in the office of chief engineer was to be filled by councils for five years. The officer was required to have five years' experience as a surveyor; the district surveyors were to have three years' experience; incompetent or unskillful surveyors might be removed on petition to the court.[4] It was made the duty of the assessors to return to the city commissioners the dimensions and quantity of each lot of ground, and when such return was insufficient the receiver of taxes might direct the surveyor to make an accurate measurement in order to recover the registered tax.[5]

In 1862 the chief engineer was directed to complete his records from the records in the recorder of deeds' office, the surveyor-general's office at Harrisburg, and from those of the court of quarter sessions;[6] the department was again reorganized with greater minutiæ of detail; reports of expenses were to be made to the controller, and warrants were to be signed by the chief.[7] It was made the duty of the surveyor to

---

[1] Ord. October 25, 1855, page 235.
[2] Ord. May 3, 1855, Digest 1856, page 583.
[3] Act April 21, 1885, P. L., 264.
[4] Act May 13, 1856, P. L., 568. [5] Act May 16, 1857, P. L., 549.
[6] Act March 8, 1862, P. L., 79. [7] Ord. June 20, 1863, page 187.

measure all repaving of cartways;[1] and he was forbidden to give stakes for paving of highways without the certificate of the chief engineer of the water works that the pipes were laid or were not required.[2] The board was given the authority to examine, confirm, or reject all plans of survey or revisions when the same were made by direction of councils; and was empowered to hear testimony and to administer oaths; no street could be added to the confirmed plan unless it was confirmed by the board of surveys; an appeal lay from their decision to the quarter sessions; petitions for widening streets were to be presented to the board and examined and passed on by them.[3]

Registry Bureau.

The registry bureau was established in 1865[4] by act of assembly which authorizes the survey department to make books or plans of the city divided into sections, which should show the dimensions, names, and situations of streets and properties thereon, with the city numbers, and who were the owners, with such a succession of blank columns as would permit the names of future owners to be entered therein, with dates of transfer, and with index for recording such names alphabetically. In order to keep up this plan it was made the duty of every buyer and seller of property to report conveyances to the survey department, and on default it was made the duty of the recorder to supply the omission; the same duty was imposed on devisees and heirs, and on the register of wills and sheriff. Owners of property and members of the bar could examine records free of charge.[5]

Building Inspectors.

Sec. 22. The act of April 27, 1852,[6] gave councils power to prescribe such regulations as they deemed needful in the

[1] Ord. May 12, 1864, page 212. [2] Ord. May 23, 1864, page 222.
[3] Act June 6, 1871, P. L., 1353.
[4] Act March 14, 1865, P. L., 321; see ord. March 26, 1865, page 196; act March 29, 1867, P. L., 600; ord. May 26, 1865, page 196.
[5] Ord. December 22, 1870, page 522. [6] P. L., 442.

construction of buildings, in order to protect and insure the health and safety of the citizens; although without such legislative action it might be safely assumed that such authority was inherent in their general police powers at common law. The main provisions of the act of 1852 were supplied the year after consolidation by an act[1] which prohibited the erection of new buildings on streets less than twenty feet wide, and directed that each new building should have an open space, either at the side or back, equal to twelve square feet; it provided for two building inspectors, to be appointed by the common pleas court, who must be either experienced bricklayers or carpenters,[2] and who were authorized to appoint two deputies respectively. Their term was for two years, and the city was divided into two districts; their duties were to inspect each house in process of erection, and see that the building was according to law; that the materials were suitable and work substantial, and to examine the foundations; they might repeat their visits if necessary; and on application furnished certificates that the building was conformable to law. They gave permits for the erection of buildings, and were paid by fees for permits and inspection. The thickness of walls was prescribed according to size and nature of building; penalties for violation of law were also prescribed; they were to notify owners or contractors of violations, and could apply to court for injunction; it was made the duty of the sheriff to enforce the decrees of the court.

It was also the duty of the inspectors to examine party-walls and pass on the fitness of the same;[3] to examine and condemn dangerous buildings or order alteration thereof; appeal lying to the board, and the action of the board being enforced by the court;[4] to examine flues;[5] to perform the duties of fence viewers imposed by act of March 11, 1862, on surveyors.[6] On information of inspectors or police, that any person was erecting an oriel window, it was made the duty

[1] Act April 21, 1855, P. L., 264. [2] Act May 7, 1855, P. L., 468.
[3] Act May 20, 1857, P. L., 590. [4] Act April 11, 1856, P. L., 319.
[5] Act February 23, 1870, P. L., 218. [6] Act May 6, 1870, P. L., 1303.

of the mayor or city solicitor to take steps to restrain the erection, or to cause its removal.[1]

By act of 1858 there were three inspectors appointed (one by the common pleas, one by the supreme court, and one by councils) for a term of three years.[2] Houses were required to be numbered on a system provided for by ordinance;[3] north and south of Market street and east of the river Delaware being initial points.

WATER DEPARTMENT.

SEC. 23. After consolidation the water department was reorganized with the other departments.[4] Councils elected the chief engineer, who held office until his successor was elected at the annual election, and had charge of the department. The subordinate officers were, registrar, who made the assessments and received the water-rents; purveyors, clerks, messengers, and inspectors, who were all appointed by the chief, with consent of select council. The joint standing committee had supervision over all the transactions and operations of the chief and other officers. All contracts, estimates, plans, bills, &c. were to be submitted to them for approval before action should be taken. An ordinance in the same year[5] made water-rents payable at the register's office annually in advance in January; added a penalty after July, and ordered that ferrules be detached on September 1 for non-payment. The expense of laying water-pipe was declared to be a lien; and no permit for the use of water was allowed till the charge was paid.[6]

The act of 1866 gave the city power to purchase and take such land as was necessary to collect and purify the water of the city, and prescribed a penalty for injury to the pipes and aqueducts.[7] Warrants were signed by the chief, who

---

[1] Ord. June 24, 1881, page 176. [2] Act April 13, 1858, P. L., 244.
[3] Ord. September 15, 1856, page 219; ord. September 30, 1880, page 144.
[4] Ord. October 3, 1854, page 104. [5] Ord. December 29, 1854, page 171.
[6] Ord. January 29, 1855, page 40. [7] Act April 11, 1866, P. L., 635.

reported to the controller; his term was three years.[1] The department otherwise remained about the same as established in 1854. The number and grade of employés were liable to be changed from year to year. The character of duty which devolved upon the chief engineer required the highest grade of professional skill to meet the growing demands for increased supply upon this overtaxed branch of municipal service. There are one hundred and twenty-nine square miles to be supplied, and a population which is rapidly increasing, and an addition of perhaps four thousand new houses annually. That increased facilities will soon be needed is patent, and to meet this want the best practical and scientific skill will be required, both for design and execution.

The waters of the Schuylkill from which comes the main supply are subject to a prior easement of the Schuylkill Navigation Company. The rights of the public for navigation of the Schuylkill are superior to those of the city, under the act of 1807, and its contract with the Schuylkill Navigation Company.[2] In time of drought the waters were used by the city to run its engines and water-wheels, and the city was held liable for injury resulting to boatmen from detention. The city being a vendor of water, its right to draw water for purposes of manufacturing, for baths, and for propelling power is subordinate to the right of navigation. The use of water by citizens, however, for domestic purposes could not be restrained by the legislature by a grant for such purposes, and the law of paramount necessity would justify the taking.[3]

Necessity for Improved Water Supply.

The question of an improved water supply has been an open one since before the Revolution. So rapid has been the growth of the city that the demand has generally kept ahead of the supply. In 1771 it was charged in a "Broadside" that "the wardens have only dug two wells since the law placing the pumps in their charge, but have raised and expended

[1] Ord. December 12, 1876, page 302.

[2] City *vs.* Gilmartin, 21 Smith, 140. [3] City *vs.* Collins, 18 Smith, 106.

£4000 in supporting and repairing the few pumps on hand." It was further alleged "that there are but four pumps kept at public charge on Water street and but thirty-four public pumps west of Third street, but that private persons maintain, in the same space at their own charge, one hundred and seventy-two wells and pumps."[1] This charge seems to have been particularly galling to the wardens, for it was promptly responded to by another "Broadside,"[2] which protested against the charges of maladministration by the wardens in matters affecting the public pumps; claimed that their cost to the city for the previous fourteen years had not been £120 per annum, and set forth the number of pumps as follows: Private pumps, eighty-six; public pumps, one hundred and twenty. This called forth a rejoinder, which sets out, "That a piece having been published addressed to the Inhabitants of Philadelphia, in answer to 'Observations on the Late Law for Regulating the nightly Watch,' the author of which labors to prove that 'the servants of the public are wrongfully and maliciously and falsely charged with misapplying the public funds,' but has only in peevish humor discovered his ignorance and the arbitrary bias of his mind," &c.; the citizen then goes on to recite how "the watch and lamps were established in 1750 and 1751 and supported by a three-penny tax about six years, when the law was renewed and it was thought necessary to vest the care of the pumps in the hands of the wardens; but as the number of pumps then in the city was not thought sufficient in case of fire, the law authorized and enjoined the wardens to take all the pumps in the public streets, lanes, and alleys into their care, and by and with the consent of the mayor, recorder, and aldermen to dig new wells and sink pumps therein where it should appear necessary; and by law one penny per pound tax was to be laid and added to the three-penny tax, which would raise £350 per annum, as the author of the above piece acknowledges, which in fourteen years would amount to £4900, a sum supposed to be sufficient for

[1] Broadsides of the Historical Society of Pa.
[2] Broadsides, Philadelphia Library, 960, folio 9.

the purpose." Our writer then goes on to advocate the necessity of returning to the private administration of the pumps, and alleges, as a question of fact, "that there are sixty-three squares from north to south, and forty-three from east to west, and that the estimated expense of putting up a proper number of pumps would be £9450."[1] Whatever may have been the merits of this controversy, it goes to show public dissatisfaction with the water supply, vigorously expressed in 1771.

The establishment of the Centre Square water works and their removal to Fairmount has been noted in section 16 of chapter III. These works having been established, Philadelphia settled down into the conviction that she had surpassed the achievements of Rome, and from this lethargic complacency it has been extremely difficult to rouse her citizens and the municipal authorities. In 1856 Mayor Vaux, in his first annual message, pointed out the necessity for better facilities. In 1867 the park commission appointed a committee to examine the question of the purity of the water, and in 1875,[2] by virtue of an ordinance, a commission was appointed to investigate the same subject. In 1882[3] a board of experts were appointed, which made a partial report indicating the imperative demand for immediate increase of the capacity of the works; as a result of this report considerable improvement was made. The final report was transmitted to councils in the report of the chief engineer for 1885.[4] In this report the commissioners state "that at the points where the water for the city is now drawn the impurity is constantly increasing and is probably approaching the limit of wholesomeness." Colonel William Ludlow, the late efficient chief of the department, gave much attention to the matter, and he, with other learned authorities, is of opinion that immediate steps should be taken looking toward the perfection of a system which would insure the city a permanent supply from sources other than the Fairmount basin.

---

[1] Broadsides, Philadelphia Library, 959, folio 53.
[2] Ord. July 5, 1875. [3] Ord. June 7, 1882.
[4] Report of the Water Department for 1885.

In a paper recently read before the Franklin Institute Albert R. Leeds, Ph. D., treats of the "Purification of the Water Supply of Cities," especially of the needs of Philadelphia, Newark, Jersey City, and other American cities. He cites his own experience in investigating the system of England and blue books of royal commissions, and most particularly the experience of London. The whole paper is interesting; but it is with his conclusions that we have to do. He states "that certain results have been obtained throughout England, which it is to be hoped will become universal.

"1. The education of public opinion to such a point as to demand sources of city water supply actually and visibly free from pollution.

"2. The construction of large, and in some cases vast, reservoirs with the object not merely of safety, but also of allowing opportunity for the dissolved organic matters to oxidize and to be carried by subsidence along with the suspended mineral matters to the bottom.

"3. Effectual filtration.

"4. The preservation of the water, after it has been filtered, in covered storage reservoirs." He shows that one of the easiest and least expensive methods of improving the quality of water is by artificial aeration. This plan has been tried in Philadelphia by Colonel Ludlow with excellent results, but only at Belmont was the process applied continuously, the other mains being too leaky to permit of its being used. "At this station the water has been charged with twenty per cent. of its volume of air, and the change in composition thereby effected is strikingly illustrated in the following results, which give the composition of the water before it enters the pumping main and as it is discharged therefrom:

	Non-aerated.	Aerated.
	Parts per 100,000.	
"Free ammonia,	0.017	0.004
Albuminoid ammonia,	0.011	0.007
Oxygen required to oxidize organic substances,	0.133	0.117
Nitrous acid,	0.0008	none
Nitric acid,	0.45	0.54
Total solids,	9.00	8.70"

The English method of filtration by use of fine sands, used very successfully in London and other towns, has been regarded as impracticable here by American engineers on account of the great operating expense. Dr. Leeds is of the opinion that an extremely simple device, recently proposed, which is yielding excellent results, may at least partially meet this objection. This device is supplementing the filter bed or top layer of fine sands by a system of double pipes which are perforated, and the annular spaces between the pipes filled in with fine quartz gravel. His concluding inference is, however, in favor of the city's turning to the pure waters of the upper Delaware, rather than continuing to look for its supply to the Fairmount basin, out of which the machinery of the law for the past twenty-five years has been practically inoperative to keep the enormously-growing volume of sewage, and where, granting the relentless operation of the legal restraints possible to keep out the worst of the pollution, the task of purifying the water from what remains must still be accomplished.

Other competent authorities are of opinion that the Schuylkill basin could still for many years be safely relied on by means of filtration and aeration. The history of the water supply of the city, the various commissions which have investigated the quantity and quality of this supply, are admirably presented by Furman Sheppard, Esq., the counsel for the South Mountain Company, in his argument before the committee of councils in behalf of the proposition of that company to lease the water works and to build an adequate aqueduct to supply the city with water from the headwaters of the Delaware. As to the expediency of this lease, it is not fitting to speak here; but it is to be hoped that the citizens of Philadelphia will not wait till the water supply falls below the line of good potable water before they become alive to the necessity of some action on this grave and imminent question, which should be settled before the actual pressure is felt; a single season of epidemic or water famine would cost the city far more than entire new works, or an aqueduct to the Delaware.

Rules for Determining Potable Water.[1]

Drinking water falls into three classes, according to the degree of organic purity, as follows:—

Class I.—Water of extraordinary organic purity, yielding from .00 up to .05 parts of albuminoid ammonia per million. This class comprises the most carefully-prepared distilled water and highly filtered waters, both natural and artificial. Occasionally river water in its unfiltered condition falls into this class.

Class II. comprehends the general quality of drinking waters. It gives from 0.05 to 0.10 parts of albuminoid ammonia per million, and any water falling fairly into this class is safe organically.

Class III. comprehends the dirty waters, and is characterized by yielding more than 0.10 parts of albuminoid ammonia per million.

Unless the water contain more than forty grains of solids per gallon no exceptions need be taken to the solids as such.

Five to ten grains of chlorine per gallon are not an absolute bar to the use of a water, but only a reason for suspicion under certain circumstances.

If water yield 0.00 parts of albuminoid ammonia per million, it may be passed as organically pure, despite of much free ammonia and chlorides; and if, indeed, the albuminoid ammonia amount to 0.02 or less than 0.05 parts, the water belongs to the class of very pure waters. When the albuminoid ammonia amounts to 0.05 parts, then the proportion of free ammonia becomes an element in the calculation, and the water should be regarded with suspicion. Free ammonia being absent, or very small, water should not be condemned unless the albuminoid ammonia reaches something like 0.10 per million. Over 0.10 per million it should render water an object of suspicion, and over 0.15 per million it ought to condemn it absolutely. The absence of chlorine, or the absence of more than one grain per gallon,

[1] Water Analysis, by Alfred Wanklyn, M. R. C. S.

is a sign that the organic impurity is of a vegetable rather than an animal origin; but it is a great mistake to allow water highly contaminated with vegetable matter to be taken for domestic use. In deciding upon the water supply of a town, the question of the possible presence of poisonous metals assumes great importance, and is far more difficult to remedy than those organic contaminations, which may be gotten rid of completely by proper filtration.

The above method of water analysis, which in one or other of its modifications has supplanted all others, is based upon the fact that the albuminoids or protein compounds, which make up the greater part of both animal and vegetable substances, and which are involved in all putrefaction, decompose under certain conditions in such a manner that the nitrogen, which forms about fifteen per cent. of them, is converted into ammonia, and as such measured. By the amount of the ammonia the quantity of putrescent matter is accurately calculated. Part of the water to be analysed is first distilled, and this distillate examined for ammonia. This is called "free ammonia." If any such be found it represents a change already effected in the organic matter of the water, and is often recognizable as due to animal excretions, and especially to urine. By the treatment of the remaining part of the water by permanganate of potassium in a strong solution of potash, the putrescent organic matter still contained in it is decomposed, and yields a further proportion of ammonia. It is this latter which is called albuminoid ammonia,[1] and which indicates the poison to be feared.

The Schuylkill water falls within the line of good potable water. A careful analysis made in 1885 shows that it does not contain of grains per gallon more than 7.20 of solids, .03 of chlorine, .046 parts per million of free ammonia, .059 of albuminoid ammonia.[2] The Academy of Natural Sciences in 1874 appointed a committee, consisting of Dr. Persifor Frazer, Professor George A. Koenig, and Mr. H. C. Humphrey, to

[1] From information furnished by Dr. Persifor Frazer.

[2] Average from Table II. by Dr. Leeds, Water Report 1885, page 388.

examine the water of the Schuylkill. From the data of these chemists the following table of dissolved inorganic matter at the several stations named is condensed.

	Millionths.	Ludlow's Report.
Roxborough dam,	105.08	135 (1884)
Fairmount,	109.07	120 (1883)
Spring Garden reservoir,	110.08	135 (1883)
River at Belmont,	91.07	125 (1883)
Schuylkill (Flat Rock dam),	91.07	125 (1883)

But the increase of population along the Schuylkill valley would seem to render it simply a question of time when the city must look elsewhere for her water supply, or adopt a thorough system of protection of Fairmount basin, supplemented by filtration and aeration.[1]

Inadequate Legal Protection of Fairmount Basin.

"While the propositions upon the question of nuisances which determine the city's legal remedies for pollution are well established, yet no adequate legal protection exists by reason of the vast amount of interest vested in manufactures which would be damaged. The remedy by indictment has been but partial and temporary, owing to the inertia of councils."[2] The question has come before the courts in various phases, as appears by the reported and unreported cases.[3]

Gas Department.

Sec. 24. The autonomy of this department was fully accomplished during the third period, and remains unchanged in this. By ordinance of 1841 the faith of the city was pledged for the debt, and it was provided that the price of

[1] See Annual Water Report for 1885. Water Supply in Relation to Sanitation. Address before the County Medical Society by Col. Ludlow, late Chief Engineer of the Water Department.

[2] Pamphlet by W. W. Carr, Esq., Philadelphia, November, 1886.

[3] Mayor *vs.* Scott, 1 Pa. St., 309; Kennedy *vs.* Board of Health, 2 Pa. St., 366; Mayor *vs.* Commissioners, 7 Pa. St., 354; City *vs.* Collins, 68 Pa. St., 106; Coal Co. *vs.* Sanderson, 18 W. N. C., 181; *ibid.*, 5 Norris, 401; City *vs.* Dobson, C. P. 2., D. T., 1879, No. 431; City *vs.* Carmany *et al.*, 18 W N. C., 152; Com. *vs.* Soulas *et al.*

gas should not be reduced till the distribution of pipes through the city was completed.[1] The courts have held that this ordinance was a part of the contract with the loanholders.[2] An early ordinance also authorized the trustees to take control and management of the several gas works and all property appertaining thereto then in possession of the city, or that might thereafter be in its possession; and to have the same power conferred by ordinance relative to the gas works built under their direction.[3] They were also authorized to purchase the gas works of the several companies in the districts at an assessed valuation, provision being made for the sinking fund to meet these purchases.[4] The purchases were effected with the exception of the Northern Liberties gas works, which is still a private company. The price of gas was made the same for the different wards; and the trustees were also authorized to continue to light, extinguish, and repair the public lamps, under the supervision and direction of the committee on gas. The location, removal, or use of public lamps was examined into by the committee on gas, who reported to councils for their decision.[5]

The amount of outstanding gas loans was, at the end of 1886, three and a half millions. The case of the Western Saving Fund *vs.* The City, 7 Casey, 175, came up on an injunction to restrain the city from interference with the management of the gas works by the trustees. The injunction was sustained, and the learned Lewis, C. J., held, that a city, in supplying gas to its inhabitants, acts as a private corporation, and is subject to the same duties, liabilities, and disabilities. It cannot impair the obligation of contracts entered into by it in that capacity because it may deem it to the advantage of the city to do so. The act of 1854 gives the city no new rights over these works, nor can the city interfere with the trustees in their control and management of the works. This case was decided in December, 1854, and gives

---

[1] Ord. June 17, 1841. [2] Saving Fund *vs.* City, 7 Casey, 185.
[3] Ord. March 20, 1855, page 111.
[4] Ord. May 10, 1858, page 194. [5] Ord. March 25, 1872, page 106.

a clear and concise statement of the history of the gas trust up to that time.

Again, in Hacker *vs.* City, 6 Phila., 94, it was held that the gas works are not a department of the city, within the meaning of the act of May 13, 1856, and that that act does not contemplate the establishment by ordinance of department regulations as to appointment of clerks, &c.

But in more recent cases, such as Wheeler *vs.* City, 77 Pa. St., 338, and Laughlin *vs.* Newlin, 17 W. N. C., 268, Com. *vs.* Culp, 42 Leg. Int., 288, the courts hold that while the trustees are intrusted with certain special duties in the interest of certain persons who have advanced money, whatever difference of opinion may have existed at one time, it cannot now be said that the gas works have any separate entity. They resemble the water works and Fairmount Park. Apart from the relations and functions of the trustees as such, the gas works may be considered as property belonging to the city, and operated not for the purpose of speculation, but to promote the comfort of the whole body of the people.

In 1885 the last gas loan created in 1855, under the provisions and subject to the obligations of the ordinance of 1841, was paid off, and a surplus of nearly $2,000,000 remained in the hands of the trustees. Councils by ordinance of June 16, 1885, directed the trustees to pay the same to the city treasurer. The commissioners of the sinking fund intervened and claimed that the money so accruing should be covered into the sinking fund under the terms of the ordinance creating them. The question came before the court on a bill in equity, and Thayer, P. J., delivered an able and exhaustive opinion bearing on the relations of the trust to its creditors or loanholders, and to the sinking fund of the city, and held, that the sinking funds established by various ordinances prior to that of March 29, 1859, for the payment of gas loans negotiated under said ordinances are not a part of the sinking fund of the city of Philadelphia, within the meaning of the act of March 13, 1857, and therefore the surplus of such sinking funds remaining in the hands of the trustees, after payment of such loans, is payable by the trustees to the city treasurer, and not to the commissioners of the sinking fund.[1]

Policy of Leasing Gas Works.

The question of the sale and lease of the gas works has recently been forced on the public attention by several propositions of a syndicate to buy or lease the same. The policy of leasing gas and water works is open to grave question, both from an economic and political point of view.

In the language of the learned judge in one of the cases above cited, "The gas works are operated not so much for the purpose of speculation as to promote the comfort of the whole body of the people." The weight of the evidence in regard to this question seems to be largely in favor of the retention of the manufacture of gas as a municipal duty.

The manufacture of gas is profitable, but it must needs be a monopoly, and that monopoly should be managed by the public in the interests of the public.

Many arguments and much evidence are ably summed up in a paper on "The Relation of the Modern Municipality to the Gas Supply,"[2] by Dr. James, of the University of Pennsylvania. The importance of the best service of light and water to a great city, considered both in a sanitary and police point of view, is so great as to seem to lay an imperative veto against any municipality parting with the paramount control of such supply. It would, indeed, seem to be a franchise which a city should be forbidden to part with. As Professor James has pithily said: "To hand over the business to private management is simply to make sure of retaining all the abuses which inhere in the public service, with no hope whatever that any of the advantages which may flow from efficient public management shall ever be attained." The possible advantages of public management,

---

[1] Gardner *vs.* Phila., 42 Leg. Int., 520.

[2] Published by The American Economic Association, July, 1886.

the certain evils of a private management, are not simply the subjects of ingenious argument, but are capable of absolute demonstration from the experience of a hundred towns at home and abroad, where both methods have been tried. To quote again from Prof. James, "The conclusion of the whole matter is, that the best form of management of the gas industry is the public one, and that if, for any reason, it is not resorted to, the community is constantly suffering a serious loss, and that, too, no matter how successful the business may seem in private hands."

Right of the City to Sell the Gas Works.

The question of the right of the city to sell the gas works has received a comprehensive review in an exhaustive opinion by Mr. John C. Bullitt, of the Philadelphia bar.[1] The summary of his conclusions, based upon an examination of all the acts, ordinances, and adjudicated cases, may be adopted without hesitation as defining the law on this subject. It is as follows: The city of Philadelphia, through its councils, has the power to alienate its real estate when no longer needed for public purposes; and if, in the judgment of councils, the lighting of the city can be more efficiently accomplished by other means, the gas works property may be sold, subject, however, to the rights of the holders of outstanding loans issued for the extension of the works. And if such a sale should now be made, the proceeds would have to be paid to the sinking fund commissioners, to be by them invested or paid out in liquidation of the funded debt. The right to lease raises another question under the Bullitt bill, since that act requires that all gas and water works now owned by the city shall be under the direction and control of the department of public works.

The Experience of Other Cities.

The experience of the other cities in America, as well as in England and Germany, which have permitted competing

[1] See Philadelphia *Record* for March 13, 1886.

gas companies to lay pipes in their streets, has been uniformly unsatisfactory. The nature of the business renders continued competition impossible, and the consolidation of competing companies has generally been accomplished after disastrous competition, which resulted in an increased capitalization, for which the consumer was forced to pay in the higher prices charged for gas. This has been the case in New Orleans, Charleston, Memphis, St. Louis, Chicago, Buffalo, Detroit, Albany, New York, and Poughkeepsie. In New York, before consolidation, the price of gas was seventy-five cents per thousand feet. The six companies came together, watered their capital from $18,308,920 to $39,078,000, and the price went up to $1.75 per thousand feet. The cities of Boston and Cincinnati have refused to allow competing companies. The cities of Philadelphia, Richmond, and Wheeling, which have for a long time owned and operated their gas works, have done so with more success than other cities on the other systems.

In England competing companies are forbidden by law; and, with the exception of London, Edinburgh, Dublin, Liverpool, Sheffield, Newcastle, Preston, Bristol, and Hull, the gas supply of the large towns of Great Britain is in the hands of the municipal authorities. A movement has already begun in London in favor of the transfer of the gas works to the municipality. The same is true of Liverpool.

The experience of one English town will serve to illustrate the effects of change of management. Leicester assumed the gas works in 1878, with the price 2s. 10d., and a consumption of five hundred and fifty-five million feet. By 1885 the price had been reduced to 2s. 4d., and the consumption increased to eight hundred million feet. The original capital of £635,000 had been reduced £19,000 from profits, £8000 put in as reserve, £3000 expended in improvements, and £121,000 paid over for the benefit of taxpayers.

In Germany much the same state of affairs exists. They began with the system of private works. In 1866 there were 266 gas works in Germany, of which 66 belonged to municipalities and 200 to private companies. In 1883 there were 600 companies, 290 public and 310 private, and even now the capitalized value of city undertakings is nearly double that of private works. Both England and Germany have given both systems a fair chance, and they are going over to the system of city ownership as rapidly as possible. They have tried competing private companies, and regulated companies with practical monopolies, and their final adoption of public control is full of significance for us in America.[1]

Fire Department.

Sec. 25. The act of 1854 gave councils ample authority to organize a fire department.[2] In 1855 it was ordered that the department should consist of all regularly-organized companies, which should, in sixty days, express in writing their willingness to be bound by the rules of the department.[3] The officers were, one chief, seven assistants, and one director elected by each company. This board had power to make rules and regulations for the government of the department, subject, however, to the control of councils; it presented three candidates for chief; the city was divided into seven fire districts; and the board also presented three candidates for assistants for each district, from which councils selected one. In the absence of the mayor and police marshal the chief had full control of the fire ground, and in his absence the assistant of the district, or the first assistant on the ground. Any company might be dismissed the service if guilty of violating the regulations of the board, or the ordinances of councils. New companies were not to be organized without consent of councils; warrants were drawn by the chief, who could suspend companies for misconduct.[4] Provision was made for the investigation of the causes of fire, examination of premises, summoning witnesses,[5] &c.

---

[1] See paper by Dr. Edmund J. James, American Economic Association, May, 1886. [2] Section 42, P. L., 43.

[3] Ord. January 30, 1855, page 52. See, also, Ord. March 5, 1856, page 41.

[4] Digest 1856, page 42. [5] Act April 20, 1864, P. L., 515.

PAID FIRE DEPARTMENT.

It was not until 1870 that the paid fire department was organized, and the whole force and system made entirely a department of the city government. This was done by ordinance,[1] which regulated in detail the organization of the department. It provided that the department should consist of seven commissioners, one chief engineer, five assistant engineers, with an adequate number of subordinates. The commissioners were required to be citizens of good moral character; they served without compensation, and were elected by councils for four years. This board was to organize a department to consist of such number of companies as councils should from time to time direct. They held at least two stated meetings a month, and kept a record of proceedings; elected one member president, who had authority to draw warrants, all bills having been first submitted to the fire committee; and they had power to suspend or expel any member of a fire company, to reorganize any company, and to prescribe a suitable uniform to be worn by officers and men; all officers and members were to be persons of good moral character, and retained their respective positions during good behavior, and for such time as they performed their duties harmoniously with their associates and satisfactorily to the fire commissioners.

No person not a legal voter of Philadelphia, and no person holding office, could be a member of the board of commissioners. The chief had sole command at fires, and it was his duty to examine the apparatus and houses and report to the commissioners. He also kept the rolls of the department, and transmitted to the commissioners all returns of officers and men. Every engine company had one engineer, one fireman, one foreman, and eight hosemen. The commissioners had power to locate and remove fire-alarm boxes, under the supervision of the department of fire-alarm and police telegraph. In the purchase of engines, hose, &c., the com-

[1] Ord. December 29, 1870, page 590.

missioners were required to advertise, and open bids in presence of the fire committee.[1] All appointments made by the commissioners were subject to confirmation by select council. Engines had the right of way in going to and from fires.

Under these ordinances the brave but turbulent volunteer firemen disappeared, and were supplanted by a force equally as brave, and rendered far more efficient by the discipline and esprit of an organized brigade.

Fire Escapes.

A recent act[2] required colleges, academies, hospitals, asylums, factories, tenement houses, &c. to be provided with adequate fire escapes, and made it the duty of the fire commissioners and the fire marshal to pass on the sufficiency. By ordinance[3] the building inspectors, chief engineer, and one person to be elected by councils were constituted a board to regulate fire escapes, with full power to order their erection on such buildings as they might deem necessary. Any person neglecting to comply with the requirements of this board was liable to a fine of fifty dollars, and a continuing fine of ten dollars per day.

In 1883 an act was passed requiring the owners of colleges, hospitals, factories, and tenement houses to keep a rope securely fastened to the inside of each of six window heads of sufficient length to reach the ground, and attaching liability for damages, as well as a penalty for disobedience.[4] This act was amended two years later,[5] requiring improved fire escapes; authorizing the fire commissioners to designate the location of the escapes; continuing the liability for damages; and making the neglect or refusal to comply with the act a misdemeanor punishable by fine or imprisonment.

---

[1] Ord. December 18, 1871, page 493.
[2] Act June 11, 1879, P. L., 128; Keely *vs.* O'Conner, 106 Pa. St., 321.
[3] Ord. December 15, 1876, page 308.
[4] Act June 1, 1883, P. L., 50.
[5] Act June 3, 1885, P. L., 65.

POLICE.

SEC. 26. As the inefficiency of the police force was one of the principal causes leading to consolidation, it is not surprising to find considerable legislation on this subject since that time. The provisions of the charter were comprehensive, and the duty of organization of a department imposed on councils was imperative.

The mayor was made the responsible head of the department. He had co-ordinate power with the sheriff for the suppression of any riot or disturbance; and he was given authority to make requisition upon the commanding officer of the military, in lieu of the marshal, as was then authorized by law.

This power of the mayor was not his at common law; and, indeed, at common law a municipality possessed little power to protect the citizens against even foreign foes. Power of taxation for the support of militia, or for purposes of public defense from invasion, had to be granted by the legislature. During the French war Philadelphia often petitioned the provincial government to take measures for the defense of the city. In the late civil war, also, the legislature passed certain acts creating a home guard, and authorizing the city to collect a militia tax for the equipment of the city militia.[1] Pursuant to these acts councils passed a number of ordinances which are now obsolete.[2]

The experience of the past in Philadelphia, however, had amply demonstrated the necessity of power in the local authorities to call upon a more powerful force than the ordinary police in emergencies.

This necessity was especially felt from 1829 to 1844, when, as has been already mentioned, the city was disturbed by numerous mobs and riots incident to the abolition agitation and other bitter political controversies of the day. The Native American riots occurred in 1844, and the police force was entirely inadequate to suppress them. The military were called

[1] Act April 11, 1862, P. L., 433. [2] See Digest 1869, page 277.

upon by the sheriff, but at first refused to respond. The following day, however, the officers met, and after consultation decided to muster; and a few days later the governor issued a proclamation ordering the general in command to call out the whole division. The immediate result of these riots, and the serious damage which ensued from the inability of the local authorities to obtain a sufficient force, was the passage of the marshal police bill, giving the marshal power to call out the military.

These mobs and riots gave rise to much litigation as to what constituted a riot, and to what extent the civil authorities might go in suppressing the same.[1] In the case of Commonwealth *vs.* Daley Judge King, in his charge to the jury, after setting out the history of the riots, defined the circumstances under which the lives of rioters might be taken in the suppression of a riot; the rule there laid down being as follows: "Rioters cannot be shot down with musketry without any previous effort to suppress them by less bloody and more pacific measures."

Marshal of Police.

By the act of 1854 it was provided that the qualified voters should every second year elect a marshal of police, who was to perform the duties vested by law in that officer. He executed the orders and warrants of the mayor, made reports to him, and held command of all the policemen and watchmen for the preservation of the peace and execution of process; he could also suspend his subordinates from service till the decision of the mayor was made.

The powers conferred by law on the police boards of the police district were to be exercised by councils, who fixed the number of policemen and watchmen for the whole city. The mayor, with the consent of select council, appointed the police.

[1] Com. *vs.* Daley, 2 Clark, 361; Com. *vs.* Wieland, 1 Brewster, 312; Com. *vs.* Hare, 2 Clark, 467; Com. *vs.* Sherry, 2 Clark, 481; Shouse *vs.* Com., 5 Barr, 83; *In re* Riots of 1844, 2 Clark, page 275.

The powers and original appointment of the marshal of police may be found at large in the act of assembly.[1] His office was speedily abolished after consolidation, and his powers not subordinate to the mayor were transferred to the mayor, while all subordinate powers were transferred to the chief of police, appointed by the mayor. The chief received such salary and performed such duties as were prescribed by councils.[2]

The department was organized under ordinance[3] passed in pursuance of the consolidation act providing "that each ward should be a police district; the station houses to be located at places selected by the mayor, having a turnkey to be appointed by him, with consent of select council."

He was to appoint in the same manner one lieutenant and two sergeants for each district. The force was to consist of eight hundred and twenty men, exclusive of officers, who were to be appointed by the mayor; and eight high constables, who should be in attendance at the marshal's office. Rules and regulations for the force were to be prescribed by the mayor, subject to the approval of councils. Councils were to elect an alderman to be a police or committing magistrate in each district, except the first and twenty-fourth, which had two, who attended daily at their offices and kept dockets. Police officers were forbidden to engage in any other business. By subsequent acts and ordinances additional duties, powers, and privileges were conferred on this department.

Policemen were allowed to receive gratuities or rewards for extra services, provided the same were not asked for or promised before the service rendered. It was made the duty of policemen to serve writs of summons and *capias* for violation of all penal and criminal acts and ordinances issued by the mayor or aldermen, &c.[4]

An ordinance[5] in the same year reorganized the department, divided the city into sixteen districts, with a station

[1] Act May 3, 1850, P. L., 666. [2] Act May 13, 1856, P. L., 567.
[3] Ord. July 28, 1854, page 38. [4] Act April 21, 1855, P. L., 269.
[5] Ord. November 15, 1855, page 248.

house in each ward; allowed each district a lieutenant and two sergeants; and reduced the rank and file of the force to six hundred and fifty men, with eight high constables as before; the powers of the mayor were left as before; and one magistrate was to be elected by councils for each district, the other provisions remaining substantially the same. Subsequently the number of police districts was increased to eighteen, and the mayor was authorized to arrange the boundaries. The number was subsequently increased to twenty-four; additional patrolmen were added from time to time, and a class known as substitutes created.[1] A detective police force was established in 1859,[2] to consist of one chief and eight subordinates, to be drawn from the force; and about the same time the mayor was empowered to add to the present force one lieutenant and ten patrolmen, who constituted the river and harbor police, being divided into two boat crews, and also one sergeant and eight patrolmen as a park police. From time to time additions were made to the force, until at length it numbered twelve hundred men,[3] while the harbor police consisted of twenty-six officers, one lieutenant, and two sergeants.

All police station houses were placed under charge of the mayor.[4] The superior officers of the police co-operated with the chief engineer at fires in reference to all matters connected with the management of the conflagration.[5] In all cases of arrest made by any officer it was his duty to take the person so arrested to the nearest alderman or magistrate for hearing, except when the arrest was made for intoxication, and then to the nearest station house.[6] The mayor was given authority to invest private watchmen with powers of policemen for the arrest of vagrants and offenders;[7] and officers were authorized to arrest on view of breach of ordinance without warrant.[8]

[1] Ord. May 11, 1865, page 191.
[2] Ord. April 29, 1859, page 235.
[3] Ord. January 18, 1877, page 31.
[4] Ord. December 7, 1867, page 370.
[5] Ord. January 3, 1855, page 46.
[6] Act April 20, 1869, P. L., 1181.
[7] Act April 26, 1870, P. L., 1269.
[8] Act May 3, 1876, P. L., 99.

The police districts were subsequently divided into four divisions, for each of which the mayor appointed a captain[1] whose duty it was to see that the ordinances were enforced, that station houses and other property were in good condition, and to report to the mayor as from time to time required.

The reserve corps was first institued by Mayor Vaux. It consisted of not less than fifty men, and was commanded by a lieutenant and sergeant and reserved for special duty; it generally consisted of a superior body of men, and, together with the river and harbor police, and special officers detailed for service at the mayor's office, was taken from the body of the force. The mayor was also authorized to appoint telegraph[2] operators, engineers, and firemen for service on the Delaware and Schuylkill police tugs.[3]

The executive force, exclusive of captains, lieutenants, and sergeants, was finally made to consist of twelve hundred and fifty men, and the pay two dollars and thirty-eight cents per *diem*, with forty dollars for clothing.[4] This force was too small in proportion to the amount of territory which had to be guarded.

Police and Fire-Alarm Department.

This department was organized in 1868; the head, called the superintendent, was elected for three years by councils; appointed his subordinates, and drew all warrants for appropriations. The mayor had full and absolute control of the wires for the transmission of messages for municipal purposes.[5]

The Poor.

Sec. 27. After consolidation the guardians of the poor were made elective, one by the voters of each ward; except that the existing arrangements for the support of the poor in

---

[1] Ord. November 24, 1871, page 465.

[2] Ord. October 8, 1874, page 297. [3] Ord. October 26, 1874, page 315.

[4] See Appendix of J. of C. C., 1884, page 216.

[5] Ord. December 9, 1868, page 470.

the boroughs of Roxborough, Germantown, Bristol, Frankford, Whitehall, Oxford, Lower Dublin, Delaware, Moreland, and Byberry were to remain as before until altered by councils; and while these provisions continued no elections were to be made in the Twenty-first, Twenty-second, and Twenty-third wards.

The board of guardians met at the almshouse and elected a president and other officers. The estates of the old guardians were vested in the city, subject to all trusts; the new board of guardians was invested with the powers of the old, subject to existing laws; all money formerly payable to guardians was to be paid to the city treasurer, and all money expended for the purposes of the poor was to be paid by the treasurer upon orders under appropriations regularly made by councils.[1] By ordinance,[2] in the following year, to organize this department, the guardians were empowered to take charge of the poor of the city, except in certain rural districts, and the board were authorized to appoint necessary officers and agents, and remove them at pleasure; fix salaries, make rules and regulations; make return of all moneys collected to the controller, and pay the same to the treasurer; to have possession of the almshouse building and the Seventh street office, and to administer the trusts vested in the late corporation of the guardians of the poor. They were directed to report annually to councils an estimate of expenses and receipts; to keep accounts with the poor districts of Philadelphia; to have warrants drawn by the president of the board, and receipts taken therefor.

This board was abolished by act of assembly, which, retaining the saving clause as to certain districts, directed that the board should organize as before, but be appointed as follows: Three by the district court, three by the common pleas, and three by councils, one each year for three years. In case of vacancy the appointing power was to fill such vacancy. Guardians were exempted from military and juror duty.[3]

---

[1] Act of consolidation. [2] March 8, 1855, Digest 1856, page 483.
[3] Act April 7, 1859, P. L., 400.

The election of the guardians was finally placed with councils, who elected four persons annually to serve three years, the minority party being represented.[1]

The guardians were invested, by act of assembly, with power to institute proceedings for desertion.[2] A pauper gained a settlement by being rated and paying either county or poor tax,[3] or by contract of hiring,[4] or by renting,[5] and the decision of the quarter sessions as to settlement is final. The board of guardians of the poor was but a department of the city, and as such was subject to the act of 1858, and could not make a contract which would bind the city, unless an appropriation sufficient to pay the same had previously been made by councils.[6]

The Twenty-first and Twenty-second wards have their own poor-houses, support their own poor, and have a rebate on their taxes of about seven cents.

Inspectors of Prisons.

Sec. 28. Inspectors of the county prisons by the act of consolidation were placed under the supervision of councils, and were elected by the voters of the wards. Soon afterwards, however, the inspectors were appointed by the courts for the term of one year; and members of the bar and clerks of the court were rendered ineligible.[7] The inspectors were forbidden to contract bills for refreshment to city officers, and were required to pay all money to the city treasurer. They had authority to make rules for the government of the prison; they might send prisoners ill with contagious diseases to the small-pox hospital;[8] and were required to send certificate of prisoners' deaths to the board of health;[9] they were authorized to discharge prisoners at the end of their term, and give

[1] Act June 2, 1871, P. L., 1316. [2] Act April 7, 1859, P. L., 400.
[3] Directors *vs.* Guardians, 5 S. & R., 417. [4] Overseers of Tioga *vs.* Overseers of Lawrence, 2 W., 44. [5] Allegheny City *vs.* Townships, 2 H., 138. [6] Matthews *vs.* City, 12 N., 147.
[7] Act May 13, 1856, P. L., 567. [8] Ord. May 19, 1866, page 162.
[9] Act March 29, 1819, 7 Smith, 219.

them a certificate of good character;[1] and they were also authorized to furnish the convicts with tobacco.[2]

Board of Port Wardens.

Sec. 29. By the act of 1854 the port wardens, sixteen in number, were elected eight each year, for two years; the master warden was appointed by the governor for three years; councils were to fix the wharf line, and the wardens performed the duties then required by law. By the acts of May 20 and March 31, 1864, one member from Bristol and one from Chester were added. The chief engineer, at the request of the port wardens, was directed to make a map of the river front; and captains of vessels were to enter and clear at the wardens' office. The harbor master and port wardens each received the sum of $2500, to be paid by the State treasurer.[3]

The board of port wardens was made a department of the city by ordinance in 1870;[4] warrants were to be drawn by the president; all receipts were paid to the city treasurer, and amounts were audited by the controller. By a later ordinance[5] it was provided that nominations for port wardens should be made in duplicate by the board of trade, commercial exchange, and maritime exchange, from which number, two at least, councils elected. The board of wardens issued pilot licenses, and took oath to support the Constitutions of the United States and Pennsylvania.[6]

Harbor Master.

By the act of March 29, 1803, a harbor master was to be appointed by the governor. He was to enforce all laws, regulations, and ordinances of the State, port wardens, and city for cleansing docks, preventing nuisances, &c. regulating, the landing of vessels, and to compel captains of ships to

---

[1] Act May 1, 1861, P. L., 462. [2] Act June 8, 1874, P. L., 278.
[3] Act May 20, 1864, P. L., 908. [4] Ord. March 26, 1870, page 170.
[5] December 31, 1878, page 326. [6] Act May 14, 1861, P. L., 745.

accommodate each other; he was to be paid by fees of vessels coming into port. There have been fifty-four acts passed by the legislature in relation to the port since the act of 1803;[1] but in this and the preceding chapter their relation to the corporation has been sufficiently set out.

Board of Health.

Sec. 30. Under the act of 1854 each ward was to elect a member of the board of health; its estates were vested in the city, and appropriations to it were made by councils, and all laws governing the board were to remain in force. The board of health was incorporated in 1818.[2] Its members, eleven in number, were elected six by councils of the old city; two by the commissioners of the district of Northern Liberties; one by the commissioners of Penn township; one by the commissioners of Southwark; and one by the commissioners of Moyamensing. It was granted power to make rules and regulations regarding the Lazaretto, and vessels and cargoes detained; for the health office, public hospitals, and for the mode of examining and visiting vessels, persons, and houses. It had power to appoint officers and servants necessary to attend the health office, the Lazaretto, and city hospital, but the governor appointed the Lazaretto physician. The captains of incoming vessels were to present certificates at the health office within twenty-four hours. The duties of the health officer and port physician were defined in detail by the act of 1818. The health officer, port physician, and quarantine master were also appointed by the governor. The buildings near Bush Hill were declared to be a public hospital for persons infected with contagious diseases; it is now known, since its removal to its present location near Germantown Junction, as the small-pox hospital. A number of supplements to this act were passed regulating divers matters of detail prior to consolidation. Since that time

[1] Laws relative to board of wardens, &c., compiled by A. P. Colesberry, Esq., Harrisburg, 1878.

[2] Act January 29th, 1818, 7 Smith, page 5.

the substance of the more important laws and, ordinances will be sufficient to give a clear idea of the scope of this department.

Councils were authorized to exempt rural districts from the provisions of the board of health.[1] Licenses to clean privies were to be obtained from this board; bone-boiling establishments were forbidden within certain limits of the city.[2] The health officer was required to keep a record of marriages, births, and deaths, and to report causes of death annually to councils; a physician or the coroner was required to give a certificate of death and its cause; magistrates, clerks, or the keeper of the records of any religious or other society were required to make return of marriages; midwives were likewise required to make return of births.[3]

By the act of 1859[4] the board consisted of twelve reputable citizens, appointed for the term of three years: three by the court of common pleas, three by select council, three by common council, and three by the district court. These elected a president and other officers; all prior laws not inconsistent therewith were to remain in force; all moneys payable to the board were required to be paid into the city treasury; and all moneys paid on account of its expenses were paid by the treasurer upon orders drawn only upon appropriations regularly made by councils. No contract was binding on the city unless a warrant was issued, and countersigned by such officer as councils directed, and such officer gave bonds.[5] The board could remove nuisances from unoccupied premises and from the streets, and the expense of such removal was made a lien; and all debts due the board were collected by the same power as that conferred on the receiver of taxes.[6] It has been the construction of councils that the board of health was only authorized to employ the fund granted for removal of nuisances, in abating nuisances on private property, where a lien

---

[1] Act March 16, 1855, P. L., 89. [2] Act May 2, 1855, P. L., 391.
[3] Act March 8, 1860, P. L., 130. [4] Act April 7, 1859, P. L., 402.
[5] Act April 21, 1858, P. L., 386; Parker *vs.* City, 11 N., 401.
[6] Act April 16, 1866, P. L., 946.

could be filed. The nuisances on the highways, it was contended, could only be removed by the contractors for cleaning the streets. The board of health frequently claimed the larger interpretation of their powers, but the matter has not been tested in the courts, and the interpretation of councils, as they held the purse-strings, has prevailed; though it is a question of grave doubt whether the board did not have the power claimed, under the acts of 1866 and 1818. The board of health had at one time the power of councils in regard to street cleaning, removing ashes, garbage, &c.; might enter into contracts therefor; and on default of contractor might order streets cleaned and draw on treasury.[1] But these duties of the board, as to the cleansing of streets, &c., were subsequently transferred to the highway department.[2]

The board may investigate and search for nuisances upon complaint of two citizens, having first obtained a warrant from a magistrate.[3] All contracts and recoveries made by the board were required to be in the name and for the use of the city of Philadelphia, and the authority of the city corporation over the board of health, as a department of the city, was recognized and emphatically affirmed.[4]

At the time of the transfer of the street-cleaning from the board of health to the highway department the contracts for the year had been given out by the board, and a bill in equity was brought on behalf of the contractors to restrain the city and chief commissioner of highways from annulling the contracts and awarding the same to others, on the ground that councils had transcended the powers to them granted by the act of May 19, 1874, section 1, which conferred on councils the power to reorganize all the departments. The bill, however, was dismissed by the court of common pleas, which ruling was sustained by the supreme court.[5]

---

[1] Act March 18, 1869, P. L., 397.

[2] Act May 19, 1874; Ord. December 22, 1881.

[3] Ord. May 19, 1866, page 162.

[4] Act March 16, 1855, P. L., 91.

[5] O'Rourke *vs.* City, C. P., No. 3, D. T. 1881, not reported.

Markets and City Property.

Sec. 31. The consolidation was followed by a transfer of the property of the several townships, districts, and corporations to the city of Philadelphia.[1] The ordinance organizing the department of city property was passed the same year,[2] and the head of the department was a commissioner elected annually by councils. He was charged with the renting and care of all real estate except that used for police and county purposes; he was to keep accounts and report to the committee on city property and to the controller semi-weekly; he was to pay all collections to the city treasurer. He appointed, with the consent of select council, his various subordinates, such as collectors, superintendents, and watchmen.

The commissioner was required to furnish the controller an annual estimate of the probable expenses of his office, and was obliged at any time to exhibit all books and papers to the mayor, controller, and committee. It was made lawful for the city, as rapidly as purchasers could be procured without sacrifice, to make public sale of the public halls, lots, and real estate vested in the city, not held upon trust, and not required for municipal purposes, and to apply the proceeds to the discharge of the city debt.[3]

Wharves and Landings.

A separate department for wharves and landings was organized by ordinance.[4] Its head was a superintendent, elected by councils; it was his duty to superintend the erection and repairs of wharves; to lease the same, and have charge of the cleansing of docks, under the supervision of the committee of port wardens. He kept accounts, drew warrants, and reported to the controller, as did the heads of other departments. In two years, however, this department was abolished, and the duties thereof charged upon the commissioners of markets;[5]

---

[1] Act February 2, 1854; act April 4, 1854. [2] Ord. August 29, 1854.
[3] Act April 21, 1855, P. L., 269. [4] Ord. December 7, 1854, page 156.
[5] Ord. September 20, 1856, page 236.

and by ordinance eleven years later[1] the department of city property was merged in the department of markets, under the title of "Department of Markets and City Property." The commissioner was elected annually by councils.

The separate department of markets, as at first established in 1854,[2] was placed in charge of a commissioner, charged with care of all market-houses, and the renting and collecting rents of market stalls and stands. This department, under supervision of the committee on markets, was to execute the ordinances of councils respecting markets.

The commissioner of city property, as finally constituted, appointed, with the consent of councils, the clerks of the markets; drew warrants; reported to controller with estimate of expenses; and paid moneys to the city treasurer. His term was ultimately made three years.[3] Among the additional duties imposed, by later ordinances, on him were those of collecting interest due the city from bonds and mortgages;[4] of causing the State House bell to be struck at midnight of July 3d one peal for each year of our national existence, and on noon of July 4th one peal for each State and territory.[5] To this department was also transferred the public bath houses, under supervision of the committee on police;[6] the city arsenal;[7] the issuing of licenses to hawkers and venders;[8] he consented to permits for fountains.[9] The morgue and public squares were placed under the charge of this department.[10]

The option of sale of city property not in use was vested in the mayor and commissioner of markets and city property; such sale to be at auction, the proceeds to go to the sinking fund; all sales to be confirmed by councils;[11] and the commissioner was enjoined to buy in any property sold by the city under mortgage at a price not exceeding the price of the mortgage.[12]

[1] Ord. December 7, 1867, page 370. [2] Ord. October 19, 1854, page 333.
[3] Ord. May 6, 1876, page 93. [4] Res. July 3, 1868, page 290.
[5] Ord. June 14, 1880, page 82. [6] Ord. September 27, 1870, page 432.
[7] Ord. June 10, 1873, page 287. [8] Ord. April 7, 1880, page 113.
[9] Ord. July 12, 1869, page 299. [10] Ord. December 3, 1870, page 538.
[11] Ord. June 5, 1877 page 151. [12] Ord. July 8, 1858.

Park Commissioners.

Sec. 32. Fairmount Park owes its origin and present dimensions to the necessity for protecting the water supply. At first it consisted of but five acres, purchased in 1812, and covered what was then Morris' Hill. Additions were made of contiguous lands; but in 1828 the area was only twenty-four acres. The Sedgely estate was added by subscription of wealthy citizens in 1857. The Lansdowne estate on the west side of the river was purchased from the Barings, an English family, a few years later by four gentlemen, who sold it to the city at cost. The acquisition of this large territory led to the necessity for its better government, the control and direction having been previously divided between the engineer of the water department and the commissioner of city property.

In 1867[1] was passed the act creating the park commission. By the act of 1868[2] the commissioners were authorized to acquire such other territory as might be necessary to protect the purity of the water; and about the same time the city was the recipient of the munificent donation of George's Hill from Jesse George and his sisters. The history of the park and the historic mansions, which date back before the Revolution, is of considerable interest, but has been amply treated elsewhere.[3] The present area is two thousand seven hundred and ninety-one and two-tenths acres; its extreme length is twelve and a half miles. It contains many miles of drives and walks, is intersected by the Schuylkill and Wissahickon, and presents scenery of great diversity and beauty.

The mayor, presidents of councils, commissioner of city property, and chief engineer of the water department, with ten citizens appointed for five years by the courts, form the

---

[1] Act March 26, 1867, P. L., 547.

[2] April 24, 1868, P. L., 1083; see, also, act April 21, 1869, P. L., 1194; act January 27, 1870, P. L., 93; March 16, 1870, P. L., 451; March 15, 1871, P. L., 363; ord. March 4, 1868, Ord. 1868, page 883; act May 15, 1871, P. L., 873; see digest of laws and ordinances relating to Fairmount Park, by Chas. H. Jones, Esq.

[3] See pamphlet entitled Lemon Hill and Fairmount Park, by Chas. S. Keyser and Thos. Cochran, Philadelphia, 1886.

commissioners of Fairmount Park.[1] They serve without compensation, and organize by the annual election of a president. The park is under their control, and they have the supervision of the expenditure of all moneys; but no contracts can be made unless an appropriation shall have been first made by councils. They have power to vacate any street within the boundaries of the park, except Girard avenue. They appoint such officers, agents, and subordinates as they deem necessary; report annually to the mayor, with a statement of their expenses; have power to lease all buildings; to govern, manage, lay out, and ornament the park; to employ and equip a park guard; to take possession of ground for park purposes, and to license passenger railroads in the park. It is lawful for councils to lay upon the commissioners the care of other park property.

Public Buildings.—History.

Sec. 33. As early as 1837 petitions were presented to councils[2] and a town meeting was held to advocate the erection of public buildings on Penn Square;[3] but although the subject was considerably discussed for several years in councils, nothing was then done;[4] and another attempt in 1847 also failed;[5] but in 1860 an act was passed[6] "providing for the erection of public buildings in the city of Philadelphia." This act appointed the judges of the district court and common pleas, the mayor, and presidents of councils, commissioners to secure the erection of public buildings—said buildings to be erected on any part of Independence or Penn Square. The opposition to the act was instant and determined. Resolutions were introduced in councils that such a debt should not be incurred without the consent and approval of councils.[7] Judges Sharswood and Hare refused to act, on the ground that the

[1] Act March 26, 1867, P. L., 548; act April 14, 1868, P. L., 1083.

[2] Journal of C. C., 1837, page 11; 1838, page 46; 1838, page 54; 1838, page 77. [3] Phila. *Ledger*, February 24, 1838; *U. S. Gazette*, March 15, 1838. [4] History of City Hall, by S. C. Perkins. [5] Act March 16, 1847, P. L., 471. [6] Act April 2, 1860, P. L., 586. [7] Journal of S. C., 1860, page 26.

duties imposed were extrajudicial[1] and against public policy for them to accept a position in regard to which they might be called upon to pass as judges. The commission, however, organized, fixed on Penn Square as the site of the building, and the contracts therefor were awarded. A bill in equity was filed to restrain the commissioners under the act from acting as such, or attempting to carry out the provisions thereof.[2] Judge Woodward, however, dismissed the bill. Another bill to the same end was filed in a few days, which met the same fate. Appeals were taken in both cases and heard together, and the supreme court dismissed both appeals with a *per cur.*[3] Other litigation was instituted in regard to the award of the contract, but it is unnecessary here to go further into the details. On October 11, 1860, the contract for the buildings was disapproved by councils by resolution, the members voting yea assigning the following reason: "We vote yea because we object to the unjustifiable interference of the State legislature with the internal concerns of this city, which ought of propriety to be considered and administered by the immediate representatives of the taxpayers."

The advent of the war served to stop any further proceedings of this commission, which may be said to have lapsed, and the matter slept till the act of 1870.

Public Buildings Commission.

The erection of public buildings at Broad and Market was finally provided for by the act of August 5, 1870.[4] The site was left open to the selection of the citizens at a popular election. Its construction and plans were placed in the hands of an independent commission, named in the act, in which were included, *ex officio*, the mayor and presidents of councils. Any vacancies in the commission were to be filled by the other members. It was made the duty of the mayor,

---

[1] Amer. Law Reg., 569; 17 Leg. Int., 174.
[2] N. P., July T., 1860, No. 29.
[3] City *vs.* Henry, 17 Leg. Int., 311.
[4] August 5, 1870, P. L., 1548.

controller, city commissioners, and city treasurer, of all other officers and of councils, to perform all such acts in aid and promotion of the intent of this act as said commission might from time to time require. The commission was authorized to employ officers and agents irrespective of any control of councils, and expend such sums in the erection of the buildings as they saw fit; and could call upon councils to levy a tax to meet the aggregate expenses for the coming year.

An Irresponsible Body.

The constitutionality of the commission came before the supreme court in 1878, where it was held that "the act of August 5, 1870, constituted certain citizens commissioners for erection of public buildings in Philadelphia, and after authorizing them to make all needful contracts for construction thereof, enacted that the commissioners shall make requisition upon the councils prior to December 1 in each year for the amount of money required by them for the purpose of the commission for the succeeding year, and said councils shall levy a special tax sufficient to raise the amount so required. Section 2, article XV., of the new constitution provides no debt shall be contracted or liability incurred by any municipal commission, except in pursuance of an appropriation previously made therefor by the municipal government. In November, 1876, the commissioners made a requisition for $1,500,000 for 1877, which the city councils refused to raise, and the commissioners then applied for a *mandamus* to compel them to levy a tax for that amount. While section 2, article XV., of the constitution prevented the commission after 1874 from making any contract until an appropriation to pay therefor had previously been made, it did not repeal the obligation imposed on councils to raise annually the amount required by the commissioners, and councils are bound to levy the tax or otherwise raise the amount. Section 20, article III., of the new constitution, providing that the legislature shall not delegate to any special commission any power to interfere with any municipal improvement, is prospective only, and does not apply to special commissions existing before the adoption of the constitution." A peremptory *mandamus* granted.[1]

This creation of an irresponsible board with power to spend vast sums of money has given rise to much discussion and many complaints. Several unsuccessful attempts were made to have the act repealed. It is to be noted, however, that such commissions were not without precedent in Philadelphia and in other cities; and, indeed, the creation of the public buildings commission was in keeping with the system of municipal government by boards and commissions which began as early as 1712, when the first board of assessors was created. Whatever objections may have been made against the commission in the past, it is now agreed that, having gone thus far with the work, it would be unwise to disturb it. The public buildings are to accommodate some State and all the city and county offices.

City Trusts.

Sec. 34. Under consolidation it was provided that all the estates then held in trust by the county, districts, townships, and other municipal corporations should be held by the city of Philadelphia, upon and for the same uses, trusts, and limitations.

The committee on trusts was at first given charge of all trusts except the Girard trust.[2] By ordinance of the same year[3] councils elected managers of The Wills Hospital, and a superintendent, who was the executive officer of the committee; drew warrants for payment of moneys, and made weekly returns to the controller, and reported quarterly to the committee on trusts.

Girard Trust Prior to 1869.

The Girard estate was managed by a joint committee of twelve, six appointed by each branch, whose duty it was to

[1] Perkins *vs.* Slack, 5 N., 270. See, also, the able and vigorous dissenting opinion of Justices Paxson and Sharswood. [2] Ord. July 3, 1854, page 22. [3] Ord. August 22, 1854, page 54.

supervise the estate according to the will. Councils also elected a superintendent, who gave bond in $50,000, and acted as secretary of the committee; it was his duty to collect all moneys arising out of the personal estate, pay over the same to the city treasurer, and furnish a written statement to the controller. An officer was also elected, called an agent, who attended to the letting and care of the real estate; also, an agent of land in Schuylkill county. Warrants for payment of bills and salaries were drawn by the superintendent, and warrants for the appropriations to the city were drawn by the city treasurer.[1]

Directors of City Trusts.

By a later act,[2] however, a decided change was made, as follows: All the duties, rights, and powers of the city concerning trusts were to be discharged through the instrumentality of a board of fifteen, which included the mayor, presidents of councils, and twelve other citizens to be appointed by the supreme court, district court, and common pleas, to serve without compensation during good behavior. The directors elected annually from their own number a president, and a secretary who received a salary. They were given power to make rules and by-laws for proper regulation of their business; to make leases, contracts, and agreements; to perform all necessary acts; and to report to councils, to the board of appointment, and to the legislature; to keep their title papers in a safe place; and to elect all their subordinate officers and fix their salaries. The city treasurer was made *ex officio* the treasurer of the directors.

Vacancies were to be filled by the board of appointment, and members could be removed by a two-thirds vote of the board. Apart from this provision there was no audit of their accounts, no power of supervision or control, and no visitation outside of a court of equity.

---

[1] Ord. June 1, 1856, page 172.
[2] Act of June 30, 1869, P. L., 1276.

Litigation over Girard's Will.

Strangely enough, the consolidation act gave rise to new litigation between the heirs of Girard and the city. The heirs came before the courts admitting that the will of Girard entirely excluded them from any claim of right to the property in question, but they contended that the consolidation act had made it impossible for any one to execute the trusts for municipal purposes, and that, as a consequence, the heirs were entitled to that portion of the estate appropriated by the testator for such uses. The court, Grier, J., dismissed the bill, holding that the corporation of the city of Philadelphia, under its amended charter, had every capacity to execute the trusts of the will of Girard which it had prior to the consolidation act.[1]

Education.

Sec. 35. The evident intent of the act of 1854 to bring home to the people the direct responsibility of all the departments is not wanting in the organization of the department of education. By the consolidation act, sections 20 and 22, each ward elected twelve school directors, except in the Twenty-first, Twenty-second, Twenty-third, and Twenty-fourth wards, where the election districts remained as theretofore. Each ward was made a school section. The directors of each section were to organize and have the powers which by law were vested in the school directors of the several sections of the first school district. Vacancies in sectional boards were filled by the other directors for the balance of the term. Each sectional board elected one controller from their own number, and those so elected formed the board of controllers, who organized by the election of a president and other officers. The city of Philadelphia, it will be remembered, was made a separate school district, with special provisions, to be known as the first school district, as early as 1818.[2] The controllers determined the number of schools, limited the expenses, and

---

[1] Girard *vs.* City, 4 Phila., 413.
[2] Act March 3, 1818, P. L., 124.

were authorized to establish a model school, provide books, and have general superintendence, and examine the accounts of money disbursed. The directors met monthly,[1] appointed teachers, kept minutes, and examined into and reported on the condition of the schools to the controllers every six months; they received no pecuniary compensation, but were exempted from duty as arbitrators, jurors, overseers of the poor, and from militia duty. By act of 1836 the controllers were directed to establish a central high school, and it was declared that the benefits of the public school act were not confined to the poor. In 1840 the controllers were ordered to report to the superintendent of public schools; and in 1846 they were authorized to open night schools for male adults; in 1845 they were incorporated. Later on, the controllers were appointed by the judges, and became members *ex officio* of their respective school sections.[2] Several acts were subsequently passed as to the number and geographical limits of the school sections, and the controllers were required to establish a system of examination of teachers.[3] Warrants for the appropriation were drawn by the president of the board of controllers.[4]

By the act of 1870[5] the board of controllers was changed to the board of education. The directors[6] of any district were to elect principals of grammar schools;[7] vacancies were filled at the next general election. When the board of education determined on the erection of a new school-house, and councils made an appropriation, the erection thereof was in the hands of the board.[8] No distinction could be made as to teachers or pupils by reason of race or color.[9] The discretion vested in board of controllers of public schools in Philadelphia, in the matter of the salaries of teachers, was to be exercised in subordination to the appropriating powers of councils. The ordinance of March 4th, 1861, which prohibited the city con-

[1] Act April 11, 1848, P. L., 526. [2] Act April 5, 1867, P. L., 779.
[3] Act February 16, 1865, P. L., 176. [4] Ord. September 20, 1854, page 188.
[5] Act March 5, 1870, P. L., 437. [6] Act May 26, 1871, P. L., 280.
[7] Act February 18, 1871, P. L., 41. [8] Act February 18, 1871, P. L., 100.
[9] Act June 8, 1881, P. L., 76.

troller from countersigning any warrant for teachers' salaries until a scale of salaries had been adopted by the controllers of public schools, which should not exceed in the quarterly payments one-fourth the whole sum appropriated for the purpose, was held to be an appropriate method of carrying out the intention of the legislature on this subject. The controllers might be compelled by *mandamus* to perform their duty in this respect.[1]

Relations of City and County.

Sec. 36. By the act of 1854 the county autonomy was preserved, and all county officers continued except the commissioners, treasurer, and auditors. The county officers are, judges, prothonotary, register of wills, recorder of deeds, clerk of quarter sessions, district attorney, and coroner; and under the new constitution the city treasurer, city controller, and city commissioners. All these officers are elected by the people at the fall elections, except the prothonotary, who is appointed by the board of judges. It was essential, for uni-uniformity of legislation, that the county should be retained intact, as it has been the unit of the Pennsylvania system since Penn. The salaries of all county officers were fixed by the legislature, and their duties regulated, except such as act in a dual capacity for county and city. Any vacancy was filled by appointment of the governor, while the vacancies in municipal offices were filled by councils. Both classes of officers were paid by the common treasury. Councils were given no control over the county offices (though the controller, as successor to the county auditors, audited all their accounts, and countersigned their warrants), except that they made appropriations for the expenses of the offices. Salaries must come within the fees and receipts of each respective office.

Liability of City for Damages.

Sec. 37. The various questions which arise regarding the liability of the city for damages, for breach of contract, negli-

[1] City *vs.* Johnson, 11 Wr., 382.

gence, and eminent domain come rather within the rules of ordinary law than the scope of a history of the city government; but a few general rules may be of interest. Broadly stated, where a municipality undertakes to do any work which it is convenient for the public good should be done by the city, such work must be done with ordinary skill and care, and kept in good repair; otherwise it is liable to its citizens or a stranger for injury resulting from such defects. Where, in other words, the city acts as an individual it is liable as an individual, but in the exercise of its governmental functions it is not liable for injuries arising from errors of judgment or excess of authority.

Reference to a few of the adjudicated cases will illustrate these principles. A municipality cannot be made liable for mistakes which may be committed by its officers in the honest, fair exercise of their discretion.[1] Any willfully illegal act committed by an officer of the city would be followed by individual and not municipal liability.

It is liable for an injury resulting from the existence of a public nuisance in a public highway, opened for public use, over which the corporation has control.[2]

Where a municipality has undertaken to construct a sewer it is its duty to construct it properly and to keep it in good condition and repair; failure to perform these duties will render the city liable in damages;[3] municipal authorities will be presumed to have knowledge or notice of a defect in a sewer or gas main, which they might have discovered by the exercise of reasonable care.[4]

But the mere omission of municipal authorities to provide adequate means to carry off the water which storms and the natural formation of the ground throw on a city lot will not sustain an action by the owner thereof against the municipality for damages arising from the accumulation of water on

---

[1] Collins *vs.* City, 12 N., 272.
[2] Norristown *vs.* Moyer, 17 Smith, 355.
[3] Vanderslice *vs.* City of Philadelphia, 7 Out., 102.
[4] Kibele *vs.* City, 9 Out., 41.

the lot by reason of the construction of a sewer that was not of sufficient size to carry off surface drainage. Where sewers were not defectively constructed, or left out of repair, the municipality cannot be made responsible for an error of judgment in the construction.[1] To like effect is Carr *vs.* Northern Liberties. An action will not lie against a municipal corporation for neglecting to construct a proper system of drainage, in consequence of which a citizen's store was overflowed from an extraordinary fall of rain, and a stock of goods therein was damaged. A power to construct sewers, given to a municipal corporation by statute, does not impose upon the corporate authority an obligation to exercise that power, nor is it liable for neglecting to provide a sufficient number of inlets to sewers which were sufficient when created, but have ceased to be so by reason of increase of the territory graded and drained.[2]

The test of the liability of the city for negligence of officers is as follows: Where the duties to be performed are of a corporate or municipal character, the municipality is responsible for their performance in a careful and thorough manner; but where, on the other hand, the functions to be exercised are of a public or governmental nature, those to whom they are intrusted, although selected and paid by the city, are not its servants but public officers, for whose misfeasance or non-feasance the city is not responsible. The right to establish and maintain a fire department is a part of the governmental power of the State.[3] The city is not liable for injuries caused by the negligent driving of a fire engine by an employé of the fire department.[4] The city is not liable for the conduct of a police officer who makes an unlawful arrest.[5] Police officers are not municipal agents but public officials, for whose neglect the municipality is not responsible.[6]

An action will not lie against the city for negligence of one

[1] Fair *vs.* Philadelphia, 7 N., 309. [2] 11 Casey, 325.
[3] Freeman *vs.* The City, 7 W. N. C., 45.
[4] Knight *vs.* City of Phila., 15 W. N. C., 317.
[5] Elliott *vs.* City, 7 Phila., 129 (25 Smith, 347).
[6] Norristown *vs.* Fitzpatrick, 8 W. N. C., 459.

of the surveyors in giving the wrong lines of allotment to an owner about to build.[1] The city and railway companies are both liable in damages for neglect to repair the streets over which the railway tracks are laid.[2]

The county was liable for injury done to any person by a mob,[3] and the city was included within the term person which might bring suit for such injury;[4] though, of course, now the city and county being one for all financial purposes, we may say the city is liable for damages done by a mob which it does not suppress. Numerous cases arose under the Native American riots in 1844, and prior to that, in the burning of Pennsylvania Hall. The liability of the city for contracts is the same as that of an individual, save in so far as any one contracting with the city does so subject to limitations imposed on the contractual power by acts of assembly and ordinances of councils extant at the time.

The Finances After Consolidation.

Sec. 38. The financial system was greatly strained at consolidation. The affairs of the old city, districts, townships, boroughs, and county had to be reorganized; and the varying state of public credit and the money market, and the heavy State debt of 1840–1842, rendered the condition complicated. Moreover, demands were made for gas, water, the park, expenses for bounties and public defense, which entered largely into the problem. But notwithstanding these palliating circumstances, the real trouble lay in most cases in the recklessness of councils and the indifference of the citizens, which, year after year, permitted the accumulation of a floating debt, which from time to time was funded.

The financial problem which every city has to solve is fourfold:—

I. Estimating the income and taxable assets, and computing the expenses for the coming year.

---

[1] Alcorn *vs.* City, 5 Phila., 130. [2] City *vs.* Weller, 4 Brewster, 24.

[3] Act May 31, 1841, P. L., 416.

[4] Commissioners of Kensington *vs.* County of Philadelphia, 1 H., 76.

II. Levying and collecting the taxes.

III. Making and supervising the contracts and expenditures.

IV. Municipal debt, powers, and limitation to create the same; objects for creating it; methods looking toward its ultimate redemption.

Estimating the City Expenses.

All departments of the city were obliged, as has been seen, to report to the city controller, both as to their expenditures and receipts. The controller made annually a detailed report to councils, with an estimate of the expenses of the city for the ensuing year. Councils also received through their various committees reports on the affairs of the city. All the reports and the estimates of the several committees were submitted to the finance committee, and its report was the foundation of the action by councils in making the appropriation and fixing the tax rate.

It will be noted that, by the act of consolidation, councils laid the tax and fixed the rate, and the city commissioners then assessed and levied the tax according to the last county assessment.[1] By the same act[2] each ward elected two assessors to perform all the duties which the law "now enjoins on assessors and assistant assessors." At such election all voters voted for but one assessor, and the two highest candidates were elected. The city commissioners, immediately after such election, issued their precepts to the assessors of the respective wards, requiring them to make out and return, within a time designated by the commissioners, a list of all taxable persons residing within their wards, and all property taxable and exempt, with a just valuation of the same. Whenever the assessors of any ward could not agree, the senior city commissioner decided.

The assessors sat in their wards for three days, after giving ten days' notice. The ordinance of 1855, establishing the

[1] Act 1854, section 13. [2] Section 17.

city commissioners, provided that they should issue their precepts to the assessors, and publish a statement of the assessment.[1]

A board of revision was constituted, consisting of the city commissioners and receiver of taxes, which heard appeals from the assessors.[2] Councils were instructed to discriminate in favor of rural property in fixing the tax rate. To the aldermen was assigned the collection of the personal taxes, which they were to pay over monthly to the receiver. City, county, and State taxes were all paid to the receiver. The State tax was transmitted to the State treasurer by the city treasurer.

By act of assembly councils were given power to levy a tax, for municipal purposes, on all subjects of taxation specified by section 32 of act of April 29, 1844, and to provide by ordinance a system for assessment thereof and collection.[3]

Receiver of Taxes.

This office of receiver of taxes was created by the act of consolidation. The receiver was elected biennially by the people; he was to give bond, and collect and receive all taxes and public assessments payable within the city; and for that purpose was invested with all powers already conferred by law; and was authorized to employ the assistance of clerks to afford facilities to citizens to pay their taxes at all business hours. The city commissioners furnished him with duplicate lists of the taxes as soon as possible. A discount of twelve per cent. was to be allowed for taxes paid prior to the end of the year; taxes unpaid by the following January remained a lien. The receiver was to render a daily account to the controller and pay over money daily to the treasurer. He also appointed an agent to receive taxes in certain outlying wards. If taxes were not paid on or before December 30 he was to give public notice, and issue his warrants, on January 15, to any constable to collect and levy delinquent taxes, as in the nature of a distress for rent. The department was organized in accord-

[1] Ord. February 12, 1885. [2] Act 1854. [3] Act August 25, 1864, P. L., 1030.

ance with the above provisions by ordinance in the same year,[1] the receiver remained its head, and the number of clerks was fixed.

Municipal Liens.

Municipal claims for taxes when filed became liens ;[2] they had priority of liens to judgments, but not to mortgages; though a tax was to be paid first out of the proceeds of a sale of real estate.[3] Taxes did not remain a lien over five years unless a suit to recover them had been brought.[4] Later on, the rates of discount for payment of taxes were changed, and councils empowered to alter the rates from time to time.[5] The rate of discount in 1886 was one per cent. per annum if paid before June 30; after June 30 there was a sliding scale of penalties from one-half to four per cent.[6]

Collector of Delinquent Taxes.

In 1870 the receiver was authorized to appoint a collector of delinquent taxes,[7] who gave security in $30,000, to whom were to be given the lists of delinquent taxes thereafter of the year before. It was made his duty to proceed to levy and collect these delinquent taxes; the costs and penalties remained the same; and he was allowed five per cent. for compensation in lieu of all costs and office expenses. By resolution of councils he was to report monthly to councils the amount collected.[8]

It was claimed by many that the creation of this office was unnecessary, for it will be remembered that the receiver of taxes was armed with ample powers for the collection of delinquent taxes, and councils had authority to furnish him with an adequate staff. In 1879 the office became the subject

---

[1] Ord. July 27, 1854, page 34.

[2] Act February 3, 1824, 8 Smith, 189; act April 16, 1840, P. L., 412.

[3] Act April 6, 1845, P. L., 488. [4] Act March 11, 1846, P. L., 115.

[5] Act April 17, 1861, P. L., 354.

[6] Ord. September 30, 1884, page 204, as amended by ord. November 3, 1884, page 251.

[7] Act March 24, 1870, P. L., 544.

[8] Res. November 6, 1871, page 444; ord. April 5, 1879, page 44.

of investigation by councils, and the report of the finance committee showed that, up to 1879, there were outstanding delinquent taxes amounting to $9,795,149; "that among the list of delinquents were many abundantly able to pay, and some holding high official position, many appearing delinquent from the creation of the office; that much money had been lost to the city by the neglect and refusal of the collector to file liens; that the moneys collected were not paid daily to the treasurer as required by law; that the emoluments accruing to the collector amounted to eleven per cent. instead of five, as allowed by law; that the net profits amounted in 1878 to $147,500." The resolution adopted by common council, though defeated in select, was to the effect, "That the retention of all fees and costs in excess of five per cent. by the collector was illegal."[1] As a result of this investigation an act was passed legalizing the previous conduct of the office. A resolution passed both branches of councils calling upon the governor to veto the act, which, despite of the protest, however, became a law.[2]

This act, besides legalizing the previous conduct, directed the collection of all delinquent taxes by sale of goods on the premises, whether belonging to tenants, executors, or trustees;[3] and the collector was authorized to proceed against real estate, &c. All registered taxes were to remain a lien until the tax bill was paid.

The enormous emoluments of this office, and its unnecessary character, at length excited a strong feeling against it, which resulted in the passage of an act to consolidate the offices of receiver of taxes and collector of delinquent taxes.[4] This repealing act was inartificially drawn, and was declared unconstitutional, as being at variance with article III., section 6, of the constitution, in that, by implication, it transferred to the receiver the powers and duties conferred by various acts without specifically re-enacting such acts.[5] Two years later

---

[1] Jour. C. C., 1879, page 646. [2] Jour. C. C., 1879, page 1030.
[3] Act of April 16, 1879, P. L., 24. [4] Act February 14, 1881, P. L., 3.
[5] Donahue *vs.* Roberts, 38 Leg. Int., 137.

another act, drawn to cover the legal objections, was passed,[1] which effectually abolished the office and conferred on the receiver the powers necessary for the efficient collection of delinquent taxes, all of which he practically had prior to the act of 1870, if the provisions of the law had been fully complied with.

In the meantime the receiver of taxes, elected on the Reform ticket in 1882, John Hunter, removed the collector of delinquent taxes, and the question was raised as to his power to do so during the term for which he had been appointed. The supreme court held, "That, by virtue of article VI. of the constitution, appointed municipal officers might be removed at pleasure of the power by which they were appointed; that the collector of delinquent taxes was such an officer, subject to removal by the receiver, and it was the duty of councils to approve the bond of such successor as might be appointed; in the event of their refusal to do so, the duty might be enforced by *mandamus*."[2] Pending the final abolition of the office, the post was filled by an appointee of the receiver, who agreed to turn the bulk of the fees beyond a reasonable salary into the treasury.

Board of Revision of Taxes.

It will be remembered that, upon consolidation, this board was made up of the city commissioners and receiver of taxes; that the assessors were elected by each ward up to 1873;[3] and that State, city, and county taxes fell upon the same class of objects. This system was bad in many respects. As is obvious, there was room for jealousy and evasion between the county and the State. The valuation of property for taxation was based on triennial assessments, made by local officers, who owed their election to the neighbors whose property they were called upon to present for the most onerous of all duties, that of tax-bearing, and to these neighbors these officers had

---

[1] Act April 10, 1883, P. L., 9.
[2] Houseman *vs.* Com., 4 Out., 222; *In re* Tener, 39 Leg. Int., 4.
[3] Act April 12, 1873, P. L., 715.

to look for re-election. This fact and the natural local jealousy lest their county should bear an undue proportion of the State taxation, often induced the assessors to assess property for taxation far below any approximate real value; abundant room was left for individual favoritism; and a higher tax rate was entailed than would have been necessary had it been based on a full valuation. This low valuation and high rate were an inducement and excuse for enlarging the list of expenses which should be met "with money borrowed, rather than by a tax on the citizens." At length it became necessary to alter the system in order to remedy those abuses. In 1866 the State relinquished to the county all real estate for the purposes of taxation, looking to other sources for its revenue; and in 1865[1] the board of revision was altered and improved in its constitution and powers and duties. Three citizens were appointed by the court of common pleas, who constituted the board, with a term of three years, and to them were granted all the powers of the old board. The act of 1867,[2] which was drafted by Mr. Thomas Cochran, who was appointed on the board and had become familiar with the deficiencies of the act of 1865, abolished the defective system of triennial assessments, which was a relic of the State board; it being rightly considered that if the citizen was entitled to have his assessment reduced in any year, the rule should work conversely in favor of the city when the rate of valuation was too low.

From time to time the board was endowed with additional powers; such as power of discrimination in deciding as to farm, suburban, and city property;[3] authority to divide the city into fifteen assessment districts, and to alter and arrange the same;[4] and power to *appoint* competent persons to serve as assessors for five years.

Three dangerous elements were thus eliminated:—

I. Triennial assessments.

II. Elective assessors.

---

[1] Act March 14, 1865, P. L., 56. [2] February 2, 1867, P. L., 137.
[3] Act May 15, 1874, P. L., 193. [4] April 12, 1873, P. L., 715.

III. The cause of jealousy between the county and State.

In 1866, before the new board had organized, Mr. Thomas Cochran, the present president of the sinking fund commission, was appointed to the board of revision. By the intelligent measures introduced by him, a decided effort was made to bring the valuation of property up to something like its real value for purposes of taxation; and in two years the taxable assets of the city, as returned, rose from $159,590,142, in 1866, to $445,563,317, in 1868. Since then the assessment has approached approximately near the real value. In 1886 it had reached $601,001,971. The tax rate fell from $4, in 1867, to $1.40, in 1868; and it is claimed by some that had the rate been then fixed at about $1.70 to $1.80, the city would not have much of its present debt to provide for. Between 1868 and 1877 the rate crept up again to $2.25, and has since been reduced to $1.85.

The board was required to return to the secretary of internal affairs, in tabular form, a statement of all real and personal property taxable for county purposes, and it was authorized to create new assessment districts and appoint additional assessors.

Income of the City from Taxation and other Sources.

Valuations of property as furnished by the board of revision for 1886.

Classified as follows.	Value.	Rate.	Product.	Aggregate Tax.
Full, . . .	$554,579,304 00	$1 85	$10,246,548 63	
Suburban, .	38,006,137 00	1 23½	462,206 79	
Farm, . . .	18,706,174 00	92½	170,365 74	
Total, . .	$611,309,615 00			$10,879,121 16

In 1885 the receipts from taxes were	$10,791,925 66
From other sources, such as collections made by the departments for fees, fines, licenses, rents, &c., the city treasurer received	3,324,691 19

The poll tax for 1885 was	11,392 00
Of the above sums the largest item was derived from water, of which over a million was net, ...	1,797,973 81
Fines and penalties amounted to	45,000 00
The city solicitor collected	165,712 00

Under the head of property, for which full rate is collected, come the items of personal property, on which a city tax is now levied; they are but three:—

Horses and cattle, amounting in 1885 to a valuation of .	$2,905,378 00
Furniture, amounting in 1885 to a valuation of	6,914,346 25
Carriages for pleasure	746,682 00

It will thus be seen that the main subject in Philadelphia for municipal taxation is real estate.

The arguments relative to the advantage of a purely real-estate basis for taxation have been frequently expounded by many writers on political economy and social science. The advantage of the real-estate or Pennsylvania system is, that this object is the most fixed and certain; the tax sooner or later indirectly reaches all other objects of value; it is more generally acquiesced in; is not inquisitorial; does not provoke fraud and deception; does not fall only on widows and orphans, through their executors and trustees, or upon those who are not willing to swear that furniture costing from $10,000 to $50,000 is worth only $300. For a valuable treatise on this subject, as applied to Philadelphia, the reader would do well to consult "Local Taxation" and "Methods of Valuation for Real Estate," by Thomas Cochran, Esq.[1]

Expenditure and Debt.

The power of the city to accumulate indebtedness was, until very recent years, practically unlimited. It is true, certain restrictions looking toward an accurate and systematic control of affairs were imposed, but all to little purpose while the power of debt-making was thus unrestricted. As early as 1856 it was made the duty of councils to state items of expenditure in making appropriations.[2] No debt or contract

[1] Social Science Association Papers for 1872 and 1874.

[2] Act May 13, 1856, P. L., 568.

was to be binding unless authorized by law, and an appropriation previously made by councils.[1] Another act limited councils in making, by ordinance, temporary loans of money, whenever they deemed it necessary, to the amount of $1,200,000 for four months, by a two-thirds vote,[2] and in issuing bonds to defray municipal expenses to the extent of $5,000,000.[3] Councils continued, however, to make liberal use of their power to provide for immediate necessities "by money borrowed, rather than by a tax on the citizens." With the power to borrow indefinitely, the excuse of the sinking fund, and the unpopularity of high taxes, they steadily accumulated indebtedness to make up for the deficiencies accruing each year.

Summary of the Loans and Deficits.

From 1854 to 1861 loans aggregating $1,630,498 had been incurred for the ordinary expenses, thus revealing an annual deficit of $271,749. From 1861 to 1867 the annual deficit was $593,896. It was then transformed into funded debt. For the decade from 1867 to 1877 the deficit averaged about $1,045,172. In 1878 the floating debt was again funded to the amount of $10,000,000, making in all $17,569,458, that had no apology for existence save the failure to collect and levy sufficient taxes each year to provide for the current expenses and the appropriations to the sinking fund. During this time the city warrants, bearing six per cent., were sold on the street at a discount, and many abuses prevailed.

Rapid Increase of the Floating Debt.

The full significance of the above statements can be better appreciated by the consideration of certain figures, taken from official records. On January 1, 1866, the funded debt was $33,837,793.96, and the outstanding warrants for 1865

[1] Act April 21, 1858, P. L., 386.
[2] Act April 21, 1855, P. L., page 264; act April 5, 1867, P. L., 831.
[3] Act March 30, 1866, P. L., 354.

amounted to $1,561,124.90. On January 1, 1878, the funded debt was $61,721,541.70, and the floating debt had mounted to the prodigious figure of $11,893,810.09, showing an increase in twelve years of more than double the total indebtedness, and all the while enormous sums had been raised by taxation.

The tax receiver had collected in this time, ...	$104,531,947 01
Received from other sources, ...	65,253,995 65
Total, ...	$169,785,942 66

The expenditures increased from $10,363,256.04, in 1865, to $15,785,158.40, in 1877; while the cost of the departments rose from $6,281,330.40, in 1865, to $10,580,393.78, in 1876. Despite the new officer for collection of delinquent taxes the record shows $2,415,648.34 delinquent on January 1, 1865, and $9,495,149 on March 15, 1879.

Prior to 1871 the balances in the city treasury rarely grew above $1,500,000, and were generally used as fast as accumulated. After that date these balances were allowed to increase to a vast amount—at times reaching over $6,000,000; and up to 1872 there were but few banks made depositories of the city money, although the treasurer was required to pay warrants when there were $20,000 in bank beyond the needs of the debt[1] and sinking fund, and not to deposit more than $300,000 in any one bank at one time.

So long as unnecessary balances were kept in the city treasury, and interest-bearing warrants were unpaid, so long the city was put to additional expense, for no reason that a business man could imagine. This evil was in a measure corrected by the ordinance of 1882,[2] requiring the city money to be deposited among the banks *pro rata* to their capital; but the great check on this extravagance and disregard of law and sound policy was created in 1879 by what is known as the "pay-as-you-go act."[3] The provisions of this were elaborate

[1] Ord. December 12, 1868, page 499; ord. March 18, 1872, page 71; ord. December 10, 1878, page 229.

[2] Ord. June 22, 1882, page 230. [3] Act of June 11, 1879, P. L., 130.

and important; but the great principle was, that when councils had made the rate and calculated what it would yield, they were obliged to keep the appropriations within the sum so yielded, and to create items for each department. Any appropriation or expenditure in excess of this total was declared to be void. No warrant could be drawn against any item in excess of said item. The only criticism on the practice under this act is, that it would seem more logical for a great city to say rather what are or should be the expenses for the coming year, and then make a rate that would insure sufficient receipts for such necessities, than to follow the present plan of fixing a lump sum to be raised, and then forcing all expenditures to come within it. It is true that the end in view in both instances is the same, *i. e.*, to keep the current expenses within the current income; but in a municipality like Philadelphia, where the income may be one, ten, or fourteen millions, just as the necessities demand, it would seem like better statesmanship to ascertain the demands for municipal improvements and current needs, and then to fix a rate accordingly, than to guess at the smallest possible figure that it is conceived will possibly answer, and then to pare down the appropriations to match. Such was not the intent of the members of councils who originally conceived and advocated the act of 1879, and who accepted it as finally passed, because it was the best measure that could be had at the time. It must be obvious that an iron-clad limit will not always meet the actual current demands, and that under such a system there are very apt to be, sooner or later, annual deficits.

Practice of Controller and Councils under Act of 1879.

Under the act of 1879 the method pursued by which the tax rate is fixed, and the appropriations ultimately made, is as follows: On the 1st of September of each year the controller submits to councils a detailed statement of the estimated receipts, expenditures, and liabilities of every kind for the next fiscal year, and it then becomes the duty of councils to fix the tax rate on or before October 1.[1]

In making his estimate the controller adopts the following plan: The valuation of property is furnished him by the board of revision. On this he calculates the estimated yield with several tax rates. Take, for example, his estimates for the year 1887. The board of revision returns taxable property of a valuation of $628,679,312.

A tax rate of	$2.41 on this would produce, gross, . . .	$14,576,907 36
"	2.00 " " " . . .	12,092,988 60
"	1.95 " " " . . .	11,487,154 87
"	1.90 " " " . . .	10,810,674 74
"	1.85 " " " . . .	10,241,595 80

From the gross amounts so calculated must be deducted an amount equal to the average proportion of the annual tax levy for each of the five years immediately preceding as had remained uncollected at the end of each of the said years. This will give the estimated amount collectible within the ensuing year. To this amount must be added the average annual income, based, also, on the experience of the five previous years, from sources other than taxes (which for 1887 is $4,122,533.75), and the result will be the total estimated income of the city. From this total it is necessary to deduct the fixed charges for 1887, which are made up as follows:—

Interest due July 1, 1887, ...	$1,685,800 00
Interest due January 1, 1888, ...	1,680,900 00
State tax on city loans, ...	100,000 00
Eighth series of city loan December 31, 1887, ...	254,825 00
Sinking fund for 1887, ...	629,600 00
Mandamuses, ...	100,000 00
Land damages Cambria reservoir, ...	294,212 97
	$4,745,337 97

This sum, deducted from the total estimated income from all sources, gives the limit for expenses of municipal government authorized by councils. The councils select from these estimates a tax rate which they think will meet the actual

[1] Act June 11, 1879, P. L., 130.

expenses, and then proceed to pare down the estimates of the various departments, which are generally nearly double what they are allowed. If the estimates of the controller are based on the lowest possible receipts and the highest probable expenses, there is no deficit. If the estimates, on the other hand, are based on the highest receipts and the lowest expenses, the deficit is in proportion to the inaccuracy. For the last few years there has been a deficit manifest by the middle of the year, which councils have had to meet by further cutting down the appropriations as first made.

After the act of 1879 the heavy returns from collections of delinquent taxes above the estimate of the five preceding years began to fall off as they became more closely collected. The surplus at the close of 1883 was reduced to $135,297.37; in 1884 there was a deficit; and again in 1885 and in 1886. Controller Page in his annual report to councils for 1883 says: "I would congratulate your honorable bodies, and the citizens of Philadelphia, upon the successful operation of the act of June 11, 1879, in limiting the expenses of our local government to the income derivable from any source, and as a remedial measure none better could have been devised. In the future it may be questioned whether the necessities of a million people are to be gauged as those of a single individual; health and life may be involved as well as convenience and prosperity. The system proposed and urged by myself and others in councils, and twice adopted by your honorable bodies, may eventually be found as more suited to our municipal business. Under the present system the income of the city is the limit of our necessities. Under the system proposed, the necessities of the city fixed the income, as that was mainly dependent upon the tax rate, which is always within the control of councils. The main idea and purpose of all at that time interested in the improvement of the business of the city was the attainment of some certainty in the sums to be annually expended. Any approach to an abandonment of that idea, and the result, so laboriously attained, is to be deprecated as a return to the chaos of the past, when debt was piled on debt without any adequate system for the expenditure of the money of the taxpayers, as though a day of reckoning was never to come."[1]

DEBT.

This subject may be treated under three heads :—

I. The power to create a municipal debt.

II. Objects for creating a debt.

III. Methods looking toward its ultimate redemption.

MUNICIPAL AUTHORITY TO CREATE DEBT.

The power to borrow money for municipal purposes is inherent in a municipality at common law, and exists without limit unless restrained or forbidden by the statute law. From 1701 the city raised money by loans on every imaginable excuse, "rather than by a tax on the citizens." After consolidation, councils were specially authorized to borrow money for temporary purposes,[2] and, when necessary to defray municipal expenses, to issue bonds to the extent of five millions.[3] The constitution of 1874, however, recognizing the growing evil of municipal indebtedness, attempted to remedy the evil. Its provisions are most important. Section 7, article IX., forbids municipalities to become stockholders in any company, or to obtain or appropriate money, or to loan its credit to any such corporation. Section 8, article IX., provides that "The debt of any county, city, borough, &c., or municipality, except as hereinafter provided, shall never exceed seven per cent. upon the assessed value of taxable property, without the assent of the electors thereof at a public election in such manner as shall be provided by law; but any city, the debt of which now exceeds seven per cent. of such assessed valuation, may be authorized by law to increase the same three per cent. in the aggregate at any one time upon such valuation."[4] Under this provision cities of

[1] Report of city controller for 1883. See editorial in the Philadelphia *Times*, February 1, 1884.

[2] Act April 21, 1855, P. L., 264. [3] Act November 30, 1866, P. L., 534.

[4] See new constitution, and act April 20, 1874, P. L., 65.

the first class were authorized to increase their debt one per cent., subject to certain conditions as to the passage of the ordinance ordaining such increase.[1]

In 1879 councils were authorized to fund the floating debt to the extent of $10,000,000;[2] and by ordinance in the same year the mayor was authorized to borrow that sum at a rate not exceeding four per cent., to be arranged in twenty-five series of $400,000, in alphabetical order, each series to be paid annually, commencing with series A on December 31, 1880.[3] The act of 1879 also provided that any old loans which should hereafter mature, for which maturity the sinking fund had failed to provide entirely, might be met and taken up by new certificates of loans, to bear interest not exceeding five per cent., and to be marked reissued.

Objects for which the Debt has been Created.

The net debt on consolidation amounted to $16,573,614. Of this amount there still remained unpaid December 31, 1885,	$2,305,245 22
For war purposes,	11,650,000 00
Railroad subscriptions,	1,275,400 00
School purposes,	3,600,000 00
Bridges,	4,853,500 00
Water works,	6,500,000 00
Park and Centennial,	8,701,600 00
House of Correction,	950,000 00
Ice boats,	385,000 00
Station houses,	450,000 00
Sewers,	3,750,750 00
Fire purposes,	200,000 00
Municipal purposes,	13,697,625 00
Gas works,	3,749,000 00
[4] Total,	$62,068,120 22

Against this the sinking fund and city hold available convertible assets amounting to the sum of $34,274,766.10.

The aggregate debt of the city reached its high-water mark in 1878, when the debt amounted to $73,615,351.79. On

[1] Act May 23, 1874, P. L., 234. [2] Act June 11, 1879, P. L., 137.
[3] Ord. October 6, 1879, page 152.
[4] Report of city controller for 1885, and Table I. for 1886.

January 1, 1887, it was, total registered debt not due, $59,-286,100; overdue and outstanding, about $83,520.22.

Sinking Fund.

As was shown in the last chapter, the idea of a sinking fund is not new, but dates as far back as 1807. The trouble has been that the sinking fund did not effect its intended purpose, because of the way in which the finances of the city were conducted; and the cause of such defect is not difficult to discover.

"The act of consolidation provided that no debt shall be incurred, or loans made, by the city without a contemporaneous appropriation of a *sufficient annual income* or tax, exclusive of loans, to pay the interest and sink the principal of such debt in thirty years;[1] and every subsequent act repeats the injunction, to raise by taxation enough to pay the principal in thirty years." The constitution of 1874 made the maintenance of a sinking fund a part of the organic law. "Every city *shall* create a sinking fund, which shall be inviolably pledged for the payment of its funded debt."[2] The faith and property of the city are pledged to the payment of the debt; the proceeds of sale of all real estate go to the same object.[3] The sinking fund commissioners were created in 1857.[4] Councils were to elect one citizen, who, with the city controller and the mayor, constituted the board. These commissioners had charge of the securities of the fund, and were virtually trustees for the city and its creditors. It was made the duty of the commissioners to cause the funds to be invested by the treasurer in the debt of the city. Subsequently the State and Federal debt were added to the list of permissible investments. It was also made their duty to keep minutes, and report quarterly to councils their proceedings and the state of the fund.

The theory of the sinking fund has been, that the annual appropriations made thereto, and kept invested for the

[1] Act of February 2, 1854, P. L., 41. [2] Const., art. XV., section 3.
[3] Ord. January 29, 1855, page 32. [4] Ord. June 19, 1857, page 225.

payment of the principal, if based on a computation of compounded interest at six per cent., and kept closely invested at that rate, would wipe out the loan at maturity. This would have been the result could the scheme have been so carried out; but, apart from every other consideration, the necessity of investing the funds received in the debt of the city, which had to be purchased in open market, would naturally force up the price of the loan, and thereby reduce its value to the city as a liquidating asset. Add to this the change in the money market, and the increased value of such trust investments by reduction of the general rate of interest, and we have an increase of this disturbing element. It may be fairly presumed, also, that the provision for the payment of the debt by certain appropriations to the sinking fund was intended to be an appropriation out of an annual income sufficient to pay this item, as well as all other annual charges; but the real facts present a far different state of affairs. Instead of paying bills at the end of the year, the city annually showed a deficiency in the current expenses, and a most extraordinary thing is, that this deficiency almost exactly counterbalanced the annual appropriation to the sinking fund.

This being so, it is obvious that the spirit of the law was not complied with, and there was no provision for reducing the debt. Obviously, on this basis, the city would never be out of debt. On the contrary, the city added to her debt one hundred per cent. in ten years, reducing the problem of paying the debt to a question of arithmetic like this: A tub half full of water has two bung-holes in the bottom capable of discharging one gallon each per minute. A faucet will pour into the tub one gallon in five minutes. How long will it take to fill the tub if you open both bung-holes and turn on the faucet?

Happily for Philadelphia, the act of 1879 stopped in great measure the yearly deficit. The sale of the Pennsylvania Railroad stock, and other assets, has enabled the commissioners to pay most loans as they matured, and the manufacturing of new debt having been closed, there is some prospect of reducing that fearful incubus. In point of fact, it is being reduced as fast as the respective loans mature.

RESULTS OF THIS THEORY OF A SINKING FUND.

To illustrate this point a little more clearly, a review of the recent experience of the sinking fund will not be out of place. At the time that the system of thirty-year loans, with annual appropriations to the sinking fund calculated to liquidate each loan as it matured, was reaffirmed by the act of 1854, the probability—nay the possibility—of the prevailing market price of such loans reaching a high premium like they command to-day could hardly have been realized. At that time the balance of trade was largely against us, as a nation, and capital could command safe investments at seven to ten per cent. For some time after 1854, the city loan often sold in open market at from $88 to $90. After the vast improvement in the assessment of property resulting from the improvement in the constitution of the board of revision, already alluded to, the bonds went up to $105, and since that time have steadily risen in value. This great rise in price, despite the enormous increase in the debt, has been due to a variety of causes. Since the war the balance of trade has set steadily in our favor, the general wealth has greatly increased, and consequently the amount of trust funds seeking investment has grown very rapidly. The limitation, in the constitution of 1874, of trust investments to city, state, and federal loans and real estate mortgages has increased the selling price of such trust securities, and lowered the general rate of interest on first-class securities to three and a half or four per cent. The fact that the commissioners were limited in their investments for a long time to the city debt, making the city a steady and the largest purchaser of its own debt, had a further tendency to keep up the price of city loans; and although the commissioners are now permitted to invest in state and federal debt, the city still remains a large purchaser of its own debt.

As a result of these various causes we have the fact that

the price of city sixes has ranged for the past six or eight years from $110 to $135, according to the lives of the respective loans, making them about a three and a half to a four per cent. investment.

The debt, exclusive of the $10,000,000 four per cent. loan, and of the assets in the sinking fund, to-day amounts to, in round numbers, say $30,000,000. If the commissioners should purchase the debt at present prices during its currency, say at an average premium of twenty per cent., the city will expend or pay, in so doing, an additional six millions. Of course, the figures just given are arbitrary, and used for purpose of illustration—there being a variable element which is incapable of being generalized or averaged from the data accessible; this variable element, of course, being the exact amount of premium paid, or to be paid, at the time of each purchase made, or to be made, by the sinking fund. It is to be regretted that it is impossible to give the prices paid for city loans purchased by the commissioners since consolidation, but these data are scattered through hundreds of bundles of papers on file in the controller's office, and have never been tabulated.

Through the courtesy of the commissioners, and with the assistance of their secretary, Col. Oliver C. Bosbyshell, the following table has been prepared, which from 1879 to date gives the amounts of city loans purchased, and the aggregate of premiums paid, during the six years covering the time when the loans have commanded the highest prices, and when, therefore, the ultimate results of the system were most fully demonstrated:—

Purchased by Sinking Fund.	Par.	Cost.	Total Premium.
Amount of city loan purchased from 1879 to 1887, ...	$9,271,214 18	$11,140,955 83	$1,869,741 65
State loans, ...	658,300 00	724,479 62	66,179 62
United States loan, . . .	1,505,000 00	1,558,665 37	53,665 37
Total, ...	$11,434,514 18	$13,424,100 82	$1,989,586 64

From this it is apparent that under the law as it stands, it is taking about thirteen millions to pay every eleven millions of our debt and it follows that, for every one hundred dollars' worth of debt purchased by the sinking fund at a premium and canceled, the city has really lost the amount of such premiums, which should have canceled just so much more of the debt.

The above result has been arrived at as follows: From the minutes of the sinking fund commissioners the record of purchases for each month has been taken off, and the totals for the eight years given. These totals will illustrate the point in question, as well as if the monthly figures were given in full. It would be impossible to say exactly what has been the average premium paid, as that could only be arrived at by ascertaining the life of each purchase, and its rate of interest; but the results shown are sufficiently conclusive, it being remembered that the city loans were either the sixes or fours; the State loans fives and three and one-half; the United States bonds, fives, fours, and threes. The times which they had to run of course varied, and premium bore direct proportion to such time and to the rate of interest, ranging from five per cent. to thirty-five per cent.

It must be observed that neither here nor elsewhere is any criticism intended as to the executive administration of the sinking fund. The commissioners have administered the law as they found it, and have done the best that the system permitted; but that under present conditions the system is a good one, neither they nor any one giving attention to the matter can contend. It is, perhaps, open to doubt whether the earlier loans could have been placed at par on any other basis; but since the time when the loan has sold above par, say from 1869 down, a plan like that of the United States Government five-twenties or seven-thirties has been feasible, and would have been suggested by a wise financial policy of the legislative branch of government. Since 1866 fully one-half of our funded debt has been incurred, say, in round numbers, over forty millions, created between 1867 and 1879.

That this system is extravagant and vicious, no one can doubt. The credit of the city has been, is, and should be, such as to enable it to borrow money at the lowest rates of interest which are usually applicable to such securities; but it has been seen that, instead of borrowing money at a low rate, it has paid an excessively high one. The question arises, how this is to be remedied. As to the loans already issued, perhaps there is no redress; the holders of the city loans have a right to insist upon the enforcement of their contract, and to require that the tax shall be levied annually and applied in the way heretofore practiced by the sinking fund commissioners. But it would have been very much wiser if provisions had been made in the loans for the drawing by lot of the amount of the bonds equal to the annual appropriation to the fund, and the payment of such bonds as were drawn out of the revenues raised by the tax for this purpose.

This mode of redeeming bonds has been usually followed with success by private corporations.

The bonds of such corporations contain a clause providing for a sinking fund in the hands of trustees, and authorizing such trustees to invest the payments to the sinking fund in the bonds themselves; purchases to be made at par and accrued interest; or, if no bonds can be so purchased in the market, authorizing the trustees to call by lot, after due notice, a number of bonds equal in value to the amount in the sinking fund on hand for investment. After notice has been given, and the bonds have been drawn by lot, all interest ceases to run. If railroad bonds, with all the uncertainties of the business, can be, and are, placed on such terms, surely the bonds of a great, wealthy, and rapidly-growing city,—the obligations of which now command a premium of thirty-five per cent.,—could be placed at par, subject to call, on some such basis, and at a rate not exceeding three to four per cent.

The last loan above described as arranged in series falling due each year, is paid by a direct appropriation. The credit of the city is now so good that any loan which it may be necessary to create to cover a deficiency caused by the failure of the antique theory of the sinking fund could probably be placed at from three to four per cent., subject to call, by the sinking fund by lot. As matters stand now, the debt and finances of the city are well in hand, and the future is not necessarily cloudy, if councilmen and citizens can be induced to meet the necessity for many needed improvements by an adequate tax rate, and can be compelled to avoid the grave heresy of banking on the future for current expenses.

It is but fair to say that, while the city may not always have received the full value of these loans, yet there stand to their credit certain valuable assets, which, while perhaps non-productive, in a pecuniary point of view, are yet beyond price for the healthy life of the city. The war debt is its own excuse, and needs no justification. Fairmount Park is an invaluable breathing space to a crowded city; and the time has gone by when any one ventures to call it the rich man's park. The gas and water works are productive assets. School-houses, like the war debt, are their own excuse. Our bridges, bad as some of them are, were necessities. The criticism is, that all of these could have been had in better shape and at less cost, had the finances and city government generally been systematically conducted on some scientific basis which would have enabled, and, indeed, forced, the citizens to look after the business of their corporation. As it is, they must charge the profit and loss to their own culpable indifference.

Municipal Claims for Paving, &c.

There is much curious learning on this subject. The books are full of laws and ordinances and adjudicated cases which are often not very clear to the court or counsel. Any treatise thereon, to be of legal value, would have to be more extended and exhaustive than our present purpose demands. The general principles, as affecting the organic law, are more easily laid down in a few lines. A municipal corporation cannot, unless authorized by law, file a lien in the nature of a mechanic's claim to enforce payment of municipal charges.[1]

[1] Mauch Chunk *vs.* Shortz, 11 Smith, 400.

Such charges are not taxes within the meaning of the act of 1824. But although municipal claims are not a tax, in the sense that a tax is generally understood to be an imposition or duty for the support of government, contradistinguished from a mere municipal charge for the improvement of property within the corporation bounds, yet it has been held that nothing is more reasonable and fair, than that the owners of property should be compelled, with their fellow-corporators, to pay for the improvement of streets.[1]

Various acts of assembly from 1829 to 1854, and later, have conferred on the city the right to provide for public improvements by assessing the cost against the property owners, on the theory that all property owners should first pay for the improvements which most immediately benefit the adjacent property; the future maintenance and repair to become a general charge. But it has lately been held that this species of taxation cannot be applied to rural property on the basis of "the front-foot rule." The general principles having been thus enunciated, the nicer points must be relegated to the special exposition of the learned profession; for, as to a complete knowledge of this particular branch of the law, the remark of Lord Coke applies most fittingly, "God forbid that one man should know all the law."

Review of the Fourth Period.

Sec. 39. While, as has been seen, the condition of affairs prior to consolidation made some decided step necessary at that time, and while it was attempted to cure the most immediate defects, which were apparent to every one, by the act of consolidation, that act made no radical change in the organic law. Its design was to adapt the machinery of government of the old city, somewhat improved, to the extended territory and increased demands of the new municipality. The evils of the financial policy of the old city must have been obvious to the framers of the act, but they still seemed to cherish the delusion that the mere existence of the sinking fund was an

---

[1] Pray *vs.* N. L., 7 C., 69.

ample provision for the ultimate payment of the debt, and no clause was inserted in the act of 1854 forbidding the city to increase its debt. The evil of the encroachment of the legislative branch upon the executive was also at that time recognized, and an attempt was made to prevent it in the future by the fiftieth section of the act of 1854, where it was provided that "no member or members of council, whether as a committee or otherwise, shall make any disbursement of corporate moneys, nor audit the accounts thereof, nor perform any other executive duty whatever." The same section, however, made it the duty of councils to provide by ordinance for the establishment and regulation of all departments, and decreed that "councils, through the mayor and proper committees, shall maintain a supervision of each department, whether corporated or otherwise," but limited their supervisory power by the following clause, "for the exposure and correction of abuses." In point of fact, however, the practice and interpretation of councils did not correspond to the intent of the act of 1854, for they neglected the exposure and correction of the abuses of the departments, and usurped in fuller measure than ever before almost every form of executive duty. If the water department wanted a pump, it was the water committee which decided on the kind, style, and horse-power; if the highway department paved a street, it was the highway committee which supervised the letting, execution, and approval of the contract. To do any thing, to obtain any thing, it was necessary to secure the ear of the appropriate committee. There was no general supervision of public work—no conference or consultation between departments; a condition of affairs which was bad enough in the old city, and became intolerable when carried into the immensely-extended business of consolidated Philadelphia, that had assumed proportions which demanded the most intelligent system and responsible supervision to obtain efficient service and adequate returns for money expended.

The financial management also became more reckless every year until the city was threatened with bankruptcy. The most noticeable features of the act of consolidation that were new, were the creation of the offices of the controller and receiver of taxes. The greatest improvements which took place during the period also had reference to finance. The constitution of 1874 placed a limit to the creation of the funded debt, and the act of June 11, 1879, by far the most important act for the welfare of the city passed in this period, put a stop to the policy, so long followed, of living beyond the income of the city, and thus year by year creating a floating debt. From time to time the powers and duties of the controller were increased, and the functions of that official were developed with intelligence and precision until he became the most potent factor in the city government. The board of revision of taxes and the tax department were also greatly improved. Fairmount Park, which owed its inception to the necessity of protecting the water supply, has grown to its present size and importance since the consolidation. The radical defect of our system of municipal government, which existed under Penn's charter and continued under the legislative charter of 1789 and was uncorrected by the act of consolidation, has been the confusion of legislative and executive functions; the absence of any centred responsibility in the appointment of executive officers, and in the supervision and control of executive duties. The neglect of the legislature to write into the organic law a peremptory denial to councils of all right or power to assume the management of executive departments has resulted in the usurpation by them of every function not absolutely placed by act of assembly beyond their reach. It may be that the framers of the act of 1854 did all that their own judgment recognized as necessary, or that the public mind demanded or would have permitted at that time. Certain it is that that act corrected few, if any, of the defects inherent in the organic law.

Very shortly after the passage of the act of consolidation, one whose position gave him every opportunity to measure the defects in our municipal system, and whose abilities entitled his opinion and observation, then as now, to the greatest weight, summed up in forcible English the radical defects in the organic law, and pointed out the necessity for intelligent legislation to cure those defects. The essence of the act of 1885 is contained in the second annual message of Mayor Vaux, which, not only as a step in the history of the Bullitt bill, but as an act of historic justice to one of Philadelphia's most meritorious mayors, is inserted here as a fitting termination to the fourth chapter.

"The experience of the past year confirms the opinion expressed in my annual communication to councils on the 8th of January, 1857, that a revision of the law establishing these departments is absolutely necessary. The duties imposed on some of them are incongruous. There is a positive necessity for a supervisory, and at the same time directing, authority, which shall have a practical as well as a theoretical existence. The nearer our municipal system of administration approaches that of our federal government, the more easily can the people comprehend it. The various and important interests which are identified and connected with municipal government, should be managed by an organism of the simplest construction. To effect this it is of the highest consequence that direct accountability, wise economy, energy, simplicity, promptness, and certainty in all administrative details should mark the character of that system which regulates and protects these interests. A revision so desirable, however, had better not be attempted, unless it is begun, carried on, and ended in a spirit of enlightened devotion to the public good. Political prejudices, partisan schemes, individual theories, contesting for control, should be condemned as at open war against the substantial welfare of the people. Any attempt at legislation on this subject, which such motives or incentives originate, will result disastrously to the public, and in the discomfiture of its originators.

"To trifle with the vast complications which create, and exist in, a municipality, is unwarranted and indefensible. Above all is such an effort indefensible when the real motive is to make these great interests, associated under municipal care and protection, the prey of mere political gambling for party aggrandizement or success. The effort may enlist the profligate or unreflecting, but they who will surely lose are the masses of the community. Their self-protection and self-interest will defeat, at the crisis of such an effort, its authors and its objects. Such an experiment is not worth undertaking. If the great ends of good government can be obtained by the revision suggested, I shall be rejoiced, but it is far better that no such attempt be made, unless the wisest and purest influences unite for its success. The government of a large city is a machinery of no inconsiderable complications. Its component compositions are not necessarily in harmonious action. Though constituting a nominal unity, they are segregations in fact, deriving their powers from different sources, and hence holding no direct responsibility to one controlling authority.

"It is unjust, therefore, to attempt to fix on an executive chief of an administration of municipal affairs, so constituted, an accountability for its imperfect or unsatisfactory results. Every sensible observer will discover defects and imperfections, but the cause of their existence should not be mistaken for the inability to prevent their development."[1]

[1] Second Annual Message of Mayor Vaux, 1858.

PRESENT SEAL OF PHILADELPHIA.

CHAPTER V.

THE NEW CITY GOVERNMENT OF PHILADELPHIA.—1887.

SUMMARY OF THE PAST.

SECTION 1. The development of the government of Philadelphia has now been traced to a period when a great change is about to take place. Neither the reasons for this change nor the real significance of it could have been even slightly comprehended were not this preceding development clearly understood. While the institutions of the nation and state have been evolved with intelligence and precision, and have been the subjects of careful historical study, the constitutions of municipalities have been maintained and transformed either with a blind adherence to traditions and theories of government long since antiquated, or in an experimental manner, with little consistent system, and until very recently they have suffered from absolute lack of historical investigation. To follow with clear understanding the long, intricate, and contradictory maze of changes the reader of the preceding pages need not be told requires accurate attention; and such is the confusion and ignorance respecting municipal institutions, that, to make sure of the ground, it has been thought proper to enter into details that, at first sight, would appear unnecessary.

The municipal institutions of Philadelphia, as well as of most American cities, from the very beginning, were founded upon an antiquated system, ill suited to modern times; and, apart from any other causes, it is not surprising that their development from such a source has caused them to be considered the only defective elements in the general system of American government.

During the first period, from 1681 to 1701, Philadelphia, as we have seen, had practically no separate existence from the rest of the county, which was the unit of local government. The charter of 1701, therefore, was not the growth of any previous institutions, but was a new creation, flowing from the sovereign pleasure of the proprietor. By that charter a close corporation was created, modeled after the pattern of the English borough. That constitution was really never better adapted to the boroughs of England than it was to Philadelphia, but was the gradual result of the intrigues of the crown for political purposes. The ancient liberties of the free burghers of the middle ages were at length curtailed, and the municipal corporation was reduced from the general body of the freemen to a close, self-elected body of a few men holding office for life, partly from a dislike of the kings of those times to popular elections, but still more in order to control the elections of members of parliament. The important characteristic of such a corporation was that, strictly speaking, the corporation proper was not the inhabitants of the place, but a close corporate body, existing, as it were, independently of the community in which it was constituted, and possessing certain powers to govern the inhabitants. Such a restricted and antiquated government was, of course, quickly found insufficient for the necessities of a modern city.

As these necessities arose from time to time with the increase of the city, it became necessary for the legislature to grant additional powers of local government. Following the precedent set in England, which arose from the distrust in which the incompetent and corrupt close corporations were naturally held by the citizens, these additional powers were not granted either to the mayor or the common council, but to boards or commissions established for the purpose. These boards acted in conjunction with the mayor and common council and with each other, but were, in the main, independent. The creation of these separate independent boards and commissions had a most important influence on the subsequent history of the city, and was the source of that absence of co-ordination and connection in the various city departments, which was the root of so much municipal mismanagement in modern times. Besides the corruption incident to the irresponsible corporation, there were perpetual jealousies and rivalries between the independent branches of the government. To distribute authority among as many different channels as possible, and to make an intricate and nice balance and division of responsibility, constituted the highest statesmanship of the period. Moreover, there was an utter absence of that division of the powers of government now considered essential—the division of executive, legislative, and judicial powers.

By the charter of 1789, a modern municipal corporation was created, sharply distinguished from the mediæval corporation in these particulars: the privileged class and every vestige of a close corporation were abolished, and the officers of the government were elected by the people; the powers over taxation, streets, and police, previously distributed among the independent assessors, commissioners, and wardens, were united in the corporation, and by them delegated to commissioners. A small beginning of a division in the executive, legislative, and judicial functions was made, and select and common councils became distinct bodies. The position of the mayor is evolved step by step. He ceases to be a member of councils. He is elected first by the aldermen, then by councils, and finally by the people; but with the last change in his election he is shorn of his power of appointment, which is transferred to councils. Along with these changes the bicameral system occurs; and the judicial duties are restricted to the aldermen, who cease to be members of the legislative branch. Such, however, was the imperfection of the machinery of government that the members of councils were slowly driven to taking the power into their own hands, by acquiring the power of appointment previously in the mayor, and stripping the city commissioners of almost all discretionary powers. The government of the city became a government by standing committees of councils, and there was complete confusion of executive and legislative powers.

At length it became necessary to consolidate the city and the outlying districts and townships within the county of Philadelphia. With the consolidation, however, there did not come any marked improvement in the municipal institutions. It is true that there was still made from year to year some progress from the original confusion toward a distribution of the legislative and executive functions; but the institutions of the city, frequently varied for political purposes, or by a kind of experimental attempt at improvement, yearly became more and more inadequate to the necessities of a large city.

The Reform Movement.

Sec. 2. The defects in the government of the city, and the municipal and political evils incident to this system, at length aroused the action of the citizens. The movement practically began with the passage of the act creating the public buildings commission. That commission, indeed, was of the same pattern as the rest of the machinery of a city government, which consisted of standing committees and unconnected departments; but there was a strong demand expressed at public meetings and elsewhere for its repeal. Although the repeal measure was defeated, an independent municipal ticket was placed in the field the following year, which did not, however, meet with much success. The feeling which had been aroused was by no means dead, and subsequent success was made possible by several improvements in the election laws. The committee of one hundred was formed in 1880, and for several years endeavored to reform municipal abuses.[1] It does not, however, fall strictly within the purpose of this history of municipal institutions to go into the details of the political events of the succeeding years. There is space only to consider them in their final results in changes in the municipal government. Many of the evils which affected municipal institutions have already been mentioned, and others will be explained in the proper place. "The principal source of abuse," said Governor Hartranft in his message to the legislature in 1876, "is not in the disposition to do wrong, but in the license to peculate and plunder. It is the power to do

[1] See Report of The Committee of One Hundred, by Thomas Leaming.

that which is done, and not those who do it, wherein we must find the evil." Following out the same idea, Mr. John C. Bullitt says: "If you would strike a real and an effective blow" at municipal abuses, "then begin at the ultimate cause. Reform the framework of the government, and thus destroy that which germinates and maintains them."

Besides the special acts, many of which have already been noticed, the framework of government was thus reformed by two measures of paramount importance—the new constitution of 1874, and the new city charter of 1885.

The New Constitution of 1874.

This constitution, the result of the work of the constitutional convention which met in Philadelphia in 1873, was ratified by the people by a general election in the same year. In interpreting the State constitution, it is important to remember that its object was not to grant legislative power, but to confine and restrain it, as, without such constitutional limitations, the power of the legislature to make laws would be absolute.[1] The construction of a State constitution, therefore, is different from that applicable to the constitution of the United States. The latter instrument, having for its object the grant of certain powers, must be construed strictly—the former liberally.[2]

The important provisions of the new constitution affecting Philadelphia, together with the other cities of the State, are those relative to special legislation, taxation, and debt. These provisions have been, or will be, explained elsewhere, and require no further notice here.

The provisions of article III., section 7, against special legislation were quickly found in practice to be extremely inconvenient, and were given a liberal construction in an important case. By that section it is provided that "The general assembly shall not pass any local or special law regulating the affairs of

[1] Nav. Co. *vs.* Coons, 6 W. & S., 117.

[2] Sharpless *vs.* The Mayor, 21 Penn. St., 147; Weister *vs.* Hade, 52 *Ibid.*, 474.

counties, cities, townships, wards, boroughs, or school districts; creating offices or prescribing the powers and duties of officers in counties, cities, or boroughs," &c., "nor indirectly enact such law by the repeal of a general law." This clause has been so construed as to permit of the division of cities by classes, and they are so divided into five classes[1] for the exercise of certain corporate powers and having respect to the number, power, and duties of certain officers. Those containing a population of three hundred thousand or over constitute the first class. Philadelphia is the only city of the first class, and the supreme court has decided that the legislature has a right to classify the cities of the Commonwealth, and to legislate for them by classes, though a single city constitutes a class by itself.[2]

The Municipal Commission.

Sec. 3. An act in 1874 vested full power in councils to modify the powers and duties of any officer or department and transfer such powers and duties to other officers and departments then existing or to be created. In other words, the act gave councils full powers to reorganize the city government, and had this power been exercised further legislation might have been unnecessary. It is not surprising, however, that councils were found unwilling to rob themselves of their extensive powers, as would have been necessary in a thorough readjustment of the branches of the city government. This power was never acted on in a systematic way, and therefore only possesses historical interest in considering the events preceding the new charter.[3] Governor Hartranft in his annual message communicated to the legislature, January 4, 1876, called attention to the condition of the municipal governments of the State, the want of uniformity in their systems, and the evils attending their administration, and recommended the appointment of a commission to consider the subject, and

[1] Act of May 23, 1874, P. L., 230; act of April 11, 1876, P. L., 20.
[2] Wheeler *vs.* Phila., 77 Penn. St., 338.
[3] Act May 19, 1874, P. L., 218.

prepare such legislation for the consideration of the legislature as would, in their opinion, meet the abuses sought to be remedied.

Among other things he said: "There is no political problem that at the present time occasions so much just alarm, and is obtaining more serious and anxious thought, than the government of cities whose administration in many sections of the country is fraught with peril, not only to the material prosperity of our people, but to the welfare and permanence of the Republic.[1] A glance at the enormous debt and stupendous schemes for public improvements, undertaken and in progress, or in contemplation by the numerous cities of the country, is sufficient inducement to this investigation, and will convince the most sceptical that a speedy and radical remedy must be found to arrest these extravagant expenditures, or the credit of our cities will be destroyed, and repudiation, to which resort some have already been driven, will be the only recourse from ruin. Experience and history alike teach that extravagance grows with indulgence, and the only safe, wise, and honest course for individuals and communities to pursue is to live within their means and pay as they go. A tendency to extravagance began to manifest itself in this country in 1867, which was exhibited most conspicuously in the innumerable propositions for public improvements of every conceivable kind. Magnificent parks, extensive water works, splendid city buildings, wide streets, with new and improved pavements, are some of the projects upon which lavish expenditures were made. In the frequent and enormous outlays of money thus authorized, numerous avenues for fraud and peculation were opened, and officers connected with the disbursement of these great amounts suddenly grew rich, and having, by reason of their control of these expenditures, scores of adherents, they soon became the arbiters of the taxation of those cities. Irresponsible themselves, they aimed to secure the election of irresponsible men to city councils, that their

[1] Message of Governor Hartranft, January 4, 1876, Senate Journal, 1876, page 13.

corrupt practices might have the process of law, and, emboldened by impunity and the supineness of respectable citizens, they endeavored to control, and it is alleged in some municipalities did corrupt, the channels of justice, and shaped its decrees to suit their nefarious ends. Honest men cannot be made by legislation, but to the power for evil of those who are dishonest and careless, a limit can and should be fixed. The principal source of abuse is not in the disposition to do wrong, but in the license to peculate and plunder. It is the power to do that which is done, and not those who do it, wherein we must find the evil.

"The contrast afforded by a comparison of the government of the Commonwealth of Pennsylvania with the government of her cities is curious and instructive. Twenty-five years ago a like spirit of extravagance and mania for public improvements prevailed throughout the State, and her policy was marked by tremendous outlays in behalf of canals and other public works, and was the parent of a debt of forty millions of dollars ($40,000,000), and of the corruptions and evil practices that aroused the people to the extraordinary effort which resulted in the constitutional amendment prohibiting an increase of the public debt, and providing a sinking fund for the payment of the interest, and an annual reduction of the principal."

Pursuant to the governor's recommendations, an act of assembly was passed on May 5, 1876, "authorizing him to appoint a commission of not more than eleven persons, whose duty it should be to consider the subjects referred to in said message, and to devise a plan for the government of cities, and to report the same to the next legislature."

On December 15, 1876, eleven commissioners were appointed by the governor, all of whom accepted the appointment, and continued to discharge the duties devolved upon them, except the Hon. D. Newlin Fell, who, having been appointed one of the judges for Philadelphia, resigned May 3, 1877. The following August, Christian Kneass, Esq., was appointed to fill the vacancy. The commission, as finally constituted, consisted of B. B. Strang, chairman, William Calder, Ch. Gibbons, John C. Bullitt, B. M. Boyer, Charles Thomson Jones, W. R. Maffet, F. M. Magee, William B. Rodgers, Christian Kneass, and Oscar L. Jackson.[1]

The result of the labors of the commission was "a uniform code, with only such variations in form and machinery as the differences in population and the necessities of the different classes of cities seem imperatively to require."

No further action was taken, however, for several years. In 1882 it was determined to make an effort to have the features of the bill applied to Philadelphia. Mr. John C. Bullitt, Henry C. Lea, E. Dunbar Lockwood, and other gentlemen prepared a bill entitled "An act to provide for the better government of cities of the first class in this Commonwealth," and the subject was taken up by the city councils of Philadelphia under resolution of May 18, 1882, entitled a "Resolution to appoint a joint special committee to prepare and present an improved method of municipal government."[2] After seven months' careful consideration the committee submitted their report providing for "A method of municipal government for the city of Philadelphia, whereby the demanded improvements in organization and administration of municipal affairs can positively be attained." The committee consisted of S. Davis Page, chairman; Effingham B. Morris, George R. Snowden, J. W. Patton, J. Dallas Hall, Charles Laurence, Alex. Reinstine, John Bardsley, John McCullough, S. S. Hollingsworth, James R. Gates, A. Haller Gross, C. H. Banes, Edward Matthews, Thomas M. Hammett, and William Thornton. A minority report was submitted at the same time, calling attention to the radical changes in the proposed plan.

---

[1] See "Report of the Commission to devise a plan for the government of cities of the State of Pennsylvania.", This valuable report is out of print and difficult to get. It has been frequently consulted in discussing the provisions of the Bullitt bill, and, in order to save needless repetition, is referred to now once for all.

[2] Resolution drafted by the Hon. Richard Vaux, and introduced in common councils by S. Davis Page, Esq.

In the meanwhile public feeling was being worked up in the press and by public meetings in behalf of the bill.[1] In his message to the legislature, February 6, 1883, Governor Pattison urged the passage of the bill then before the legislature. A petition for the passage of the Bullitt bill was presented to the legislature at the session of 1883 signed by many prominent citizens. Among other matters it recited some of the evils and abuses incident to the then condition of the city government. "The affairs of the city of Philadelphia," the memorial declared, "have fallen into a most deplorable condition. The amounts required annually for the payment of interest upon the funded debt, and current expenses, render it necessary to impose a rate of taxation which is as heavy as can be borne.

"In the meantime the streets of the city have been allowed to fall into such a state as to be a reproach and a disgrace. Philadelphia is now recognized as the worst-paved and worst-cleaned city in the civilized world.

"The water supply is so bad that during many weeks of the last winter it was not only distasteful and unwholesome for drinking, but offensive for bathing purposes.

"The effort to clean the streets was abandoned for months, and no attempt was made to that end until some public-spirited citizens, at their own expense, cleaned a number of the principal thoroughfares.

"The system of sewerage and the physical condition of the sewers is notoriously bad—so much so as to be dangerous to the health and most offensive to the comfort of our people.

"Public work has been done so badly that structures have

---

[1] For editorials illustrating the various arguments brought at the time for and against the bill, see *The Times*, December 21, 1877; January 3, 1878; January 8, 1878; November 11, 1882; May 25, 1878; *The Evening Telegraph*, January 13, February 9, March 29, April 9, April 10, April 12, and April 16, 1883; *The Philadelphia Record*, April 7, April 24, April 27, April 30, and May 1, 1883; *The Inquirer*, January 24 and 25, February 5, April 4, 7, and 11, 1883; *The Press*, January 14, April 5, 7, 9, 12, 13, and 29, 1883; *The Public Ledger*, April 18, 1883; *The Sunday Dispatch*, April 8 and 15, 1883; also, a paper on the "Form of Municipal Government of Philadelphia," by John C. Bullitt, Esq., 1882.

had to be renewed almost as soon as finished. Others have been in part constructed at enormous expense, and then permitted to fall to decay without completion.

"Inefficiency, waste, badly-paved and filthy streets, unwholesome and offensive water, and slovenly and costly management have been the rule for years past throughout the city government."

The memorial further declared, "It has often been alleged that this state of things is due to the failure of the people to elect good men to office. This may in part be the cause. But the real cause is to be found in the system of government itself."

The bill originally introduced by W. C. Bullitt, Esq., of Philadelphia, however, failed to pass in 1883, but was at length passed by the legislature in 1885, to go into effect April 1, 1887. The provisions of this bill are radical and far-reaching. A complete readjustment of the branches of the city government is attempted; and a long advance is made from the heretofore recognized traditions and theories of municipal government in which, after the original model established in London six centuries ago, councils made the appropriations, levied the taxes, and managed the executive departments through its unpaid committees.

The Mayor.

INFERIOR POSITION OF THE OLD MAYOR.

Sec. 4. One of the leading features of the bill is the altered position of the mayor in the city government. Notwithstanding the progress which had been made in the functions of the mayor, from the time when, apart from his judicial functions, he was little more than the nominal head of the common council, his powers were very limited, and there was a consequent absence of co-ordination among the city departments. There was no responsible executive head of the city government. The mayor was little more than a chief of police. With the exception of the police and a few unimportant officers, he did not appoint and consequently could not suspend or remove. In fact, he had practically no control over the other officers and departments of the city, and was, consequently, powerless to restrain corrupt practices, however eager he might be to do so.

POWER GRANTED TO THE MAYOR.

Following the plan pursued successfully in the state and national governments, the executive and legislative functions of government are separated. The mayor is made the real head of the government. He is granted the fullest executive powers, and can, therefore, be held fully responsible for their administration. He is elected for the term of four years, and is not eligible to re-election. It is his duty to see that the ordinances and laws are enforced; to communicate annually to councils a statement of the finances and general condition of the affairs of the city; to make such recommendations to councils as he may deem expedient; to call special meetings of councils when necessary; to perform such duties as may be prescribed by law or ordinance; and, finally, "to be responsible for the good order and efficient government of the city."

To this end he is given ample and effective powers. He may call for reports from the heads of departments; he is an *ex-officio* member of all boards, except the board of building inspectors; he can remove any officer appointed by him; he may disapprove of items of appropriation bills; and he may appoint three persons to examine, without notice, the accounts of any city department or employé.[1]

RESTRAINTS ON THE MAYOR.

While possessing these powers, however, the mayor is not without due restraints. His appointments and removals are subject to the approval of select councils, and he is liable to impeachment for malfeasance in office.

---

[1] Article I. of new charter. See appendix.

Departments.

EVILS OF THE OLD SYSTEM.

Sec. 5. Throughout the history of the government of Philadelphia the separation and independence of the departments has been one of the most obvious and serious evils. Although after the Revolution, as has been seen, the powers distributed among the common council, assessors, commissioners, and wardens were united in the corporation, yet the influence of the past was too strong, and there never was a real connection and co-ordination among the various branches of the government. There were in Philadelphia, before the passage of the Bullitt bill, some twenty-five separate and distinct departments of municipal government, which collected and disbursed many millions. They had no proper relations with each other. They were not brought together for consultation in reference to the affairs of the city, and they were not accountable to any general head. Each one managed its own business in its own way, without reference to any other; and each was naturally led to seek as much money as it could get from the city treasury for its own expenditures. Confusion and waste frequently resulted from the action of one department without consultation with another department. "Frequently, when an ordinance had been passed providing for the paving of a street and the construction of a sewer and laying of water-pipes, the street would be paved. It would then be opened to construct the sewer. When this was done it would be repaired, and then be opened again to put down the water-pipe, and after this was done it would be paved again, and then it would be again opened and gas-pipes laid, and then be paved a fourth time." The most signal instance of want of harmony between two departments of the city exists as a permanent monument to the present system in the bridge for a large water main over the Wissahickon. This was built, under the supervision of the water department, to carry water from the Roxborough water works to Germantown, at a large cost; and a public bridge was then and is now needed at this point, or near it, to connect Ridge avenue and Roxborough with Germantown. At a moderate outlay, in addition to the present water-pipe bridge, one could have been built that would have answered as an aqueduct and roadway; but there was no conference between the two departments."[1]

Departments Under the New Charter.

The duties and powers of these departments are distributed by the bill among the following executive departments:—

I. Department of public safety.
II. Department of public works.
III. Department of receiver of taxes.
IV. Department of city treasurer.
V. Department of city controller.
VI. Department of law.
VII. Department of education.
VIII. Department of charities and correction.
IX. Sinking fund commission.

While the mayor is the executive head of the government, the heads of the departments are his advisers, after the model of the federal government.

A Few Connected Departments.

Following that model, it was the object of the framers of the bill to make the departments of government as few and as well concentrated as is consistent with the duties to be performed; while the various departments are so related to each other, through a common head or chief, that they can have proper consultation with each other, and administer their several affairs in harmony and with reference to each other.[2]

---

[1] A paper read before the Social Science Association and the Civil Service Reform Association on the Form of Municipal Government of the City of Philadelphia, by John C. Bullitt, Esq., 1882.

[2] Art. II. Executive departments.

A Uniform System of Appointment.

A uniform system of appointment is followed, by which responsibility is graded from the mayor down through the heads of departments to the subordinate officers, in the place of the varied former methods by which some of the city officers were elected by the people, some by councils, some appointed by the courts, while in the case of the "public buildings commissioners" the board fills the vacancies as they occur.

Department of Public Safety.

Sec. 6. The department of public safety is under the charge of a director.[1]

Police.

To its charge have been committed all the affairs of the city appertaining to its police powers in its largest sense, including matters relating to the public health. Careful provisions are made to obtain an efficient and well-disciplined force. A pension fund is maintained by monthly charges on the officers. No policeman shall be discharged without cause and trial.

The Mayor Relieved from Immediate Charge of Police.

One important change in this department is to be noticed. The mayor is relieved from the immediate supervision of the police force. Previously he had been little else than the chief of police, and the duties devolving upon him in this connection have usually absorbed the greater part of his time. As he is now charged with such extended powers and duties, he is relieved from the details of the police business, which, if properly attended to, would absorb all his time. At the same time he is robbed of no power necessary for the preservation of the peace and good order of the city, as he has the appoint-

[1] Article III. Department of public safety.

ment of the head of the department and general supervision over its conduct and management. Upon any emergency, or apprehension of riot, he may take command of the police force, and appoint as many special patrolmen as he may deem advisable.

Board of Health.

As it was designed to include the most comprehensive police powers, under the department of public safety, the board of health is placed under its charge. The number of the board is reduced to five, appointed by the mayor. The director of public safety is a member of the board, and chief executive officer thereof; and has supervision and control over all the subordinate employés of the board.

Building Inspectors.

Under the department of public safety is also placed the board of building inspectors, which consists of three members, appointed in this case by the director himself.

Department of Public Works.

Sec. 7. No special principle is involved in the construction of the department of public works.[1] Under it are consolidated all the affairs of the city in the nature of public works, such as the water works, gas works, the control, repair, and lighting of the streets, the construction and maintenance of public buildings, bridges, and other public structures, and control over public squares, real estate (except such as is used for educational or police purposes), surveys, engineering, sewerage, drainage and dredging, highways, wharves, and docks of the city.

The Public Buildings Commission excepted.

One important exception, however, in this department is to be noticed. The public buildings commission is expressly left as it is. Whatever may have been the objection to this

[1] Article IV. Department of public works.

commission in the beginning, it is obvious that it would be a serious mistake to make a change in the management of the construction of the buildings when they are nearly finished in a satisfactory manner.

It is to be noted, also, that the operations of the city ice boats are under the control of this department.

SURVEY DEPARTMENT.

The survey department is also under the control of the department of public works; and councils are authorized to divide the city, by ordinance, into such survey districts as to them may seem proper. Until the expiration of the respective terms of office of the present district surveyors, such surveyors are attached to the department of public works.

FINANCE.

SEC. 8. As can be easily seen throughout the past history of Philadelphia, the finances have been, from the very beginning, when the old mediæval corporation struggled along with its inability to lay any kind of tax, down to the present time, the most important matter in the city government. The experience of this past history, and, indeed, the past history of all American cities, is, that the accumulation of municipal indebtedness is justly and universally ranked as overshadowing all others in importance.

NOTE.—The following table was carefully prepared by the municipal commission, showing the increase of population, valuation, taxation, and indebtedness of fifteen of the principal cities of the United States from 1860 to 1875:—

Increase in population,	70.5 per cent.
Increase in taxable valuation,	156.9 " "
Increase in debt,	270.9 " "
Increase in taxation,	363.2 " "

See, also, appended to the message of Governor Hartranft of 1876, a detailed statement of the debts of a number of prominent cities of the country in 1867 and 1875. The table also shows the cost of the several departments of those city governments, and is a valuable help to a proper understanding of the expenditures of the various cities named. —*Journal of the Senate*, 1876, page 32.

It must be borne in mind that this alarming increase in debt and taxation occurred during a period of great apparent national prosperity, when money was plenty, when property commanded enormous prices, and when it was easier to apply the maxim "pay as you go" than at any other period. As has been previously admitted, many of these debts were contracted for needed permanent improvements; but, making due allowance for all such considerations, these figures are justly alarming. In the language of a distinguished writer on the subject, "When we take into consideration that the most careful analysis of the amount of annual accretions of capital by the economy of a great community in prosperous times is somewhat less than three per cent. of its gross products, it is quite obvious that the inhabitants of American cities are rapidly approaching the point where they will sacrifice to their city administrations the whole annual increase of their combined labor. When it is considered that the payment of the interest, in many cases the principal, of these debts must be provided for in the face of decreasing values and depreciating securities, and of the attendant diminished receipts, the significance of these figures is still more apparent."[1]

Constitutional and Legislative Restraints on Indebtedness.

Various kinds of restraints have been imposed upon the power of cities to contract indebtedness, but, in the main, without much success. All attempts to protect the property of the citizen by constitutional or legislative provisions, limiting or regulating the amount of city indebtedness, have thus far proved a failure.

By the constitution of 1874, section 8, article IX., it is provided that the debt of a county, city, borough, township, or school district, or other municipal or incorporated district, shall never exceed seven per centum on the assessed value of

[1] See Report of the Pennsylvania Municipal Commission.

the taxable property therein.' This provision was, of course, intended to prevent the encumbering of the property of any citizen for public purposes to a greater extent than seven per cent. It was demanded by public sentiment, and, no doubt, largely influenced the popular vote in favor of the constitution. In its workings, however, it has been an absolute failure.

In every city of the State, except Philadelphia, the city is part of the county government. The county has the power to borrow money to the extent of seven per centum; the city to the extent of seven per centum; the general school district, to the extent of seven per centum; and the ward school district to the extent of seven per centum,—making twenty-eight per centum in all,—which can be lawfully imposed, and has been authorized by the act of 1874.[1]

But there is still another cause of failure, to which Philadelphia is more peculiarly liable. In order to evade the provision of the constitution limiting the power to contract debts to seven per centum, the assessed value of property in nearly every city of the State was largely increased, in some instances, incredible as it may seem, to the extent of one thousand per centum. It is, therefore, clear that no sufficient protection against an undue increase of municipal debt can be found in constitutional and legislative provisions of this kind.

Property Qualification for Electors.

A property qualification for electors has also been proposed as a remedy for the accumulation of municipal indebtedness. This proposition, however, had a theoretical rather than a practical value; because it is extremely doubtful whether any such limit in the suffrage would be tolerated in this country. A property qualification was proposed by a commission appointed by the governor of the State of New York —at least for that branch of the city government having power to levy taxes and disburse money.[2] While, however,

[1] Report of Pennsylvania Municipal Commission.

[2] See section 19, chapter V., of this book.

such a qualification might prove effective in a city like New York, yet no important results could be expected in a city like Philadelphia.

The city of Philadelphia, appropriately called the city of homes, contained in 1878, at the time of the report of the municipal commission, about one hundred and fifty thousand dwellings and about one hundred and thirty-five thousand voters.[1] It is thus obvious that the great mass of voters are either owners of houses or tenants paying rent. Hundreds of blocks of comfortable homes, renting from twelve to twenty dollars per month, are scattered throughout the city, and are occupied by an intelligent class of mechanics and operatives. The provision recommended by the New York commission, therefore, requiring the payment of an annual rental of $250 as a qualification for voting, would in Philadelphia exclude this very large and reputable class of citizens, while it would not exclude many objectionable tenants who, in many cases, pay a higher rent. Moreover, while no doubt it would exclude some of the irresponsible class, it would also exclude very many of the sons of reputable property-holders, who would exercise the franchise honestly and intelligently.

On the contrary, it is justly noted by the Pennsylvania commission as a remarkable but notorious fact, that the accumulations of debt in Philadelphia and other cities in the State have been due, not to a non-property-holding, irresponsible element among the electors, but to the desire for speculation among the property-owners themselves. Large tracts of land outside the built-up portion of the city have been purchased, combinations made among men of wealth, and councils besieged until they have been driven into making appropriations to open and improve streets and avenues, largely in advance of the real necessities of the city. Extraordinary as the statement may seem at first, the experience of the past shows clearly that frequently property-owners need

---

[1] Report of municipal commission.

more protection against themselves than against the non-property-holding class.

Prohibition of Local Legislation.

The prohibition of local legislation on the part of the State legislature by constitutional enactment has proved a most effective and beneficial measure. There has been frequent occasion to comment on the financial evils of Philadelphia from mismanagement or from the defects of the city government; but it is only fair to say that in many cases the largest debts have been contracted, not by authority of councils or any department of the city government proper, but under the provisions of special acts of assembly, appointing commissioners to open streets, park commissioners, building commissioners, bridge commissioners, &c. This kind of legislation arose under the first charter, as will be remembered from the despotic powers of the close corporation and the distrust in which it was held by the citizens; and partly from necessity in consequence of the inefficiency of the machinery of the city government, partly from habit in the past, and partly from ignorance of the evils of the system, it was continued down to the present time. These local acts were frequently passed, not only without the request of councils, but very often against their very earnest protest. By the constitution of 1874 careful provisions are made in reference to local and special legislation; and these, with the effective provisions concerning the methods and subjects of legislation in general, have had happy results. By section 7 of article III. it is provided that the general assembly shall not pass any local or special laws, among other subjects, regulating the affairs of counties, cities, townships, wards, boroughs, or school districts; authorizing the laying out, opening, altering, or maintaining roads, highways, streets, or alleys; relating to ferries or bridges, or incorporating ferry or bridge companies, except for the erection of bridges crossing streams which form boundaries between this and any other State; vacating roads, town-plots, streets, or alleys; locating or changing county seats; erecting new counties or changing county lines; incorporating cities, towns, or villages, or changing their charters; erecting new townships or boroughs; changing township lines, borough limits, or school districts; creating offices or prescribing the powers and duties of officers in counties, cities, boroughs, townships, election or school districts. In such cases as local and special legislation is not forbidden by the constitution it is provided by section 8 of article III. that "No local or special bill shall be passed, unless notice of the intention to apply therefor shall have been published in the locality where the matter or thing to be affected may be situated; which notice shall be at least thirty days prior to the introduction into the general assembly of such bill, and in the manner to be provided by law. The evidence of such notice having been published shall be exhibited in the general assembly before such act shall be passed."

Commissions for Municipal Improvements forbidden.

By section 20 of article III. it is provided that "The general assembly shall not delegate to any special commission, private corporation, or association any power to make, supervise, or interfere with any municipal improvement, money, property, or effects, whether held in trust or otherwise, or to levy taxes or perform any municipal function whatever." Thus the creation of these independent boards and commissions was absolutely prohibited for the future.

Subscriptions to Railroads forbidden.

Another source of the accumulation of municipal indebtedness, more prominent formerly than to-day, subscriptions to railroads and other schemes of internal improvements, was provided against by section 7 of article IX., providing that "The general assembly shall not authorize any county, city, borough, township, or incorporated district to become a stockholder in any company, association, or corporation, or to obtain or appropriate money for, or loan its credit to any corporation, association, institution, or individual."

In addition to the provision already noticed, limiting the debt of cities, &c., to seven per centum, it is further provided by the same section—section 8 of Article IX.—that no new debt to an amount exceeding two per centum upon the assessed value of the taxable property should be incurred without the assent of the electors thereof at a public election; but any city, the debt of which exceeded seven per centum at the time of the adoption of the constitution, can be authorized by law to increase the same three per centum, in the aggregate, at any one time.

By section 9 of article IX. the Commonwealth is forbidden to assume the debt of any city, county, borough, or township, unless such debt shall have been contracted to repel invasion, suppress domestic insurrection, defend itself in times of war, or to assist the State in discharge of any portion of its present indebtedness. By section 10 of the same article a very important and effective provision was made for the discharge of any debt accumulated within the limits allowed by the constitution. This section provided that "Any county, township, school district, or other municipality incurring any indebtedness shall, at or before the time of so doing, provide for the collection of an annual tax sufficient to pay the interest, and also the principal thereof, within thirty years." To a similar end it is provided by section 2 of article XV., that "No debt shall be contracted, or liability incurred, by any municipal commission, except in pursuance of an appropriation made therefor by the municipal government;" and by section 3 of the same article it is provided that "Every city shall create a sinking fund, which shall be inviolably pledged for the payment of its funded debt."

Improved Methods in the City Government.

Finally, it has been attempted to prevent the incurring of debts and extravagant expenditures by cities, by improved methods and systems in the city government. The successive important changes, especially within the decade preceding the passage of the Bullitt bill, having been carefully traced, it now remains to note the provisions made by that bill, having in view a more thorough system of accountability, and a more economical administration of affairs.

Department of the Receiver of Taxes.

Sec. 9. The department of the receiver of taxes is under the control of a receiver of taxes,[1] who is elected for the term of three years, and gives security as provided by law. All officers charged with the duty of collecting taxes, and the receipt and collection of funds derived from loans, licenses, water-rents, water-pipe, frontages, permits and rents from markets, landings, wharves, and other public property and interests, are attached and subordinate to this department. The receiver of taxes is charged by the controller with the full amount of all tax duplicates of the several wards, and also with all other accounts placed in his hands by the proper officer for collection, and makes daily returns to the controller of all moneys paid, and by whom paid.

Directors of City Trusts and Board of Revision excepted.

It is to be noted that two departments of the city government, which properly fall under this department according to the spirit of the bill, have been expressly omitted from its operation, as they have been well managed in the past, and it seemed best not to disturb them. These are the boards of directors of city trusts and of revision of taxes, which are left as created by acts of assembly.

Department of City Treasurer.

Sec. 10. The head of the department of city treasurer is the city treasurer,[2] who is elected for the term of three

[1] Article V. Department of receiver of taxes.
[2] Article VI. Department of city treasurer.

years, and gives security. No person shall be eligible to the office of treasurer except a citizen of the city resident therein for seven years next preceding his election, and he shall not be eligible to election for next succeeding term. It is his duty to demand and receive from the proper officers all moneys payable to the city from whatever source, and pay all warrants duly issued and countersigned.

Important Regulations.

The methods to be pursued in the discharge of his official duties are laid down with the greatest care. He is to keep the accounts arising from the usual sources of revenue and income separate and distinct from one another. He must make daily deposits of all moneys received by him in such bank or institution as may be designated by councils, and shall make specific reports daily to the city controller of all receipts and deposits, and of all moneys withdrawn from the treasury, and shall present and verify his cash account in such manner and as often as may be required. It is also expressly provided that "all the moneys of the city received by any officer or agent thereof shall be deposited daily in the city treasury." It is also provided that "no money shall be drawn from the city treasury, except by due process of law, or upon warrants on the treasurer signed by the head of the appropriate department and countersigned by the controller, which shall state the consideration of the same, and the particular fund or appropriation to which the same is chargeable."

Department of City Controller.

Sec. 10. The provisions thus made, taken in connection with the powers of the controller, and the general supervising authority of the mayor over the accounts and administration of all the departments, are the safeguards over the public moneys and property provided by the bill.[1]

The head of the department of city controller is the city controller. He is elected for the term of three years.

[1] Article VII. Department of city controller.

DUTIES OF CONTROLLER.

His duties are most carefully defined by the act. The controller shall—

I. Prescribe the form of reports and accounts to be rendered to his department, and shall have the inspection and revision of the accounts of all other departments and trusts.

II. Audit the accounts of the several departments and trusts, and all other accounts in which the city is concerned, and submit an annual report to councils of the accounts of the city, exhibiting the revenues, receipts and expenditures, the sources of revenue and the manner of disbursement of the same, which report shall be published.

III. Keep separate accounts for each specific item or appropriation made by councils to each department, and require all warrants to state specifically against which of said items the warrant is drawn. Each account shall be accompanied by a statement in detail, in separate columns, of the several appropriations made by councils, the amount drawn on each appropriation, the unpaid contracts charged against it, and the balance charged to the credit of the same.

IV. He shall not suffer any appropriation to be overdrawn, or the appropriation for one item of expense to be drawn upon for any other purpose, or by any department other than that for which the appropriation was especially made, except on transfers made by ordinance of councils, or unless sufficient funds out of which said warrant is payable shall actually be in the treasury at the time.

V. If any warrant presented to the controller contain an item for which no appropriation has been made, or there shall not be a sufficient balance of the proper fund for the payment thereof, or which, for any other cause, should not be approved, he shall notify the proper department of the fact; and if the controller shall approve any warrant contrary to the provisions of the bill, he and his sureties shall be individually liable for the amount of the same to the holder thereof.

VI. Whenever a warrant or claim shall be presented to

him he shall have power to require evidence that the amount claimed is justly due, and for that purpose may summon before him any officer, agent, or employé of any department of the city, or any other person, and examine him, upon oath or affirmation, relative to such warrant or claim.

VII. He shall also perform all duties required of him by law or ordinance.

His Duties relative to Contracts.

It is also provided by the bill that "Every contract involving an appropriation of money shall designate the item of appropriation on which it is founded, and shall be numbered by the controller in the order of its date, and charged as numbered against such item, and so certified by him before it shall take effect as a contract, and shall not be payable out of any other fund; and if he shall certify any contract in excess of the appropriation properly applicable thereto, the city shall not be liable for such excess, but the controller and his sureties shall be liable in damages to an amount not exceeding such excess, which may be recovered in an action on the case for negligence by the contracting party aggrieved."

The provisions respecting the controller have been minutely recited because he is the most important and responsible officer in the city government; and, as the liberties guaranteed in the bill of rights have been obtained by the heroic struggles of our ancestors, beginning with *Magna Charta*, so each of these carefully-framed provisions respecting the controller, after many struggles and hard experiences in the past, have been framed to guard against various abuses in the management of the city finances.

Department of Law.

Sec. 11. Few important changes are made by the Bullitt bill in the construction of the department of law.[1] The department of law consists "of a city solicitor, who shall be the

[1] Article VIII. Department of law.

head thereof." He is elected for the term of three years, and shall have such assistants and clerks as are authorized by ordinance.

City Solicitor to prepare all Contracts.

Perhaps the most important provision made by the bill is, that the city solicitor shall prepare all contracts to be made with the city, or any of its trusts and departments, and endorse his approval of the form thereof on each before it shall take effect as a contract; and further, that he shall prepare in his office all contracts, bonds, and other instruments in writing in which the city is concerned, and shall receive a reasonable fee therefor for the use of the city, to be fixed by ordinance. The purpose of these provisions is to secure correctness and uniformity in the preparation of such instruments, to protect the citizen from imposition in charges, and to prevent the city solicitor from receiving any compensation other than the salary fixed by law for his services.

No Department to employ any other Solicitor.

Another important provision is, that no department of the city shall employ any other solicitor, but assistant counsel may be employed in any particular matter by the mayor, with the consent of councils, but he shall be selected by the city solicitor. As will be remembered, formerly the mayor had his solicitor, as had several boards and departments of the city.

Recovery of Judgments against the City.

The provisions respecting the recovery of judgments against the city are intended to prevent a serious difficulty. Formerly, upon the recovery of a judgment against the city, the plaintiff had been able, by *mandamus*, to take out of the city treasury any funds he might find there, whether needed for other purposes or not. Thus when the city had accumulated a fund in its treasury for the purpose of paying interest on its debt, or to pay its school teachers, or other employés, a creditor could take the money by *mandamus*, and thus prevent its application to the purposes for which it was raised. But more than this, all arrangements made by the city for the payment of its current and necessary expenses became deranged. It was, consequently, impossible for councils to provide for that adjustment of its current revenues to its current expenses, and that application of the funds raised by taxation to the purposes for which they were intended, which the experience of the past has proved conclusively must prevail in any well-ordered system of municipal finances, and which was one of the leading objects aimed at by the theory of the Bullitt bill. Judgments against the city are therefore to be reported to councils by the city solicitor, and if there are no funds in the city treasury provided for and applicable to the payment of them, the amount is to be raised in the next levy of taxes. Such judgments shall be paid, in the order of their priority, out of the first moneys paid into the city treasury on account thereof by reason of such levy. If, however, there are any moneys in the treasury not otherwise appropriated, councils are to direct the payment therefrom of the judgments in the order of their priority. But while the creditor of the city is thus deprived of the power to force the payment to him of money raised for other purposes, or which, by right, should be paid to other persons quite as deserving, he still has his remedy by *mandamus*, or other proper process, to enforce compliance with the above provisions.

Department of Education.

Sec. 12. The department of education continues as already established by law.[1]

Department of Charities and Correction.

Sec. 13. The department of charities and correction is under the charge of a president and four directors.[2] To this

---

[1] Article IX. Department of education.

[2] Article X. Department of charities and correction.

department is confided the management of the charities, almshouses, hospitals, houses of correction, and all other similar institutions belonging to the city, and formerly, for the most part, under the control of separate independent boards.

As in several other cases, already noted, the board of directors of city trusts, and the board of inspectors of the county prison, are not changed; and the Lazaretto remains under the control of the board of health.

The record of its proceedings, which the board of charities and correction is required to keep, is open at any time to the examination of the mayor, and of any committee of councils. All officers and servants required for the several institutions are appointed by the board. So vast and intricate are the subjects committed to its charge, varying so greatly with the financial and sanitary condition of the city, that it was not deemed advisable by the framers of the bill to provide in detail for the performance of its duty. Councils are authorized to provide by general ordinance for all things needful for the efficient management of the institutions and department.

Sinking Fund Commission.

Sec. 14. The sinking fund commission remains as established by law.[1]

Appointment of Department Officers, Clerks, and Employés.

Sec. 15. The provisions made by the bill respecting the appointment of officers are intended to carry out the leading thought of, the new system, which is to mould city governments on the plan of the State and National governments.[2]

The mayor, who was formerly little more than a chief of police, is now made the real executive head, and is, consequently, held responsible for the good government of the

[1] Article XI. Sinking fund commission.

[2] Article XII. Appointment of department officers, clerks, and employés.

city. To this end the mayor is given power to appoint, with the consent of select councils:—

I. The director of the department of public safety.

II. The director of the department of public works.

III. The president and directors of charities and correction.

The director of the department of public safety and the director of the department of public works hold office during the term for which the appointing mayor was elected; while the president and directors of the department of charities and correction hold office for the term of five years.

Only Partial Concentration of Power in the Mayor's Hands.

It is to be noted that, while it was the intention of the framers of the bill to concentrate executive authority in the hands of the mayor by giving him the appointment of the heads of executive departments, yet, for various reasons, that concentration has not been carried nearly to the extent originally intended and demanded by the theory of the system. The remaining executive heads of departments—the receiver of taxes, the city treasurer, and the city controller—remain elected by the citizens; and while the mayor is given a certain supervision and control over them, yet, it is to the people directly, and not to him, to whom they are responsible for the discharge of their duties. The mayor, therefore, as far as these three departments extend, cannot be held wholly responsible, and to this extent the theory of the bill is not carried out.

As far as regards the city controller, there are many reasons for having him elected by the people. He is, so far as the accounts of the city are concerned, "the tribunal of last resort." He is to audit and settle the accounts of all the departments, and all the accounts in which the city is concerned. His position is peculiar, and, as he acts as a check to all other departments of the city, he may justly be considered as being apart and outside of the general system of city government. The city treasurer and receiver of taxes, however, are executive officers, and, according to the theory of the system, should be appointed by the mayor. They were, indeed, to be appointed by the mayor in the code originally framed by the municipal commission; but when the bill was finally framed as a practical measure, it was thought best, for many reasons, to leave them, as formerly, elective officers. Besides, in the case of the county officers, a constitutional amendment would have been necessary. Carrying out the theory of responsibility, it is provided that all subordinate officers and clerks shall be appointed by the directors or chief officers of departments. Careful provisions are made for a strict system of civil service.

Executive Heads and Discretionary Boards.

The following principle is also found in the scheme—that where the duties are of an executive character they are placed in the hands of one man, as in the case of the department of public safety; but when they require rather judgment and discretion they are placed in the hands of a board, as in the case of the president and directors of charities and correction. Moreover, it is to be noted that the members of this board hold office for five years, so that the board is not changed immediately under a new mayor.

Arguments for and against the System.

The commonest argument against the system is, that too much power is placed in the hands of one man; and the attempt was made in 1883 and 1885, when the bill was before the legislature, to take away from the mayor the power of appointing the heads of the departments and make them elected by the people. It is the very essence of the theory of the system, however, that this power can be safely lodged with the mayor, and that his direct responsibility to the people will be amply sufficient to restrain any man, however ill disposed.

"There is a force in public sentiment," says Mr. Bullitt,[1] which, when it is properly utilized, no man can resist. It is that which controls the actions of men in responsible public positions, more than all things else. I care not how bold, how reckless, how defiant a man may be, let him be placed in the chief executive office of a government where public sentiment can be concentrated upon him, and he can be held up to the censure and scorn of his fellow-citizens if he departs from the path of rectitude, and he will quail under its rebuke. No man who has ever yet attained high office in this country has had the hardihood to brave it. This responsibility to public sentiment, and its recognized power, should be at the very foundation of all our governmental structures. The only departure from it is found in city governments."[2]

The large powers of appointment lodged in the mayor, so far from being a dangerous power, is expected to be frequently a source of weakness, in consequence of the wide extent of his responsibility before the people, and the difficulty he will have in distributing such patronage as is at his disposal, without exciting bitter hostilities. Moreover, it is argued, the very sensitiveness of the people, with reference to the deposit of such large powers in a single hand, is an additional safeguard. It puts upon the mayor, say the advocates of the system, almost unavoidably the necessity of showing by positive action that he and his party merit it. Besides, two results are accomplished: the office is made such as any man is glad to hold; it is worth any man's while to be mayor of a large city under such a charter, because he has the chance of serving the community to some purpose; and, in the next place, the question to be decided at the election is shorn of the complex and not generally known details of the bearing of one office on another, and is reduced to the simple question, which of two

---

[1] A paper read before the Social Science Association and the Civil Service Reform Association, on the Form of Municipal Government of the City of Philadelphia, 1882, by John C. Bullitt, page 17.

[2] See arguments to the same effect relative to New York, section 21, page 302.

men is best fitted for the responsibility of the whole city government for four years.

To render the heads of the departments elective would be really to constitute several independent mayors within the city, whatever other merits might be left in the system. In the language of Mayor Low, of Brooklyn, the change "involves the complete loss of unity in the city government. Responsibility on the part of all heads of departments to the mayor serves the same function in the city government as gravity in the solar system. One might as well expect the planets without gravity to avoid collision in the skies, as to expect the different departments to work efficiently together if they feel completely independent of each other. And another objection to this plan, equally fatal, is, that experience has proven abundantly that the more important an office is, the larger the number of people who will vote concerning it. Greatly to multiply important elective offices, therefore, is not to increase popular control, but to lessen it. The expression of the popular will at the ballot-box is like a great blow struck by an engine of immense force. It can deliver a blow competent to overthrow any officer, no matter how powerful. But, as in mechanics, great power has to be subdivided in order to do fine work, so, in giving expression to the popular will, the necessity of choosing among a multitude of unimportant offices involves inevitably a loss of power to the people."[1]

Impeachment of Municipal Officers.

Sec. 16. While these great powers are given to the mayor and heads of departments, and the subordinate officers and employés are protected by stringent civil service regulations, careful provisions are made for the simple and speedy impeachment and removal of unfaithful city officials. The cumbersome machinery usually employed in such cases is dispensed

[1] Municipal Government. An address by Hon. Seth Low, mayor of Brooklyn. Delivered in City Hall, Rochester, N. Y., 1885, and published by the Municipal Reform League, Arthur S. Hamilton, Sec., 26 Exchange street, Rochester.

with, and the means of impartial and thorough investigation brought within the reach of any twenty freeholders of the city who can satisfy the court that there are reasonable grounds for proceeding.[1]

CONTRACTS.

SEC. 17. Careful provisions have been made by the bill in order to throw around the making and execution of contracts every possible guard against improvidence and fraud, having in view the fact that the welfare and financial condition of the city depend, in a great measure, upon the manner in which these contracts are made and executed. Among the other limitations it is provided[2] that "every contract for public improvements shall be based upon estimate of the whole cost furnished by the proper officer through the department having charge of the improvement, and no bid in excess of such estimate shall be accepted." Every contract is required to contain a clause that it is subject to the provisions of the act. Formerly, if the city wished to suspend the work contracted for, because it was not expedient to levy the taxes to pay for it, or for any other reason, the contractor could go on with the work, and compel councils to raise the money by taxation; or, if it happened to be in the treasury, he could take it out by *mandamus*. Accordingly, it is provided that the liability of the city on contracts shall be limited by the amounts which shall have been, or may be, from time to time, appropriated for the same.

It is also provided that "in all contracts, the cost of which is to be paid by assessment upon the property abutting or benefited, the city shall not be liable to any claim for the amount to be collected from such assessment, but the contractor shall look to the assessment for his compensation." It was expected by the framers of the bill that this clause would bring about a great saving to the city. "Contractors," says the report of the municipal commission, "are ready enough

---

[1] Article XIII. Impeachment of municipal officers.

[2] Article XIV. Contracts.

to urge the opening and improving of streets, and to make contracts therefor, if they can only look to the city for their pay; but if they are obliged to look only to the property benefited, then the owners will be most careful to prevent such improvements until the necessity for them has actually arisen, and the inducement to contractors to urge the making of such improvements prematurely is taken away. This clause will relieve the cities of many of the most oppressive burdens under which they have heretofore been laboring."

General Provisions.

Sec. 18. Among the general provisions of the bill it may be mentioned that councils are given the necessary and important power to compel the attendance of witnesses and the production of books, papers, and other evidence, at any meeting of the body, or of any committee thereof. The previous grant and importance of this power has already been noted. It is also provided that no officer or employé of any department, trust, or commission, or employé of any contractor under any such department, trust, or commission, shall be a delegate to any political convention, or be present at any such convention, except in discharge of his duties, on penalty of forfeiture of his position.

Following the principle adopted in the new constitution, and fully established by the experience of the past, it is further provided that "no officer or employé of the city shall collect any fees or perquisites for his own use, but all such fees or perquisites now collectible under the law shall be paid into the city treasury, and councils by ordinance shall provide for the payment of proper salaries to all officers or employés of the city," except for such as serve without compensation.

Councils Deprived of all Executive Power.

Sec. 19. The greatly-diminished power of councils is one of the most prominent changes wrought by the bill. Since 1839, when nearly all the appointments made by the mayor were transferred to councils, the development of the government, as has been seen, was a steady progress toward the concentration of all legislative and nearly all executive powers in councils, who acted through standing committees. The heads of the departments appointed by councils were merely the agents of those committees, not only in the administration of the trusts supposed to be committed to departments, and in the appointment of subordinate officers, but in the payment of bills and current expenses not embraced in special contracts, thus affording opportunities for corrupt combinations between the two branches of the city government. This was a condition of things existing only in the city government. It is not found either in the state or nation, and is believed to constitute a principal reason why the government of cities has proved the only failure in the republican system.

It is argued that the divorce of city councils from all executive functions will enable them to devote themselves with greater advantage to their proper duties of legislating for the efficient administration of the departments specially charged with executive functions, and will, to a great extent, remove the necessity for standing committees, and the perpetual meetings of such bodies. It is hoped that it will then be possible for "men of business, competent and trustworthy, who have, with all honest citizens, a common and personal interest in the public welfare, to take part in the legislative branch of municipal government. It will not be asking too much of them to give a limited portion of their attention to the honorable service of protecting and promoting the true interest of a community of which they form a part, whose character and credit, at home and abroad, are matters of deep and common concern."[1] Under the old system, which "gave to joint standing committees the practical control of all municipal executive departments, the councils or their committees were in almost perpetual session. The two branches of the councils of Philadelphia met at least four times in every month, except during a short summer recess, and vigilant members

[1] Report of the Pennsylvania Municipal Commission.

devoted two or three days of nearly every week to public affairs. Under such conditions very few citizens who were engaged in business demanding their personal supervision were found willing to assume the absorbing duties imposed upon a member of councils.

Property Qualification proposed for one Branch of Councils.

In the report of the municipal commission it was proposed that the members of select council should be owners of real estate within the city, assessed and taxed in their own names, for municipal purposes, for not less than three years previous to their election. It was argued in behalf of the provision that municipal governments affect the general absolute rights of citizens to a very limited extent, their main object being to secure a faithful administration of financial trust, and to secure the proper application of large sums of money to their proper uses. In this respect, and to this extent, it was maintained, a city government is, to all intents, a partnership between the citizens, who own the property to be affected, and contribute the money to be expended for municipal purposes, and that, therefore, it did not seem too much to require that one branch of councils should be composed of owners of property within the limits of the city they were selected to govern. It was the only branch of the city government in which property was to have a distinct representation.

This and other qualifications for members of councils proposed by the commission were omitted when the general code came to be fitted to the practical necessities of the city, and took shape as the Bullitt bill. In the first place, it is idle to consider propositions in restraint of the suffrage, as such propositions would never be adopted by the people. In the second place, it is a mistake to hold the constitution of the legislative branch of the city government wholly responsible for the evils of the past, and to argue that these evils are capable of cure by the election of good men to councils. It is true that councils have been largely responsible, and that a great improvement might be made; but it is the essence of the theory of the new system, that the fault lies principally with the constitution of the executive branches of the government. Separate the executive branch from councils, it is argued, and the councils will be good enough. A property qualification is peculiarly inapplicable to Philadelphia, for the reason that the number of freeholders or rentpayers is nearly equal to the number of voters.

Contemporaneous Municipal Reforms in other Cities.

Sec. 20. It would be impossible for the reader to have a thorough understanding and a broad comprehension of the changes recently effected in the government of Philadelphia without some knowledge of the similar changes effected at nearly the same time in neighboring cities. These changes have all been the result of similar agitations; they have been based upon similar modern theories of municipal institutions; and the peculiar development of the institutions of one city furnishes instructive illustration and explanation of the development of institutions in the other. Such a comparative study, moreover, will have the advantage of still further elucidating the modern ideas of municipal government, since in one city one theory has predominated, such as the property qualification in New York, while in another city it has been subordinated to another theory, as in Philadelphia, where the property qualification for electors was not considered; and the main remedy for municipal abuses was held to be the concentration of executive power and its separation from the legislative. It is proposed, therefore, to give a brief sketch of some of the contemporaneous municipal reforms in other states in order to illustrate the reforms made in Pennsylvania.

Brooklyn.

The charter of Brooklyn, until recently, was justly entitled to the description given by its mayor, Hon. Seth Low, that it was "a new type, substantially, among the charters of American cities."[1] The principle of concentrated power and responsibility in the hands of the mayor has recently been more thoroughly carried out in that city than anywhere else. The people of Brooklyn elect, besides the board of aldermen, only three city officials,—the mayor, who is the chief magistrate and chief executive of the city; the comptroller, who is the financial officer of the city and its book-keeper, and the auditor, who performs the duty which his name implies. To the mayor, as the chief magistrate and the chief executive of the city, is given the appointment of all city officials that are not elected, with a few minor exceptions. The mayor appoints the corporation counsel, the city treasurer, the collector of taxes and assessments, the registrar of arrears, the police commissioner, the fire commissioner, the health commissioner, the commissioner of city works, the commissioners of buildings, the president of the department of assessment, the excise commissioners, the park commissioners, the board of assessors, the board of education, and the board of elections. Moreover, it is to be noted that all these appointments are made by the mayor without confirmation by the board of aldermen. With certain minor exceptions, the executive officers are appointed by the mayor on February 1, after he takes office. The mayor is elected at the annual election in November, assumes his office on January 1 following, and one month after taking his office is given this opportunity of organizing the city government in a way to insure its being in sympathy with himself, and to make it one for which he is willing to be responsible in all its parts, because he is held strictly responsible for it all.

Five Principles in the Government of Brooklyn.

Five principles are involved in the scheme thus briefly sketched. First, the mayor exercises the right of appoint-

[1] Municipal Government. Address by Hon. Seth Low, mayor of Brooklyn, delivered in the City Hall, Rochester, N. Y., February 19, 1885, and published by the Municipal Reform League, Arthur S. Hamilton, Secretary, 26 Exchange street, Rochester, N. Y.

ment without confirmation by the board of aldermen. Second, all the executive heads of departments are appointed by him, within one month of his taking office, for a term substantially the same as his own. "That is to say, each incoming mayor has the different departments carried on for him for one month by the appointees of his predecessor, and when he has had four weeks' opportunity to familiarize himself with the details of his office, he is given the chance to organize the city government, on its executive side, in sympathy with himself." Third, all the great executive departments of the city are confided to the care of a single executive—a single commissioner, and executive boards and commissions are abolished. Fourth, when the work is not executive, but requires rather discretion and judgment, it is put, not into the hands of one man, but confided to a board, like the board of education. Fifth, the executive heads of departments appointed by the mayor hold office for a term the same as the mayor's; while, on the other hand, the boards and commissions appointed by the mayor, whose duties are not executive, have terms of different length from the mayor's; so that in the case of the board of education, for instance, no mayor would have the appointment of the whole board unless re-elected to another term.

Concentration of Power in the Mayor the Essence of the Brooklyn Plan.

The essence of the scheme is the concentration of power and responsibility in all executive matters in the mayor and his subordinates, the heads of departments. "The people of Brooklyn have cause to believe," says Mayor Low, "that the judgment of mankind is sound when it teaches that *one man for executive work* is better than a larger number. There may be wisdom in a multitude of counselors, but there is not efficient action when you have to consult more than one." For instance, the department of city work contains six bureaus, one of which has the care of the water-works, another the collection of the water rates, another the care of the streets, their paving and repaving, cleaning and lighting; another the construction of sewers, and the cleaning and care of them; and another the purchase of supplies. In other words, whenever special work—whenever construction or care or maintenance is called for on the part of the city, it is all attended to, no matter what its nature, by the one department of city works, divided into these six bureaus, at the head of each of which is a single man—all responsible to the head of the department. There are not, as in Philadelphia, six different authorities, each having the right to tear up the streets, and no authority on whom the duty was specifically laid to put them in repair again. In the Brooklyn system, on the other hand, every sort of work calling for the opening of a street is under the same charge—under the care of the commissioner of city works; and if the bureau of sewers, for instance, wishes to tear up the streets to fix a sewer, the bureau of street repairs, as soon as they are made, puts the street in order again.

Limitations to the Mayor's Power.

Among the limitations to the great power granted to the mayor—that most relied on—is the provision for the expenditures. The purse-strings are not held by the mayor. He is a member of a board of estimate, consisting of five—the mayor, controller, and auditor on behalf of the city, and the county treasurer and supervisor at large on the part of the county. This board recommends the amounts to be raised in the budget for the ensuing year. Their recommendations then go to the board of aldermen, who, while not given the power to increase any item, can cut down any item they see fit. Whatever power and duty of administration the mayor has in the current year, must be within the limit of the appropriation given him by others, and not made up by him.

The Legislative Branch.

The constitution of the legislative branch in Brooklyn is interesting, as an extreme instance of the tendency of the new system to concentrate all power, in opposition to the old system which, as has been seen in the history of Philadelphia, aimed at as minute a distribution of power as possible. It was in consequence of this tendency to distribution that the town meeting in New England and the old corporation in Philadelphia came to be split up, and the legislative branch to be still further divided, after the model of the federal legislature, into two branches. Thus, in Philadelphia, there were created the select and common councils. Boston had a board of aldermen and a common council. In the system of Brooklyn, however, the opposite tendency of the new school is carried out to the extreme, and the legislative powers are concentrated in one chamber.[1]

The system of government adopted in Brooklyn has so far been eminently successful.[2]

NEW YORK.

SEC. 21. About the same time that questions of municipal government were being agitated in Pennsylvania, similar questions were likewise agitated in New York. The governor in a special message, communicated to the legislature May 22, 1875, called attention to the evils of the municipal

---

[1] Charter amendments, city of Brooklyn, N. Y. Single-head act. Confers upon the mayor the sole and exclusive power to appoint any commissioner or head of department. Chapter 377. An act in relation to the government of the city of Brooklyn. May 25, 1880.

Single-head act amended. Chapter 457. Laws, 1881.

Board of estimate, to prepare annual budget limiting expenditures. Chapter 532. An act to create a board of estimate for the county of Kings and the city of Brooklyn, and to prescribe the manner in which appropriations shall be made for the support of the government of said county and said city, and the appointment of court officers. May 31, 1880.

Chapter 447, board of aldermen to serve without pay, "An act in relation to the common council of the city of Brooklyn." May 21, 1883. See, also, municipal home rule—an argument for it in the city of Brooklyn. Speech by Mayor Seth Low, at the rink, Friday evening, October 6, 1882.

[2] Fourth annual message of Hon. Seth Low, mayor of Brooklyn, January 5, 1885. Also, speech of Mayor Low, at Masonic Temple, Tuesday evening, October 16, 1883.

systems of the State, and the necessity for adopting a permanent and uniform plan for the government of the cities of the State, and recommended the appointment of a commission to consider the subject. On the same day a concurrent resolution was adopted by the senate and assembly, authorizing the governor to appoint a commission of not more than twelve persons to consider the subject referred to in the message, and to report a plan for the government of cities to the next legislature. Twelve persons were appointed by the governor under this resolution. The commission organized immediately, and Hon. William M. Evarts was chosen president. The commission made their report to the legislature in 1877.

The report declared, in enumerating the evils which infest the administration of city governments, "No statement or illustration of these is requisite to a conviction of their existence."[1] The most important and obvious of these evils were declared to be the accumulation of permanent municipal debt, and the excessive increase of the annual expenditure for ordinary purposes.

"The direct, immediate, and palpable" causes of these evils are enumerated as follows:—

First.—Incompetent and unfaithful governing boards and officers. "The various forms of mischief resulting from a public service thus filled are numberless; but they uniformly present the common feature of increasing either debt or taxation, or both. These unworthy holders of public trusts gain their places by their own exertions. The voluntary suffrage of their fellow-citizens would never have lifted them into office. Animated by the expectation of unlawful emoluments, they expend large sums to secure their places, and make promises beforehand to supporters and retainers to furnish patronage or place. The money expended to secure election must be paid. The corrupt promises must be redeemed. Anticipated gains must be realized. Hence old and educated

---

[1] Report of the commission to devise a plan for the government of cities in the State of New York, presented to the legislature March 6, 1877.

subordinates must be dismissed and new places created to satisfy the crowd of friends and retainers. Profitable contracts must be awarded and needless public works must be undertaken. The forms of law are evaded or shaped for the purpose of conferring the patronage upon favorites; and the various departments of administration, instead of striving to make the burden of government as light as possible, engage in a contention to draw within their own control the largest possible part of the public resources. The amounts required to satisfy these illegitimate objects enter into the estimates upon which taxation is eventually based; in fact, they constitute, in many instances, a superior lien upon the moneys appropriated for government, and not until they are in some manner satisfied do the real wants of the public receive attention. It is speedily found that these unlawful demands, together with the necessities of the public, call for a sum which, if taken at once by taxation, would produce dissatisfaction and alarm in the community, and bring public indignation upon the authors of such burdens. For the purpose of averting such consequences, divers pretenses are put forward suggesting the propriety of raising means for alleged exceptional purposes by loans of money, and in the end the taxes are reduced to a figure not calculated to arouse the public to action, and any failure thus to raise a sufficient sum is supplied by an issue of bonds." It was estimated that more than one-half of the city debts of the State of New York belongs to the species of intentional and corrupt misrule above described.

Second.—The introduction of State and national politics into municipal affairs. The causes for this well-understood evil are: (1.) The paramount importance which the great issues of State and national politics possess in the minds of ambitious party leaders and the desire to strengthen their forces by patronage, which can only be gained by the control of local affairs. (2.) Next to the small number of leaders are those who, by habit and temperament, are led to take a wholly partisan view of city affairs, and those who follow politics and office-holding for a living. (3.) The rest of the community, containing the large majority of the more thrifty classes, averse to engaging in what they deem the "low business" of politics, or hopeless of accomplishing any substantial good in the face of such powerful opposing elements, content themselves, for the most part, with acting in accordance with their respective parties.

The third cause of the evils of municipalities, in the opinion of the New York commission, is the assumption by the legislature of the direct control of local affairs. The evils of special legislation in the case of Philadelphia have already been noted, and the remarks in the report of the New York commission are equally applicable. Special legislation is open to objection: (1.) Because the legislature has not sufficient time, in the great number of their general duties, to devote the requisite attention to local matters. (2.) They have not the requisite knowledge of details, and, consequently, local affairs are left entirely to the representatives from the different localities, and local bills are "log-rolled" through the houses. (3.) The general representatives have not that sense of personal interest and personal responsibility to their constituents which are indispensable to the intelligent administration of local affairs; while the judgment of the local governing bodies in various parts of the state and the wishes of their constituents are liable to be overruled by the votes of legislators living at the distance of a hundred miles. (4.) The occupation by the central legislative body with the consideration of a multitude of special measures relating to the local affairs. To this cause are to be ascribed the haste, error, and imperfection which frequently characterize special legislation.

The extent of the mischief in this direction is shown by the illustration of a single session. Of the eight hundred and eight acts passed in 1870 by the New York legislature, two hundred and twelve are acts relating to cities and villages, ninety-four of which relate to cities, and thirty-six to the city of New York alone. A still larger number have reference to the city of Brooklyn. These two hundred and twelve acts occupy more than three-fourths of the two thousand pages of the laws of that year. If the time requisite for the members of the legislature to comprehend their provisions and acquire the information necessary to form a judgment concerning the expediency of adopting them had been given to the work, the entire session would hardly have sufficed for the purpose. A similar illustration is furnished in the experience of Philadelphia. From 1816 to 1874 there were over one thousand special acts of assembly passed for the government of municipalities, exclusive of the laws relating to Philadelphia, passed prior to 1854, the act of 1874, relating to the government of cities, and its several supplements, and all other general laws relating to the cities of the state.[1] The multiplicity of laws relating to the same subject thus brought into existence is itself an evil of great magnitude, and leads to confusion, litigation, expense, and endless troubles. (5.) The worst phase of special legislation, however, is, that corrupt cliques and rings have been enabled to get through schemes which might otherwise have been impossible. "Cities were compelled by legislation to buy lands for parks and places because the owners wished to sell them; compelled to grade, pave, and sewer streets without inhabitants, and for no other purpose than to award corrupt contracts for the work. Cities were compelled to purchase at the public expense and at extravagant prices, the property necessary for streets and avenues, useless for any other purpose than to make a market for the adjoining property thus improved. Laws were enacted abolishing one office and creating another with the same duties, in order to transfer official emoluments from one man to another; and laws to change the functions of officers, with a view only to a new distribution of patronage, and to lengthen the terms of offices, for no other purpose than to retain in place officers who could not otherwise be elected or appointed."

---

[1] See report of commission to devise a plan for the government of cities of the state of Pennsylvania. See also section 7, article III., New Constitution; provisions against special legislation in Pennsylvania.

CONCENTRATION OF POWER NOT HELD TO BE A REMEDY IN NEW YORK.

In considering the remedies for existing municipal evils it is interesting to note that the New York commission strongly condemn the principal feature of the Bullitt bill. "It has of late years frequently been suggested," says the report, "that the corrective proposed by frequent popular elections fails of its intended effect, for the reason that, under present arrangements, there is such a division of power that the people are unable to discern the officials upon whom maladministration is really chargeable. The remedy suggested is, to clothe the mayor with full authority to appoint and remove all the principal executive officers, and then to vest in the officer so appointed the control of the business of raising and appropriating moneys. It is argued that, under such civil arrangement, the people could always hold the mayor responsible for wasteful or inefficient administration, and would be sure to apply the proper remedy by changing the head of the government. We have no confidence in such a scheme. It finds no support in the established principles of popular representative government. The important functions of determining how much money shall be raised by tax, and of its distribution among the various local objects and purposes, are essentially discretionary, and the officers who are to exercise them should be sensible of no obligations, restraints, or fears, except such as proceed from their convictions of the public welfare. Few men, deserving of public confidence, would accept such places at the hands of a master who could make and unmake them at pleasure. But, more than this, the scheme suggested places the control of vast sums of money—in the city of New York thirty millions of dollars, a larger revenue than that of some kingdoms—in the hands of a single man. No such control over the public resources is lodged even with the sovereign in any constitutional government. The disposition of such a fund, absolute when once gained, whould become the contention, not so frequently of those who would prove faithful to the trust, as of those who sought only to betray it. The assumption that, with frequent elections, the people would very soon dispose of an unworthy chief officer, is altogether illusory. The master of the revenues and patronage of a million people might not suffer himself to be displaced. The notion that the present failure of municipal elections to remove unworthy officers is mainly attributable to an inability to trace the responsibility for maladministration to its true source, is erroneous. The real difficulty is, that the mass of the citizens, however strongly they may be convinced of the necessity of a political change, are not willing to enter upon a campaign against thoroughly-organized political combinations, for the reason that there is not sufficient prospect of success."

A Property Qualification for Voters held to be the only Remedy.

After considering the various remedies proposed for municipal evils, the commissioners are led to "the fundamental quesion, whether the general application of universal suffrage in the election of the local guardians and trustees of the financial interests of these public corporations is in accordance with sound principles, or suitable to our present condition. Entertaining, however, a natural jealousy of any suggestion that might wear the appearance of a departure from the principles of American polity, they preferred to direct their first efforts toward the discovery of some mode of rearranging the local administration, which, without disturbing the elective system, would give promise of a reform of existing abuses. As already shown, all such efforts appeared to them, after the fullest consideration, to be misdirected; and the question remained, whether the election, by universal suffrage, of the local guardians of the financial concerns of cities can be safely retained. This report has thus far been largely directed to a recapitulation of the discussions and conclusions through which they were led, or rather forced, to a consideration of the principal question above stated. We have pursued this method because we recognize and appreciate the natural disinclination of our citizens to attribute the disorders of our political system to the operation of general suffrage. After the most careful deliberation our conclusion is, that the choice of the local guardians and trustees of the financial concerns of cities should be lodged with the taxpayers. To admit to a participation in such choice those who make no contribution to the funds to be administered, is not in conformity with the principles on which human affairs are conducted, and is a departure from the general policy of this State, as frequently declared by the legislature."

It is interesting to note that, while the only plan suggested by the New York commissioners, among all others proposed for the remedy of municipal abuses, was to limit the exercise of the right of suffrage, on questions of expenditure and taxation, to the taxpaying portion of the community,[1] this plan was considered by the Pennsylvania commissioners to be not only unnecessary and impracticable, but as ill-suited to the social condition of the people.

History of the Property Qualification in New York.

Such a limitation on the suffrage, however, in the municipalities, the larger part of the administration of which consists in the raising by taxation, from the owners of property therein, of a common fund for carrying out the local purposes above referred to, and the due application of that fund, is by no means a new scheme in the history of local government in New York. The legislature in framing the local governments for the one hundred and twenty villages in the State, possessing the general features of city charters, has intrusted the control of the financial concerns to the taxpayers alone. The village executive officers, the board of trustees, the local

[1] See article on the administration of American cities, favoring a limitation of municipal suffrage, in the *International Review* for September and October, 1877, pages 631–646, by Simon Sterne, a member of the commission appointed by Governor Tilden.

legislature of the village, were elected by voters possessing the ordinary qualifications; but the vote of the taxpaying electors was, with certain exceptions, requisite to confer the authority to raise money by taxation. In the cases of the first village charters, no tax whatever was permitted to be raised, except by the authority of a vote of the taxpayers; but it was found that there were certain annually recurring expenses, small in amount, and usually of about the same sum, which it was a matter of course to supply; and the legislature, in many instances, to save the inconvenience of a separate vote of a separate body of electors at a village meeting, introduced into numbers of the village charters carefully-guarded provisions, authorizing the boards of trustees to raise by tax sums limited in amount, usually a few hundred, sometimes a few thousand, dollars, for these regular and inevitable expenditures; but for any unusual object, requiring the expenditure of any considerable sum, the authority to levy a tax was carefully restricted to the taxpayers; and it is to be observed that any proposition for the raising of an unusual tax, when submitted to the taxpayers, was required to state the purposes to which the money was to be applied, so that the contributors to the fund could pass judgment upon the objects of the expenditure, as well as upon the amount to be raised.

Provisions adopting this method are found in the charters of nearly all the villages of the State prior to the passage, in 1847, of the general law for the incorporation of villages. The constitution of 1846 made it the duty of the legislature to provide by general law for the incorporation of villages, and accordingly the general act of 1847 was passed, and continued in force until it was superseded by the general village incorporation act of 1870. Both these acts reaffirmed and adopted the same principle of discrimination in the exercise of the suffrage, giving the election of officers to the electors generally, but committing questions of expenditure, with the exception of small amounts for ordinary purposes, to the taxpayers alone. Many of the cities of the State grew out of village organizations, and their charters usually contained the same discrimination, as in the case of Binghamton, Kingston, Oswego, Ogdensburg, Elmira, and Long Island City.

That the same discrimination was not applied to the large cities in the State of New York, was the result rather of accident than design. The question whether the financial concerns of municipalities should be intrusted to the control of universal suffrage, or to that of the taxpayers only, could not arise in the convention which framed the constitution of 1821, since that convention preserved the restriction of the right of suffrage in all cases to owners of property. In 1826, however, the property qualification was almost wholly abrogated by the amendment to the constitution. The convention of 1846 did not adequately deal with the questions arising respecting the local government of cities and villages. At that time, as already explained, the control of the financial concerns was, in all villages and most of the cities, lodged with the taxpayers through the instrumentality of a system of direct voting upon the questions themselves. In respect to the metropolis, the legislature itself annually passed upon the question of all the expenditures, and as to many of the expenditures of other large cities. Moreover, the evils of wasteful and corrupt administration had then scarcely begun to develop themselves to a degree sufficient to command attention; and the convention contented itself with an express delegation to the legislature of the duty of providing by general law the requisite legislation for cities and villages. That duty, so far as it related to villages, was performed in the manner indicated; but in respect to cities, especially the larger ones, it could hardly be performed by the legislature alone. To commit the control of financial affairs, even in respect to extraordinary expenditures and debt, to a direct vote of the taxpayers, was hardly possible. This method is applicable only to small communities, and to extend it to great cities like the metropolis would be impracticable. The establishment of a representative body, to be chosen by the taxpayers, was, indeed, a practical method by which could be controlled the question of expenditure and taxation in large cities; but the provisions of the constitution, declaring in effect that all elective officers should be chosen by universal suffrage, stood in the way of such a scheme. The result was, that the legislature, while carefully guarding the concerns of debt and taxation in the smaller municipalities, by limiting them to the general body of the taxpayers, was compelled to leave the great concerns of debt and taxation, for the most part, to the municipal councils chosen by the voters at large.[1]

Scheme of Government proposed by the New York Commission.

Having principally in view the limitation of the suffrage to the taxpayers in matters of expenditure, a constitutional amendment was recommended by the New York commission, of which the following are the principal features:—

First.—The delegation of the entire business of local administration to the people of the cities, free from legislative interference therewith; reserving to the State its functions of making the general laws under which the local affairs are to be administered, and also a supervision of the manner of administration.

Second.—A chief executive officer, clothed with the authority of general supervision, and with the unfettered power to appoint the other principal executive officers, except those two (the chief financial and chief law officers), whose duties immediately affect the matter of the public expenditure, and with the power of removal, subject, however, to the approval of the governor.

Third.—A board of aldermen, clothed, as now, with all the legislative powers, *except such as relate to taxation and expenditure,* and elected—as at present—by the people.

Fourth.—A separate body, called the board of finance, to be elected by tax and rent payers, with such powers only as relate to taxation, expenditure, and debt; its principal function being to determine the amount of the annual expendi-

[1] See report of New York commission.

ture and to appropriate it to its various objects and purposes. The assent of this body was made requisite to the appointment of the chief financial and law officers.

Fifth.—A detailed plan, designed to be complete in itself, for securing efficiency, order, and frugality in the financial administration, and to be executed by the board of finance. Its main features were:—

1. The determination, in each year, of the sum of money requisite to be expended for all objects and purposes, and what part thereof should be raised by taxation, and the levying of the latter sum.

2. The appropriation, at the same time, of the whole sum to be expended to the several objects and purposes.

3. The certain realization of the entire amount appropriated, by compelling the relevying of deficiencies in the collection of taxes.

4. The prohibition of any expenditure beyond the sums appropriated, by making all contracts and engagements in excess thereof void.

Sixth.—A further enforcement of the maxim, "pay as you go," by a prohibition against borrowing money, or incurring debt, except under certain specified conditions, not likely to arise often.

The leading features of the report of the New York commission, thus briefly sketched, give a fair idea of the condition of municipalities and position of municipal questions in that State. As in Pennsylvania, reform in the government of New York city continued to be the subject of agitation for many years.[1] Indeed, tinkering with the charters of the great cities of the State, either in the interest of or against their citizens, occupied a large part of the time of successive sessions of the legislature. It is not the purpose of this brief sketch to go into the details of this legislation, or to give more than a sketch of the salient features in the development of municipal

---

[1] See the recommendations of reform in the inaugural message of Mayor Grace to the board of aldermen, January 5, 1885, document No. 1.

questions, as affording a useful and instructive illustration of similar questions in Philadelphia.[1] In 1884 the New York legislature passed several important bills, known as the "New York reform bills." The first of these bills is the one known, variously, as the "mayor's," the "aldermanic," or the "mayoralty responsibility bill." This important act is as follows:—

"An act to centre responsibility in the municipal government of the city of New York.

"The people of the State of New York, represented in senate and assembly, do enact as follows:—

"SECTION 1. All appointments to office in the city of New York, and made by the mayor and confirmed by the board of aldermen, shall hereafter be made by the mayor without such confirmation.

"SEC. 2. This act shall take effect January 1, 1885."

Governor Cleveland, in signing this bill, filed, among other reasons, the following: "If the chief executive of the city is to be held responsible for its orders and good government, he should not be hampered by any interference with his selection of subordinate administrative officers, nor should he be permitted to find, in a divided responsibility, an excuse for any neglect of the best interests of the people. The plea should never be heard, that a bad nomination had been made because it was the only one that could receive confirmation. No instance has been cited in which a bad appointment has been prevented by the refusal of the board of aldermen of the city of New York to confirm a nomination. An absolute and undivided responsibility on the part of the appointing power

[1] An act to reorganize the local government of the city of New York, April 30, 1873, chapter 335, and the supplementary acts; chapter 400, laws of 1873; chapter 304, laws of 1874; chapter 305, laws of 1874; chapter 757, laws of 1873; chapter 300, laws of 1874; chapter 120, laws of 1875; chapter 476, laws of 1875; chapter 125, laws of 1878; chapter 726, laws of 1873; chapter 839, laws of 1873; chapter 759, laws of 1873; chapter 383, laws of 1878; chapter 631, laws of 1875; chapter 758, laws of 1873; chapter 808, laws of 1874; chapter 303, laws of 1874; chapter 326, laws of 1873.

accords with correct business principles, the application of which to public affairs will always, I believe, direct the way to good administration and the protection of the people's interests. The intelligence and watchfulness of the citizens of New York should certainly furnish a safe guarantee that the duties and powers devolved by this legislation upon their chosen representative will be well and wisely bestowed; and if they are ever betrayed, their remedy is close at hand. I can hardly realize the unprincipled boldness of the man who would accept at the hands of his neighbors the sacred trust, and, standing alone in the full light of public observation, would willfully prostitute his powers and defy the will of the people. To say that such a man could by such means perpetuate his wicked rule, concedes either that the people are vile, or that self-government is a deplorable failure."

Some time prior to 1872 these appointments were made by the mayor without confirmation, as was contemplated by the act of 1884. In that year a measure passed the legislature, giving the power of appointment to the common council. Gov. Tilden vetoed the bill, giving reasons similar to those of Gov. Cleveland. "Nowhere," he said, "on this continent is it so essentially a condition of good government, as in the city of New York, that the chief executive officer should be clothed with ample powers, have full control over subordinate administrative departments, and so be subject to an undivided responsibility to the people and to public opinion for all errors, shortcomings, and wrongdoings by subordinate officers." * * * "Give to the city a chief executive, with full power to appoint all heads of administrative departments. Let him have power to remove his subordinates, being required to publicly assign his reason." Again, in 1876, he said in a public address, when suggesting a scheme of municipal government: "Have, therefore, no provision in your charter requiring the consent of the common council to the mayor's appointments of heads of departments; *that only opens* the way for *dictation by the council,* or for *bargains.* This is not the way to get good men, nor to fix the full responsibility for maladministration upon the people's chosen prime minister."[1]

The remaining reform bills signed by Governor Cleveland, although of great local importance, merely require mention here. They were the county clerk's bill,[2] the sheriff's bill,[3] the county register's bill,[4] and the surrogate's bill.[5]

PRESENT GOVERNMENT OF NEW YORK.

The following is a brief sketch of the present government of New York:—

The mayor is elected at the general state election, to hold office for two years. The executive power of the corporation is vested in the mayor and the officers of the departments. The legislative power is vested in a board of aldermen, consisting of twenty-two members, elected annually,—sixteen elected by districts and six at large. No voter shall vote for more than four of the aldermen at large; and in districts from which three aldermen are elected no voter shall vote for more than two.

There are the following executive departments:—

Finance, the head of which is the comptroller; law, the head of which is the corporation counsel; police, with four commissioners; public works, one commissioner; public charities and correction, three commissioners; fire department,

[1] See article by Charles Nordhoff, on the misgovernment of New York (*North American Review*, October, 1871), recommending that the mayor be elected by the people for a short term, with power to appoint all his subordinates, but for his own term of office only; a city judiciary, to be appointed by the mayor for life or good behavior; a common council, with full legislative powers over municipal matters, and over the appropriations for carrying on the city government.

[2] "An act in relation to the office of the clerk of the city and county of New York."

[3] "An act to regulate and provide for certain expenses of conducting the office of sheriff of the city and county of New York."

[4] "An act in relation to the office of the register of the city and county of New York."

[5] "An act in relation to the office of surrogate of the county of New York."

three commissioners; health department, consisting of president of police board, health officer of port, and two commissioners; public parks, four commissioners; taxes and assessments, a president and two commissioners; department of docks, three commissioners; street-cleaning, one commissioner.

The comptroller, the commissioner of public works, the corporation counsel, and the president of each department are entitled to seats in the board of aldermen, with the right to participate in discussions, but not to vote.

Removals from office are made by the mayor for cause, subject to the approval of the governor; except that the head of the department of street-cleaning shall be subject to removal by the mayor, with the approval of the board of health, whenever the mayor shall certify that in his judgment such removal is required in the public interest.

The board of estimate and apportionment consists of the mayor, comptroller, president of the board of aldermen, and the president of the department of taxes and assessments. Between the 1st of August and the 1st of November the board meets, and, by affirmative vote of all the members, makes a provisional estimate of the amounts required to pay the expenses of conducting the public business of the city and county of New York in each department and branch thereof, and of the board of education. The heads of departments are required to furnish a statement in detail of what they severally require. A duplicate of the estimate made by the board is submitted to the aldermen. Any objections or suggestions made by the board of aldermen are transmitted in writing to the board of estimate, and that board then proceeds to consider the same and make a final estimate. If the action of the aldermen is overruled, the reason shall be published in the *City Record*. The taxpayers then have an opportunity to be heard. After the final estimate is made, it is signed by the members of the board, and the several sums named therein become appropriated to the several purposes and departments therein named.

"The board of education consists of twenty-one commissioners of common schools, appointed by the mayor for a term of three years each, seven members to be appointed each year. The board annually appoints, for each ward, one trustee of common schools, to serve for five years. The trustee is required to be a resident of the ward for which he is appointed. The board appoints a city superintendent of schools; and it appoints the school teachers, "upon the written nomination of a majority of the trustees of the ward, stating that the nomination was agreed to at a meeting of the board of trustees, at which a majority of the whole number in office were present."

Boston.

Sec. 22. The original government of the city of Boston was, as in the surrounding New England townships, the government of the town meeting. As the city increased in population, however, this general meeting of the citizens annually, to legislate for their local concerns, was found cumbersome and inconvenient.[1] Accordingly, in 1822, the first charter was granted, by which the executive powers of the corporation generally, together with all the powers formerly vested in the selectmen of the town, either by general or special laws, or by usages, votes, or by-laws, were given to the mayor and aldermen.

First Charter of Boston.

The mayor was simply a member of the board and its chairman. He had a vote, but no veto power. The city council, that is, the mayor and aldermen and common council, sitting as separate boards and acting by concurrent vote, had the powers formerly exercised by the town meetings. The city clerk and the city treasurer were elected by the two boards in convention. In the case of all other officers necessary for the good government of the city, the city council had power to provide for their "appointment or election," prescribe their

[1] See Quincy's Municipal History of Boston.

duties, and fix their compensation. Wardens, clerks, and inspectors of elections, firewards, overseers of the poor, and school committeemen were elected by popular vote in the several wards. By an act passed three years later (1825), the power to choose firewards was given to the mayor and aldermen.

Revised Charter.

In 1854 a new act of incorporation was granted by the general court, and accepted by the legal voters. The mayor was deprived of his vote on matters coming before the board of aldermen, and was given a qualified right to veto all acts of the city council, and all acts of either branch in which an expenditure of money was involved. The administration of the police and the executive powers of the corporation, and all the powers formerly vested in the selectmen of the town and in the mayor and aldermen, were given to the board of aldermen. It was supposed at the time that the new charter gave greater power to the mayor, but practically it curtailed his powers. As an *ex-officio* member of the board of aldermen it had been customary for the mayor to act as chairman of the most important committees of the aldermen and city council; and as chairman of the board which had not only succeeded to all the executive powers formerly exercised by the selectmen of the town, but which had equal powers with the common council as a legislative body, he was in a position to exert, and, following the popular precedent set by Mayor Quincy, did exert, a controlling influence in the management of city affairs. The grant of the qualified right of veto did not in practice compensate him for what he had formerly possessed by law and custom.

Subsequent Legislation.

No general revision of the charter was made until recently; but the powers and duties of the mayor, the aldermen, the city council, and certain heads of departments, have been amended and enlarged by numerous special acts of the general court. Some of the more important of these changes will be specified: In 1864 the city council was authorized to elect overseers of the poor. In 1870 a board of street commissioners was established, the members to be elected by popular vote, with authority, subject to certain qualifications, to exercise the powers formerly held by the board of aldermen concerning the laying out, altering, or discontinuing the streets and ways of the city, and the abatement of taxes. In 1871 a department for the survey and inspection of buildings was established, the chief officer to be appointed by the mayor, subject to confirmation by the city council. In 1874 a board of registrars of voters was established, the members to be appointed by the mayor and confirmed by the aldermen. In 1875 a board of park commissioners was established, consisting of three persons, to be appointed by the mayor, with the approval of the city council. In the same year the school committee was reorganized. The number of committeemen was reduced from one hundred and fourteen to twenty-four, elected on a general ticket (eight each year for a term of three years) instead of by wards. In 1878 the mayor and aldermen were authorized to appoint the wardens and clerks for service at all elections; and in 1881 the power to appoint inspectors of elections was also transferred to the mayor and aldermen. In 1875 the Boston water board was established, the members to be appointed by the mayor with the approval of the city council. In 1878 the control of the police department was transferred from the board of aldermen to a board of three commissioners, appointed by the mayor, with the approval of the city council.[1]

In 1873 a commission was appointed, under an order of city council adopted 1873, to revise the charter and other laws relating to the city, and report the same in a new draft. The report was presented in June, 1875, and was accompanied by a proposed new act of incorporation, drawn with great care, and covering many of the details of municipal business. The draft of the act accompanying the report pro-

[1] Report of the commission on the city charter, 1884.

vided, in substance, that the terms of office of the mayor and members of the city council should be extended to three years; that the city council should have the entire control over all appropriations of public money, and the purposes for which it was to to be expended; that the heads of the several executive departments of the government should be selected and nominated by the mayor and confirmed by the city council; that no member of the board of aldermen or common council, acting either individually or as a committee, should make any disbursement of public money or perform any executive duty whatever, except as specially authorized by law.

It will be observed that in many respects this scheme was up to the latest theories of municipal government. The recommendation of the commissioners, however, failed to receive favorable action as a whole; but in the subsequent reorganization of some of the departments these ideas were carried out.

Under an order of the city council, approved June 24, 1884, commissioners were appointed to "examine the act incorporating the city of Boston, and all other general and special statutes now in force concerning the government of the city, and report to the city council, on or before the first Thursday of November next, what, if any, changes are necessary or expedient by reason of the increase in area and population of the city." The commission promptly organized, with Samuel C. Cobb as chairman, and a report was made in the following November.[1]

"If any evidence were needed," says the report, "to prove the necessity for a change of the present loose and irresponsible methods of administering our local affairs, it would be found in these statements and communications; but, unfortunately, the evils of the present system are so conspicuous and grievous, that the commission may well take note of them without formal proof. The lack of harmony between the different departments, the frequent and notorious charges of

[1] Report of the commission on the city charter, Boston, November 6, 1884. Document 120.

inefficiency and corruption made by members of the government against each other, and the alarming increase in the burden of taxation are matters within the knowledge of all who have taxes to pay, or who read the proceedings of the city council." The remedies suggested are many and widely at variance; but it will be noticed that there is a substantial agreement upon the following points, namely, that the "executive should be separated from the legislative department; that the power and responsibility of the executive should be increased; that the number of departments, and especially the number of heads of departments, should be reduced; and that the work of the different departments should be so arranged as to secure concert of action."

It was complained in the first place that the different city officers were elected or appointed "without regard to any system, and in a manner calculated to destroy all responsibility." The mayor, three street commissioners, and twenty-four school committeemen were elected at large; twelve aldermen by districts; seventy-two councilmen by wards; the remaining city officers being appointed by the mayor, elected by the city council in convention, appointed by the mayor and confirmed by the city council, elected by the concurrent vote of the two branches of the city council, appointed by the mayor and confirmed by the aldermen, or appointed by the board of aldermen.

The influence of the standing committees of the city council was another evil. By rule of city council every joint standing committee had general management and supervision of the department assigned to it, subject to the special instructions of the city council, and to the provisions of all statutes and lawful ordinances.

The various appropriations for the departments were substantially controlled by the respective committees. Of the total appropriation of $12,291,000 for city purposes during 1884, the expenditure of something over $4,000,000, or one-third, was controlled directly or indirectly by committees of the aldermen or city council.

City Taxes.

"It has been stated," says the report, "and the statement appears to be fully sustained by the facts, that property, both real and personal, is more heavily taxed in Boston than in any other large city in this country." The following statement and comparison with other cities is extremely interesting, and is taken from the report.

The rate in Boston of $17 on a thousand for 1884 exceeded by about eight per cent. the highest rate in any previous year, namely, $15.80 in 1865, the year following the war, when the State tax levied on this city was $1,592,501, against $578,055 the present year. The total valuation in 1865 was $371,892,775, and for 1884 it was $682,648,000. The increase over the rate of 1883 is about seventeen per cent.

During the last thirty years, covering the period since the revision of the city charter, the population increased from one hundred and forty thousand to about four hundred thousand, or one hundred and ninety per cent. The valuation of real and personal property increased from $227,000,000 to $682,648,000, or two hundred per cent. The expenditures of the city increased from $2,135,000 to about $12,000,000, or four hundred and fifty per cent.

The appropriations to carry on the government in Boston during 1884, exclusive of payments on account of interest and city debt, State tax, and county expenses, amounted to $9,909,019, equal to $27.30 for each inhabitant, census of 1880.

The appropriations in New York for 1884, excluding State tax, interest on debt, payments for redemption of debt, and maintenance of judiciary amounted to $20,232,786, equal to $16.76 for each inhabitant, census of 1880.

The appropriations for city purposes in Baltimore for the year 1883 amounted to $3,878,804, equal to $11.67 for each inhabitant.

The appropriations for city purposes in Philadelphia for 1884 amounted to $8,599,196, equal to $10.15 for each inhabitant.

The appropriation for city purposes in Cincinnati for the year 1883 was $2,718,804, equal to $10.63 for each inhabitant.

The assessors' valuation of real estate in New York appears to be about sixty per cent. of the market value. An estate, taken by chance, on one of the well-known streets of that city is taxed for $280,000. The actual cost to the present owners is $431,500,—valued much higher. Net amount of rent, exclusive of taxes, general and special, $40,000. Another estate, valued by the assessors at $34,000, yields an income of $6025 per annum, and pays a tax (with customary discount off) of $757. The tax rate is 22.90 on $1000.

When the difference in the valuation of real estate in Boston and in New York is taken into account, and the fact that personal property in New York, including bank shares, is valued at only $197,546,000 (less than one-fifth of the real estate valuation, against two-fifths in Boston), it is clear that the burden of taxation, especially on capital invested in mercantile and manufacturing business, is much heavier in Boston than it is in New York.

In the city of Chicago the valuation of property is between one-fifth and one-third of the actual value. The following instances are fairly representative :—

A piece of well-known hotel property is valued on the assessors' books for $120,000. It is actually mortgaged to-day for $325,000, that mortgage being taken at one-half its true value, $650,000. Rent under lease in 1884, $40,000, in 1885, $56,000, or fifty per cent. of the assessed valuation.

A business block actually cost, in 1874, $43,500. Valued on assessors' books, 1883, at $9000. Actual present rental, $6000. Actual value, as shown by the sale of a similar adjoining lot, $60,000. Average tax for the last ten years, including all taxes of every kind (general and special), about $575. An estate, occupied as a residence, sold in 1881 for 25,000. Valued in 1882 on assessors' books, $7000, and in 1883, $5500. Average tax, including all special assessments of every kind, $370.

A piece of tenement property, appraised in 1882 at $12,-000; estimated to be worth in 1884, $15,000. Actual rents for the last four years, $2000. Average actual tax for seven years, about $170. Valued on the assessors' books, $1980.

An estate on Chestnut street, Philadelphia, used for business purposes (twenty-seven feet front by eighty-seven feet deep, building five stories high), was in 1884 valued for purposes of taxation at $27,000. Tax on the estate for the same year, at $18.50 on $1000, $499.50. Mercantile tax (for State purposes) on sales of merchandise in the store during the year, say from $85,000 to $100,000, as per schedule, $80. Total on real estate and business, $579.50.

The tax in Boston on an estate and business similarly situated would be as follows:—

Tax on estate (the assessors' valuation is higher there in proportion to the market value than it is in Philadelphia, but in this comparison we will presume it is the same), $27,000, at $17 on $1000, $459. Tax on stock in trade, say $25,-000, $425. Total on estate and business, $884. From which it appears that a man carrying on business in Boston pays an annual local tax amounting to fifty per cent. more than a man doing business of the same extent and value in Philadelphia, and in addition to this he is liable to a tax on his income exceeding $2000.

Real estate in the suburbs of Philadelphia is assessed at two-thirds, and the farming lands at half, the rate levied upon the portion of the city fully covered by buildings. That is to say, for 1884 the rate of taxation on property in the business portion of the city was $18.50 on $1000; in the suburbs, $12.33; on farm lands, $9.25. The total valuation of personal property in Philadelphia for the same year amounted (for city purposes) to only $9,884,578, about one fifty-fifth of the real estate valuation, as against two-fifths in Boston.

The rule established by the board of revision in Philadelphia is to assess city property at ten times the annual rental, unless, of course, it appears that a fair market rental is not obtained. In the case of manufacturing or industrial works, which are deemed an advantage to the community, a liberal discount is made on the real estate, and the machinery is not assessed at all. It is stated that, as a general rule, the selling value of property in Philadelphia is twenty-five per cent. above the assessed value, and numerous instances have been furnished to sustain the statement.

The revenue derived from special assessments for public improvements is considerably larger in the other cities than it is in Boston. The expense of laying out and building new streets in Philadelphia is substantially borne by the property which is benefited; but when a street is once made, the city bears the expense of keeping it in repair; so that in the case of the estate on Chestnut street, to which we have referred, there are no special assessments for paving or other street improvements.

The law in regard to special assessments in Boston provides that the abutters shall pay half the cost of sidewalks for foot passengers, three-fourths of the expense of constructing new sewers, and half the estimated value of the benefit from laying out, widening, or changing the grade of any street.

The amount of special assessments during the ten years previous to 1884 was $3,691,938.

The taxation of personal property for municipal purposes is also complained of.[1] Moreover there were thirty-seven different departments controlled by one hundred and five persons, not including assistant assessors, superintendents of bridges, and numerous committees of the city council which as already mentioned exercised executive powers.

The Plan Proposed in Boston.

In the plan proposed by the commissioners the legislative power of the local government was to be vested in the city council, which was reduced to one chamber, on the ground that "one body having the responsibility is more amenable

[1] See "Taxation," by William Minot, Sr., Boston, 1881.

to public opinion than two." The executive powers of the corporation were to be vested in the mayor, an executive council consisting of five persons from the citizens at large, and in the heads of the departments.

The Executive Council.

The executive council is a feature peculiar to this scheme. Objections were made to giving the mayor the sole power of appointment. There were, also, in the opinion of the commissioners, "serious objections" to placing the power of confirmation in the legislative branch. The question was, how could a check be placed upon the arbitrary exercise of power without unduly interfering with the executive power and responsibility? "The satisfactory solution of the problem was the establishment of an executive council composed of a small number of persons, elected from the citizens at large upon the minority representation plan. The executive council was to act upon the mayor's appointments, and possess certain executive powers." Another feature of the scheme was, to pay the members of the city council and the executive council. The executive appointments in the new plan were considerably reduced in number. Each department, with certain exceptions, was placed under the charge of one person, who had power to appoint his subordinates; while the heads of the departments were appointed by the mayor with the consent of the executive council. It was further proposed by the commission that the mayor should have power to veto distinct items in any ordinance; that the mayor, or any other municipal officer, might be indicted, and, if found guilty, fined or removed from office for misconduct; that the mayor should, once a month or oftener, call the heads of the departments together for consultation, and advice upon the affairs of the city; and that the estimates for carrying on the several executive departments of the city should be examined and revised by the mayor and executive council before being submitted to the city council.

Present Government of Boston.

"The temper in which the majority report of the commissioners was discussed by the city council showed that nothing in the way of an adequate reform of existing abuses could be expected from that body.[1] A citizens' association was formed, with a view to securing some measure of reform by direct application to the general court. The scheme finally adopted by the association included many of the important recommendations made by the commission. As it seemed necessary, in order to secure favorable action, that whatever scheme was presented should have the support of the entire organization, and as there were differences of opinion as to the expediency of reducing the legislative department of the government to one body, and also as to the expediency of giving the mayor the sole power of appointment, a compromise was agreed upon by which the two branches of the city council were retained in their original form, but without executive power, and the mayor was authorized to appoint all city officers, subject to confirmation by the aldermen, and to remove any of them for such cause as he might deem sufficient, a distinct statement of the cause being given in his order for removal. The mayor was also authorized to veto, subject to the usual qualifications, the separate items in any ordinance or order involving an appropriation or expenditure of money.

"The scheme prepared by the association was adopted by the general court without material alteration. Another important measure, which originated with the then mayor, and which was favored by the Reform Association, was also adopted at the same time, limiting the rate of taxation to a sum not exceeding nine dollars (exclusive of the State tax, and of the sums required by law to be raised on account of the city debt) on every $1000 of the average of the assessors' valua-

[1] City Government of Boston; by James M. Bugbee. Johns Hopkins University Studies in Historical and Political Science. Fifth Series. No. III. Page 42.

tion of taxable property for the preceding five years. In connection with this restriction, the limit of municipal indebtedness, which, by an act passed in 1875, had been fixed at an amount not exceeding three per cent. of the last preceding valuation, was further reduced to two per cent. on the average valuation for the preceding five years.

"The general court of the same year (1855) passed another act, which was prepared by those specially interested in the cause of temperance and the suppression of vice, establishing a board of police for Boston. In 1878 a special act of the general court authorized the mayor to appoint, subject to the approval of the city council, three commissioners to have charge of the police department, with power to appoint all the officers, and to grant licenses for the sale of intoxicating liquors. It was represented that the influences under which the commissioners were appointed prevented them from properly executing the state laws for regulating and restraining the sale of liquor and for the suppression of gambling and prostitution. There was a good deal of evidence to sustain the charge. But it was evident that a majority of the voters of Boston, including many substantial citizens who were eager to support any legitimate measure for the restriction of the liquor traffic, were opposed to the principle of allowing the state to take possession of, and govern, the most important department of the local government—a department which, although it had shown some laxity in the enforcement of certain laws, had not failed, on the whole, to preserve order and protect life and property. The act provided for the appointment, by the governor and council, of three citizens of Boston, to constitute a board of police, with power to 'appoint, establish, and organize' the police of Boston, and to license, regulate, and restrain the sale of intoxicating liquors. The city is required to pay, on the requisition of the board, all expenses of maintaining the establishment. In case of a riot, or violent disturbance of public order, the mayor is authorized for the time being to assume control of the force, and the police board is required to execute his orders."

OTHER CITIES.

SEC. 22. The above sketches of some of the features in the municipal development of Brooklyn, New York, and Boston will give the reader an idea of the tendency and character of modern theories of municipal government, and furnish a useful comparison and illustration to the reforms in Philadelphia. It may serve a similar useful purpose to give, as briefly as possible, the present governments of four other important cities.

BALTIMORE.

The mayor is elected for a term of two years. He is required to be twenty-five years of age, ten years a citizen of the United States, five years a resident of the city, and assessed on property within the city to the amount of $500.

The city council consists of two branches. The first is composed of one member elected annually from each ward, who shall be a citizen of the United States, a resident of the city three years, a resident of the ward of which he is elected, and assessed to the amount of $300. The second branch is composed of one member from every two contiguous wards, elected biennially, who shall be twenty-five years of age, a resident of the city four years, and assessed to the amount of $500. The members of the city council receive $1000 each per annum.

City officers are appointed by the mayor, by and with the advice and consent of a convention of the two branches of the city council. The principal city officers are, the comptroller, the city counsellor, the city solicitor; five fire commissioners; a commissioner and assistant commissioner of health; a superintendent of streets for each of the five districts into which the city is divided by the health commissioners; three commissioners for opening streets; a water board consisting of the mayor, *ex officio*, and six residents of Baltimore.

The board of police commissioners consists of three persons elected by the Maryland legislature, to hold office for six years each. The public schools are managed by twenty commissioners elected by the two branches of the city council in convention, to serve for a term of four years each. Three persons are appointed by the mayor, with the approval of the city council, to constitute the appeal tax court, with the general powers of assessors of taxes in Massachusetts.

St. Louis.

The mayor is elected for a term of four years. The following heads of departments are also elected by the qualified voters for a term of four years each, namely: A comptroller, auditor, treasurer, register, collector, recorder of deeds, inspector of weights and measures, sheriff, coroner, marshal, public administrator, president board of assessors, and president of the board of public improvements.

The members of the board of public improvements, with the exception of the president, are appointed by the mayor, and known as street commissioner, sewer commissioner, water commissioner, harbor and wharf commissioner, and park commissioner. These titles show what bureaus are included in the public improvement department. The mayor also appoints the following officers for terms of four years each, namely: A city counsellor, such district assessors as may be provided by ordinance, superintendent of the workhouse, superintendent of house of refuge, superintendent of fire and police telegraph, commissioner of supplies, assessor of water rates, two police justices, attorney, jailer, and five commissioners on charitable institutions. All appointments made by the mayor require the confirmation of a majority of members of the council. Any elected city officer may be suspended by the mayor and removed by the council for cause; and any appointed officer may be removed by the mayor or council for cause.

The legislative power of the city is vested in a council of thirteen members, elected on a general ticket for four years, and a house of delegates, consisting of one member from each ward, chosen by the voters in the several wards, to serve for two years each. Members of the council are required to be thirty years of age, citizens of the State for five years, inhabitants of the city, and freeholders therein. A member of the house of delegates is required to be twenty-five years of age, a citizen of the United States, an inhabitant of the city for three years, and a taxpayer for two years next before the day of election. The two bodies together constitute the municipal assembly. The members are paid $300 per annum for their services. Members absent from any meeting forfeit a dollar.

The "president and directors" of the public schools consist of as many members as there are wards in the city, each ward electing one director to serve for three years. The directors levy the school tax, which is assessed and collected by the officers who have charge of the assessment and collection of other taxes.

Chicago.

The city council consists of the mayor and thirty-six aldermen, elected for two years each. The aldermen are elected on the minority representation plan.

The city clerk, city attorney, and city treasurer are elected on a general ticket. The other city officers are appointed by the mayor, with the advice and consent of the city council. The commissioner of public works has charge of all public improvements, and appoints and removes, with the consent of the mayor, the heads of bureaus in his department, as follows: the city engineer, the superintendent of streets, the superintendent of water, the superintendent of sewerage, the superintendent of special assessments, and the superintendent of maps. The building department is under the charge of one commissioner, who appoints inspectors of buildings and an inspector of elevators. The law department is under the charge of the corporation counsel, appointed by the mayor; the city attorney, elected by the people; and the prosecuting attorney, appointed by the mayor upon the recommendation of the corporation counsel and the city attorney. The health department embraces the commissioner of health, the superintendent of police, and the city physician. The health commissioner has substantially the powers and duties of the board of health in Philadelphia. The city physician performs his duties under the direction of the commissioner. The superintendent of police is the head of the police department. With the consent of the mayor he appoints all officers and members of the department. The fire marshal is head of the fire department. All officers and members of the department are appointed by him with the consent of the mayor. The board of education consists of fifteen members appointed by the mayor, with the advice and consent of the council, to serve for a term of three years each.

The city council is required annually, before the third Tuesday in September, to ascertain the amount of appropriations required for all corporate purposes; and, by an ordinance specifying in detail the purposes for which such appropriations are made, levy the amount upon all the property subject to taxation. A certified copy of the ordinance is then filed with the county clerk, whose duty it is to ascertain the rate per cent. which will produce a net amount not less than the amount directed to be levied; and the clerk then enters the tax on the books of the collector of state and county taxes. The aggregate amount of taxes levied for any one year, exclusive of the amount for the payment of bonds or interest thereon, shall not exceed two per cent. upon the aggregate valuation of all property subject to taxation. The mayor can veto separate items or appropriations in any ordinance.

San Francisco.

The city of San Francisco has no charter, but is governed under what is known as the "consolidation act," which consolidated the city and county of San Francisco under one government. The main feature of the "consolidation act" is the "one-twelfth act," which divides the fund devoted by the supervisors to any special department of the city government into twelve equal parts, one for each month of the fiscal year, and provides that the expenditures for any one month shall not exceed the amount set aside for it.

The mayor is elected for two years. He has little power in appointing municipal officers. He is *ex officio* president of the board of supervisors and board of health. The municipal council consists of a board of supervisors of twelve members, elected every two years, representing the twelve wards of the city. Their powers are derived entirely from the legislature, and their duties are largely executive. The mayor has the veto power; but the veto may be overruled by the votes of nine members of the board of supervisors. He cannot veto parts of appropriation bills. The finance committee of the board of supervisors makes the necessary appropriations for carrying on the city government, subject to the approval of the whole board.

Conclusion.

The tendency of the recent theories of municipal government, illustrated in Philadelphia and the other cities already mentioned, may thus be briefly summarized: All executive power is concentrated in one head, responsible directly for the whole administration to the people who elect him; a few subordinate heads of departments are appointed by and responsible to this head; a complete separation is made between the executive and legislative branches of government; and a stringent limitation is placed on the power to accumulate indebtedness, while careful regulations are framed for the financial system and methods. Much of the immediate success in Philadelphia will depend on the wisdom exercised by councils in framing the operating ordinances, and on the character of the men who are first called upon to administer the provisions of the system.

APPENDICES.

An Act

To provide for the better government of cities of the first class in this Commonwealth.

Article I.

THE MAYOR.

Section 1. *Be it enacted, &c.,* That on and after the first Monday of April, one thousand eight hundred and eighty-seven, in cities of the first class in this Commonwealth, the executive power shall be vested in the mayor and in the departments authorized by this act.

The mayor shall be the chief executive officer of the city, and shall be at least twenty-five years of age, and have been a citizen and inhabitant of the State five years, and an inhabitant of the city for which he may be elected mayor five years next before his said election, unless absent on the public business of the United States, or of this State, and shall reside in said city during his term of service.

The mayor shall be chosen by a plurality of the votes cast at the municipal election, and shall hold his office for the term of four years from the first Monday of April next ensuing his election, and serve until his successor is duly elected and qualified, but shall not be eligible to the office for the next succeeding term.

If two or more candidates be equal and highest in votes one of them shall be chosen mayor by a vote of the majority of all the members of the incoming councils in joint convention assembled, immediately upon their organization.

When a vacancy shall take place in the office of mayor, a successor shall be elected for the unexpired term at the next municipal election occurring more than thirty days after the commencement of such vacancy, unless such election should occur in the last year of said term, in which case a mayor *pro tempore* shall be chosen by councils in joint convention by the votes of the majority of members elected, and the person elected mayor shall hold office until the expiration of said term and until his successor shall be duly elected and qualified, and it shall be the duty of the president of the select council to issue the proclamation for such joint convention to be held not less than ten, nor more than twenty days, after such vacancy shall take place.

Until the vacancy is filled the president of select council shall act as mayor.

It shall be the duty of the mayor:

I. To cause the ordinances of the city and the laws of the State to be executed and enforced.

II. To communicate to councils at least once a year a statement of the finances and general condition of the affairs of the city, and, also, such information in relation to the same as either branch of council may, from time to time, require.

III. To recommend by message in writing to the councils all such measures connected with the affairs of the city and the protection and improvement of its government and finances as he shall deem expedient.

IV. To call special meetings of councils, or either of them, when required by public necessity.

V. To perform such duties as may be prescribed by law or ordinance, and he shall be responsible for the good order and efficient government of the city.

The mayor shall call together the heads of departments for consultation and advice upon the affairs of the city at least once a month, and at such meetings he may call on the heads of departments for such reports as to the subject-matters under their control and management as he may deem proper, which it shall be their duty to prepare and submit at once to the mayor. Records shall be kept of such meetings, and rules and regulations shall be adopted thereat for the administration of the affairs of the city departments, not inconsistent with any law or ordinance, which regulations shall prescribe a common and systematic method of ascertaining the comparative fitness of applicants for office, position, and promotion, and of selecting, appointing, and promoting those found to be the best fitted without regard to their political opinions or services.

The mayor shall be *ex officio* a member of all boards herein provided for, except the board of building inspectors, and shall have the right as such to participate in their deliberations and proceedings, and vote whenever he may deem it advisable so to do.

The mayor may, by a written order to be transmitted to select councils giving his reasons therefor, remove from office any head of department, director, or other officer appointed by him.

During the recess of select council he shall have power to fill all vacancies that may happen in offices to which he may appoint subject to the approval of the said select council at their next session, and if such appointment shall not be rejected within thirty days after said select council shall have convened, the same shall be considered confirmed.

The several heads of departments shall present to the mayor annually on or before the first Monday of February, a report of their proceedings during the preceding year, and he shall transmit the same to councils with any recommendations he may think proper to make.

The mayor may disapprove of any item or items of any bill making appropriations, and the part or parts of the bill approved shall be the law, and the item or items disapproved shall be void, unless repassed according to the rules and limitations prescribed by law for the passage of bills over the mayor's veto.

The mayor shall, as often as he may think proper, appoint three competent persons to examine without notice the accounts of any city department, trust officer, or employé, and the money, securities, and property belonging to the city in the possession or charge of such department trustees, officer, or employé, and report the result of such investigation.

Article II.

THE EXECUTIVE DEPARTMENTS.

Section 1. There shall be the following executive departments:

I. Department of public safety.

II. Department of public works.

III. Department of receiver of taxes.

IV. Department of city treasurer.

V. Department of city controller.

VI. Department of law.

VII. Department of education.

VIII. Department of charities and correction.

IX. Sinking fund commission.

No department shall be created other than those herein enumerated.

Councils shall provide by ordinance for such bureaus, clerks, or other subordinate officers, as may be required for the transaction of the business of the department.

Each department shall have power to prescribe rules and regulations, not inconsistent with any law or ordinance, or with the provisions of article one hereof, for its own government, regulating the conduct of its officers, clerks, and employés, the distribution and performance of its business, and the custody, use, and preservation of the books, records, papers, and property under its control.

Each department shall furnish to the mayor or councils, or either branch of councils, such information as he or they may at any time demand in relation to its affairs.

Article III.

DEPARTMENT OF PUBLIC SAFETY.

Section 1. The department of public safety shall be under the charge of one director who shall be the head thereof.

The care, management, administration, and supervision of the police affairs, and all matters relating to the public health, to the fire and police force, fire alarm telegraph, erection of fire escapes, and the inspection of buildings and boilers, markets, and food sold therein, shall be in charge of this department.

No person shall be employed in this department as a policeman or fireman who is not a citizen of the United States, or who has been convicted of crime unless pardoned, or who cannot read and write understandingly in the English language, or who shall not have resided within the State at least one year preceding his appointment.

The superintendent of police, whenever directed by the department, shall appoint and cause to be sworn in any number of additional patrolmen to do duty at any place in the city designated, by and at the charge and expense of the person or persons who may ask for such appointment. They shall be subject to and obey the orders, rules, and regulations of the department, and conform to the general discipline and special regulations thereof.

The mayor may, upon any emergency or apprehension of riot or mob, take command of the police force and appoint as many special patrolmen as he may deem advisable. During their services the special appointees shall possess the powers and perform the duties of regular employés of the department, and shall receive such compensation as shall be authorized by the mayor, not exceeding that of the regular officers of the force performing corresponding duties.

The department shall make suitable regulations, under which the officers and members of the fire telegraph and police force shall be required to wear an appropriate uniform. It shall be a misdemeanor punishable by fine not exceeding five hundred dollars, and imprisonment not exceeding six months, or either or both in the discretion of the court, for any person to falsely personate by uniform, insignia, or otherwise, any officer or member of the department.

There shall be created and established by ordinance a pension fund to be maintained by an equal and proportionate monthly charge made against each member of the fire and police force, which fund shall be safely invested and held in trust by the commissioners of the sinking fund and applied upon such terms and regulations as councils may by ordinance prescribe, for the benefit of such members of the fire and police force as shall receive honorable discharges therefrom by reason of age or disability, and the families of such as may be injured or killed in the service; but such allowance as shall be made to those who are retired by reason of the disabilities of age shall be in conformity with a uniform scale.

No policeman or fireman shall be dismissed without his written consent, except by the decision of a court either of trial or of inquiry duly determined and certified in writing to the mayor, which court shall be composed of persons belonging to the police or fire force equal or superior in official position therein to the accused. Such decision shall only be determined by trial of charges with plain specifications, made by, or lodged with, the director of the department of public safety, of which trial the accused shall have due notice, and at which he shall have the right to be present in person. The persons composing such court shall be appointed and sworn by the director of the department of public safety to perform their duties impartially and without fear or favor, and the person of highest rank in such court shall have the same authority to issue and enforce process to secure the attendance of witnesses, and to administer oaths to witnesses, as is possessed by any justice of the peace in this Commonwealth.

Such charges may be of disability for service, in which case the court shall be one of inquiry, whose decision may be for the honorable discharge from the service of the person concerned, or of neglect or violation of law or duty, inefficiency, intemperance, disobedience of orders, or unbecoming official or personal conduct, in which cases the court shall be one of trial, and its decision may authorize the director of the department of public safety to impose fines and pecuniary penalties, to be stopped from pay, or to suspend from pay or duty, or both, for a period fixed by them not exceeding one year, or to dismiss from the service.

It shall be lawful for the director of the department of public safety at his discretion, to suspend from duty before trial any person charged as aforesaid, until such trial can be had, with or without pay as such court shall afterward determine, but no trial shall be delayed for more than one month after charge made.

The finding of the court of trial or inquiry as aforesaid, shall be of no effect until approved by the mayor.

In cities of the first class the board of health shall continue with the powers and duties now vested in it by law, but the members thereof shall be five in number to be nominated by the mayor and confirmed by the select council for the period of three years. The present members thereof shall serve until the expiration of their terms of office respectively, but when their number shall be reduced below five, then the mayor shall nominate persons to fill the vacancies resulting therefrom so that the number shall be always five, but the board of health shall be attached to the department of public safety. The director of public safety shall *ex officio* be a member and president of the board of health, and, as chief executive officer thereof, subject to the resolutions and orders of the said board, appoint, supervise, and control all the subordinate officers and employés attached to the board.

The board of building inspectors shall continue with the powers and duties now vested in it by law, and shall consist of three members. After the expiration of the respective terms of office of the several present building inspectors, their places shall be filled by appointment by the head of the department, in the manner pointed out in article twelve hereof; but it shall be attached to the department of public safety, and shall perform the duties now by law allotted to it under the supervision and control of the director of public safety. The said board shall be composed of practical bricklayers and carpenters, but the three members thereof shall not all be of the same occupation.

Article IV.

DEPARTMENT OF PUBLIC WORKS.

Section 1. The department of public works shall be under the charge of one director who shall be the head thereof.

Water works and gas works owned and controlled by the city, the supply and distribution of water and gas, the grading, paving, repairing, cleaning, and lighting of streets, alleys, and highways, the construction, protection, and repair of public buildings, bridges, and structures of every kind for public use, public squares, real estate (except such as now or hereafter may be used for educational or police purposes), surveys, engineering, sewerage, drainage, and dredging, and all matters and things in any way relating to or affecting the highways, footways, wharves, and docks of the city, shall be under the direction, control, and administration of the department of public works: *Provided*, That nothing in this section contained shall be construed to repeal or conflict with any special acts of Assembly providing for the erection and construction of public buildings, or an act, entitled "An act appropriating ground for public purposes in the city of Philadelphia," approved the twenty-sixth day of March, one thousand eight hundred and sixty-seven.

The operations of the city ice boats shall be under the direction of this department.

The provisions of section twenty-seven of an act, entitled "A further supplement to an act, entitled 'An act to incorporate the city of Philadelphia,'" approved February second, one thousand eight hundred and fifty-four, and of section three of an act, entitled "A supplement to the act consolidating the city of Philadelphia," approved April twenty-first, one thousand eight hundred and fifty-five, are hereby repealed, and councils are hereby authorized by ordinance to divide the city into such survey districts as to them may seem proper. Until the expiration of the respective terms of office of the present district surveyors, such surveyors shall be attached to the department of public works and shall perform their duties under the direction of the said department, and at the expiration of their said respective terms, subject to such ordinances as councils may make upon the subject, their places shall be filled in the manner pointed out in section four of article eleven hereof.

ARTICLE V.

DEPARTMENT OF RECEIVER OF TAXES.

SECTION 1. The receiver of taxes shall be the head of this department; shall be elected and give security as now provided by law, and shall hold his office for a term of three years, and until his successor is chosen and qualified.

All officers charged with the duty of collecting taxes, and the receipt and collection of funds derived from loans, licenses, water rents, water pipe, frontages, permits and rents from markets, landings, wharves, and other public property and interests, shall be attached and subordinate to this department, and be subject to its supervision, control, and direction. But boards of directors of city trusts now existing, and boards of revision of taxes created by any acts of Assembly of this Commonwealth, shall be appointed and perform their functions as heretofore.

No person shall be eligible to the office of receiver of taxes except a citizen of the city, resident therein for seven years next preceding his election, unless he shall have been absent on public business of the United States or of this State.

The receiver of taxes shall be charged by the controller with the full amount of all tax duplicates of the several wards, and also with all other accounts placed in his hands by the proper officer for collection, and shall make daily returns to the controller of all moneys paid and by whom paid.

ARTICLE VI.

DEPARTMENT OF CITY TREASURER.

The city treasurer shall be the head of this department; he shall be elected and give security as now provided by law, and shall hold his office for a term of three years and until his successor is chosen and qualified. The duties of the city treasurer shall remain as now provided by law except as modified by the provisions of this act.

No person shall be eligible to the office of treasurer except a citizen of the city, resident therein for seven years next preceding his election, unless he shall have been absent on public business of the United States, or of this State, and he shall not be eligible to election for the next succeeding term.

The city treasurer shall demand and receive from the proper officers all moneys payable to the city from whatever source, and pay all warrants duly issued and countersigned.

No money shall be drawn from the city treasury except by due process of law, or upon warrants on the treasurer signed by the head of the appropriate department and countersigned by the controller, which shall state the consideration of the same, and the particular fund or appropriation to which the same is chargeable.

The treasurer shall keep the accounts arising from the several sources of revenue and income separate and distinct from one another, and shall make daily deposits of all moneys received by him in such bank or institutions as may be designated by councils, and shall make specific reports daily to the controller of all receipts and deposits, and of all moneys withdrawn from the treasury, and shall present and verify his cash account in such manner and as often as may be required.

All the moneys of the city received by any officer or agent thereof shall be deposited daily in the city treasury.

Article VII.

DEPARTMENT OF CITY CONTROLLER.

Section 1. The city controller shall be the head of this department; he shall be elected as now provided by law and shall hold his office for a term of three years, and until his successor shall be duly chosen and qualified.

The city controller shall

I. Prescribe the form of reports and accounts to be rendered to his department, and shall have the inspection and revision of the accounts of all other departments and trusts.

II. Audit the accounts of the several departments and trusts, and all other accounts in which the city is concerned, and submit annually to councils in such manner as may by ordinance be directed, a report of the accounts of the city verified by his oath or affirmation, exhibiting the revenues, receipts, and expenditures, the sources from which the revenues and funds are derived, and in what manner the same have been disbursed; which report shall be published in pamphlet or book form.

III. Keep separate accounts for each specific item or appropriation made by councils to each department, and require all warrants to state specifically against which of said items the warrant is drawn. Each account shall be accompanied by a statement in detail in separate columns of the several appropriations made by councils, the amount drawn on each appropriation, the unpaid contracts charged against it, and the balance standing to the credit of the same.

IV. He shall not suffer any appropriation to be overdrawn or the appropriation for one item of expense to be drawn upon for any other purpose, or by any department other than that for which the appropriation was specifically made, except on transfers made by ordinance of councils or unless sufficient funds out of which said warrant is payable shall actually be in the treasury at the time.

V. If any warrant presented to the controller contain an item for which no appropriation has been made, or there shall not be a sufficient balance of the proper fund for the payment thereof, or which for any other cause should not be approved, he shall notify the proper department of the fact; and if the controller shall approve any warrant contrary to the provisions hereof he and his sureties shall be individually liable for the amount of the same to the holder thereof.

VI. Whenever a warrant or claim shall be presented to

him he shall have power to require evidence that the amount claimed is justly due, and for that purpose may summon before him any officer, agent, or employé of any department of the city, or any other person, and examine him upon oath or affirmation relative to such warrant or claim.

VII. He shall also perform all duties required of him by law or ordinance not inconsistent with the provision hereof.

Detailed statements of the receipts and expenditures of the several departments shall be made on the third Monday of each month to the controller.

Every contract involving an appropriation of money shall designate the item of appropriation on which it is founded, and shall be numbered by the controller in the order of its date and charged as numbered against such item, and so certified by him before it shall take effect as a contract, and shall not be payable out of any other fund, and if he shall certify any contract in excess of the appropriation properly applicable thereto, the city shall not be liable for such excess, but the controller and his sureties shall be liable in damages for an amount not exceeding such excess, which may be recovered in an action on the case for negligence by the contracting party aggrieved: *Provided,* That so much of this section as enacts that a contract certified by the controller shall not be payable out of any other fund than the item of appropriation against which it is numbered, shall not apply to such contracts for public improvement as are referred to in article fourteen, section one hereof.

The controller shall, at the end of each fiscal year, or oftener if so required by councils, and, also, upon the death, resignation, removal, or expiration of the term of any officer, audit, examine, and settle the accounts of such officer, and if he shall be found indebted to the city the controller shall state an account and file the same in the court of common pleas of the proper county, together with a copy of the official bond of such officer, and give notice thereof to him or his legal representatives; and if any person or persons affected thereby shall be dissatisfied with such settlement he or they may appeal therefrom. The appeal, with his or their exceptions to the account as stated, verified by the oath of the person or persons appealing, shall be filed in the office of the prothonotary of said court, within ten days after the service of notice. The appellant shall, within ten days, enter security to be approved by the court to prosecute the appeal with effect and pay the costs and the debt and interest, which may appear by the judgment of the court to be due to the city. The balance of account as shown by the settlement filed as aforesaid, shall constitute a lien on the real estate of the officer so indebted and his sureties from the date of the filing thereof, which lien shall continue for the period of five years from the date of filing. A writ of *scire facias* to enforce the lien shall be issued thereon within six months, which shall contain a clause warning the sureties or the executors or administrators of the officer or of his sureties to appear and make defense, and the case shall thereupon be proceeded with to final judgment according to law.

Notice of the audit shall be given by the controller to the officer or his legal representatives before the final statement of the account, and if desired by such officer or his legal representatives, opportunity shall be given for a hearing. A copy of such notice with an affidavit of the proof of service thereof, shall be filed with a statement of account as evidence of service of notice.

Article VIII.

DEPARTMENT OF LAW.

Section 1. The department of law shall consist of a city solicitor who shall be the head thereof; he shall be elected as now provided by law and shall hold his office for a term of three years and until his successor shall be duly chosen and qualified; the department shall have as many assistants and clerks as may be authorized by ordinance. The solicitor and assistant solicitors shall be attorneys at law, admitted and qualified to practice in the courts of this Commonwealth.

The city solicitor shall

I. Be the legal adviser and act as attorney and counsel for the city and all its departments and officers, and the authorization in writing of the mayor in all cases be a sufficient warrant of attorney for representing the city, its departments and officers.

II. Prepare all contracts to be made with the city or any of its trusts and departments, and endorse on each his approval of the form thereof before the same shall take effect, and be the custodian of all such papers and records as may be designated, and perform such other duties appertaining to his department as may be required by law or ordinance.

III. He shall make a return daily to the city controller of each item of money or moneys received by or through him or his assistants by virtue of his office, including all fees and perquisites for the preparation of any contracts, bonds, or other instruments of writing, or such as may be derived from any other subject-matter connected with the city or its affairs, and shall pay daily such amount to the city treasurer.

All contracts, bonds, and other instruments of writing, in which the city is concerned, shall be prepared in the office of the city solicitor, and he shall receive for the city a reasonable fee from the persons for whom such contracts, bonds, or instruments may be drawn, to be fixed by ordinance, and he shall approve all security required to be given for the protection of the city, and a proper registry shall be kept by him of all such contracts, bonds, and instruments.

No department of the city shall employ any other solicitor, but assistant counsel may be employed in any particular matter or cause by the mayor, with the consent of councils, but he shall be selected by the city solicitor.

Judgments recovered against and payable by the city, remaining unpaid with the interest due and to become due thereon, shall be reported to the councils by the city solicitor at their first session after the same shall become payable, and if there shall be no funds in the city treasury provided for and applicable to the payment thereof the amount shall be raised in the next levy of taxes. Such judgments shall be paid in the order of their priority out of the first moneys paid into the city treasury on account thereof, by reason of such levy, but if there be any moneys in the treasury, not otherwise appropriated, councils shall direct the payment therefrom of the judgments in the order of their priority, and the plaintiffs in such judgments shall have the right to enforce compliance with the provisions hereof by mandamus or other proper process, but shall not have the right to collect or compel the payment of any such judgments in any other manner or out of any other funds of the city.

Article IX.

DEPARTMENT OF EDUCATION.

Section 1. The department of education shall continue as now established by law.

Article X.

DEPARTMENT OF CHARITIES AND CORRECTION.

Section 1. The department of charities and correction shall be under the charge of a president who shall be the head thereof, and four directors, to which department shall be confided the care, management, administration, and supervision of the charities, almshouses, hospitals, houses of correction, and all other similar institutions, the control or government of which is intrusted to the city: *Provided,* That no part of this section shall interfere with the Municipal Hospital or Lazaretto as now under the control of the board of health, or with the functions of any board of directors of city trusts now existing, created by any acts of Assembly of this Commonwealth.

The board shall keep a complete record of all its proceedings which shall always be open to the inspection and examination of the mayor and of any committee appointed by councils, or either branch thereof, and shall appoint all officers and servants required for the several institutions under its management.

Councils shall have power to provide by general ordinance for all things needful for the proper and efficient management of the said institutions and the said department, not inconsistent with the provisions of this act, and all able-bodied paupers, vagrants, and other persons admitted or committed to any of the said institutions may be required to work upon the public streets or roads, or elsewhere.

The board of inspectors of the county prison shall continue as now constituted by law.

Article XI.

SINKING FUND COMMISSION.

Section 1. The sinking fund commission shall continue as now established by law.

Article XII.

APPOINTMENT OF DEPARTMENTAL OFFICERS, CLERKS, AND EMPLOYÉS.

Section 1. The mayor shall nominate and, by and with the advice and consent of the select council, appoint the following officers who shall hold office during the term for which the appointing mayor was elected, and until their successors shall be respectively appointed and qualified.

I. The director of the department of public safety.

II. The director of the department of public works.

III. The president and directors of the department of charities and correction shall also be appointed by the mayor, but their term of office shall be five years from the date of their appointment if they shall so long behave themselves well.

Sec. 2. The directors or chief officers of departments shall appoint all subordinate officers and clerks.

The directors or chief officers of departments may, by written order, giving their reasons therefor, remove or suspend subordinate officers and clerks, provided the same is not done for political reasons.

In case of such removal the director shall appoint a successor who shall hold office subject to confirmation within ten days after such appointment by the select council, if then in session, or within ten days after the beginning of the next succeeding session, if such appointment be made during a recess.

SEC. 3. All officers, clerks, and employés, except the assistants of the city solicitor, in the several departments and subdivisions thereof, or of any board attached thereto, shall be appointed by the head of the said department, but from and after the passage of this act, no such appointment or any promotion of any subordinate official, excepting only of assistants or laborers employed for special or temporary purposes, and professional experts, and such others as are specially excepted by this act, shall be lawful except when made under and in pursuance of rules and regulations providing for the ascertainment of the comparative fitness of all applicants for appointment or promotion, by a systematic, open, and competitive examination of such applicants, which rules and regulations it shall be the duty of the mayor and the heads of departments to make and promulgate within sixty days after the passage of this act. One of the said rules shall provide that any personal solicitation of the officers of said board or of the appointing power in favor of any candidate, by any person whomsoever, unless fraudulently done in order to injure him, shall be taken and deemed to have been done at the instance of the candidate himself, and shall disqualify him from competing at any such examination or appointment for and during one year thereafter: *Provided*, That no officer, clerk, or employé shall be appointed in any department, subdivision thereof, or any board attached thereto, until such rules and regulations have been promulgated, except to fill a vacancy caused by death or resignation.

ARTICLE XIII.

IMPEACHMENT OF MUNICIPAL OFFICERS.

SECTION 1. Municipal officers shall be liable to impeachment, suspension, and removal from office for any corrupt act or practice, malfeasance, mismanagement, mental incapacity, or incompetency for the proper performance of official duties, extortion, receiving any gift or present from any contractor or from any person seeking or engaged in any work for, or furnishing material to, the city, or from any incumbent or occupant of, or candidate or applicant for, any municipal office, and for willfully concealing any fraud committed against the city.

Complaint in writing may be made to the court of common pleas of the proper county by not less than twenty freeholders of the city, each of whom shall write his occupation and residence opposite his signature, charging any municipal officer with any offense, setting forth the facts on which the said charge is founded, supported by the oaths or affirmations of at least five of the complainants according to the best of their knowledge, information, and belief. If in the judgment of the court there appears to be reasonable ground for such proceeding, the court shall direct the complaint to be filed of record, and grant a rule upon the accused returnable on a day certain to appear and answer the same.

If on the return day of the rule the court shall find sufficient cause for further proceedings, it shall appoint a committee of five competent and reputable citizens to investigate the charges contained in said complaint, who, having been first severally sworn or affirmed to perform the duties of their appointment with fidelity, shall have full authority for that purpose to examine the books of the office held by the accused, and any papers, contracts, letters, or documents filed therein, and examine witnesses under oath or affirmation, whose attendance the court shall enforce, if necessary, by subpœna and attachment.

It shall be the duty of the committee to make a written report to the court of the facts found by them, which shall be filed of record, accompanied by the testimony taken, within three weeks next after their appointment, unless the time shall be extended by the court upon their application. In any stage of the proceedings if the public interest so require the court may, by an order to be filed of record in the case, suspend the accused from office until he shall be tried and acquitted.

If the committee, or any three of them, shall find that any charge made as aforesaid is well founded they shall, in their report, so state in specific form, and in such case the court shall cause a certified copy of the whole record, with the specifications of the charges against the accused, to be transmitted to the select council, which shall be assembled within ten days thereafter in special and open session as a court of impeachment, and the members shall be severally sworn to try and decide the same according to the evidence. A copy of the specifications shall be served on the accused or left at his last place of residence, at least five days before the commencement of the trial, and he shall be entitled to be heard therein in person or by counsel, and to produce evidence in his defense, and the prosecution before the select council shall be conducted on the part of the city by the city solicitor.

The president judge of the said court of common pleas, or in his absence an associate judge thereof, shall preside during the trial and decide finally all questions of law and evidence that may arise in the case. He shall have the power to issue subpœnas for witnesses and compel their attendance by attachment, and the production of books, papers, and documentary evidence required or called for by the said court of impeachment, and to punish witnesses and others for contempt as fully as any court of this Commonwealth may lawfully do in any case.

The decision of the court of impeachment shall be entered upon the record of its proceedings and certified by the clerk to the court in which the complaint was filed. If the accused shall be found guilty on any of the specifications the said court of common pleas shall enter judgment accordingly and declare the said office vacant.

Article XIV.

CONTRACTS.

Section 1. All contracts relating to city affairs shall be in writing, signed and executed in the name of the city by the officer authorized to make the same after due notice, and, in cases not otherwise directed by law or ordinance, such contracts shall be made and entered into by the mayor. No contract shall be entered into or executed directly by the city councils or their committees, but some officers shall be designated by ordinance to enter into and execute the same. All contracts shall be countersigned by the controller and filed and registered by number, date, and contents in the mayor's office, and attested copies furnished to the controller and to the department charged with the work.

Every contract for public improvements shall be based upon estimate of the whole cost furnished by the proper officer through the department having charge of the improvement, and no bid in excess of such estimate shall be accepted. Every such contract shall contain a clause that it is subject to the provisions of this act, and the liability of the city thereon shall be limited by the amounts which shall have been or may be, from time to time, appropriated for the same.

No contract for work to be done for, or property or materials to be sold or supplied to, any city of the first class, or any department thereof, shall be made with any councilman, officer, or employé of such city, or with any firm, copartnership, or association of which such councilman, officer, or employé is a member, and if any councilman, officer, or employé during the term for which he shall have been elected or appointed, knowingly acquire an interest in any such contract he shall forfeit his office.

In all contracts for improvements the cost of which is to be paid by assessment upon the property abutting or benefited, the city shall not be liable to any claim for the amount to be collected from such assessments, but the contractor shall look to the assessment for his compensation.

Article XV.

GENERAL PROVISIONS.

Section 1. The first elections under this act shall be held on the third Tuesday of February, immediately preceding the expiration of the term of the mayor in office at the time of its approval.

For the purpose of enacting legislation to properly carry out the provisions of this act the councils shall, prior to the first day of January one thousand eight hundred and eighty-seven, enact ordinances providing for the reorganization of the several departments of the city, so as to conform to the requirements of this act. All executive powers and duties of the several officers of the city not hereinbefore otherwise distributed, shall be assigned by ordinance to the appropriate department hereby created, and when so assigned all other departments now existing shall be abolished.

Each branch of councils shall have power to compel the attendance of witnesses and the production of books, papers, and other evidence, at any meeting of the body, or of any committee thereof, and for that purpose may issue subpœnas and attachments in any case of inquiry, investigation, or impeachment and cause the same to be served and executed in any part of the Commonwealth, and if any witness shall refuse to testify as to any fact within his knowledge, or to produce any books or papers within his possession, or under his control, required to be used as evidence in any such case, the clerk of that branch of councils, by whose authority such witness was subpœnaed, shall forthwith report the facts relating to such refusal to that one of the courts of common pleas of the county to which current new actions and proceedings may at the time be distributed, apportioned, and assigned, and all questions arising upon such refusal, and also upon any new evidence not included in said clerk's report (which new evidence may be offered either in behalf of or against such witness), shall at once be heard by said court. If the court determine that the testimony or evidence required by such witness is legally and properly competent, and ought to be given or produced by him, then said court shall make an order commanding such witness to testify or to produce books and papers (or both, as the case may be), and if said witness shall thereafter refuse to testify or to produce books or papers as aforesaid, in disobedience of such order of the court, then the said court shall have power to order the commitment of such witness to the county jail of the proper county for contempt.

No witness shall be excused from testifying in any criminal proceeding, or in any investigation or inquiry before either branch of the councils, or any committee thereof, or any officer of the city having the right to conduct the investigation touching his knowledge of any offense committed against the provisions of this act. But such testimony shall not be used against him in any criminal prosecution whatever, and the accused shall not be convicted in any court on the testimony of an accomplice unless the same be corroborated by other evidence or the circumstances of the case.

All persons who at the time of the passage of this act shall be employed by any department of the city government, which is abolished by this act, shall be transferred by operation hereof to the appropriate department hereby created, and shall perform such duties as may be required of them by the head of such department.

All salaried officers, whose offices are not abolished by this act, shall serve out the several terms for which they were respectively elected, except where the right of removal already exists. They shall perform their several duties subject to the supervision and control of the appropriate department, and shall receive the same salary, fees, and emoluments to which they were severally entitled before the passage of this act.

The board of managers of the house of correction and the board of guardians of the poor are abolished from and after the first day of April, one thousand eight hundred and eighty-seven.

No person shall hold more than one office of profit in any city department, and no person shall hold any office of profit under the city or any department thereof while holding any other official or representative position of profit in or under the Government of the United States, of this Commonwealth, or of such city except in the militia service of this Commonwealth.

If any officer or employé of any department shall receive or share in any present, fee, gift, or emolument for official services other than his regular salary or pay, except by the consent of the director of the department given in writing, he shall be dismissed from the service.

No officer or employé of any department, trust, or commission, or employé of any contractor under any such department, trust, or commission, shall be a member of, or delegate to, any political convention, nor shall he be present at any such convention except in the performance of duty relating to his position as such officer or employé; and any violation of these provisions shall work a forfeiture of his position, and it shall be the duty of the department to dismiss him from office and enter upon their record the cause of such dismissal.

No officer or employé of the city shall collect any fees or perquisites for his own use, but all such fees or perquisites now collectible under the law shall be paid into the city treasury, and councils, by ordinance, shall provide for the payment of proper salaries to all officers or employés of the city, except for such of them as it is herein provided shall serve without compensation.

Article XVI.

Councils shall, by general ordinances, provide for the proper and efficient conduct of the affairs of the city by the mayor and several departments, and the boards thereof, but they shall not pass any ordinances directing or interfering with the exercise of the executive functions of the mayor, departments, boards, or heads, or officers thereof.

Approved the first day of June, A. D. 1885.

ROBT. E. PATTISON.

An Ordinance

To carry into effect the act of assembly entitled "An act for the better government of cities of the first class in this commonwealth," approved June 1st, 1885.

Section 1. *The Select and Common Councils of the City of Philadelphia do ordain,* That on and after the first Monday of April, A. D. 1887, the executive power of the city of Philadelphia shall be vested in the mayor and the departments authorized by the act of assembly, entitled "An act for the better government of cities of the first class in this commonwealth," approved June 1st, 1885.

Sec. 2. The following departments are hereby established in accordance with said act:—

I. Department of public safety.
II. Department of public works.
III. Department of receiver of taxes.
IV. Department of city treasurer.
V. Department of city controller.
VI. Department of law.
VII. Department of education.
VIII. Department of charities and correction.
IX. Department of sinking fund commission.

DEPARTMENT OF PUBLIC SAFETY.

Sec. 3. The department of public safety shall be under the charge, direction, control, and administration of one director, who shall be the head thereof. He shall be at least thirty years of age, and have been a citizen and inhabitant of the State five years, and an inhabitant of the city for five years next before his appointment, unless absent on the public business of the United States or of this State, and shall reside in said city during his term of service.

Said director shall receive a salary of seven thousand five hundred (7500) dollars per annum, and give to the city satisfactory security, in the sum of twenty-five thousand (25,000) dollars, conditioned for the faithful discharge of his duty.

Before entering upon his duties, the said director shall take and subscribe the oath or affirmation in Article VII. of the Constitution of the State of Pennsylvania, which shall be filed with the city controller.

This department shall embrace the present departments of police, health, fire, electrical, erection of fire escapes, building inspectors, inspectors of steam engines and boilers, and shall have charge of inspection of markets, food, and all other matters connected with the health of the people.

SEC. 4. The board of building inspectors shall be attached to, and under the control and direction of the department of public safety, and shall consist of three members, who shall perform the duties now by law allotted to it, and at the expiration of the term of the present inspectors the director of said department shall appoint their successors: *Provided*, Said board shall be composed of practical carpenters and bricklayers; but the three members shall not all be of the same occupation.

SEC. 5. The enforcement of regulations concerning fire escapes shall be in charge of the board of building inspectors, fire marshal, and chief engineer of the fire department. They shall elect their own chairman, and adopt such rules and fire escapes as they may think desirable, subject to the approval of the director of public safety.

SEC. 6. The care, management, and control of the police station houses, police tug boats, and patrol houses shall be under this department.

SEC. 7. Whenever the department of public safety shall direct the chief or superintendent of police to appoint additional patrolmen at the charge and expense of any persons asking such appointments, the director thereof shall forthwith report the same, with the names of the appointees and the place where they are to perform duty, to select council. And whenever the mayor, in case of an emergency or apprehension of riot or mob, shall appoint special patrolmen, he shall report forthwith the names, number, and rate of pay of such appointees to select council.

DEPARTMENT OF PUBLIC WORKS.

SEC. 8. The department of public works shall be under the charge, direction, control, and administration of one director, who shall be the head thereof. He shall be at least thirty years of age, and have been a citizen and inhabitant of the State five years, and an inhabitant of the city for five years next before his appointment, unless absent on the public business of the United States or of this state, and shall reside in said city during his term of service.

Said director shall receive a salary of seven thousand five hundred (7500) dollars per annum, and give to the city satisfactory security, in the sum of twenty-five thousand (25,000) dollars, conditioned for the faithful discharge of his duty.

Before entering upon his duties, the said director shall take and subscribe the oath or affirmation in Article VII. of the Constitution of the State of Pennsylvania, which shall be filed with the city controller.

This department shall embrace the present departments of water, gas, highways, bridges and sewers, surveys and the district surveyors, markets, wharves, city property, and city ice boats. The erection of public lamps, and the lighting and care of same, whether gas, gasoline, or electric lights, the construction, protection, care, and repair of public buildings, squares, market-houses, wharves and docks, bridges, real estate, and structures of every kind for public use (except such as now or hereafter may be used for educational or police purposes, the control of, or the erection of the new public buildings, at Broad and Market streets), shall be under the direction of this department.

SEC. 9. The city shall be divided into survey districts as at present, and until the expiration of the respective terms of office of the present district surveyors, such surveyors shall be attached to the department of public works, and shall perform their duties under the direction of said department. At the expiration of their respective terms, the director of public works shall, by appointment, subject to the approval of select council, fill the vacancies for a term of five years, with the same duties and responsibilities as is now provided by law.

SEC. 10. The board of highway supervisors shall be composed of the director of the department of public works, the chief officer of the bureaus of highways, water, gas, electrical, city property, and surveys. The director of the department of public works shall be president of said board.

DEPARTMENT OF RECEIVER OF TAXES.

SEC. 11. The receiver of taxes shall be the head of this department; he shall be elected, and give security, as now provided by law, and shall hold his office for a term of three years, and until his successor is chosen and qualified. He shall receive a salary of ten thousand (10,000) dollars per unnum.

The duty of collecting taxes and the receipt and collection of funds derived from loans, licenses, water-rents, water-pipes, frontages, permits, and all receipts connected with the manufacture of and sale of gas, and rents from markets, landings, wharves, and other public property and interests, shall hereafter be performed by this department.

The receiver of taxes shall be charged by the controller with the full amount of all tax duplicates of the several wards, and also with all other accounts placed in his hands by the proper officers for collection, and shall make daily returns to the controller of all moneys paid, and by whom paid.

SEC. 12. From and after the first Monday of April, 1887, all moneys due to the city of Philadelphia, whether for taxes, loans, licenses, water-rents, water-pipes, frontages, permits, and rents from markets, landings, wharves, and other public property and interests, or from any source whatever, shall be received and collected by the department of the receiver of taxes, and from and after the first Monday of April, 1887, the registrar of the water department and the clerks employed in the collection of funds derived from water-rents, water-pipes, frontages, and permits, shall be transferred to the department of the receiver of taxes, for the performance of similar duties, and the books of accounts then in use by the said registrar and his clerks shall be continued for the same purposes until the close of the year 1887.

SEC. 13. The receiver of taxes shall furnish the city solicitor with a list of all claims unpaid within the time prescribed by law, that liens may be entered and the interest of the city protected.

DEPARTMENT OF CITY TREASURER.

SEC. 14. The city treasurer shall be the head of this department. He shall be elected, and give security, as now provided by law, and shall hold his office for a term of three years, and until his successor is chosen and qualified. The duties of the city treasurer shall remain, as now provided by law and ordinance.

DEPARTMENT OF CITY CONTROLLER.

SEC. 15. The city controller shall be the head of this department, and shall perform the duties as now prescribed by law or ordinance.

SEC. 16. The city controller is hereby authorized, prior to December 31st, 1887, to prepare proper warrant books for the departments of the city government as reorganized under the provisions of this ordinance; he is hereby authorized to continue the accounts in his office as they now are until January 1st, 1888, and have prepared such books and to open such accounts as will be necessary to carry into effect the requirements of this ordinance, and of the act of assembly entitled "An act to provide for the better government of cities," &c., approved June 1st, 1885.

DEPARTMENT OF LAW.

SEC. 17. The city solicitor shall be the head of this department, and shall perform the duties as now prescribed by law or ordinance.

DEPARTMENT OF EDUCATION.

SEC. 18. The department of education shall continue as now established by law and ordinance.

DEPARTMENT OF CHARITIES AND CORRECTION.

SEC. 19. This department shall be under the charge, management, control, and administration of a president and four directors. They shall be at least thirty years of age, and have been citizens and inhabitants of the State five years, and inhabitants of the city for five years next before their appointment, unless absent on the public business of the United States or of this State, and shall reside in said city during their term of service. Said president and directors shall serve without compensation, but shall not be required to give any security.

Before entering upon their duties, the said president and directors shall take and subscribe the oath or affirmation in Article VII. of the Constitution of the State of Pennsylvania, which shall be filed with the city controller.

This department shall embrace the present department of house of correction and the department of the guardians of the poor. They shall manage and control all almshouses, charities, hospitals, houses of correction, and all similar institutions wholly under the control of the city. All the powers vested in the board of guardians of the poor and the managers of the house of correction shall be vested in this department: *Provided,* That no part of this section shall interfere with the municipal hospital or Lazaretto, as now under the control of the board of health, or with the functions of any board of directors of city trusts now existing, created by any acts of assembly of this Commonwealth.

SINKING FUND COMMISSIONERS.

SEC. 20. The sinking fund commissioners shall continue as now established by law or ordinance.

GENERAL PROVISIONS.

SEC. 21. The salary of the mayor from and after the first Monday of April, 1887, shall be twelve thousand (12,000) dollars per annum.

Before entering upon his duties, he shall take and subscribe the oath or affirmation in Article VII. of the Constitution of the State of Pennsylvania, which shall be filed with the city controller.

SEC. 22. Upon the removal by the mayor of any head, director, or other officer appointed by him, he shall transmit to select council, at its next meeting, his reasons therefor, and shall, within thirty days thereafter, nominate to that body a successor. During any vacancy the mayor shall designate the officer to serve *ad interim*, who shall have the same powers and perform the same duties the officer removed performed and discharged.

SEC. 23. The boards of fire commissioners, guardians of the poor, managers of house of correction, fire escapes, as now constituted, and the trustees of the Philadelphia gas works, be, and are hereby, abolished from and after the first Monday of April, 1887. All the books, papers, records, and all other property connected with each of said boards shall be turned over to the new department created to take the place of the boards hereby abolished.

SEC. 24. All heads of departments in the employ of the city on the first Monday of April, 1887, shall hold their respective positions and receive their present salaries until the expiration of the terms for which they were elected, but they shall be attached to and become a part of the departments herein created, and they and each of them shall be subject to the director of the department to which they are hereby assigned.

SEC. 25. The following joint committees shall be appointed by the presidents of select and common councils immediately after the organization of councils in April, 1887, and annually thereafter: Finance, water, highways, surveys, charities and prisons, railroads, schools, police and boiler inspection, law and election divisions, verify cash accounts of the city treasurer, gas and fire departments, electrical, city property and printing and supplies, compare bills, and commerce and navigation, and municipal government, each of above to consist of twelve members of each body, nine members of which shall constitute a quorum; except the committee to verify cash accounts of the city treasurer, five members of which shall constitute a quorum. The presidents of select and common councils shall be members of all standing committees and shall be entitled to a voice and vote therein.

The chairman of the committees on finance, highways, surveys, charities and prisons, police and boiler inspection, gas and fire department, and municipal government, shall be a member of common council.

The chairman of the committees on water, railroads, schools, law, and election divisions, verify cash accounts of the city treasurer, electrical, city property, and printing and supplies, compare bills, and commerce and navigation, shall be a member of select council. No member of either branch of councils shall be chairman of more than one standing committee.

SEC. 26. From the first Monday of April, 1887, to December 31st, 1887, all warrants presented to the city controller, from the departments placed under the control of the directors of public safety, public works, and charities and correction, shall be approved by the directors and president of said departments, before being countersigned by the city controller.

SEC. 27. All discharges, appointments, and engagements of laborers and employés, in the departments of public safety, of public works, and of charities and correction, whether salaried or per diem, shall be made by the directors of said departments (excepting only of assistants or laborers employed for special or temporary purposes, and professional experts): *Provided*, That in all cases of discharge of salaried officers, the head of such department shall notify select council at their next meeting of such discharge with the reasons or cause therefor, and shall submit to select council, within thirty days, the name of the person appointed in place of the one discharged.

Sec. 28. Upon the abolition of any of the departments, boards, or commissions of the city of Philadelphia, or the transfer of the same to any of the departments created by the act of assembly, approved June 1st, 1885, by virtue of said act or this ordinance, all the powers, duties, incidents, and functions of said abolished or transferred department, board, or commission shall become vested in the department which shall thereafter have charge of the same subject-matters, which departments, boards, or commissions so abolished or transferred, shall be hereafter respectively called bureaus under the several departments to which they have been assigned.

Sec. 29. From and after the first Monday of April, 1887, it shall be the duty of each department of the city government and the clerks of councils to furnish the receiver of taxes with a list of all accounts due the city, on or before the day the same may accrue and becomes due, from any and every source, giving such information as will fully enable him to collect the same. And it shall be the duty of each department to furnish the city controller with a duplicate of such return made to the receiver of taxes; whereupon the controller shall forthwith charge such return to the receiver of taxes. All moneys due the city of Philadelphia shall be paid to the receiver of taxes, and it shall be unlawful for any person to pay moneys to any one for the city, except as above stated.

Sec. 30. All ordinances or parts of ordinances inconsistent herewith be, and the same are, hereby repealed.

Approved December 30th, 1886.

INDEX.

A.

B.

C.

D.

E.

F.

G.

H.

I.

J.

K.

L.

M.

N.

O.

P.

R.

ACTS OF ASSEMBLY.

NOTE.—It will be observed that for the sake of uniformity and to increase the facilities for finding the ordinances cited above, that Lowber's, Duane's, and Lowber & Miller's Digests have been cited as far as they covered the ground; from 1814-1854, under the head of "Ordinances," reference is made to "Ordinances of the Corporation," published by the authority of councils. Copies of this publication are now very scarce, but the publication, bound in two volumes, is in the possession of the Law Association of Philadelphia. After 1854 the annual volumes of ordinances have been cited. The Manuscript Laws are to be found only in the Historical Society of Pennsylvania.

CASES CITED.

ORDINANCES CITED.

JOHNS HOPKINS UNIVERSITY STUDIES

IN

Historical and Political Science.

HERBERT B. ADAMS, Editor.

PROSPECTUS OF FIFTH SERIES.—1887.

The Studies in Municipal Government will be continued. The Fifth Series will also embrace Studies in the History of American Political Economy and of American Co-operation. The following papers are ready or in preparation:—

I-II. City Government of Philadelphia. By EDWARD P. ALLINSON, A. M. (Haverford), and BOIES PENROSE, A. B. (Harvard). January and February, 1887. 72 pages. *Price, 50 cents.*

III. City Government of Boston. By JAMES M. BUGBEE. March, 1887. 60 pages. *Price, 25 cents.*

City Government of Baltimore. By JOHN C. ROSE, B. L. (University of Maryland, School of Law). *In preparation.*

City Government of Chicago. By F. H. HODDER, Ph. M. (University of Mich.), Instructor in History, Cornell University.

City Government of San Francisco. By BERNARD MOSES, Ph. D., Professor of History and Politics, University of California.

City Government of St. Louis. By MARSHALL S. SNOW, A. M. (Harvard), Professor of History, Washington University.

City Government of New Orleans. By Hon. W. W. HOWE.

City Government of New York. By SIMON STERNE and J. F. JAMESON, Ph. D., Associate in History, J. H. U.

The Influence of the War of 1812 upon the Consolidation of the American Union. By NICHOLAS MURRAY BUTLER, Ph. D., and Fellow of Columbia College.

The History of American Political Economy. Studies by R. T. ELY, WOODROW WILSON, and D. R. DEWEY.

The History of American Co-operation. Studies by E. W. BEMIS, D. R. RANDALL, A. G. WAGNER, *et al.*

FOURTH SERIES.—Municipal Government and Land Tenure.—1886.

I. Dutch Village Communities on the Hudson River. By IRVING ELTING, A. B. (Harvard). January, 1886. 68 pages. *Price, 50 cents.*

II-III. Town Government in Rhode Island. By WILLIAM E. FOSTER, A. M. (Brown University).—The Narragansett Planters. By Edward CHANNING, Ph. D., and Instructor in History, Harvard University. February and March, 1886. 60 pages. *Price, 50 cents.*

IV. **Pennsylvania Boroughs.** By WILLIAM P. HOLCOMB, Ph. D., J. H. U., Professor of History and Political Science, Swarthmore College. April, 1886. 51 pages. *Price, 50 cents.*

V. **Introduction to the Constitutional and Political History of the Individual States.** By J. F. JAMESON, Ph. D., and Associate in History, J. H. U. May, 1886. 29 pages. *Price, 50 cents.*

VI. **The Puritan Colony at Annapolis, Maryland.** By DANIEL R. RANDALL, A. B. (St. John's College). June, 1886. 47 pages. *Price, 50 cents.*

VII-VIII-IX. **History of the Land Question in the United States.** By SHOSUKE SATO, B. S. (Sapporo), Ph. D., and Fellow by Courtesy, J. H. U. July-September, 1881. 181 pages. *Price,* $1.00.

X. **The Town and City Government of New Haven.** By CHARLES H. LEVERMORE, Ph. D. (J. H. U.), Instructor in History, University of California. October, 1886. 103 pages. *Price, 50 cents.*

XI-XII. **The Land System of the New England Colonies.** By MELVILLE EGLESTON, A. M. (Williams College). November and December, 1886. *Price, 50 cents.*

THIRD SERIES.—Maryland, Virginia, and Washington.—1885.

I. **Maryland's Influence upon Land Cessions to the United States.** With minor papers on George Washington's Interest in Western Lands, the Potomac Company, and a National University. By HERBERT B. ADAMS, Ph. D. (Heidelberg). January, 1885. 102 pages. *Price, 75 cents.*

II-III. **Virginia Local Institutions:—The Land System; Hundred; Parish; County; Town.** By EDWARD INGLE, A. B. (J. H. U.) February and March, 1885. 127 pages. *Price, 75 cents.*

IV. **Recent American Socialism.** By RICHARD T. ELY, Ph. D. (Heidelberg), Associate in Political Economy, J. H. U. April, 1885. 74 pages. *Price, 50 cents.*

V-VI-VII. **Maryland Local Institutions:—The Land System; Hundred; County; Town.** By LEWIS W. WILHELM, Ph. D. (J. H. U.), Fellow by Courtesy, J. H. U. May, June, and July, 1885. 130 pages. *Price,* $1.00.

VIII. **The Influence of the Proprietors in founding the State of New Jersey.** By AUSTIN SCOTT, Ph. D. (Leipzig), formerly Associate and Lecturer, J. H. U.; Professor of History, Political Economy, and Constitutional Law, Rutgers College. August, 1885. 26 pages. *Price, 25 cents.*

IX-X. **American Constitutions; The Relations of the Three Departments as Adjusted by a Century.** By HORACE DAVIS, A. B. (Harvard). San Francisco, California. September and October, 1885. 70 pages. *Price, 50 cents.*

XI-XII. **The City of Washington.** By JOHN ADDISON PORTER, A. B. (Yale). November and December, 1885. 56 pages. *Price, 50 cents.*

SECOND SERIES.—Institutions and Economics.—1884.

I-II. **Methods of Historical Study.** By HERBERT B. ADAMS, Ph. D. (Heidelberg). January and February, 1884. 137 pages. *Price, 50 cents.*

III. **The Past and the Present of Political Economy.** By RICHARD T. ELY, Ph. D. (Heidelberg). March, 1884. 64 pages. *Price, 35 cents.*

IV. **Samuel Adams, The Man of the Town Meeting.** By JAMES K. HOSMER, A. M. (Harvard), Professor of English and German Literature, Washington University, St. Louis. April, 1884. 60 pages. *Price, 35 cents.*

V-VI. **Taxation in the United States.** By HENRY CARTER ADAMS, Ph. D. (J. H. U.); Professor of Political Economy, University of Michigan. May and June, 1884. 79 pages. *Price, 50 cents.*

VII. **Institutional Beginnings in a Western State.** By JESSE MACY, A. B. (Iowa College); Professor of Historical and Political Science, Iowa College. July, 1884. 38 pages. *Price, 25 cents.*

VIII-IX. **Indian Money as a Factor in New England Civilization.** By WILLIAM B. WEEDEN, A. M. (Brown University). August and September, 1884. 51 pages. *Price, 50 cents.*

X. **Town and County Government in the English Colonies of North America.** By EDWARD CHANNING, Ph. D. (Harvard); Instructor in History, Harvard College. October, 1884. 57 pages. *Price, 50 cents.*

XI. **Rudimentary Society among Boys.** By JOHN JOHNSON, A. B. (J. H. U.); Instructor in History and English, McDonogh Institute, Baltimore Co., Md. November, 1884. 56 pages. *Price, 50 cents.*

XII. **Land Laws of Mining Districts.** By CHARLES HOWARD SHINN, A. B. (J. H. U.); Editor of the *Overland Monthly.* December, 1884. 69 pages. *Price, 50 cents.*

FIRST SERIES.—Local Institutions.—1883.

I. **An Introduction to American Institutional History.** By EDWARD A. FREEMAN, D. C. L., LL. D., Regius Professor of Modern History, University of Oxford. With an account of Mr. Freeman's Visit to Baltimore, by the Editor. *Price, 25 cents.*

II. **The Germanic Origin of New England Towns.** Read before the Harvard Historical Society, May 9, 1881. By H. B. ADAMS, Ph. D. (Heidelberg), 1876. With Notes on Co-operation in University Work. *Price, 50 cents.*

III. **Local Government in Illinois.** First published in the *Fortnightly Review.* By ALBERT SHAW, A. B. (Iowa College), 1879.—**Local Government in Pennsylvania.** Read before the Pennsylvania Historical Society, May 1, 1882. By E. R. L. GOULD, A. B. (Victoria University, Canada), 1882. *Price, 30 cents.*

IV. **Saxon Tithingmen in America.** Read before the American Antiquarian Society, October 21, 1881. By H. B. ADAMS. 2d Edition. *Price, 50 cents.*

V. **Local Government in Michigan and the Northwest.** Read before the Social Science Association, at Saratoga, September 7, 1882. By E. W. BEMIS, A. B. (Amherst College), 1880. *Price, 25 cents.*

VI. **Parish Institutions of Maryland.** By EDWARD INGLE, A. B. (Johns Hopkins University), 1882. *Price, 40 cents.*

VII. **Old Maryland Manors.** By JOHN JOHNSON, A. B. (Johns Hopkins University), 1881. *Price, 30 cents.*

VIII. **Norman Constables in America.** Read before the New England Historico-Genealogical Society, February 1, 1882. By H. B. ADAMS. 2d Edition. *Price, 50 cents.*

IX-X. Village Communities of Cape Ann and Salem. From the Historical Collection of the Essex Institute. By H. B. ADAMS. *Price, 50 cents.*

XI. The Genesis of a New England State (Connecticut). By ALEXANDER JOHNSTON, A. M. (Rutgers College), 1870; Professor of Political Economy and Jurisprudence at Princeton College. *Price, 30 cents.*

XII. Local Government and Free Schools in South Carolina. Read before the Historical Society of South Carolina, December 15, 1882. By B. J. RAMAGE, A. B. *Price, 40 cents.*

The first annual series of monthly monographs devoted to History, Politics, and Economics was begun in 1882–3. Four volumes have thus far appeared.

The separate volumes bound in cloth will be sold as follows:—

VOLUME I.—Local Institutions. 479 pages. $4.00.

VOLUME II.—Institutions and Economics. 629 pages. $4.00.

VOLUME III.—Maryland, Virginia, and Washington. 595 pages. $4.00.

VOLUME IV.—Municipal Government and Land Tenure. 610 pages. $3.50.

The set of four volumes will be sold together for $12.50 *net.*

VOLUME V.—Municipal Government and Economics. (1887.) *This volume will be furnished in monthly parts upon receipt of subscription price,* $3.00; *or the bound volume will be sent at the end of the year* 1887 *for* $3.50.

EXTRA VOLUMES OF STUDIES.

In connection with the regular annual series of Studies, a series of Extra Volumes is proposed. It is intended to print them in a style uniform with the regular Studies, but to publish each volume by itself, in numbered sequence and in a cloth binding uniform with the First, Second, Third, and Fourth Series. The volumes will vary in size from 200 to 500 pages, with corresponding prices. Subscriptions to the Annual Series of Studies will not necessitate subscriptions to the Extra Volumes, although they will be offered to regular subscribers at reduced rates.

EXTRA VOLUME I.—The Republic of New Haven: A History of Municipal Evolution. By CHARLES H. LEVERMORE, Ph. D., Baltimore. This volume, now ready, comprises 350 pages octavo, with various diagrams and an index. *It is sold, bound in cloth, at* $2.00.

EXTRA VOLUME II.—Philadelphia, 1681-1887; A History of Municipal Development. By EDWARD P. ALLINSON, A. M. (Haverford), and BOIES PENROSE, A. B. (Harvard). This volume, now ready, comprises 400 pages, octavo. *It will be sold, bound in cloth, at* $3.00; *in law-sheep at* $3.50.

EXTRA VOLUME III.—Baltimore and the Nineteenth of April, 1861. By GEORGE WILLIAM BROWN, Chief Judge of the Supreme Bench of Baltimore and Mayor of the City in 1861. *Price,* $1.00.

All communications relating to subscriptions, exchanges, &c., should be addressed to the PUBLICATION AGENCY OF THE JOHNS HOPKINS UNIVERSITY, BALTIMORE, MARYLAND.

CHAPTER III. Maryland's desire for Peace.—Events which followed the Election of President Lincoln.—His Proclamation calling for Troops.—The City Authorities and Police of Baltimore.—Increasing excitement in Baltimore.

CHAPTER IV. The Sixth Massachusetts Regiment in Baltimore.—The Fight.—The departure for Washington.—Correspondence in regard to the Killed and Wounded.—Public meeting.—Telegram to the President.—No Reply.—Burning of Bridges.

CHAPTER V. April 20, increasing Excitement.—Appropriation of $500,000 for defense of the City.—Correspondence with President and Governor.—Men Enrolled.—Apprehended Attack on Fort McHenry.—Marshal Kane.—Interview with President, Cabinet, and General Scott.—General Butler, with the Eighth Massachusetts, proceeds to Annapolis and Washington.—Baltimore in a state of armed neutrality.

CHAPTER VI. Session of the General Assembly.—Report of the Board of Police.—Suppression of the Flags.—On the 5th of May, General Butler takes position six miles from Baltimore.—On the 13th of May he enters Baltimore and fortifies Federal Hill.—The General Assembly will take no steps toward secession.—Many young men join the Army of the Confederacy.

CHAPTER VII. Chief Justice Taney and the Writ of Habeas Corpus.—A Union Convention.—Consequence of the Suspension of the Writ.—Incidents of the War.—The Women in the War.

CHAPTER VIII. General Banks in Command.—Marshal Kane Arrested.—Police Commissioners Superseded.—Resolutions passed by the General Assembly.—Police Commissioners Arrested.—Resolutions passed by the General Assembly.—General Dix in Command.—Arrest of the Members of the General Assembly, the Mayor, and others.—Release of Prisoners.—Colonel Dimick.

CHAPTER IX. A Personal Chapter.

APPENDIX I. Account of the alleged conspiracy to assassinate Abraham Lincoln on his journey to Baltimore, from the Life of Abraham Lincoln by Ward H. Lamon, pages 511–526.

APPENDIX II. Extract from the Opinion of the Supreme Court of the United States, delivered by Chief Justice Taney in the case of Dred Scott *vs.* Sandford, 19 How., 407.

APPENDIX III. The Habeas Corpus Case. Opinion of the Chief Justice of the United States, *ex parte* John Merriman.

APPENDIX IV. Message of the 12th of July, 1861, to the first and second Branches of the City Council, referring to the events of the 19th of April, and those which followed. The first paragraph and the concluding paragraphs of this document.

APPENDIX V. As a part of the History of the Times, Reproduction from the *Baltimore American* of December 5, 1860, of the Reception of the Putnam Phalanx of Hartford, Connecticut, in the city of Baltimore.

APPENDIX VI. Visit of a portion of the members of the Sixth Massachusetts Regiment to Baltimore on the 19th of April, 1880, and an Account of its Reception, from the *Baltimore Sun* and the *Baltimore American*.

PRICE.

The volume will comprise about 150 pages, octavo, and will be sold, bound in cloth, at $1; and at reduced rates to regular subscribers to the "Studies."

Orders and subscriptions should be addressed to THE PUBLICATION AGENCY OF THE JOHNS HOPKINS UNIVERSITY, BALTIMORE, MARYLAND.

/

BALTIMORE

AND THE

NINETEENTH OF APRIL, 1861.

A STUDY OF THE WAR.

By GEORGE WILLIAM BROWN,

Chief Judge of the Supreme Bench of Baltimore; Mayor of the City in 1861.

THE editor of the *Johns Hopkins University Studies in Historical and Political Science*, announces the above-work for early publication (March, 1887) as an EXTRA VOLUME of the Series. The position of Judge Brown as Mayor of Baltimore in 1861 gave him exceptional opportunities for observing and understanding the municipal situation. His unflinching devotion to official duty in marching through Pratt street at the head of the Massachusetts Sixth Regiment, on the 19th of April, in the midst of a furious mob, will inspire confidence in his account of the events of that day. The concurrent testimony of Baltimoreans, of different political opinions, confirms Judge Brown's historical statement as the most accurate that has thus far been written. The events leading to the 19th of April and immediately following that date are frankly discussed. Judge Brown's point of view is that of many leading citizens of Maryland. He has attempted to describe the position of the middle, or peace party. Judge Brown's Study is a contribution to a better understanding of the state of society and of public feeling in the border land between the North and South in 1861. After the lapse of a quarter of a century, American citizens have learned to hear with interest and appreciation both sides in the story of battles and campaigns. A Maryland view of past Politics may serve to enlighten the Present and instruct the Future.

The following table of contents will give some idea of the nature and scope of the work :—

CONTENTS.

CHAPTER III. THE LAND QUESTION.—Official Control over Alienations and Dwellings.—Divisions of the Outland.—New Haven a Village Community.—Evolution of Subordinate Townships.—The Delaware Company.

CHAPTER IV. THE UNION WITH CONNECTICUT. THE BIRTH OF NEWARK.—A New Party within the Colony.—Terms of Admission of Strangers.—Increasing Importance of Townsmen.—The Village Question.—New Haven and the Restored Stuart.—Hegira to New Jersey.

CHAPTER V. THE WORK OF THE COURTS IN JUDICATURE AND LEGISLATION.—Drunkenness.—Sabbath-breaking.—Spiritual Discouragements.—Quakers and Witches.—Lewdness.—Models of Civil Procedure.—Legislation concerning Trade and Prices.—Arbitration.—Magisterial Interest in Trade.—Revival of the Common Law and English Usage.

CHAPTER VI. NEW HAVEN A CONNECTICUT TOWN, 1664–1700.—Changes in Constitution.—Hopkins Grammar School.—Minister's Tax.—Tithingmen.—Justice of the Peace.—Divisions of Land.—Indian Reservations.—The Village Controversy.—Public Benevolence.—Indian Wars.—Villages again.—Tyranny of Andros.—Local Enactments.—Intemperance.—Funeral Customs.

CHAPTER VII. NEW HAVEN A CONNECTICUT TOWN, 1700–1784.—The Quarrel with East Haven.—Yale College.—The Walpolean Lethargy.—Sale of the Town's Poor.—First Post Office.—First Oyster Laws.—Sketch of the Town's Commerce.—The Approach of the Revolution.—New Haven during the War.—Committees.—Articles of Confederation.—Treatment of Tories.—Final Division of the Township.—The Church the Germ of the Town.

CHAPTER VIII. THE DUAL GOVERNMENT. TOWN AND CITY. 1784–1886.—Town-Born *vs.* Interloper.—First Phases of City Politics.—First Charter.—Description of the City.—Municipal Improvements.—Fire Department.—Adornment of the Green.—Public Letters to the Presidents and Others.—Downfall of Federalism.—Slavery and Abolition.—Municipal Growth.—Sects.—Administrative Changes.—Windfall from Washington.—Liquor Traffic.—Light in the Streets.—High School.—Era of Railways.—Needs of the Poor.—The City Meeting.—Charter of 1857.—Town Officers.—City Improvement.—Police and Fire Departments.—In the Civil War.—Recent Charters.—Conservative Influences in the Community.

CHAPTER IX. THE PRESENT MUNICIPAL ADMINISTRATION.—School District.—Town Government.—Town-Meeting.—Consolidation.—City Government.—City Judiciary.—City Executive.—City Legislature.—Legislative Control over the Commissions.—Conduct of Commissions.—Executive Organization.—Administrative Courts.—Frequent Elections.—Board of Councilmen.—Choice of Aldermen.

Appendix A.—Mr. Pierson's Elegy.
" B.—The Town of Naugatuck.
" C.—Dr. Manasseh Cutler's Diary.
" D.—A Town Court of Elections. New Haven, A. D. 1656.

The volume now ready comprises 350 pages octavo, with various diagrams and an index. It will be sold, neatly bound in cloth, at $2.00. Subscribers to the STUDIES can obtain at reduced rates this new volume, bound uniformly with the First, Second, Third, and Fourth Series.

THE REPUBLIC OF NEW HAVEN.

A History of Municipal Evolution.

BY CHARLES H. LEVERMORE, PH. D.

Fellow in History, 1884-85, Johns Hopkins University.

THIS work is a new study, from original records, of a most remarkable chapter of municipal development. Beginning with an English germ in the parish of St. Stephen, Coleman street, London, Dr. Levermore has traced the evolution of the Rev. John Davenport's church into a veritable commonwealth, in which the life-forces of Old England circulate anew.

The Republic of New Haven is unique and one of the most interesting of all American commonwealths. It was a city-state, self-contained, self-sufficing, like the municipal commonwealths of antiquity. It is impossible to measure the greatness of Greek cities or of the Italian republics by their extent of territory. It is equally impossible to estimate the colonial and municipal life of America by any standards of material greatness. And yet few persons realize how far-reaching in American history is the influence of a single town like New Haven. Not to speak of the intellectual forces which have gone forth from that local republic, from its vigorous church-life and from Yale college, born of the church, New Haven, like her mother England, is the parent of a wide-spread colonial system, not unworthy of comparison with that of Greek cities. A glance at the accompanying diagram will illustrate the wonderful evolution of New Haven.

The following table of contents will serve to indicate the scope and character of the topics treated in Mr. Levermore's History of New Haven:—

www.ingramcontent.com/pod-product-compliance
Lightning Source LLC
Chambersburg PA
CBHW031054110726
47900CB00003B/925
* 9 7 8 3 3 3 7 3 3 8 5 9 6 *